A Glimpse of the Dream

A Glimpse of the Dream

L.A. FIORE

Published by Montlake Romance, Seattle

www.apub.com

ISBN-13: 9781503944299
ISBN-10: 1503944298

Cover design by Laura Klynstra

Printed in the United States of America

To the men and women who put their lives on the line in the service and protection of others

prologue

Blue Hill, Maine: 1997

My knees shook, and my stomach ached with fear. The silent car contained only me and the woman driving—social services, she'd said to the priest when she'd picked me up that afternoon to drive me to my new home.

I had taken care to wear something really nice that day—my best black dress that Mom and I had purchased for a birthday party I'd wanted to go to. I had even combed my hair until it shined like copper. That's how my dad described my hair: copper. But I wasn't wearing it for a party; instead, I'd stood in a graveyard as the rain misted around us and watched as my parents were lowered into the ground, two holes right next to each other. At least they would be together. I didn't want to go into a box in the ground, didn't want the darkness or the cold. I hated that when I thought of them now, that was how I'd see them. The tears in my eyes burned almost as painfully as the throbbing in my head.

Christmas lights lit the houses we passed, but I didn't look; the sight of them would forever be a reminder of this awful day. My parents had been out Christmas shopping, the roads had been slick from the rain, and their car had lost control on a turn only a mile from our house. I had heard the sirens from my room, but didn't know whom they were for. As I sat watching *Doctor Who*, my parents were dying.

The car turned down a long drive, but it was so dark I couldn't see the house that would now be my home. Grammy and Gramps's best friend, Mrs. Marks, was the only family I had left. Grammy had died two years before from cancer, and then Gramps a year later from a broken heart. And now my parents were gone. Chills spread goose bumps over my skin. I had never met these people, didn't know anything about them, and now I had to leave my home near Boston and go live with them in Maine.

Lightening crackled against the pitch-black sky, and I caught my first glimpse of Raven's Peak, but it wasn't a house; it was like a gothic castle, and it scared me. Big and ugly, and, considering how much of the trip we were going uphill, I could only assume the house looked down on the town that surrounded it. A small cottage with a picket fence in Newton, Massachusetts, had been my home. Mom had loved flowers, had grown them everywhere, including in window boxes. Dad had sworn something fierce—that was how Mom put it—hanging them, but, in the end, he'd loved them as much as she had.

The car came to a stop, but I didn't get out immediately—I took a moment or two to breathe deeply, because my heart hurt it was beating so fast. The house looked even bigger when I was sitting just in front of it. The almost-full moon cast a creepy glow, making the mansion seem almost haunted, like something you'd see on *Scooby-Doo*.

Stepping up to the biggest front door I'd ever seen, thick wood and iron, I'd barely knocked before it opened. An old man stood there, dressed in black, and, though he gave the appearance of sternness, a kind light shone in his eyes. He held the door for us and we entered a space so large I think my old house could have fit right there next to the stairs. It had high ceilings, paneled walls, and the dark space was illuminated by only a few lights on the wall. A coldness crept into my bones, probably from my fear as well as the temperature. The inside felt almost as cold as the outside.

"This is Teagan Harper." That was how the social services lady introduced me in what was the most frightening moment of my life. An elderly woman, who had to be Mrs. Marks, approached, taking my hands into her wrinkled ones. She wasn't as old as I was expecting, despite the gray hair, which was pulled up into a bun. Her black dress looked like something women wore in the old days, like in those black-and-white films my mom had loved to watch. Her eyes, a dark blue, were kind but really sad too.

"I'm very sorry for your loss, Teagan."

I wanted to cry, but I knew that if I started, I might never stop. My lower lip trembled and, despite my best efforts, tears started leaking from the corners of my eyes. "Thank you."

"Are you hungry?"

My stomach answered for me. Mrs. Marks smiled. "This is Mr. Clancy, and he makes a mean sandwich. Let's get something in that belly." Her gaze then moved to the woman who had brought me, the kindness fading to anger.

"Thank you for bringing her" were her only words before she touched my shoulder and led me away. Even I understood that had been a dismissal. Was she angry because the woman had been kind of abrupt? Mrs. Marks said to me, "I will be making a call. Her manner was completely unacceptable."

I didn't know how to respond to that, so I remained silent. We entered the kitchen. There were two stoves, three refrigerators, and so much counter space my mom would have been tickled, since our kitchen had been very small. The memory caused a stabbing pain in my heart.

"Do you have a preference for what's on your sandwich?" Mrs. Marks asked as she started toward the refrigerator; Mr. Clancy entered the kitchen and walked to one of the cabinets for a plate.

"Ham and cheese is my favorite."

"Well, you're in luck, because that's one of my favorites too." She poured me a glass of milk as Mr. Clancy prepared the sandwich.

While I watched Mr. Clancy, Mrs. Marks settled on the chair next to me.

"This is all very difficult, and I can't imagine what you're feeling right now, but please, if you need anything, I'm here."

My eyes were leaking again, and my throat got so tight I didn't think I'd get any words past it, but I did manage to say, "Okay."

"If you need to talk, I've been told I'm a great listener."

I could only nod, because speaking past the painful lump in my throat was now impossible. Mr. Clancy placed the plate in front of me, and I understood no words were expected as I dug into my sandwich. I couldn't eat the whole thing, even though my stomach was empty, so he wrapped the rest in case I got hungry later. Mrs. Marks led me to my room, a pink room fit for a princess. A canopy bed sat against the far wall; in my room, it would have taken up the entire space and then some, but in this room it looked almost lost. The furniture was all old, not like from a dingy flea-market, but beautiful pieces that surely belonged in a museum. A fire was burning in a big fireplace.

"Your clothes have been put in the dresser and closet. Your nightgown is on the bed. There is a bathroom right through those doors. Towels are in the closet. Do you need anything else?"

"No." Looking around the room, I felt like Alice in Wonderland: overwhelmed. Despite its size, it was cozy. "It's a pretty room."

"I'm glad to hear you like it. Sleep well, Teagan. I'll see you in the morning."

She closed the door quietly behind her. Standing there in the prettiest room I had ever seen, I'd never felt more alone and afraid. Still dressed in my best clothes, I curled up in a ball on the bed and cried. And that was when *he* entered my life. I didn't know anyone had come into the room until I felt a small hand on my back. Lifting my head, I looked into the bluest eyes I had ever seen.

He immediately took a few steps away from me. "I'm sorry about your mom and dad."

Sitting up, I wiped at my eyes and stared at the boy. I'd never had a boy in my room—hadn't even known any boys from home well enough to call them friends. I waited for the nervousness that I usually suffered when I was around boys, but I didn't feel it. Dressed in sweatpants and a tee, he looked to be a few years older than me. His black hair was kind of long and messy, but it was his eyes that I couldn't stop looking at. They were so blue—the clearest, brightest blue I had ever seen. "Who are you?"

"I'm Kane, Teagan."

He said it just like that, a simple statement. An odd swishy sensation stirred in my chest hearing that he knew my name. I asked, "Do you live here too?"

He looked even sadder at my words. "Yeah."

My heart hurt thinking about what had brought me there and what likely had brought him too. "Did your parents die?"

"No, I never knew my dad, and my mom . . . I don't know where she is."

Why wasn't he living with his relatives? There had to be someone. He must have seen that in my expression, so he added, "She used to work here. Growing up, I spent more time here than my own house. I have no one else, so when my mom left, Mrs. Marks adopted me."

"Oh." His mom had left. How could a mom leave? "I'm sorry."

He kind of ignored that and said, "You know, it's okay to cry."

"I haven't stopped all day. My stomach hurts from crying so much." And even then, just thinking about my parents, I felt the tears stinging the back of my eyes. Needing to change the subject so I didn't start blubbering in front of Kane, I said, "This place gives me the creeps."

"I get that; it's a bit overwhelming, but despite its size, it's really not creepy. It's been in Mrs. Marks's family for generations: her great-great-grandfather built it. It's fun exploring, because there are lots of hidden rooms and it's filled with really cool stuff like the suit of armor in the entrance hall."

I had noticed the suit of armor, which only furthered my belief that I had somehow stepped into an episode of *Scooby-Doo*. "How many people live here?"

"Four." A small smile touched his lips before he corrected himself, "Five now."

"Seems like an awful lot of house for so few people." I couldn't imagine how long it took to clean it, remembering the hours Mom and Dad had spent on our small house. The thought brought pain again. Seeming to sense that, Kane took a step closer, and, oddly, I found that small act of concern comforting.

"It is, but Mrs. Marks won't sell. It's like a part of her."

"What's it like living here?"

A little smile appeared on his face. "Different, but Mrs. Marks and the others are really nice—a bit strange, but that's what makes it fun."

"Strange, how?"

"You'll see."

"How long have you lived . . ." I couldn't bring myself to finish, seeing understanding and pain in his eyes at my thoughtless question. Asking him how long he had lived there was another way of asking how long it had been since he'd been abandoned. He surprised me, though, when he answered.

"Two years."

"And there are no other kids?"

"No."

"Don't you get lonely?"

"Maybe sometimes, but you're here now. You should get some sleep," he said as he started for the door.

I didn't mean to grab his hand so hard, but for the first time all day I didn't feel so lost. "Please don't leave me alone."

He seemed to think on that for a minute and, making up his mind, said, "Get changed into your pajamas and meet me in the hall."

"Okay."

I changed so fast because I feared that he wouldn't be there when I yanked open the door, but he was. He took my hand and led me down the long hallway to the massive stairs.

"Have you ever seen such a big staircase?" Kane asked, and I knew he was trying to take my mind off my parents.

"No." And, in an attempt to do the same, and because I really thought so, I said, "I bet it would be fun sliding down the railing."

He glanced down at me. "You wouldn't be scared?"

"Probably, but that would only add to the adventure."

A smile flashed over his face, and I knew he liked my answer even before he said, "Agreed."

We walked down another hallway until we reached the library. As soon as he turned on the lights, I gasped. It was like the library in *Beauty and the Beast*, books as high up as you could see.

"What a room." I said.

"This is my favorite room. I can't tell you how many times I come down here when I can't sleep and start counting the books."

"What's the highest you've counted?"

"Got up to two thousand once, and I wasn't even halfway through the room."

"That's amazing." Even more amazing, his taking my mind off my parents was working. A small sofa sat in a corner.

"It's more comfortable than it looks," Kane said before he led me to it. We curled up on the sofa with a blanket.

"You okay? Do you need anything? Tissues, a drink?" he asked.

"I'm okay, thanks."

"I don't really know what you're feeling, my situation is a little different, but I do know that a time will come when you can remember your parents and not be overwhelmed with the pain of losing them."

I whispered to him my biggest fear, "I'm afraid that I'll forget them."

"You'll always be able to see them." He sounded so confident and, having lost his mom, maybe he really did know what he was talking about. But I wasn't convinced.

Shifting so I could stare into those blue eyes, I said, "But not in the way I want. When I think of them, all I see are the boxes being lowered into the ground, the tombstones with their names: Amy and Christian Harper. Every time I think of them, that's what I'll remember. And I hate it, hate that my last memory of my parents is seeing them being put into the ground."

"I'm sorry for that, but you can see your parents again, because you can see with more than your eyes, Teagan."

"No, you can't."

"I'll prove it. Did you ever go on vacation with your parents?"

"All the time."

"Do you have a favorite?"

"Yeah, we went to Hawaii once."

"Close your eyes and think about that vacation."

I didn't want to, but I closed my eyes anyway. "Can you see them?" he asked.

I could. They appeared so clearly, my throat hurt from the tears that wanted to fall. "Yes."

"In your memories, your parents are there. See with your heart and you'll always see them."

"Is that what you do with your mom?"

"Yeah." He sounded really sad, and I couldn't blame him.

It was the most natural thing for me to rest my head on his shoulder. In any other situation, with any other boy, I would never have even thought to do it, but with Kane it felt so perfectly right. I whispered, "Thank you for that."

"Try to sleep. I won't leave you alone."

"Why are you being so nice to me?"

"Because I remember what it feels like to be scared and alone, but we don't have to be scared and alone because now we've got each other. Sleep. You'll feel better in the morning."

And with him at my side, I did sleep all through the night. In the morning when I woke, Kane wasn't there, but sitting on the table just in front of the sofa was a large glass of chocolate milk with whipped cream. I liked chocolate milk and whipped cream, but it was the meaning behind the offer—Kane's attempt to comfort me, knowing how I must have felt waking up for the first time in a home that wasn't my own, a place where my parents weren't and never would be—that had my heart beating funny.

He understood and sought to help ease me through that difficult first morning. Hearing voices, I took my milk and followed them into the kitchen. Mrs. Marks was there, as were Mr. Clancy and Kane. There was another woman there, heavy with white hair.

"Teagan. How are you, honey?" Mrs. Marks asked, joining me by the door but hesitating to touch me.

"Okay."

"You've met Mr. Clancy and Kane, and this is Mrs. Terry, the housekeeper. She also does the cooking."

Nervousness sent my eyes drifting toward the floor. My underarms were sweating. I felt someone right next to me and, from the corner of my eye, I saw Kane. He reached for my fingers, not holding my hand, but touching me, comforting me. And it worked. Lifting my head, I gave Mrs. Terry a shaky smile.

"Hi."

She didn't force me to talk. She seemed to understand.

Mrs. Marks spoke up. "We have a few rules in this house. Everyone helps with the cleaning, because my ancestor was crazy when he built this massive place and it can be rather taxing, especially to clean. If you ever need anything, you ask. Don't go without because you're afraid to speak. And lastly, we eat cake for breakfast most mornings."

I think my jaw might have dropped at that last rule. She winked at me. "So, Mrs. T, what cake is it this morning?"

"Kane's favorite, triple chocolate."

Grabbing my hand, Kane dropped me into a chair at the table before he went for the plates and forks. Sitting down next to me, pushing his chair closer so that our legs brushed, he held up his fork. "I get two slices."

And in that moment, I knew I was going to be okay.

The Early Years
Teagan

My palms began to sweat as the car pulled up in front of a stone building; it wasn't very big, but it was intimidating. A new school.

Mrs. Marks turned from her spot next to the driver, whose name I learned was Sam. "You'll be fine, Teagan. I know it's scary, but you'll adjust and maybe you'll even make a friend or two."

My throat worked as I attempted to keep myself from bursting into tears. I hated this, every bit of it.

"Come on, Teagan," Kane called as he climbed from the car. Starting fourth grade in a different school midyear was not going to be fun. At least Kane was in the same school as me, even if he was a sixth grader.

His head poked back through the open door. "Come on."

"Bye," I said to Mrs. Marks and Sam.

"See you after school," Mrs. Marks said, her voice kind, her smile encouraging. Dragging myself across the seat, I climbed out, but my feet refused to move me any farther. Kane grabbed my hand and started pulling me toward the building.

"You'll be fine, don't worry," Kane said.

Easy for him to say. The smell of chalk and disinfectant filled my nose as soon as I stepped through the front doors. My stomach was already churning with nerves, and the added scents didn't help. Continuing down the hall, we stopped just outside one of the classrooms.

"Mrs. Texler is very nice, so relax. When the day is over, they'll call for car riders first—that's us. I'll meet you out front. You'll be fine. And after school, I'll take you out for something to eat. Mrs. Marks gave me money and cleared it with the office that we'll be walking into town after school."

I took a few deep breaths as Kane yanked the door open for me. He seemed to know I needed reassurance, so he smiled. "Ice cream after school."

Nodding, since words would not come, I stepped into the classroom and every eye turned to me. Mrs. Texler rose from her seat at her desk and walked around to join me. Her hand on my shoulder felt surprisingly comforting, her smile reassuring.

"Class, this is Teagan Harper, she will be joining us for the rest of the year. Please make her feel welcome."

And they did. I think the other students knew what had happened to my parents, because everyone in class stopped by my desk to say hi. And even though I still had butterflies in my belly, I wasn't as terrified.

When the bell sounded for the end of the day and the lady over the speaker called for car riders, I didn't run from the room like I thought I would that morning. For a first day, it had been pretty okay. Stepping outside, I looked around for Kane. When I saw him, something moved through me, an emotion I'd never felt before. He was talking to a girl with long brown hair and big blue eyes. She was older—his grade, I was sure. Kane leaned against a tree, laughing at whatever she'd just said.

I supposed I should have realized that he had a life, friends outside of Raven's Peak. Now that school was back in session, he'd probably start playing with his friends and forget about me. That hurt, though he *was* two years older than me. Why would he want to hang with a little kid? My feet moved a little slower at the thought, because I wanted him all to myself. He was my only friend so far. Selfish, that's what my mom would say. I was being selfish. And just thinking of her sent tendrils of pain through my chest, squeezing so hard my eyes burned.

Turning from Kane and his friend, I started down the path toward home. He should take his *friend* into town for ice cream. Yet I hadn't gotten very far when I heard Kane calling my name. He appeared at my side, breathing hard from running after me.

"Where are you going?"

"Back to the house."

"I thought we were going to get ice cream."

"You don't have to."

"I know I don't. I want to."

"But what about the girl you were just talking to?" I said.

Absently, he glanced behind him. "Camille? What about her?"

"Don't you want to go with her?"

"No." He said it as if it were obvious. The feeling in my belly eased. "The parlor makes the best sundaes. We'll get one and share."

"Okay." I sounded almost giddy—I was happy he wanted to get ice cream with me.

His eyes found mine and he flashed me a smile. "And then you can tell me all about your first day of school."

"Let's go. Murder waits for no one." Mrs. Marks was in rare form that evening. We were all heading to the library, because it was time to play our monthly game of Clue. She was Miss Scarlet, of course, dressed in a red gown, her hair up like it usually was. She was carrying one of those cigarette holders, minus the cigarette, because smoking was a "dreadful habit." Her first name was Veronica, but she never let anyone call her that. I often wondered why, because she wasn't stuffy or overly formal. It felt odd that she preferred Mrs. Marks, especially since I didn't think there was ever a Mr. Marks. I had asked Kane if he knew the reason, but he didn't know either.

Mr. Clancy was Colonel Mustard; Mrs. T was Mr. Green, dressed in an eighties leisure suit. I was Mrs. Peabody. Mrs. Marks found me the ugliest tweed suit with old lady shoes to wear, and not even Mrs. Marks wore pumps like the ones she forced on me. Kane was Professor Plum in an ascot and khakis and a corduroy jacket with patches on the elbows. He was not happy. In the months since I had come to live at Raven's Peak, he and I had become inseparable. Mrs. Marks and the others often teased us; if you saw one, the other was surely close behind. Despite how close we had become, I grinned at his discomfort, because he looked ridiculous.

"I hate that I have to wear an ascot. Only Fred from *Scooby-Doo* can pull that off. I look like a dork."

"You are a dork, Kane. Deal."

His head snapped in my direction. "Careful, Teagan."

"Or what? You'll lecture me to death?" Having recently turned ten, I'd just learned the word "lecture" and, since he was Professor Plum, I thought I was being very clever.

He started for me, but Mrs. Marks stopped him. "There will be no bloodshed until the game begins. Now, everyone must assume their positions. Once the lights go off, it's action. Does everyone remember their parts?"

Mrs. Marks loved this, loved mysteries and whodunits. I enjoyed watching her enthusiasm for the game. It created lightness in the sad circumstances.

"I have just polished the candlesticks, so if one of them is the murder weapon, I would appreciate that whoever uses it cleans it," Mr. Clancy said. He was trying to sound serious, but I saw the way his lips turned up on the one side. They really were the strangest group of people, and yet Kane had been right: they were a lot of fun.

"Well, we'll have cake when this is all done. Nothing works up an appetite like murder," Mrs. T suggested.

"You can say that again," Kane agreed, but he was looking at me, and I had a terrible feeling he was the murderer and I was the victim. The look he was throwing at me was sinister.

"All right. Remember, only the murderer knows who the victim will be. As soon as the lights are out, make yourself scarce, because even if you're the target and you're about to die, your murderer should have to work for it. If you're the victim, be sure to scream loudly, so we can find your body, and then the game begins." The lights went out. "Action!" Mrs. Marks called.

I took off, almost running, but I felt Kane behind me gaining with every step. I reached the kitchen before he caught me, his arms coming around me and pulling me back against him.

"Sorry, Teagan." But he didn't sound sorry at all.

I laughed through my entire death scene because Kane's method for killing me was to tickle me to death.

Walking down the sloping backyard of Raven's Peak, I glanced back at the huge house—although, "house" didn't even seem to be the right word. The place was just that big. Grass and trees wrapped around the property, and then it just dropped off as the ocean met the land. It wasn't a long drop, but even still, it was scary. A set of stairs, with railings on both sides, led down to the beach below. Raven's Peak sat on a point; a walkway had been carved into the cliffside, curving around the point as another way for people to get to the beach. Taking the walkway, I started down. The sound of the waves crashing against the rocks was music to my ears. White sand, that I bet felt wonderfully warm in the summer, met the cliff, but only for a small stretch. In the distance, the water crashed up against the cliffs, the sight violent but pretty.

Walking along the beach, I held my coat closed tightly around me. Though spring was coming, it was still cold. I looked out at the island that sat just off the beach. It wasn't very big, maybe the size of a couple football fields, oddly shaped, and about a half mile from where I stood. There were trees—I could see them even from my distance. I wondered how it had formed there, so close to the mainland and yet off on its own. It seemed like it would sink if anyone ever stepped on it.

"Nice, isn't it?" I hadn't heard Kane approach, so I jumped a few feet in the air when he spoke.

"Kane!" I smacked him on the arm.

"Sorry, I thought you heard me coming." He turned his face to the sea. "Mrs. Marks owns that."

"Really?"

"I'm going to swim out to it when I'm older. When I'm a strong enough swimmer."

My eyes went wide. "You're going to swim out there?"

"Yep." His focus turned to me. "You can come."

"I can't swim."

I couldn't lie. I wanted to swim out there with him, but I was afraid of the water. "When you're ready, I'll teach you to swim. Deal?"

I could do that, when I was ready. "Deal."

"Dinner's ready."

We started back to the stairs. "Did Mrs. Marks have the steps and walkway added?"

"The steps. The walkway was done when the house was built back in the day. Pretty neat the way they carved it right into the stone. I like taking the steps, they're scarier."

"I like the walkway."

"Then we'll take the walkway. Mrs. T is making potpie for dinner. I love her potpies."

Since I hadn't yet had one of Mrs. T's potpies, I couldn't comment, but since everything else she made was the best I'd ever tasted, I couldn't wait. I wondered if Kane's obsession with food started after he'd come to Mrs. Marks's to live. I could understand that if it were the case. "You and food. Do you ever think of anything else?"

His smile was just a bit wicked. "Sometimes."

"You're not going to share what else in your world could possibly compete with your love of food?"

"I shouldn't need to share it, I think it's pretty obvious," he replied.

In response, my body turned warm all over and my heart rolled in my chest. Could he possibly be talking about me?

He answered my unasked question. "On the Kane's scale of likes, you are neck and neck with food."

It didn't sound like a compliment, but knowing Kane as I did, it was the highest compliment he could give. He looked a bit uncomfortable, and I knew he was feeling it too when he changed the subject. "You doing okay?" His question surprised me. As did his steady stare. Maybe studying me was a better word, since he looked like Mrs. T looked when she was reading through a problem in my math book.

"About my parents?"

"Yeah."

"I miss them, but when I think about them, I don't feel like I have to cry as bad as I did before."

"That's good."

"What about you? Are you still sad when you think about your mom?"

His head turned away, and I think he was trying to hide tears. "She left me, and I don't know why, so it's still as hard now as it was then."

I reached for his hand, and his closed tightly around mine. "I'm sorry she left you, Kane, but in some ways I'm not."

His head jerked to me with tears in his eyes. "Why did you say that?" He sounded mad.

"Because if she hadn't, we probably wouldn't be as close as we are."

I watched as his anger faded and a little smile curved his mouth. "Looking at it that way, I'm glad for it too."

Mr. Clancy was sitting in the kitchen having tea when I came home from one of my walks on the beach. Kane was off at the boatyard, shadowing Mr. Miller to learn about boat building, a dream of his. He had invited me to join him, but the few times I had previously, I could tell he felt as if he needed to entertain me. He didn't, of course, but that was Kane's way. Mr. Miller was willing to apprentice Kane, so he needed to focus on that, not me.

"Teagan, would you like a cup of tea?"

I never drank tea. My parents had been coffee drinkers, but I was willing to give it a try. It smelled good. "Okay."

With the skill of someone who did it often, he poured the fragrant liquid into a china cup. "Milk? Sugar?"

"I've never had tea," I confessed.

"Have a touch of sugar."

Seemed like a good plan to me. "Okay."

He smiled at me as he prepared my tea and then studied me as I took my first sip. It was delicious. His smile turned even wider. "Good, isn't it?"

"Yes."

"It's a special brew I get from Harrods in London."

"Tea all the way from London. Fancy."

Mr. Clancy winked.

"Can I ask you something?" I asked.

"Sure."

"How long have you worked here?"

"I grew up here. My father used to be the butler when Mrs. Marks's father was alive. As I do now, he lived here with my mother and me."

"You've lived here your whole life?" I liked the thought of that, being connected to the same place through your entire life's journey.

"Yes. Back in the day, the house was filled with people—immediate and extended family. Almost every room was occupied, but it didn't feel crammed, just the opposite, in fact. Mrs. Marks had two brothers who were significantly older than her, but we all played together when we were kids. Some of my fondest memories are the days the four of us had our adventures."

"Where are her brothers now?"

"They died in World War II. I remember when the telegram came for Robert, the younger of the two. I'd never seen her father cry, but he cried that day. Only two weeks later, a telegram came for Gerald. The house had always been one of laughter, but after their deaths, a solemnity settled over it and never really lifted until Kane's arrival."

I wanted so badly to know more about Kane, but I didn't know if I had a right to ask. Mr. Clancy obviously had no trouble reading my thoughts.

"Kane's mother worked here. Rebecca kept the house—cleaning, doing the linens. When she learned she was pregnant, she was thrilled and terrified because she was a single woman who needed her job. But there had never been a question that we would all help with Kane so that she could have both. I remember the first day she brought him here. Even as an infant, his eyes were the exact shade of blue they are now. Watching him grow, hearing laughter in the house again, brought life back into this old place.

"Rebecca leaving took me completely by surprise, because she adored Kane. But she had been a rolling stone in her youth. She had dreams of leaving this town and making a name for herself. I'd thought she had moved past that, but clearly I was wrong. I didn't know her as well as Mrs. Marks had, though I always had the sense that Rebecca's decision to leave surprised even her."

I heard the anger and censure in his tone, and I had to agree. Leaving your child was wrong.

"And now you're here. I'm sorry for the circumstances that brought you to us, but I love watching as you and Kane take up where Mrs. Marks and I left off."

Touched, I couldn't form any words in reply, so I offered a weak smile and took a sip of my tea.

"Kane Doyle, that's it, you creep. I am getting you back. That is the last toad you will be putting in my bed." I heard him laughing, even though I didn't know where he was hiding in the massive house. I had been living at Raven's Peak for seven months and for four of those I had found toads in my bed, usually in the early evening when I liked to come to my room and read before dinner. I had named all of them—I was up to Kane 102.

I really didn't mind the toads, and I didn't think Kane was a creep for doing it either. I didn't know how I would have gotten through those months without him. He had the uncanny ability to know when I wasn't happy, when a memory of my parents came out of nowhere. He was always there at my side. Most times he did no more than offer a shoulder, but he was always there.

Even still, I had to get him back for the toads. In the four months since he started with his gross joke, I'd attempted to get even with him: spraying all his clothes with perfume and adding hot sauce to the ketchup, knowing how much he loved that on his fries, but my efforts didn't deter him. It was time to kick it up. Running to the kitchen, I saw Mrs. T behind the stove creating something wonderful as usual. "Mrs. T, I was wondering if I could help you with making a special dinner for Kane tonight."

Her old gray eyes twinkled at me. She knew that Kane and I dedicated our lives to getting the better of each other. "How special, dear?"

"Well, you know how he loves his potpie. I was thinking we could try a different kind of potpie with worms. Is there a way to do that without harming the worms?"

Her cackle of laughter filled the kitchen. "That is really gross."

"I know. It's awesome."

"Worms in my kitchen? You do ask a lot of me. You found another toad, I'm guessing."

"Yep."

"Very well, get me the worms, and I'll whip them up into a pie of sorts. No harm will come to them."

"You're the best." And then I hurried off to do just that.

At dinner, we all sat in the kitchen like we always did. Mrs. Marks preferred its coziness over the cavernous space—that's what Kane called it—that was the dining room. The staff usually ate with us.

"That smells delicious, Mrs. T. You seem to have outdone yourself," Mrs. Marks said. And then she winked, so she knew about the joke we were playing on Kane. It was not surprising, because she knew everything. Mrs. T looked as if she had just sucked on a lemon, and Mr. Clancy was careful to keep his focus away from Kane.

"God, I'm hungry."

"You're always hungry, Kane. It's amazing you're not the size of a barn with the amount of food you eat," I said.

His eyes narrowed at me and I just knew he was plotting again. "Jealous."

I was, of course, since I didn't eat like that and yet I was a little round. Didn't seem fair. Instead of answering him, I just stuck out my tongue. I couldn't wait to see his expression when he saw all those worms squirming around in his dinner.

Mrs. T placed Kane's pie in front of him. It was like a ritual, the way Kane ate a potpie. He always pulled the top crust off to eat the insides before eating the crust with melted butter. Trying not to grin was hard as I watched Kane dig in and saw the anticipation on his face. It took a minute, once he removed the top crust, to understand. His eyes grew wide and he jumped back from the table.

"You better run, dear," Mrs. Marks said as Kane's gaze met mine. I ran right out of the kitchen, down the hall, and through the front door. I didn't get far before I felt his arms around me. He pulled me to the ground, wrestling me until he was on top. I tried to knock him off, but he was stronger and bigger.

"Good one, Teagan." I didn't even get to gloat before he smashed a fist full of mud in my face. "That's a good look for you."

After our showers, Kane and I walked down to the docks. He loved looking at the boats and I loved looking at the water.

"I can't wait to build my own boat one day," he said as we sat side by side on the pier, our feet dangling.

"Do you see it in your head—the boat you want?"

"Yeah. And I'd like to do it in teak. I'll drive it all over, from here down the coast." Peering at me from the corner of his eyes he said, "You can come with me if you want."

"I want."

He seemed to like that answer. His lips turned up at the sides.

"What are you going to call your boat?"

"I don't know, but the name of a boat is very important. It has to be meaningful, special, because the boat is like a part of you. I'll figure it out."

In the next second, Kane jumped up and started jogging down to the end of the pier where an older man was trying to carry too much at once.

"Let me help you with that, Mr. Miller."

"Thank you, Kane. You're a good boy."

Kane flashed him a smile in reply. He did that a lot, offering a hand when someone needed it. He didn't even need to be asked. Mrs. Marks said he had a big heart. They loved him, Mrs. Marks and the others. I envied the closeness they had with each other. They would do anything for him, and he would do anything for them. He had a family again and, even though I felt like an outsider sometimes, I didn't begrudge him what he had found.

I had been searching for Kane for almost an hour, retracing my steps because I couldn't find him. When I circled back around to the beach, he was there, but he wasn't alone. Camille Bowen had joined him. Had they just been to the island? Kane and I often spoke of that island and how we would explore it together. Had he forgotten that promise because his interest in Camille was stronger than his friendship with me?

She was trying to hold his hand, and the fact that she was even reaching for it made it seem like they had held hands before. Were they dating? Had they dated? Remembering my first day of school, seeing the two of them talking, I couldn't deny they had looked good together: friendly and comfortable. Maybe they were an item, and I had misunderstood him that day. Maybe it wasn't disinterest in taking her for ice cream in general, just that day in particular, since he had already made plans with me.

I hadn't made a sound, and I was quite a distance from them, but Kane's head snapped in my direction and his gaze seared me. Embarrassed for getting caught, I hurried back up the path to the house. He didn't need his privacy invaded by me, especially since he had given so much of his time already to help me fit into my new life.

"Teagan, where are you going?" I heard from behind me.

Turning to Kane, I knew my cheeks were flushed because I felt awkward. "I'm sorry, I didn't know you had company."

"Yeah, that." He sounded disgruntled. "Camille and I—"

"Kane, you don't owe me an explanation. It's none of my business."

"I know I don't owe you one, but I'd like to give you one just the same. Camille sees us as a couple, but I'm not sure I want to go there with her."

"Why not? She's very pretty."

"Yeah, she is—there doesn't seem to be much more to her than that."

The question was out of my mouth before I truly knew I was planning to ask it. "Did you go out to the island together?"

He looked hurt at that. "No. I promised to take you."

Relief, waves of it, washed over me. "I couldn't find you, and then there you were on the beach, so I just assumed I couldn't find you because you were over there."

"That island is ours, Teagan. We explore it first."

"I feel the same. I just wasn't so sure you still did."

"Because of Camille?" he asked, his eyes bugging out in disbelief.

"Yeah."

"Well, that's just stupid. You're you and Camille is just a girl."

I couldn't stop from smiling. "Where is Camille now?"

"On her way home. She had a minor temper tantrum over having our 'moment' interrupted, as she puts it."

I felt the heat creeping into my cheeks again. "Sorry."

"Don't be. I'd much rather be hanging out with you. You said you were looking for me. What's up?"

"Oh, right, I almost forgot. Mrs. T is baking peanut butter cookies."

He grabbed my hand and started pulling me toward the house. "I'd definitely rather be hanging out with you."

Had someone told me when I'd first arrived at Raven's Peak that I would find contentment, happiness even, I would have thought they were crazy. I had, though, and I owed that mostly to Kane. I'd never had a best friend, but I had one now. We understood each other, almost as if he were an extension of me and me of him. My eyes drifted to my nightstand. A small smile touched my lips. Every morning, for the year that I'd been there, I had awoken to find a glass of chocolate milk with whipped cream waiting for me. That first morning, Kane had brought it hoping to help ease the pain he knew I was feeling. I loved that he still did it—it was such a small gesture, but one that meant a lot to me.

I wasn't as happy as I usually was, because it was exactly a year ago that Raven's Peak had become my home, which brought my parents' deaths front and center in my thoughts. I reached for the picture of them and felt my heart twist in my chest. It was my favorite photo, taken during their university years. Dad was smiling down at Mom as she lovingly looked up at him. She was wearing her Boston University sweatshirt, one she wore often, one that I now owned. I missed them, but I had learned to live without them, and I owed that to Kane. Without him, I would never have survived that first night, let alone the 364 that followed. I climbed out of bed, as I did every morning, before I walked to my door and held it open for him. He was usually leaning up against the wall waiting for me so we could start our day.

"Morning, Tea." That was what he called me, because he thought Teagan didn't fit my personality. I liked that he'd given me a nickname—one that was only his.

His bedhead indicated he'd only just gotten up, time enough to bring me the milk.

"Morning."

Taking the milk to the balcony off my room, we sat together on the little sofa with the blanket from my bed wrapped around both of us. I handed the milk to him after I took a sip. The sun breeched the horizon, the large sphere casting an orange hue to the sky. A lightness filled my chest, from the view and from feeling Kane next to me. We did this every morning. Sometimes we just sat there in silence, sometimes we talked about anything and everything.

I had started contemplating what I would be when I got older. The one clear goal I had was that I wanted to attend Boston University, wanted to follow in my parents' footsteps. Outside of that, I didn't have a clue. Kane, two years older than me, must have figured it out already. "What do you want to be when you grow up, Kane?"

He shrugged, which was his usual response until he thought about a question. "I don't know, but whatever I do, I want it to be here. I can't imagine any place on Earth better than this."

I followed his stare. He wasn't wrong. We could hear the sound of the waves crashing against the cliff of Raven's Peak. Mrs. Marks spoke of her house as a bird sitting on the topmost branch of a tree, and she was right, it really was.

"Sometimes I think it would be neat if Mrs. Marks would turn this place into one of those family-run inns. There are so many rooms that I don't think even we've discovered them all, and we've really looked. It seems like a waste that so much of the house goes unused. We could run it, you and me."

I thought of the conversation I'd had with Mr. Clancy over tea a few months back. To know there had been a time when the house was filled with family was as comforting as it was sad.

"Would you really want to be around strangers all the time?" I asked.

His head turned to me, those clear blue eyes looking into my green ones. "No, we would live on our island in a little house."

I sighed. "I like that idea. A little blue house."

"No, green."

"Blue, with window boxes just like my dad made for my mom."

His hand found mine under the blanket. "Window boxes, but a green house."

"Fine, if I get the window boxes, you can paint the house green."

"What about you, what do you want to be?" He looked very grown-up all of a sudden.

"I don't know. I do know that I want to go to BU, want to find a connection to my parents by experiencing something they had."

He squeezed my hand in understanding. "Sounds like a good plan."

"And after college, I think I'd like to travel, so maybe I'll get a job where I can travel a little, but what I really want is to be near you." And it was true. I didn't really know what I wanted to do for a career, but I did know that I always wanted to be close to Kane.

His shoulders relaxed and the biggest smile covered his face. "We can travel, since I'd like to see places with you, but we would come home here."

"Sounds perfect."

He jumped up from his spot and took the glass from me. "Come."

"Where are we going?"

"You'll see."

He pulled me through the house until we ended up in the library. My feet just stopped in the doorway, my focus on the Christmas tree, the biggest one I'd ever seen, all lit with white lights. Mrs. Marks and the staff were in the room, all of them smiling at me.

"We know this time of year, this day in particular, is very difficult for you, Teagan, but the day doesn't have to be a reminder of your parents' deaths. We can celebrate the memory of their lives." Mrs. Marks was wearing one of her lacy dresses, this one green, and she held two porcelain angels. "One for each of your parents," she said. "We thought you'd like to hang them on the tree."

My throat hurt, my stomach felt all funny, and my hands were shaking. Before I reached for them, she added, "It was Kane's idea."

Kane watched me with a sad little smile, and in that moment my young heart was no longer my own.

⁂

"It's not that hard, Tea. Just relax."

Three years after Kane and I had discussed swimming out to our island, I was finally ready to learn how to swim, but I wasn't having much luck. "I'm trying, but I'm scared."

"We're in three feet of water. I won't let you drown."

"Okay." Resting on my back, I tried to float like he'd showed me, but I kept sinking.

"Too many cakes, Tea. You're dropping like a rock."

"Are you calling me fat, Kane Doyle?"

"Round, not fat. Come on, you want to swim with me out to the island, but to do that, you need to know how to swim."

"Okay. Let's try it again." I forced myself to relax, took a couple deep breaths, and almost felt lighter. For the first time all morning, I really thought I could do it. "You can let go."

"I did already." My eyes flew open and he was grinning at me. "Way to go, Tea."

For the next hour I did float, for some of the time anyway. Though Kane was as eager as me to swim out together to our island, he never got angry or frustrated. Later, we did go to our island, taking the boat that was docked on the beach of Raven's Peak.

We pulled the boat up on the sand, something we had done countless times. Kane fell silent, unusual for him. We started walking along the beach, but instead of engaging me in conversation as he always did, he just stared off at the horizon.

"You okay?" I asked.

"Yeah, I was just thinking about my mom."

As much as I knew about Kane, he rarely talked about her. "Why don't you ever mention her?"

"This is going to sound strange, but I don't really remember much about her. What I have are impressions more than memories. She could be so happy sometimes, wanting to bake two hundred cookies, and we'd laugh and throw flour at each other, and she'd hug me and tell me how much she loved me. And then she'd be so sad, she wouldn't climb out of bed for days. Mrs. Marks tried to explain to me that my mom was manic-depressive or something."

"What happened to her?"

"She just left one day. I was in the hospital. I had tripped down the stairs and broken my leg. She never came to see me, and then the social worker came with Mrs. Marks, who adopted me."

I couldn't imagine my parents just leaving me without a word, being in the hospital scared and alone and having the one you needed to see the most not showing up. "I'm sorry, Kane."

His next words were so softly spoken I almost didn't hear him. "Don't ever leave, Tea. You and me. Promise?"

Linking my fingers with his, I made the promise. It was an easy one to make, since I never wanted to leave him. "Promise."

We returned to the house just before dinner, but Mrs. Marks didn't join us. In the four years that I'd lived there, every year on the same day Mrs. Marks didn't leave her room. Whenever I asked Mr. Clancy why, he only ever replied that she just needed a day to herself.

Kane and I were in the bathroom washing up for supper. I asked, "Why do you think she stays in her room?"

"I don't know. I've asked her about it, but she never answers, but you know that tomorrow she'll be her normal self. I heard her crying through the door last year. She sounded so sad that I was going to walk in and check on her, but Mr. Clancy stopped me. He told me that she just needed the day."

"That's so sad. I wish she'd talk with us about it, especially since she's seen us through our own heartbreaks."

"I know, but the best thing we can do for her is exactly what Mr. Clancy asked: give her space." He started from the room. "Race you to the table, winner gets the other's dessert."

"Cheater!" I screamed after him, but later I watched as he devoured my pudding too.

I sat on the front steps of Raven's Peak, my attention on Kane as he walked to his car with his friends. He was seventeen now and had worked a bunch of odd jobs so he could afford the car. It wasn't much to look at, but he was convinced the heart of a panther lived in his dilapidated blue Camaro. I wanted to go with them to the movies, but I was only fifteen and felt uncomfortable.

His black hair was messy, even though I knew he had just been to the barber and it had grown out almost overnight. He used to be only a few inches taller than me, but now he was at least a head taller. He had a bar in his room where he did chin-ups. It mesmerized me, watching his muscles move under his skin; he had a lot of them. I couldn't do it. I'd tried but couldn't even get my chin to the bar.

The leather jacket he was wearing had been a gift from me. Mrs. Marks had helped me buy it; it suited him and his collection of faded jeans. And even with all the changes he'd been through the past year, his crystal-blue eyes were still my favorite; I saw my Kane in them. But at the moment, those eyes were staring down at Camille.

Camille had started coming around the house a lot asking for him the past year. I had thought she'd gotten over her crush on him but apparently not. She walked around the place like she owned it. You could see her thoughts: She was imagining living with Kane in the house that overlooked the town. Her family came from money, lots of it, and they had the fanciest house in town. Actually, it was the second fanciest house after Raven's Peak, and that burned her ass. She wanted Raven's Peak as much as she wanted Kane. I didn't like that he was going to the movies with her. He claimed they were just friends, but the way she looked at him was anything but friendly. Regardless, he was my Kane. But I looked like a boy with my flat chest and non-existent hips, and she looked like a woman. I hated Camille.

"Want me to bring you back an ice cream?" Kane called. I knew he was trying to be nice, but it only made me feel more like a kid.

"No." I jumped from my spot at the door and ran to my room. I didn't stop running until I reached my bed, threw myself on it, and cried. I didn't even really understand why I was crying, only that seeing him go off without me really hurt.

Later that night, Kane came to my room. Sitting on the edge of my bed, I rolled to face him, my hands under my cheek.

He brushed my hair from my eyes. "Are you still mad?" he asked.

"I wasn't mad, I was upset."

"Okay. Are you still upset?"

"I guess not. Did you have fun?"

"No. Camille tried to put her tongue in my mouth."

My muscles tensed, and I tried to tell myself it was just a reaction to the idea of her tongue in his mouth—gross—but I knew there was more to my response than that. "You didn't like it?"

"It's not that. I just didn't want a kiss from her."

"Why not? She's pretty." Why was I encouraging this? I'd been secretly jealous of Camille for years, so why was I almost telling him to kiss her? Clearly I was insane.

"I guess, but I wasn't into it." He lowered his head and I knew he had something on his mind.

"What are you thinking?" I asked.

"I wanted a kiss, just not from her."

Oh. He liked someone. I understood, he was really cute and sweet, but I kind of always hoped that one day he would like me in that way. He was my friend, though, so I tried to be his.

"If there's someone you want to kiss, you should just kiss her."

His head snapped up at that. "Seriously?"

"Well, yeah, but she better be deserving of you."

A strange look passed over his expression, like he wasn't sure if I was teasing him. "I want to kiss you, Tea."

I understood the expression "fluttery heart" in that moment; mine felt as if it had wings. "Me?"

"Yeah."

"Okay." Sitting up, I tucked my hair behind my ears as I attempted to calm down, because I was equal parts nervous and excited. I'd fantasized about Kane kissing me for years. To know that he'd been thinking the same made me feel giddy. He shifted so we were facing each other.

His finger touched my cheek before running down along my jaw, and goose bumps immediately appeared on my skin. It felt different, the way he touched me—unlike the countless times he had before.

"Are you sure? This isn't just a kiss. It'll be different between us."

"What do you mean?" I didn't want to lose him; he was my best friend.

"I don't want to just kiss you, Tea. You're not ready for the rest, so I'll wait, but I feel different about you. And I think you feel it too."

"I do. Have for a while."

"So when I kiss you, I'm not just kissing you. You're mine. I want you to be mine."

My heart moved into my throat; his words mirrored exactly how I felt. "I want that too, I really want that."

His eyes turned dark, and the sexiest look swept his face. Fearing I was about to faint—I felt so lightheaded—I sought to ease some of the intensity. "Okay, you can kiss me now. Wait, did you brush your teeth? Maybe you should rinse your mouth with disinfectant."

And then his mouth was on mine, despite my joke, his lips brushing mine lightly. My eyes closed on their own and my heart sighed. His hands framed my face before his tongue ran along my lips, just the tip tracing the curve. Wanting to taste him, my mouth opened and he pushed his tongue in. It was awkward at first, I wasn't sure what to do with my tongue, and then it was as if our bodies took over, fueled by the emotions we were both feeling. His tongue swept my mouth as my tongue sought his. It felt incredible, stirring feelings that I had felt before around Kane, but heightened. When Kane pulled his mouth from mine, he looked hungry.

"Are you okay?" I asked, because he looked a bit like the Big Bad Wolf at that moment.

"Yeah. You should probably get some sleep." He stood and started from my room.

"Was that bad?" I asked, because he'd sounded almost curt.

His head turned to me when he reached the door. "No, Tea, it was not bad. It was perfect. You're mine. Remember that."

"Forever, Kane."

"Good. See you in the morning."

And then he was gone, his words still rolling around in my head. He'd kissed me. He'd liked that he'd kissed me. Take that, Camille.

In the morning, I woke with butterflies in my stomach. Kane had kissed me. My fingers unconsciously brushed over my lips, the memory of his mouth on mine caused chills to shoot down my arms. My feet didn't quite seem to touch the floor as I walked to the door. He was standing there, like normal, but the look in his eyes was anything but. He moved to me without speaking a word, his fingers threading through my hair as he tilted my head for his kiss. Unlike the night before, there was nothing awkward about the way his mouth claimed mine, his tongue stroking my own. Reaching for him, I fisted his shirt in my hands to keep myself upright. My scalp tingled, as did the rest of me. Clearly I wasn't the only one who had spent the night thinking about our first kiss.

"Good morning," he whispered.

"It really is a good morning. That was a great way to start off the day."

He chuckled. His thumb brushed over my lower lip, his eyes tracking the motion. His gaze lifted and he whispered, "Mine."

My heart skipped a beat.

❧

After the last bell rang, I headed for my locker. Kane was in my thoughts, as he had been for every second in the weeks since our relationship had started. I loved him, had for a long time, but I realized it wasn't just love, not like you'd love family. I was *in* love with him. The tragedy that had sent me to Raven's Peak had also given me Kane. Talk about a silver lining.

"Tea."

Chills raced down my arms. Turning, I watched as Kane made his way to me. His legs were clad in faded denim and the Henley shirt he wore so perfectly hugged the muscles of his chest and arms. He walked right into me, his mouth fusing to mine. Fear accompanied my joy, because Kane was graduating soon and I worried over what was next for us. He must have seen something in my expression when he pulled away.

"What's wrong?" He tilted his head and really studied me. "Not here. Get your stuff, and we'll go somewhere to talk."

It was uncanny how well he knew me. Swapping my books to his other hand, Kane reached for my hand as we walked to his car. He drove to the docks, a place we often visited, sometimes together and many times alone. It was a great place to think.

We walked to the end of one of the piers. Pulling me into his arms, he turned so my back rested up against the railing. His focus was completely on me. "What's going on?"

"You're graduating."

"Yeah. So?"

"Are you going to college?"

His focus shifted to just over my shoulder, his expression thoughtful. "I don't think so."

I couldn't help the joy I felt, since I wanted him with me, but I was also curious. "Why not?"

"Maybe I'll feel differently in a year or two, but right now, I'm just not interested. I want to work, want to start putting money away, so when we're ready we can start a life together."

Happiness filled me, so intense it brought tears to my eyes. "Are you serious?"

"Yeah. I meant it, Tea. You and me forever."

Burying my face in his chest, I felt the worry that had weighed me down instantly lift. He touched my chin and forced my focus on him. "You thought I was going to leave you?"

"I did."

"First, I wouldn't make that kind of decision without talking with you. Second, even if I did go to school, there are places close enough to home that I could commute to."

And that thought brought back my fear, because I still wanted Boston University, had been working really hard to get the grades that would get me in. If he had a life here, how could I ask him to give it up? As was his way, he read my thoughts perfectly.

"If you go to Boston, I'm coming with you. There was never a question."

"Are you sure?"

"Absolutely."

"And you would be okay with that, even if you had a job?"

"I can always find another job."

"And if you're in school?"

"I can transfer. Jobs and schools are plenty, there's only one you."

"We're young. You might feel differently in a few years."

His expression turned serious. "I've known you for six years, Tea, and my feelings for you have only grown deeper in that time. A few more years and I'll really be sunk."

Love for this boy washed over me for how easily he spoke those words. "That's a good answer, Kane."

His grin was adorable. "You good?"

"Yeah."

"Time for ice cream." But instead of releasing me, he moved his body closer and bent his head for a kiss that turned my bones to goo.

Kane had been right. In the two years that we'd been dating, we had grown even closer, and not just romantically. There was something to be said for dating your best friend. He had started working full-time at the boatyard and, though he wanted to get his own place, he would only consider actually doing it if I moved in with him. As much as we wanted to take that step, I was only seventeen, and we suspected that Mrs. Marks wouldn't approve. I finally learned how to swim, and we swam out to our island every week. Kane usually beat me, since he was a much stronger swimmer, but I held my own. That day, we took the boat so we could bring a picnic. After eating, we went to play in the water, and Kane tried to dunk me against my will. The only way I could stop him was by wrapping my arms and legs around him and squeezing tight. He went dead still.

"Kane?"

"You win. You can let go."

"What's the matter with you?"

"Nothing. I think maybe I'll take a swim." But he climbed out of the water and reached for his towel, wrapping it around his waist. As I followed him out, he turned to me.

"You have the same look on your face that you get when looking at one of Mrs. T's cakes. What's going on with you?" I asked, my hands moving to my hips. His black hair partially covered his face, and those blue eyes, usually so cool, looked hot, sizzling hot.

"It's just, you're different."

"I'm different. What are you talking about?" He looked down to my chest. "Oh, these. I know, right, they grew overnight."

He swallowed as if that was hard for him.

I had breasts finally, and my roundness, as Kane called it, had thinned out so I could wear a bikini. It was about time. There were a few boys at school interested in taking me out, but I was Kane's. We kissed a lot but we never did anything more. Partly because I hadn't been ready and partly because we lived together and we weren't sure how Mrs. Marks would feel about it. I could admit that I was ready now. I wanted to go all the way with Kane.

"What? I'm not the only one who has changed. Look at that." I poked his shoulders. "Your arms never looked like that before. And that"—I ran my hand down his stomach over the muscles, all six of them—"I like that."

My hand brushed over something hard, and I pulled away at the same time he did.

"Are you okay?" I asked.

"Yeah." It came out in a strangled voice.

"Did I do that?"

"Yeah."

"Does that happen often?"

"Yeah, whenever you're around."

"It happens to me too."

He looked almost hopeful. "What do you mean?"

"Sometimes when you hold me or kiss me, I feel tingles in my belly and my breasts feel fuller and I get an ache . . . down there."

He was gulping, like he was trying to draw breath into his lungs without much success. "You shouldn't be telling me this."

"Why not?"

"Because I want you, Tea. You know I do."

I wanted him too, but I couldn't help teasing him. "You want to poke me with that?" I pointed, since he wasn't really covering it very well with his towel. "I don't think so." And yet my toes curled.

He laughed. "It'll feel good for both of us."

"For you, maybe, but for me it'll be like getting impaled." Which it probably would the first time—and yet I still wanted him.

"No, it won't. I promise you, you will want it. You'll beg me for it."

I would, I knew I would, but I wasn't going to relent that easily. "Not likely."

"I'll prove it. Let me kiss you."

I knew exactly where this was going, wanted it to go there, was thrilled that he'd waited to go there with me, so it was easy to agree. "Okay."

He walked to me, reached for my arms, and wrapped them around his waist. Cradling my face in his hands, he kissed me. Just his lips at first, a slight brushing that I felt all the way down to my toes. When the tip of his tongue touched the corner of my mouth, I wanted more of it, more of him. Pressing myself against him, I opened my mouth and he slipped his tongue inside. He tasted so good, his tongue sweeping my entire mouth and, as if on cue, my breasts felt fuller and the ache started.

I pulled my mouth from his. "Kane?"

"Yeah, Tea?"

"You're right, I do want you to poke me."

He laughed, wrapped me in his arms, and carried me to the blanket. "Told you."

"Can we?"

His eyes went wide. "Seriously?"

"I want it to be with you and I'm ready now."

"Ah, well, I would like that too."

He seemed nervous, so I kept teasing him because, despite what we were about to do, it was still us. "I only want you poking me."

The grin caught me by surprise. "Stop calling it poking. You really want to do this now?"

"I really do. Did you bring a condom?"

Color bloomed on his cheeks. I giggled. "You planned this."

"No, but I was hopeful, very, very hopeful."

"To be with me?"

"Only you, Tea."

Sitting up, I reached for the string of my bathing suit, but he stopped me. "Let me."

His fingers shook as he lightly brushed them over my shoulders, then up my neck. I felt the slight tug before my suit top slipped to my waist. I was a little embarrassed, being exposed to him, but the heated look on his face made the uncomfortable feeling fade.

"So beautiful, Tea," he said while his fingers brushed me, his touch making the ache between my legs intensify.

"Lie back." His voice had gone all rough.

Lying back, he settled next to me on his side, his head on his hand, while his free hand cupped one of my breasts, his thumb brushing across the tip.

"How's that feel?"

"Really good."

"How about this?" he asked a second before his mouth replaced his fingers.

"Oh my God, Kane."

A wetness accompanied the ache between my legs. My hips started to move, seeking relief. His hand moved down my body, slipping under my bathing suit, and his mouth continued to drive me wild. As soon as he touched the place that was aching, my hips lifted off the blanket.

Reaching for him, I touched the hard bulge in his swim trunks. He exhaled on a moan.

"I want to see."

I didn't have to ask twice. He jumped up and pulled his shorts off, his erection bobbing to attention. I giggled.

"What's so funny?"

"It's like it's on alert."

"You sure you want to do this?"

"With you, yes."

He settled on top of me. Spreading my legs, I felt him right where his fingers had been, and he was so hard and smooth, it was my turn to moan.

"It'll hurt the first time."

"I don't care."

And then he was kissing me, full on the mouth, his tongue pushing past my lips, tasting and claiming. The ache was back, even stronger than before. His hands moved everywhere, touching and learning. And then his finger was pushing into me.

"Oh."

"Does that hurt?"

"Yeah, but it feels good too."

Our eyes were locked when he did it again, pushing his finger in slow and deep. The sound that came from the back of my throat was one of pain and pleasure. He worked me, in and out until my body adjusted to the intrusion, and then he shifted and reached for the condom. I was fascinated as he slid it on. He was so hard, and kind of purple with bulging veins, and yet he was beautiful.

Settling between my thighs, he wrapped his hand around himself and guided it right where it needed to be.

"I'm sorry," he whispered right before his hips shifted and he pushed himself in. It hurt, he was only a quarter of the way in, but it hurt.

"Want me to stop?"

"No. Just do it fast."

"I don't want to hurt you."

"It'll hurt less if you just do it fast."

And he did. With one powerful thrust of his hips, he was fully inside of me. Tears smarted in my eyes, because it really hurt. I almost told him to pull out, but as long as he didn't move, it didn't hurt.

His face was pinched, and I wondered if he was in pain too. "Does it hurt you too?"

He laughed out loud. Not the answer I was expecting. "No, it feels really good. It will feel even better when I start to move."

"You have to move?"

"We're not going to come if I don't."

The pleasant ache was gone; I doubted I was going to feel anything but pain, but I wanted him to come. Wrapping my legs around him, I pulled him deeper. His eyes closed on a groan.

"Move, Kane."

He didn't wait to be told again; he moved slowly and I felt the tingles in my stomach and my breasts started to feel heavier, but the ache between my legs was not the good kind. His hips moved faster, and I winced each time he thrust, filling me completely. And then his body stilled, but his expression, the look of euphoria, took my breath away. We stayed like that for a while, and when his eyes opened there was more than euphoria in his gaze—I saw love.

"Did you?" I asked just to be sure.

"Yeah, that was incredible. You didn't, but I am nothing if not persistent."

I laughed. He was such a clown. "I liked watching you."

He pulled out of me and, as much as it had hurt, I missed being connected to him. "I'll be right back."

I wasn't a virgin anymore and I was okay with that. I really wanted to feel whatever it was Kane had felt, but having him inside me, pain or not, had been perfect.

My eyes flew open when I felt a soothing coolness between my legs. Kane was there, back in his trunks, with a towel soaked in seawater, pressing it where I hurt.

"How badly did I hurt you?"

"Not so much."

"Sorry you didn't come."

"I didn't expect to the first time."

"We'll try it again when you're not so sore."

He looked down, his eyes where his hand was, before his gaze lifted back to me. "Love you, Tea."

My heart stopped for a second and my chest got all tight, hearing this boy say those words to me.

"You don't have to say them back."

Sitting up, I moved to kneel in front of him, my hands coming to rest on his shoulders. "I lost my heart to you the day we hung the angels on the Christmas tree."

His eyes widened. "Seriously?"

"Totally."

Wrapping me into his arms, he kissed me so long that I begged him to poke me again. And this time, when he came, so did I.

As I sat on the sofa on the balcony off my bedroom, my thoughts remained on the day before: the day Kane and I had sex. He told me he loved me. I knew he did, but I kind of thought it was like the love someone had for a dog. Not that I was comparing myself to a dog, but *I* was a trusted companion. It wasn't that kind of love he felt for me though—he *loved* me. I saw it in his face; even though he was very good at keeping his thoughts private, I saw it. He let me.

I can't lie, that first time we had sex it hurt, and the second time too, but then the feelings swept in—the tightening in my belly, the rush, like a wave just getting ready to break, my body feeling suspended for just a beat or two. When I did fall, it wasn't in fear, but in the most incredible sensation. I liked sex, loved it with Kane.

I think I might have been walking a little funny that day, but considering how I had become sore, I was okay with that. Kane didn't want to have sex again until I stopped hurting. Earlier, he'd brought me a warm compress for the ache between my legs, wanted to help me place it, but I think that might have led to the very act he wanted to avoid.

I wondered if Mrs. Marks knew that Kane and I had had sex. She seemed to know everything, but I didn't how she would feel about that, us both being her charges. I kind of thought we were a foregone conclusion. We'd been thick as thieves for eight years. I'd loved him for almost as long as that.

He had left an hour or so ago to put out a small kitchen fire in the diner. I really hated that he was a firefighter—one of the three volunteers in the town who helped the regular squad. He'd signed up as soon as he'd turned eighteen. He had witnessed a boat burning as a kid, and he couldn't believe how fast it had gone up, how quickly the fire had itched to spread. Thoughts of that happening to people's homes, with all of their possessions inside, was what motivated him to volunteer. I understood. It was who he was, after all, but we had fought about it. He promised he would be careful, focused. Yet every time he was called, I waited for his return with my heart in my throat.

Mrs. T was baking something sinful. The smell wafted up to me. Maybe it was pastries. I could eat them all before Kane got home, another downside to his foray into fire management. I didn't actually reach the kitchen, because I heard voices coming from the library, rather loud voices, so I went to see what was up.

Before I stepped into the room, I heard Kane. That little bugger, he was probably already eating the pastries. I started into the room to give him a piece of my mind, and then I heard the second voice, Camille. My body just froze, except for my heart, which was pounding in every part of my body. What was she doing there?

"The way you handled that fire was very sexy," Camille purred at my boyfriend. Sexy? Putting out a fire was sexy? He'd probably used a fire extinguisher. What the hell was so sexy about that?

"You said you needed to ask me something, so ask." He sounded pissed. Pissed was good. I could work with pissed.

"Not here. Maybe we could take a ride out to your little island."

No! I screamed in my head. That island was our special place—even more so now that we'd had sex there. Camille wasn't welcome. I knew he felt the same way, and yet I still held my breath for his response. "Are you fucking out of your mind?" he asked.

He always was better at comebacks than me.

I could hear her pouting. "I miss us, miss you. Why can't we give it another try?"

"We never gave it a first try. Despite your best efforts, the closest we got to a try was you sticking your tongue down my throat."

"It's her, isn't it? You're like her lap dog. Everywhere she goes, you're right there at her side."

"Lap dog." Kane sounded as if he was pondering that expression. "If it's Tea's lap, I'm okay with that. She always wanted a dog anyway."

My tummy flipped. He was my trusted companion too.

"What is it you really want, Camille?"

"You. And I want to be mistress of Raven's Peak. I've wanted that since I was a little girl, and I'm used to getting what I want."

Kane started laughing; he actually laughed at her. "You're seriously fucked up. I live here. I'm not related to Mrs. Marks. I have no claim on this house. She was just kind enough to give me a place to stay. So even if I did lose my mind and marry you, I wouldn't get the house. If anyone were to inherit, it would be Tea. And I know you are not her type."

"Mrs. Marks adopted you. You would inherit."

"She adopted me so I wouldn't be put into foster care. Tea's grandparents were Mrs. Marks's best friends. She's more family to Mrs. Marks than I am."

I didn't agree with Kane. He was like a grandson to Mrs. Marks.

"That old lady would give it to you if you wanted it." The way she said that was like she knew something, hanging the carrot and hoping for Kane to bite. I would have; he didn't.

"Let me make this clear to you. I love Tea, I want a life with Tea. Even if I didn't have Tea, I wouldn't want you. You will never have this house, so move on."

"You'll be sorry, Kane Doyle. You'll be sorry you crossed me. I promise you that."

"The door's that way. Use it."

Stepping into the shadows, I watched her leave the room and storm off. Her face flamed purple, not at all attractive. The sound of the front door slamming echoed throughout the house.

"You heard all of that?" My head whipped around to see Kane leading against the doorjamb.

"Yeah, sorry. I didn't mean to eavesdrop until I heard it was Camille, and then I was wishing I had a glass to put against the door."

"Meant every word I said."

"That you love me and want a life with me?"

"Yep."

"Well, as it happens, I want that with you, so we're good." My eyes twinkled. "I always wanted a dog."

Sincerity turned mischievous and, in the next second, he started down the hall.

"Where are you going?" I asked.

"Do you smell that?"

"What?"

"The delicious smell coming from the kitchen."

"The pastries?"

"Yup. I'm going to eat them all." And this was why I loved him so much; despite the fact that our relationship had evolved, we were still just us: the same people we'd been as kids. I smiled.

"Oh, no you're not," I called to him halfway to the kitchen.

But he did eat the majority.

Kane and I were at the ice cream parlor, sharing a sundae, when the bell over the door jingled, announcing Camille's entrance. Her eyes scanned the room, landing on Kane and me. She looked smug. Why, I had no idea, since the last time she'd seen Kane, he told her no way in hell would they ever be together.

She settled at the counter, her legs swinging, smiling and laughing with the boy behind the counter, but every once and a while her eyes darted back to us.

"What's up with Camille?" I asked Kane, which made him halt devouring his ice cream for a moment, his gaze turning toward the counter.

"Who knows, who cares."

True, who did? We finished our ice cream, Kane leaving the money and tip on the table, before we started outside toward his car. Walking around to my side, he reached for the door, but stopped as if frozen. In the next second he said, "What the fuck!"

Following the direction of his scowl, I understood his anger. His tires had been slashed.

The door of the ice cream parlor opened and Camille stepped out and leaned up against the wall—her gaze in our direction, her expression satisfied.

"Fucking Camille." Kane started toward her, but I grabbed his arm.

"We don't know she did it."

"We can't *prove* she did it, but she fucking did it."

I had no doubt he was right. "It's what she wants—the reaction. Don't give it to her."

Kane seethed, his face turning red with anger, but he turned from her and moved back to his car. He reached for my hand. "You're right."

"Are you going to call the police?"

"Her dad's a lawyer. What the hell is the point? Let's see if the auto body shop has my tires in stock."

"How will you pay for them?"

"I'll figure it out. Looks like we're walking home."

"I like walking."

He grinned. "I like you." And then he kissed me. As we walked to the garage, Camille was nowhere to be seen.

chapter 2

The College Years
Teagan

Sitting on the beach by Raven's Peak, I looked toward the horizon, excitement and sadness battling inside me. I had been accepted to Boston University. I was able to go, thanks to money from my parents that I'd gained access to when I'd turned eighteen, and so my excitement. The sadness came from the thought of leaving Kane. We had discussed him coming with me to Boston, and he still wanted to, but he was currently working on a boat at the boatyard that he wanted to see finished. He also wanted to wait until the fire department found his replacement. Our town didn't see many fires, but the force was small, and he didn't like leaving them high and dry.

This meant that I was going to be heading off without him. In the nine years that I had lived at Raven's Peak, Kane had never been far away. He was more than my boyfriend; he was my best friend. With him, I felt stronger and more confident.

I couldn't lie, I was looking forward to returning to Boston and attending the school where my parents had met, ready to take that next step in my life. I just wished I could take that step with Kane at my side. And there was another thought that had started to fester. What if we were only as close as we were because of convenience? We had both been orphaned: scared and lonely. What if during our separation he realized that it wasn't so much me but the proximity of me that he liked? I decided never to mention it to him, but that negative thought lingered in the back of my mind.

I knew Kane was near before he even sat down.

"Thought I'd find you out here," he said. "Nice sweatshirt."

I was wearing my mom's Boston U sweatshirt.

"You all packed?" he asked.

"Yep."

Sensing my turmoil, he lifted my chin to meet his gaze. "What's wrong?"

"You are going to come, right?"

"Yes."

"I mean it, Kane, you're not going to change your mind, are you?"

"Where's this coming from? I love you, Tea. I want to be with you, but I've got to finish what I started here before I can do that. Six months, that's all I need, and then I'll be crashing in your dorm and eating all of your takeout."

"Clown." But there was a part of me that didn't understand why he hadn't already finished up with the boat and arranged for his replacement at the fire department. It wasn't as if my move had been sprung on him; he'd known it was coming for a while, years, in fact. This negative thought also lingered, and I was worried that he was having second thoughts, especially considering how adamant he had been just a few years before about jobs and schools being plenty but there being only one me.

"Seriously, before you know it, I'll be there, waiting for you every night after class." He wiggled his eyebrows. "I might even cook you dinner if you play your cards right."

"I'm going to miss you."

"We'll talk every night."

"Okay."

"Six months, Tea, and then you won't be able to get rid of me."

Resting my head on his shoulder, my gaze drifted back to the horizon. "Never. I would never want to get rid of you."

"Good, since I would never have allowed it." And then he changed the subject. "You're excited."

He wasn't asking. "I'm nervous, but I am excited and not just for the education but for the whole experience. I've lived a pretty sheltered life, so getting out and being on my own, despite how much I hate that you aren't coming with me now, I want that. I want to know I can make it on my own. Does that make sense?"

"Yeah."

"My parents often talked about college and how much it helped form the people they became. They took me once to one of their reunions; I was only five, but I remember the day so vividly. I feel like I'll be able to connect with them again, walking the same campus they did, eating in the same dining halls, being in the place that meant so much to both of them."

"They'd be proud of you," he said softly.

"Thank you for saying that. I think they would be too. Do you regret your decision to not go away to college?"

"No. I got two more years with you."

Happiness burned through me in response, and then he added, "But maybe watching you, I'll be inspired to give college a try."

"It'd be nice to go through the experience together," I said softly.

"We'll still be together, Tea, regardless."

I liked that answer.

His arm slipped around my waist, and for a good long time we just sat there, content in our silence.

Kane climbed from my bed the following morning and grabbed his boxer briefs. He slept in my room every night now, ever since that day a year ago when we'd made love. He waited until everyone was asleep before he snuck in and crawled into bed with me. I loved having him next to me, his body pressed against mine. Feeling him slide into me, moving against me, kissing and touching me. I couldn't get enough of him, would never have my fill.

"Hurry up. Mr. Clancy will be up any minute to get my bags," I tried to say, but I was laughing too hard watching Kane hopping on one foot trying to pull up his shorts. "You really should just walk around naked, it's a good look for you."

"You're ridiculous. Only you get to see this."

"I so don't have a problem with that."

"What time is your flight?"

"Two."

"All right, I'll be back in about an hour and I'll take you."

He wrapped my face in his hands and kissed me long and hard. "One hour."

"I'll be ready."

My bags were on the driveway an hour later, and I was sitting on the front step. Shopping for college had been an experience. Mrs. Marks had been on a mission, and it had felt nice bonding with her over even something as small as bedspreads for my dorm room. She was proud of me, I could see it in her expression. She wouldn't let me pay for anything either, even though I had the money from my parents. I had the sense that there was more to the moment than just me going off to school, as if something in her own past fueled her exuberance now.

"You have your phone and computer?" Mrs. Marks asked.

"Yes."

"Your checkbook and credit card?"

"Yes."

"Remember to call as soon as you get there."

"I will."

"Enjoy yourself. I know you'll work hard, you always do, but enjoy yourself too." Her tone turned serious. "I know about you and Kane. I think we all knew where you were both heading. But while you are separated for the next few months, have fun. Live the college experience, because it only happens once."

"We wondered if you knew. We weren't sure how to broach the subject."

"The same for me. I suspected early on that you two were going to develop an attachment. Had you been younger when your relationship changed, I would have said something, but you were on the cusp of eighteen. You've known each other since you were nine and eleven—I think you both knew what you wanted and what you were doing. But with that being said, this time apart will be good for both of you. You've only ever known each other, and forever is a long time. Take this opportunity to make sure of your feelings."

Dread moved through me at her words. Was she encouraging me to date? Did she not appreciate just how much Kane meant to me? Or did she know something about Kane that I didn't? I wanted to ask, but I didn't want to hear her answer.

Mrs. T chimed in, thankfully changing the subject. "I've packed a few slices of cake in your bag." I loved her cakes almost as much as Kane did.

"Thank you for your contribution to the freshman fifteen."

"I do what I can," she said with a smile.

Kane's car pulled up the drive. He hopped out all smiles. "You ready?"

Just looking at him, I knew I had no doubts about my feelings. I didn't need to play the field, I had the one I wanted. And I hoped, truly hoped, he did too. "Yep."

Mr. Clancy helped Kane load the car while I said my good-byes. Mrs. T hugged me hard and slipped me two hundred bucks. "Emergency fund."

The memory of my first day at Raven's Peak flashed in my mind, and how my eyes had burned with fear. And now they were burning because I was leaving the place that really had become my home.

"It's only four years, and then you'll be back. Besides, there are holidays. We'll see you in November."

"I know. I don't know why I'm being so sentimental."

"It's a big step. You're entitled. Be safe, Teagan."

Mrs. Marks was next, kissing me on each cheek and taking a moment to just stare. "I remember the scared little girl who appeared that first night . . . and now look at you, a confident young woman heading off to college. I'm really proud of you."

I was about to cry, so I quickly hugged her and kissed her cheek. Mr. Clancy was holding the car door for me, and I pecked him on the cheek, which earned me a smile, before I climbed in.

Kane turned the car around and, as we started down the drive, I looked back at the three of them all waving me off. I waved until I couldn't see them anymore, and when I turned forward, my cheeks felt damp.

"You okay?"

"Yeah, I guess I'm just realizing that they really are our family. We're lucky, Kane. Our lives could have turned out so very differently."

"I know. We're an odd group, but we work."

"Yes, we do."

"Classes start on Monday?"

"Yeah, new student orientation is this weekend."

"You and your roommate are going to do that together, right?"

"Yeah. She seems nice, at least on the phone. I would rather have you as my roommate."

"Next year, apartment off campus, you and me."

"Promise?"

"I'll do one better." He pulled the car over and shut down the engine before climbing out without saying another word. He came around to my side as I stepped out of the car.

"What are you doing?"

He dropped to one knee and my heart moved up into my throat.

"I love you, Tea. I want my life with you. I want to wake up next to you every morning and go to sleep next to you every night. Marry me."

My yes came out as a sob, a happy sob—he felt the impending distance too. With his proposal, my lingering worries faded.

Reaching into his pocket, he pulled out a little black box. Inside was a diamond ring, the small brilliant-cut solitaire framed in white gold. "It's not as big as I would have liked, but I'll upgrade it when I'm making more money."

"No! It's perfect."

He grinned and slipped it onto my finger. "You're stuck with me now."

Dropping to my knees, I threw my arms around him and held on tight. "Exactly where I want to be."

Kane got me to the airport just in time. We said our farewells at the security checkpoint. "Call as soon as you get to your room."

"I will."

"Have fun, Tea. This is a big deal, and you've worked hard for it."

"And you put in double time so you cut the six months to three."

"Deal." He wrapped my face in his hands, his thumbs brushing my cheekbones, while we looked our fill. Our good-bye kiss was just a brushing of our lips, and still my entire body sighed. Reaching for my bag, he handed it to me. "See you in November." He lifted my hand and kissed the ring.

"Love you." My feet felt like lead as I walked away from him, staring back over my shoulder at the sight of him standing there, hands in his pockets, and a small smile on his face. The image burned into my memory. My fiancé. Thanksgiving was in three months; that wasn't so long a wait.

New student orientation was surprisingly fun. My roommate, Eleanor, was as sweet in person as she had been over the phone. She was also very shy, so it took a bit to get her to talk in the beginning. But after the first few hours together, she warmed up to me—even going so far as to initiate conversation. Our first weekend was packed with activities, learning the campus, getting introduced to the school's organizations, learning how to use our meal cards, and meeting our advisors. It was during lunch that first day that I met Simon Dale.

The dining hall made the most amazing chocolate chip cookies. I wasn't the only one to think so, since the platter emptied quickly. There was only one cookie left, and just as I stepped up to it, a large hand reached over me and grabbed it.

"Hey," I said, turning to see a boy standing there holding my cookie. He grinned. He actually grinned at me. He had a Mediterranean look: golden-brown skin, hair on the long side and so dark a brown it looked almost black, which matched his eye color perfectly. Standing several inches over six feet, he was all muscle. He was undeniably hot, and yet there wasn't even a spark of interest in me, only irritation.

"That's mine," I whined.

"I got it first."

"Seriously?"

"Yep, they're that good, but I'm willing to share." Aside from Kane, I didn't have a lot of experience with guys, so I was surprised at how comfortable I felt talking to *this* guy. Comfortable enough to even tease him despite his imposing stature.

"How magnanimous of you."

He broke the cookie in half, but before he handed it to me, he said, "I'm Simon Dale."

"Teagan Harper."

"You from Boston?" he asked.

"Maine. What about you?"

"Beacon Hill. I'm pretty sure one of the standard questions we're suppose to ask is, what's your major?"

I couldn't count how many people had asked me that. "Undecided. You?"

"Art history."

"Really? That actually sounds kind of cool. Are you interested in working in a museum?"

"I'm not sure, but I love art in all forms and the history behind it."

"It must be nice to have a general idea of what you want to do. I'm so not there yet." An odd look swept his expression, so I asked, "What's that look for?"

He kind of snorted in reply. "It'd be even nicer if my parents would get on board with it."

"So their aspirations for you don't include the study of art?"

"Far from it. They want me to major in political science for my future career in politics, but I have no interest."

"Do you think they'll eventually come around?"

"Yeah, eventually. But I could do without all the drama now."

It had been years since the thought of my parents had brought me pain, but I couldn't deny being at Boston U had pulled those feelings close to the surface. If I had the chance to see them again, I'd welcome conflict, even an argument, over my choice of major.

Not knowing where my thoughts were, Simon asked, "What about you? Are your parents pushing a major on you?"

The pain was no longer under the surface, but right there and clearly very easy to see—Simon's smile faded. "Did I say something wrong?"

"My parents died when I was nine."

"Oh. I'm sorry."

"No, it's okay. It was so long ago. I'm feeling a little more tender than normal because they both attended this school." Just as I'd hoped, walking in their footsteps really did make me feel connected to them, but it was heartbreaking too. I wasn't living in one of the dorms they'd once called home, but I passed by them. In my head, I could see my parents walking up the steps, loaded down with books, so young and eager. The reality that they were both gone only fourteen years after they graduated broke my heart every time I allowed myself to think about it.

"Carrying on the tradition, that's cool."

I hadn't really thought of it as carrying on the tradition, but I guess I kind of was—and he was right, it was cool. And then Simon reached for my hand and squeezed it very gently. He said nothing, but I could tell he knew where my thoughts were and was offering silent comfort. The gesture was one that Kane would have done, and in that moment I missed him terribly.

"Did you leave a boyfriend behind? Because that looks like an engagement ring," he said as his focus shifted to my finger.

I missed Kane, but thinking about him always warmed me, and this time I felt it on my cheeks. "I did. He's moving here in a few months after he ties up some things he's working on."

"How long have you been engaged?"

"He proposed on the way to the airport, so only a day, but I've known him since I was nine."

"Since you were nine? I'm guessing you've got a good story to tell."

He wasn't wrong; the story of Kane and me, though unfinished, was pretty freaking great. "I do."

"I love a good story. Let's get some coffee and you can tell me all about this guy so I can live vicariously through you."

It was the way he emphasized *this guy* that clued me in that Simon was gay. Though, in fairness, I'd already suspected it.

"What's this guy's name?"

"Kane, but surely you aren't serious about hearing our story. It'd bore you."

"Is it love?"

"Yeah."

"Then I won't get bored. Besides, isn't that what today is all about? Making friends. I don't know about you, but I think it'll be more fun experiencing all this with a friend."

Teasing him again, I asked, "You want to be my friend?"

"We both share a love for the chocolate chip cookie. Friendships have been built on far less."

Simon was a bit goofy, and yet he reminded me a lot of Kane. "I agree."

He reached for my elbow and started guiding me to the counter for our coffee. "Excellent. Coffee first and then the story. I want to hear all about this Kane."

After orientation, Simon and I began to hang out regularly. It started with meals in the dining hall, but it didn't take long before we found ourselves in each other's room: studying, watching television, or just talking. We even hit a few parties, though neither of us were really that into it.

A couple of weeks after orientation, Simon appeared at my door, but it wasn't for our standard meal breaks. His normally sunny personality was replaced with a look of dejection.

"Simon, what's wrong?"

"I told my parents I was gay. They didn't take it well."

Reaching for his hand, I drew him into my room, where we settled on my bed. Eleanor was at a study session, so we had privacy. "I thought they already knew."

"So did I. I mean, I never confirmed it, but I thought it was pretty clear."

"So what happened?"

"My mom was mentioning a girl I grew up with, they often do that, and I'd had enough with what I thought were their passive-aggressive feelings toward my sexual preference. But apparently they didn't have a clue. My mom cried and my dad . . . he couldn't even speak."

"And I'm guessing you weren't expecting that response from them."

"No. They've always been very supportive, if demanding, but I never thought they'd have an objection to me being gay. They love me, so it shouldn't matter. Should it?"

"Of course it shouldn't matter."

"What if they can't get over it?"

"There's nothing to get over. Being gay is who you are and your parents love you. They'll eventually come around."

"I hope you're right."

"Me too."

Four weeks. Three full weekends. That's how long it'd been since I'd left Raven's Peak, since I'd left Kane. Eleanor, being a Bostonian, went home every weekend. I missed Kane something fierce, despite having to work so hard for my classes. We talked every night, and I told him he should come down for a weekend, because we'd have the room all to ourselves. Blue Hill was far, so I didn't think he'd be able to visit, but how I wished he would.

Friday night and the whole weekend stretched ahead of me, most of it to be spent studying. Simon had gone home to some family function, so I wouldn't even see him for our normal meal breaks. His parents had apologized, but things were still a bit awkward. It was partly why Simon went home, an attempt to show his parents that he was still Simon regardless of his sexual orientation.

Sitting on my bed, dressed in one of Kane's tees, I pulled my knees up and rested my cheek on them. I didn't know how I would manage being away from Kane for five more months. At least it was only five months and not the full four years. I'd never make four years. It wasn't even because I missed the sex and the kissing—which I did—I just missed *him*.

Thinking about him prompted me to call, but disappointment filled me when his phone went to voice mail. I had a test on Tuesday, so I might as well start studying. I grabbed my backpack and unloaded my books on my bed and got lost in work.

A knock at my door pulled me from my reading—the clock read almost ten p.m. I hadn't realized how long I'd been at it, but I'd gotten a lot done. Dropping my book on my bed, I walked to the door and pulled it open. It took me a beat or two to react, since I wasn't sure that what I was seeing was real. Kane stood there with a bag over his shoulder and a grin on his face.

"Hey, Tea. Surprise!"

I threw myself into his arms. His bag dropped to the floor, his arms wrapped around me, and he held me so close. "I've missed you," he whispered into my hair.

"I've missed you more."

"Maybe we should do this inside," he said, then added, "because I want to make love to you and I don't think you want your dorm mates to see what a fine specimen of a man you've got yourself."

I stepped back. "You're a clown. How did you get in?"

"Charmed one of the girls as she was leaving." With a wicked look, he reached for his bag and followed me into my room. The door had only just closed when I heard the lock, and then his mouth was covering mine. Our lips molded, my tongue pushing between his lips, and his hands roamed over my back and down to my ass while we moved toward my bed.

Pressing hot kisses down my neck and shoulder, his fingers gripped my shirt and lifted it over my head. "I like that you're wearing my shirt."

"I sleep in it," I managed before his tongue was in my mouth, his hands on my breasts, the ache between my legs accompanied by a wetness.

At my bed, Kane stepped back, eyeing me from head to toe, as I stood there in only a pair of pink panties.

"God, I've missed you. You're going to want to clear your bed off because in another minute, I'm knocking everything on the floor."

Bed? So lost in him, I'd completely forgotten that all of my homework was spread out on my bed. With one sweep, I knocked everything to the floor before jumping into the middle of the bed, lying down on my back and resting on my elbows with my knees up and legs slightly spread.

His laugh rang around the room.

"You're wearing too many clothes, Kane."

"Noted." He watched me as he stepped out of his jeans and yanked his shirt forward over his head. Naked and aroused, he was beautiful.

Climbing onto the bed, he settled between my legs, his mouth meeting mine. My arms wrapped around his neck, his weight pushed us deeper into the mattress. "Kane, the condom."

He pulled his mouth from mine, chuckling as he looked down at me. "Impatient?"

"It's been too long."

His gaze sizzled. "Agreed." He climbed from the bed, grabbed his jeans, and pulled out several condoms from his front pocket.

"Optimistic."

"Determined is a better word," he said as he joined me on the bed and handed me the condom. I loved slipping the condom onto him, loved feeling how hard he was and knowing it was because of me. Gently pushing me flat against the mattress, he settled himself right where we both needed him.

"Next time, we'll go more slowly," he promised, and then he was filling me, my hips lifting, my back arching, and everything in me sighing at being connected to him again.

"Missed this," he whispered.

"Me too. Now move."

But I didn't need to say that, he already was. Oh, did I miss this.

❧

It was close to two in the morning when we finally settled in for sleep. Tucked up against Kane's side, his fingers running patterns over my bare belly, he asked, "You okay with me just showing up?"

Shifting so I could see him, I gave him my best "duh" face. "Yes."

His lips turned up on the one side but the smile didn't quite reach his eyes. "I didn't want to intrude, but I needed to see you."

"You could never intrude. I called you earlier, wanted to ask you to come for the weekend."

His eyes lit with his smile this time. "Really?"

"Why would you doubt it, Kane? I love you. I miss you like hell."

"It's just that you're here, with so much to do and see. I'm just the guy you left at home. Maybe I can't compete with that."

Sitting up, I stared at him like his head was spinning in circles. "Compete? So if it had been you who went away, I should be concerned that you would move on?"

"No!"

"That's how I feel."

"I needed to hear that." He reached for my finger where the diamond winked up at him.

"I never take it off."

He pressed a kiss on it, his gaze meeting mine. "Five months."

"I'm counting the days."

"Eight weeks until Thanksgiving," he added.

"We'll get a long weekend; I can't wait."

"That makes two of us. I think we might actually have a dinner guest this year."

"Really? Who?" In all the years that I lived at Raven's Peak, it was only ever the five of us.

"Mrs. T's grandniece. She's attending the University of Maine at Farmington, and she's been coming to Raven's Peak for the weekends to spend time with Mrs. T."

A coldness swept through. Stupid, probably, but I didn't like that someone had taken my place, even if it was just for the weekends. Did Kane treat her like he treated me? Did they spend time together too? The idea sent jealousy burning through me.

"You okay, Tea?"

I wasn't, but I didn't want to get into that now, so I lied, my first ever lie to him. "I'm great."

Thanksgiving loomed. Midterms were kicking my ass. I had a D in my econ class; I needed the extra study sessions the professor was offering. I had become so consumed with studying that I had started missing Kane's phone calls, either losing track of time or falling asleep waiting for him to call. I hated missing his calls, looked forward to them all day. Usually when I missed him, I called the next morning to apologize, but he never answered. I didn't know if he was busy or if he was punishing me because I hadn't answered.

I needed to tell Mrs. Marks I wouldn't be coming home the following week for the holiday, so I made that call first; it was the easier of the two. She answered on the second ring. "Teagan, I was just thinking about you. When is your flight?"

My throat actually hurt from the tears that wanted to fall. "I'm not going to make it home. My professor is offering an extra study session on the Friday after Thanksgiving, and I really need to go."

"Oh. Are you sure you can't just come for the day?"

I could. I'd thought about it, but I knew if I went for just the day, I wouldn't want to come back. I'd blow off the study session, and I couldn't afford to do that. "I really want to be with you, but I know myself well enough that if I come home, I won't come back for the session."

"Have you told Kane?"

"He's my next call."

"We'll miss you. What will you do about eating?"

"One of the dining halls is staying open for the students, mostly foreign, who aren't going home. They're even making turkey and all the trimmings."

"Well, at least there's that. How are you?"

"I'm good. I really love it here and, once I get my grade up, I'll be even better."

There was silence on the line for a beat before she said, "I know how much you want to come home, but you're taking responsibility for your schooling, and, as much as I hate to say it, that is the right priority at this point in your life."

"I hope Kane feels the same."

"He'll be upset, Teagan, but he'll understand."

"Happy Thanksgiving, Mrs. Marks."

"Happy Thanksgiving to you. Don't work too hard and make sure you take a break and eat some turkey on Thursday."

"I will."

I dreaded making the next call. My hope was that Kane would come to Boston, and we could have a dining hall–style Thanksgiving together and then spend the rest of the weekend in my room. There was no point in delaying the inevitable. I settled back on my bed and called him.

"Hey, Tea. What time's your flight?" My heart twisted in my chest; he sounded so excited. I didn't immediately answer. "You're not coming home."

"I'm sorry. I want to come home, but I got a D on my midterm. I have to attend the study sessions over the break or I'm going to fail. Is there any chance you can come here?"

"Mrs. Marks has been preparing for your return for weeks. You know how she is about the holidays."

"Please don't make me feel worse than I already do."

Frustration and a little contrition came across the line. "I'm sorry, it's been seven weeks since I've seen you. I'm going crazy."

"I am too, but Christmas is right around the corner, and I'll be home for a month. I was thinking of inviting my friend Simon home for part of it. Do you think Mrs. Marks would be okay with that?"

Silence.

"Simon's gay, so whatever you're thinking, please don't. He knows all about you."

"I'm sure she'll be fine with him coming here."

"Are you?"

"He's your friend."

"Kane, what are you thinking?"

"Nothing."

"Please, I've known you since you were eleven, so stop bullshitting me."

"I'm jealous. Is that what you want to hear? I'm jealous. The fact that your friend is gay is of no importance. He gets to see you when I don't."

"In under three months, that's going to change."

"I know, but I can't help it. I've only ever been completely truthful with you, so why deny what I'm feeling," he added.

"That's fair."

"I'll let Mrs. Marks know it will only be five for Thanksgiving this year."

"I already spoke to Mrs. Marks. Five, you mean four?"

"No. Doreen, Mrs. T's grandniece, is joining us. I told you about her."

Now I hated it even more that I wasn't going home.

"Tea?"

"I'm jealous of Doreen."

"Why?"

"For the same reason you're jealous of Simon. Is she pretty?"

Silence.

"I'll take that as a yes."

"Tea, you're being silly."

"Is she gay?"

"Not that I'm aware of."

Definitely wished I were going home.

"You sure you can't come here?" I asked. It may have sounded more like a plea.

"I already promised I'd show Doreen around—the happening spots. I thought we'd be doing that together."

So not only was Doreen going to be there, she was going to be spending quality alone time with my fiancé. I felt ill, but I couldn't change my mind; I had to get my grade up, and if I went home now, it would be obvious to Kane that I was only going home because I was jealous. I didn't want to give him the satisfaction.

"Miss you, Tea."

And even drowning in jealousy, I couldn't deny that I missed him too. "Miss you."

Thanksgiving came and went. I had called home and spoken to everyone on the actual day, Kane detailing the scents coming from the kitchen to rub it in. He sounded happy, which I thought was surprising with how upset he'd seemed about me not coming home. I tried not to think about why he'd be happy, namely by spending time with Doreen, but I did anyway. A pain had started in my stomach, an ulcer most likely, and I called it Doreen.

After my study session on Friday, Kane and I talked, but I hadn't heard from him since. Each day that went by without word, the more worried I got. He'd had a long weekend with Doreen, and now he wasn't calling me. It seemed like a reasonable jump to believe he wasn't calling because he was spending time with her. There weren't words to describe the sensation that moved through me when I thought about Kane moving on with someone else.

As the days turned into weeks, I began to get scared that it was something more, that something bad had happened. I couldn't get through to him or anyone at the house, which never happened. Focusing on anything at school was impossible, so I made arrangements with my professors and headed home using the open-ended tickets Mrs. Marks had purchased for me to use at Thanksgiving.

As soon as I landed, I called for a cab, which was going to cost a fortune, but I wanted to get home as fast as possible. Until the moment Raven's Peak came into view, I hadn't realized how much I'd missed being there. After paying the cabbie, I grabbed my bags and ran up the front steps. Mr. Clancy wasn't there to open the door, but then, he wasn't expecting me.

As I placed my bags just inside the door, I was met by silence. I ran up the stairs right to Kane's room, but when I entered, my feet just stopped. His room wasn't just unoccupied, it looked nearly cleared out. Most of his personal stuff, things he didn't use but didn't want to part with, was boxed in the corner, but all his clothes and those things he used daily like his iPod and speakers were gone. I didn't know how long I stood in his room that was no longer his room. Where the hell was he? Had he moved to Boston already and was waiting to surprise me? But it seemed like a cruel joke to not contact me. We never went so long between calls.

I searched the house for the others, but the place was empty, and, from the look of the pile of mail on the kitchen counter, it had been for a while. Reaching for my phone, I called Mrs. Marks, but as was the case lately, her phone went to voice mail. An uneasy feeling moved through me. Something was definitely not right.

Someone was bringing in the mail; they'd know what was going on. I started from the house to head to town to find that person. Halfway down the drive, a car I didn't recognize pulled in. I recognized the driver—Camille. Pulling over, she climbed out. Surprise filled me, because Camille had gone off to school only just the year before. The timing of her decision, not long after Kane had told her no way would they ever be together, made it clear to both of us that she was off licking her wounds. Considering her motivation, I guess it wasn't a surprise to discover she hadn't stuck with it.

"Teagan? What are you doing here?"

I was tempted to ask the same of her, but I honestly didn't care. "Came home for a visit. Do you know where everyone is?"

"Oh." I didn't sense understanding or even sympathy in that one word, but I did see a giddiness that turned my stomach. "You don't know?"

"Know what?" What the hell did she know about my family that I didn't?

"They've been gone for a while, getting Kane settled in his new apartment."

I wasn't sure I heard her correctly, but excitement mingled with my confusion, because it sounded like he was in Boston. I was going to kill him for the way he did this, but I was thrilled with the end result. "New apartment?"

"Yeah, to be closer to his girlfriend."

"You mean me?"

"No, his new girlfriend."

All the air left my lungs. New girlfriend, what the hell was she talking about? Kane had a new girlfriend? "Doreen?" The name passed my lips before I even really knew I'd meant to say it.

"Yes. You should see them together. Every weekend they're inseparable. A lot like how you and he used to be before you got all consumed with school. It's not surprising that their feelings grew into something more, especially since you seem to have moved on."

Pain sliced through me; as much as I wanted to dismiss every word from her mouth as a lie, I couldn't. Deep down I'd feared this very thing. Yet despite the ache in my chest, I was certain that Kane would have told me if he'd moved on. He'd never leave me adrift.

"Mrs. Marks and the others went to help get him settled. I'm sorry. I thought you knew, being his best friend and all."

Somehow I knew she'd said that on purpose to dig the knife in. It should have hurt, it should have eviscerated me, and there was a part of me shattered at the possibility, but I refused to believe that my Kane would act so selfishly.

"What are you doing here?" I asked.

"Collecting their mail." She tilted her head, surveying me like she would a lost puppy. But it wasn't pity in her gaze—she was enjoying every second. Turning from her, I started back to the house. "I've already brought in the mail, so you can leave."

Kane had found someone else. I couldn't bear to think it, but then, where was everyone? I thought to continue on into town as planned, if for no other reason than to disprove Camille's hateful lies, but Mrs. Marks and the others rarely socialized in town so the likelihood that someone there knew the details about their impromptu trip was unlikely. I did try calling the boatyard a few times because Mr. Miller, as Kane's employer, would know Kane's whereabouts, but as was my luck lately, I wasn't able to get through to him.

I returned to Boston and stewed over the conversation with Camille for days. Kane and Doreen had been spending weekends together since September, almost three months. He was an easy guy to like, an even easier guy to love. Entertaining the possibility that Kane had moved on caused a pain so severe it was staggering, but he would have never handled the situation so callously; he was too thoughtful. The realization that something could have befallen Mrs. Marks, Mr. Clancy, or Mrs. T, because they were elderly, made me call the hospital, but none of them had been admitted.

I honestly didn't know what to make of the situation. The state of his room bugged me. It had looked like he'd been in the middle of packing, so where the hell was he? I couldn't deny that Kane was intrigued by Doreen. I knew him well enough to be able to tell by his tone. Remembering Camille's comment about me having moved on, I wondered if it were possible that Kane felt that way too? Was that why he hadn't called to tell me that he'd found someone else? Was he pissed and bitter at my believed defection? Was it a coincidence that, after spending many weekends with an adoring Doreen, they had a long weekend together, and then he suddenly stopped calling his fiancée, who rarely took his calls and couldn't be bothered to come home for Thanksgiving? Or was he feeling guilty?

He'd told me he was jealous of Simon, that he was going crazy not seeing me. Was that true? Or was he so quick to anger during that phone call because he knew he had been too quick to propose. Had he finally realized that I'd been a convenience because he had now found the real thing with Doreen? A sob burned up my throat. As much as I wanted to deny it, when I looked at the situation logically, the facts supported Camille's story.

I tried for that whole week following my trip home to get in touch with anyone, to no avail. And that hurt too, the freeze-out from people I thought of as my family. If Kane had moved on, shouldn't the family be rallying behind *me*, knowing how devastated I'd be? Or were they pissed at me, believing that I had also moved on? I had always known they were more Kane's family than they were ever mine.

It was a week and a half after I returned to Boston when I finally heard from Kane, making it nearly a month since his last call.

"Kane?" My voice shook, and my stomach twisted in knots.

"Teagan."

He sounded funny, distant maybe. And what was up with the Teagan? He never called me that.

"Kane, where have you been? I've been calling you for a month."

"Sorry," he said, his words clipped like he was angry, like this was a conversation he didn't want to have but had to.

"Is everything all right?"

"Teagan, I'm sorry to tell you this over the phone, but I'm not moving to Boston."

It took a minute for those words to sink in and another for me to react. Devastation hit me first, and then I felt dead inside. *I'm not moving to Boston.* Who would have thought that so short a phrase could have such a catastrophic impact? And, even though I didn't want to hear it, I needed to: "Why?" My voice cracked.

An uncomfortable silence fell. Never had silence been uncomfortable between us. Dread filled my belly. I knew what was coming and, even knowing that, hearing the confirmation from him shattered me. "I met someone. I'm sorry, I really didn't mean for it to happen."

The first time I'd ever seen him flashed into my head—the boy who offered comfort to the broken girl who had just lost her parents—and that image was followed with the one of him standing at the airport security check after having just asked me to marry him. And now his smiles and kisses, his laughter and hugs, would all be for someone else. Camille had been telling the truth.

"Doreen."

"Yes. I'm sorry, Teagan, I can't marry you."

I looked down at his ring, which I hadn't taken off since he'd put it there. The symbol of our life together, a symbol I drew strength and comfort from. The words barely passed the lump in my throat. "You don't want to marry me?"

"I'm sorry."

I had never understood the expression "going numb," but now I did. At that moment, I felt absolutely nothing, not sorrow, not anger, not pain. I felt nothing except broken. My next words came out automatically, because my brain was struggling to make sense of a situation that made no sense. "Do you want your ring back?"

"No."

"Are you happy?" That question was directed at my best friend, not my lover, because despite everything, I wanted him to be happy.

"I am. And you'll be again too."

"No, Kane, I won't, not now. Be happy. I really do hope you'll be happy." I wasn't going to say it, but I felt it, even if he didn't anymore, and this would be the last time I could. "I love you, Kane."

My thumb pressed the "End" button, the action so final. Not

just the end of the call but the end of us. I sat there, staring down at my phone, the tears welling up and over my lower lids, because I didn't know where to go from there. He had been my life; all of my happiest moments were with him, my whole world's happiness was him. And he had found someone else.

Simon found me looking out at the Charles River, watching the sunrise. It had been two days since Kane's call, two days since learning that the future I'd wanted so much to have with him wasn't to be. It hadn't really hit me yet, because there was a part of me that just didn't believe it. Every time I thought of him moving on, the image of him on one knee on the side of the road flashed in my head. I truly believed his actions had all been genuine: his love for me, the sincerity of his proposal, and the absolute certainty in his expression that what he was asking, what we were committing to, was what he wanted.

"Teagan?"

Simon stepped up next to me, touching my chin with his fingers and forcing my gaze to his. He always had a smile on his face, but not now. Something dark moved over his expression. "What happened?"

"Kane's found someone else."

"What?" That one word was snarled and filled with contempt.

"I'd convinced myself that Camille had lied to break us up. You know I don't trust her. She's always wanted Kane."

"I'm sensing a 'but.'"

"Kane called me two days ago and confirmed it." Tears streamed down my face, but I just didn't have the energy to wipe them away. "He stopped calling, and he isn't at home, because he moved to be closer to her."

"Son of a bitch."

"Part of me, a big part of me, doesn't believe him either, and yet why would he lie? I thought I had it all figured out, you know. We got engaged early, but it felt right in every fiber of my being. And it hurts so fucking much to know I wasn't enough. It took him years to fall for me, and he fell for her in only months. I feared that I had just been a convenience, and then he asked me to marry him and those fears dissolved. But I really must have only been a convenience, and a rather boring one at that, if he could move on so quickly."

"He's an asshole."

"That's just it, Simon, he isn't. I want to hunt him down, even though I haven't a clue where he's living now, and demand that he tell me how he could so easily move on. And yet I can't bear the thought of seeing him again. With five words, he took away every happy memory I've had since my parents died."

"Have you spoken to Mrs. Marks?"

"I haven't been able to get through to anyone at the house. And I can't lie, if they really are helping to get him settled, why didn't anyone help *me*? Kane is Mrs. Marks's adopted child, but I thought we were a family. You're not suppose to show favoritism, right?"

His arm came around me, tucking me close to his side. "I'm sorry, Teagan. Lame-ass words, I know, but I am sorry."

Resting my head on his shoulder, I closed my eyes, thankful that I had him, that I wasn't completely alone.

~

A week after talking to Kane, I finally got through to Mrs. Marks. She sounded tired, her voice raw as if she'd been crying.

"Are you okay? You don't sound so good."

"Oh, Teagan, I'm sorry I haven't called. It's just that . . ." Whatever she was going to say, she seemed to have second thoughts. "Damn it, I hate this. I'm okay. How are you? How's school?"

She never cursed. "Did Kane move away to be closer to Doreen?"

Her shock lined with anger could not have been faked. "Who told you that?"

"Camille said he moved away to be closer to her at school."

"That girl should mind her own damn business."

Another curse, but I couldn't focus on anything but the answer to the question that hadn't stopped pounding in my brain. "Mrs. Marks, did Kane follow Doreen?"

She sounded resigned in a way I'd never heard in her before when she replied, "Yes."

And that was when I finally admitted to myself that Kane and I were over.

Lying very still in bed, eyes closed and taking only shallow breaths, I wondered if it were possible to just fade out of existence. When you felt dead inside, shouldn't you just die? I felt nothing. Never in my life had I felt such an absolute sense of nothing, not even when my parents had died.

Every time I closed my eyes I saw him, his smile, those eyes sparkling with love, and I felt him like he was really next to me, holding me, touching me. Like a living torment, his proposal was always right there, the sight of him dropping to one knee. *I love you, Tea. I want my life with you. I want to wake up next to you every morning and go to sleep next to you every night. Marry me.* But he didn't want to marry me. He'd dropped everything and moved to be closer to *her*, when he had told me he needed time before he could join me. My future, once so full of possibilities, now felt like it would only contain days alone, a constant reminder that I hadn't been enough.

I didn't know what I had done, what had turned him from me and so completely. The idea that it was because of me trying to adjust to college life and being overwhelmed and overworked seemed unfair. I had to have done something, though, because he wasn't even my friend anymore. He didn't love me, and that hurt like hell, but I could probably have survived that. But cutting me from his life completely, the most vital part of *my* life for nearly ten years, left a hole that was too big to be filled. And he had cut himself out of my life. His number had been disconnected. I knew this, because I had broken down and called him during one particularly bad night. I never got through—talk about a kick in the gut.

Simon pulled the covers from my head with a quick flick of his wrist, the sunlight streaming in through the windows. I now understood how vampires felt when hit with sunlight.

"Stop." I grabbed for the blanket. He was faster and pulled it clear off the bed.

"You're getting up today."

"No, I'm not."

"Damn it, you are not spending another minute mourning for that asshole."

"I wish it were that easy."

Settling on the bed, he brushed my hair from my face. "I know you're hurting, but you've got to get past it and him."

"I don't know how. He was family, Simon. After my parents died, he became my family. Whatever happened in my world, I knew it would be okay as long as I had Kane. He saved me when I was younger; he pulled me from my despair. I never saw this coming. There were never any warning signs, no indication at all that he was feeling restless. He asked me to marry him four months ago, got down on one knee and pledged himself to me. How do you find someone else after that? I don't understand. I don't know what I did wrong. I don't know why I wasn't good enough."

"Fucking asshole. He's the one not good enough. He's the one who did something wrong, not you. The way I see it, it's better to learn now the kind of man he is and not after you have kids and a house."

"I wanted kids and a house with him. I really, really wanted that."

The anger arrived days later. Pulling out every stitch of clothing I owned, I tossed all the pieces he had given me. The few T-shirts I had of his—the ones I'd taken so I could feel him with me—I burned. I deleted his messages on my phone. I tore up the pictures I brought with me. All but one. My plan was to use it as a dartboard.

And even as my rage burned through me, I mourned. What if I never got past this? What if I couldn't find my way without him? How quickly life could turn. I'd loved Kane, and now I hated him. And yet, it didn't make me feel any better.

Maybe if I hadn't worked so hard, or if I hadn't gone away, or if I had stayed close, he wouldn't have lost interest. Had I brought this on myself?

As I sat in class, the teacher was talking about something, but I just couldn't pay attention. A couple sitting a few rows in front of me had their heads together talking. Kane and I used to do that, especially at dinner or when we were forced to go to church. We'd always found a way to make a situation fun. It was easy, because we just genuinely liked each other. Even before there was romance, we had been the best of friends. He knew me better than anyone, including my parents. He was the one I always ran to.

Had I known my friendship with him would be put on the line by falling in love, I may not have allowed myself to feel that way for him. Boyfriends came and went, but a best friend, someone who knew all of your secrets, was rare. I had been lucky because Kane had been both to me, but that had proved to be remarkably unlucky, because in losing one, I had lost the other.

chapter 3

Starting Over
Teagan

The long road to Raven's Peak loomed before me. I didn't want to return, but Mrs. Marks was throwing me a graduation party. Despite the memories I so wanted to avoid, she and the others were the only family I had. I wanted to see them and share my accomplishment with them.

In the years since learning about Kane, I'd made excuse after excuse for why I couldn't come home. I even went so far as to find summer work in Boston to avoid summers in Maine. I knew Kane was no longer living at Raven's Peak, but Raven's Peak was synonymous with him. There were just too many memories there to haunt me. Mrs. Marks had tried to persuade me to visit home, but every time I thought about packing a bag, I couldn't.

We spoke on the phone all the time. Mrs. T and Mr. Clancy and I exchanged e-mails regularly, but physically going home, until now, had just been too damn hard. I had invited them to come to Boston, but they were older now, so I knew the journey was too much for them. And even knowing this, it still hurt that they never made the trip. Especially since they had made the trip for Kane when he'd moved out.

Even with the perspective of almost four years, I hadn't bounced back as well as I should have. Simon had insisted I see a therapist, and she helped me realize I wasn't coping well. I needed closure. I needed to understand how I'd lost not just my boyfriend but my best friend. And until I understood how I could have lost both so completely, I was adrift and afraid that I'd never be able to hold on to another relationship.

If not for Simon, I think I would have done something really stupid once the reality of my life had settled in. I almost flunked out that first year. My focus on my schoolwork had cost me Kane, and I'd almost failed out anyway. Ironic.

Pulling around the circular drive, I slammed the car into park, but I couldn't seem to get myself to leave it. I didn't want to go inside, where all those memories were just waiting to bombard me. I wasn't staying long—a few weeks to get the rest of my stuff packed and then I was gone, back to Boston and my new life. Simon and I were getting a place together and starting a business. Antiques. Mrs. Marks was thrilled with this idea, especially because she loved all things old. Simon's parents insisted on purchasing us the building we had our eyes on. His father was a retired investment banker, and his mother a very successful event planner. They were very nice people, if a little uptight. But they adored their son. He believed they'd offered to buy us the building due to their lingering guilt about not handling the news of him being gay well. I wasn't so sure that was the case; I think it was just love for their son. Either way, having that financial burden removed from our shoulders was very much appreciated.

I climbed from the car, then grabbed my bags and headed for the door. As was his way, Mr. Clancy pulled the door open before I'd even knocked. "Welcome home, Teagan."

I dropped my bags, then wrapped him in my arms. "Hi."

"How are you doing?" he asked.

"I'm okay."

"Congratulations—graduating with honors. Mrs. Marks hasn't stopped bragging."

It was true, after that first year, I'd dedicated myself completely to my schoolwork and managed to not only pull my grades up but to graduate with honors. I was proud of myself. I did it for myself, and yet I still hadn't quite found happiness again.

"How is she?" I asked. Mrs. Marks had taken Kane's defection almost as hard as I had.

A slight hesitation followed my question, and when he did answer he sounded almost curt. Odd. "She's fine. Come, let me show you to your room."

"Could I have another room? I don't think I'm ready to be in there yet. Too many memories."

Sadness swept his expression, but the other emotion I saw, anger, surprised me. Before I could ask what he was thinking, he said, "I understand. I'll make up the lavender room for you. Leave your bags at the stairs. Come, Mrs. Marks is waiting for you."

"I'll help you make the bed," I offered almost absently, because there was something I just had to ask. "Mr. Clancy?"

He turned back to me. "Yes?"

"Why did you all go with Kane to help him settle into his new apartment, but no one came with me to settle me into my dorm?"

Pain flashed over his face this time. A deep pain that was startling to see. "Are you okay?" I asked.

His hand shook as he reached for my arm. He started to say

something and then stopped himself. "He needed us more than you did. And, honestly, we had the sense you wanted to take that step without us, but, had you asked, we all would have been there."

He wasn't wrong that I'd wanted to take that step without them. After learning that Kane wasn't joining me for a few months, I'd made the decision to try to make it on my own, needed to know I could. But I didn't agree with his comment that Kane needed them more. Kane was way more self-sufficient than me. And then the thought popped into my head: *What if he hadn't been as careful with Doreen and had gotten her pregnant?* My stomach twisted painfully, and I wished I'd kept my mouth shut.

"Never mind," I whispered.

Mr. Clancy shook his head. A heaviness fell over him that hadn't been there before.

I wanted to cry—the idea that Kane could have a child, a family—I just wanted to cry. Instead, I put on my game face and pushed my ugly thoughts away, because they really could just be ugly thoughts. I didn't know anything about Kane's life now. Mrs. Marks was waiting. She was sitting in the reading room, a pretty room done completely in white embossed wallpaper, with pastel-toned furniture and dark walnut floors.

"Teagan, you're home." She stood to hug me. Even in her late seventies, she still moved around like a woman half her age. "How are you?"

"Okay." Miserable, heartbroken, and sick in the stomach at the possibility that Kane had a child with someone else.

"We've missed you. Staying in touch through the phone and e-mail is wonderful, but it isn't the same as face-to-face. I know why you stayed away for so long, though I wish you hadn't."

"It was too hard to come home. Even now, it hurts being here."

"I . . . about Kane."

"Please. I don't want to talk about him." I really didn't need to know any more than the basics. He'd found someone else and moved on. Enough said.

"It's just, oh, Teagan, I wish you knew everything."

"I don't care to know everything. He moved on, and that's what I'm trying to do. Please, Mrs. Marks, it's hard enough being back here. Putting Kane front and center in my thoughts is going to make this so much harder."

She nodded in understanding but looked conflicted, angry.

I changed the subject. "You look pretty. Is that a new dress?" I asked.

"New for me."

Mrs. Marks wore only vintage, didn't like herself in anything made after 1930. Her salt-and-pepper hair was always pulled up in a Gibson Girl–style bun, and her feet were always in small heels of some kind. I'd asked her about it once, and she replied that life was short and so one needed to live each day to the fullest. She loved heels and, though she never really had a cause to wear them, she wore them anyway. Remembering the conversation I'd shared with Mr. Clancy about Mrs. Marks's brothers, I understood her desire to live each day like it was her last.

She gestured to a chair and waited for me to sit before she followed. Mrs. T appeared, wheeling a tea tray.

"Teagan."

"Mrs. T." She hugged me for so long, and her eyes searched mine when she pulled back. But it was when she pressed her hand to my cheek that I nearly lost it. I hadn't realized how much I'd missed being home until that moment. Mrs. T stepped back and immediately busied herself with making the tea.

I was happy to see Mrs. T and Mr. Clancy take a chair, but the feeling was tempered by the odd atmosphere in the room, which I attributed to the glaring absence of Kane. Even Mrs. Marks seemed affected, uncomfortable or maybe nervous. Her hands twisted in her lap, and her focus shifted a few times to the sofa where Mrs. T and Mr. Clancy were sitting. And then she said, "So tell us all about this idea of yours for an antique shop."

Two nights later, I couldn't sleep with the memories pushing to get in, to be remembered. And, while trying to hold them back was exhausting, I still couldn't find sleep. The party earlier had been lovely—Mrs. Marks and the others had gone to a lot of work, but celebrating without Kane felt wrong. And I knew I wasn't the only one to feel it. He didn't even come home to celebrate my achievement, even though he had been more excited for me than I had been when I got my acceptance letter. How thoroughly he'd removed himself from my life. What I found even more unbelievable was how he had distanced himself from Mrs. Marks and the others. Avoiding me I understood; it hurt, but I understood. Knowing how much Mrs. Marks and the others loved him, I thought it seemed cruel for him to distance himself from them too.

Climbing from bed, I pulled on a robe and headed downstairs. I was just passing the large terrace doors that overlooked the ocean when I noticed a light on the water. A light that appeared to be coming from the island that Kane and I had often snuck off to. Anger filled me. The intensity of it was surprising. Had Mrs. Marks sold her island? Even so, how dare someone claim that land? It was Kane's and mine, even though those dreams had died long ago. Without even a conscious thought, I grabbed a flashlight, flew out of the house and ran down to the small boat docked on the beach.

The engine moved me across the water and, even though it was dark, as I got closer I realized the light was for a house—a house built on our spot. I wanted to rage. Why couldn't things just be left as they were? Why couldn't I have that one private reminder of Kane and all that he had been to me? I knew I was being unreasonable, but I didn't care.

Driving the boat right up onto the shore, I climbed out and stalked to the house. As I approached, I heard a crash, followed by muffled swearing. I knocked on the front door, and a woman in her midtwenties answered. She was pretty, with long blond hair and green eyes that looked annoyed or maybe overwhelmed.

"Can I help you?"

What could I say to her? *Get off. This is my land, not yours.* I just stood there, staring at the woman living in a house that was built in the exact place where Kane and I had first made love. Embarrassed by my behavior, I started to turn away, and then I heard another curse, and this time there was no mistaking that voice. My breath froze in my throat as I pushed into the living room—it had been tossed. Had there been a fight? A movement caught my attention just as a man stepped into view. His black hair was long and messy, falling over his shoulders. His strong jaw and upper lip sported a five-o'clock shadow that had been allowed to grow an extra few days. Wide shoulders, flat stomach, and narrow hips—the body of man. The room pitched, and I felt my vision dim around the edges. Kane. There was no recognition on his face at the sight of me, but that barely registered, because in that moment the most profound sense of anger tore through me, like sharp talons sinking into my flesh.

"Kane. What a pleasant surprise. I thought you moved away, so eager to be free you left in a hurry, severing all ties in the process."

Shock flashed over his face. "Teagan. What are you doing here?"

A coldness settled over me when I heard the hardness in his voice. He was calling me Teagan still. Moving back from him like I'd been burned, I just stared, unable to understand the coldness that was directed at me.

"Shouldn't that be my question? You're the one who took off."

As he looked at me, his eyes, those beautiful eyes that had only ever looked at me with love, were not even bothering to connect.

"Why are you back?" Bitterness rang in my tone.

"Always loved it here, never intended to stay away for long."

"And me, did you plan on seeing me again? You may not have wanted me anymore, but we were friends once. There was a graduation party earlier today. Couldn't bother to get your ass up to the house to see your onetime BFF?"

"Thought it'd be easier this way, a clean break. We didn't want the same things."

I couldn't get my brain around any of this. The man standing before me, who looked like the boy I loved, was not at all the boy I loved. "We got engaged, seems to me we were pretty much on the same page."

"Look, Teagan, we were kids—scared and alone and we grew attached. Some would probably say too attached. You were already pulling away from me. You felt it as much as I did. What we had was great for what it was, but it wasn't real love, it wasn't lasting love. It was just young love. I realized that after we were separated for a while, so yeah, I wanted a clean break."

The memory of my conversation with Camille flashed in my head, and how I had struggled to make sense of what was not understandable in the days that followed. I had been right. Kane had thought I had moved on but he had also felt guilty because he had moved on too. "You told me never to leave. Forever, remember?"

"At the time, I felt that way. I don't anymore."

Luckily my walls were solid fucking concrete 'cause I felt nothing, but I did want answers. He owed me that. "What changed? You bought me an engagement ring."

"That was what changed. Seeing the ring, the permanency of what I was doing, a lifetime with one person: the only girl I ever knew, it made it real and I realized I didn't want that."

"Is that her, Doreen, your girlfriend?" I couldn't even look at the woman who was silently witnessing this nightmare. Was there a child here somewhere? That thought penetrated the wall—nearly doubling me over in pain.

His next words destroyed me. "My wife now."

Another crack in the wall, a sob ripped from my throat; I couldn't have stopped it even if I'd wanted to. "So it wasn't that you didn't want a lifetime with just one woman, you just didn't want a lifetime with me. You didn't want me."

I felt it, even with how hard I had barricaded it in, my heart split open and I was bleeding out, my whole world collapsing around me. My happy memories of the past crumbled to dust.

"You promised me this house, our world away from the world. We made love, fumbled through it, right under where this house is built. Was the memory so repugnant to you that you had to cover it up? You weren't just my boyfriend, my first love, and my best friend—you were my family. I lost my family once, and it hurt like hell. Didn't think anything could hurt worse, but I was wrong. Every happy memory I have since coming here is with you, every single one. You can have those memories now, because I don't want them. I don't want to remember you, because in remembering the good, I'll be forced to relive the bad." I started for the door. "Don't worry, you won't see me again."

His last words to me felt like a knife to my heart. "No, I won't."

I stopped moving, my head dropped in mourning for the life I had still secretly hoped would come to pass, but now I knew that it never would. Lifting my head again, holding it high, I walked from his house. The thought of walking into the water, and not stopping, was so tempting it terrified me.

The sun was starting to rise when I finally made it back to the house. Mrs. Marks was waiting for me.

Shock had set in but I was furious too. Mrs. Marks had wanted to discuss Kane when I first arrived and considering the news, she should have fucking insisted I listen. "He's married and living in our house and no one thought to tell me that?" She looked shattered in response, almost as destroyed as me, but I was too angry to care. "I can't stay."

"I know, dear girl, I wish it didn't have to be this way."

Her voice cracked and tears slid down her cheeks but I was dying inside so her pain didn't penetrate my own. I packed my bags and called a cab. That afternoon I was back in Boston.

Simon pulled his door open and, at the sight of me, he grabbed my arms. "What the hell happened?"

"I saw Kane."

"Fuckhead. Come in." He grabbed my bags and dropped them on the floor before dragging me to the sofa, since my legs weren't working right. I understood now the odd tension at home—they all knew that Kane was living our dream with someone else and no one told me. I thought he hadn't bothered to come home for my party, but he had been home, right there in walking distance, and yet he had made no attempt to see me. Anger was giving way to the familiar gut-wrenching pain that never seemed to ease.

"What did he have to say for himself?"

"He's married."

"What?"

"And living in the house we had talked about building."

"I say again—fuckhead."

"Simon, no one told me. I discovered that fun fact all on my own."

"Jesus."

On the flight home, pushing past the stunning betrayal from those I held most dear, I could think of nothing but how different Kane was. The boy I loved was gone, the man in his place was bitter and cold. It was this more than anything that churned my anger and my heartache. What the hell had happened to change him so much? "I'm angry and I'm hurt and there's a part of me that feels nothing. What happened to the boy I grew up with, the one who laughed and teased, the one who was so kind to everyone? That boy's gone. And I honestly don't understand why. He didn't want a life with me, fine, but he pushed me out of his life completely. He was so cold, so unfeeling. There was nothing in his eyes. The warmth and sparkle that I so loved seeing was gone. His eyes were dead."

"I'm so sorry, Teagan."

Jumping up from the sofa, I reached for my phone. Mrs. Marks answered on the first ring.

"What happened to him?"

"Teagan?"

"What happened to Kane? Why is he so different?"

She hesitated and I knew she knew more about Kane than she was saying, even more than the crushing secret about his wife. "Tell me, damn it. I have a right to know. The man living in that house is not Kane. He's altered. What the hell happened to make him that way?"

"Sometimes people change."

"Bullshit."

"Language."

"No, seriously bullshit. Kane, the big-hearted Kane, as you've said yourself. Where is that Kane?"

"I don't know."

"And you're not alarmed that he's so drastically different? What do we know about his wife, except for the fact that she has changed him so completely? Relation to Mrs. T or not, who the hell is she?" And then a thought made me worry. "Do you think he's on drugs?"

"I think he needs time to deal."

"With what?"

"Whatever happened that's changed him."

"Do you know what happened?"

"I know that he's been through a great deal, and, when he's ready, I'm sure he'll reach out to you. You are still his best friend."

"You do know. He told you, but he won't tell me. I'm tired of trying to understand when no one is offering me a damn thing. Take care of him, Mrs. Marks."

"Teagan?"

"I'm sorry, but I just can't do this anymore. Now I'm the one who needs time."

"You will come home."

"My home is here in Boston. Thank you for everything you've done for me. Good-bye, Mrs. Marks."

I hung up before she could reply. It was time to move on.

Looking around the space that would one day be Simon's and my antique store, pride burned through me. Six months after I'd severed all ties with my past, I was finally healing, and a huge part of that was due to this store. The building was much like the TARDIS—bigger on the inside. When the contractor started work, his crew discovered walnut floors under the carpeting. Why someone would cover hardwood with carpeting, I didn't know. The load-bearing columns added a nice touch to the open space. Simon was working with the painter on custom colors, because apparently there was a science behind the colors used: colors that soothed, excited, and even encouraged people to buy.

I had tapped into more than half of the money my parents had left me between my schooling and the store, but I really did believe we were going to be a success. Simon had a real knack for finding treasures. He was a natural salesman, and we both genuinely loved antiques.

Checking my watch, I called to Simon, "I have to go. Meeting Erik."

"Okay. Have fun."

Erik and I had met at the local coffee house, both of us coming in at the same time for our morning coffee. It took him a month to work up the nerve to say hi. We'd been to dinner countless times, which had evolved to where our relationship was now—great sex, dinner optional. I enjoyed his company. As much as I had healed in the past six months after learning that Kane had married, it had been four and half years since Kane had ended us, and I was still unable to commit to someone. I could admit to myself that I was broken and suspected a part of me always would be.

Hurrying home, I showered and dressed in one of my flowing skirts and a Lycra top, slipped on my sandals, and pulled a brush through my hair. Erik had offered to pick me up, but I didn't want to give him the wrong impression. This was fun, this was sex, nothing more.

He opened the door of his apartment dressed in faded jeans, a tee, and bare feet. Erik looked comfortable and sexy as hell. "Hey."

"Hi."

"Come in."

I liked his apartment—dark walls, masculine furniture, sparse but nicely done.

"You want a glass of wine?" he asked.

In answer, I pressed myself against him, my mouth finding his. His arms immediately wrapped around me and pulled me close. His tongue pushed into my mouth, tasting me with a thoroughness that left me weak. I liked sex. It made me feel—for just a little while, I was content.

"I'll take that as a no." He lifted me into his arms and carried me to his bedroom. Dropping me on his bed, he looked wicked. "I've been thinking about this since the last time I saw you."

In answer, I lifted my skirt and spread my legs.

Two hours later found me on the floor searching for my panties. Erik rested back against his pillow, his arms behind his head, his eyes on me. "Stay the night."

"I can't."

"You mean you won't."

Finding my panties, I pulled them on before the search began for my bra. "Where's the fire, Teagan?"

"There isn't one. I just like sleeping in my own bed."

Silence met that as I continued to find my clothes and get dressed.

"He really did a number on you."

Everything inside me froze with those words. He wasn't wrong, Kane had destroyed me, but I thought I had been better at hiding it.

"You gonna leave me some money on the dresser?" He was only partly teasing.

Guilt moved through me, because I didn't want to hurt him. I liked him, but I couldn't give him more of me, because there really wasn't any more of me left. I settled next to him on the bed. "We talked about this. I'm not looking for a commitment."

He brushed his finger down my arm, and I was sure he was going to tell me he didn't want to see me anymore. He surprised me.

"I won't call you. You want to see me again, you know my number."

Leaning into him, my lips brushed lightly over his. "I'll call."

And I did. For six months, we had fun, but he wanted more, and I was unable to give it to him. As much as I liked him, my heart could not be reached. Kane had done that to me—irrevocably changed me—but life went on, and so did I.

2015
Teagan

"Damn, that's beautiful. Where did you find that?" The rosewood French Napoleon rolltop desk that Simon found was from the mid-1800s, I would guess, the leather inlay with nailheads in pristine condition.

"Some farmhouse in Concord. They were spring cleaning."

"How much did you pay for it?"

"Three thousand."

"You stole it."

"I gave them their asking price."

"Well, why not? We'll get fifteen thousand for it easily."

"You know it. Who's the king of antiques?"

I bowed, like I did every time he made a great deal, which was fairly often. "You are, O mighty one."

"I think you should take me to dinner."

"Absolutely, anywhere you want to go."

In the five years since we'd graduated, Simon and I had built a wonderful antique business located on Massachusetts Avenue in the Back Bay of Boston. For the past two years, we'd run firmly in the black. The store was set up like a home, with furniture arranged in clusters, and every part that made up those clusters—the rugs, the lighting, the knickknacks—was for sale. A large glass case where our ancient brass cash register sat was filled with vintage jewelry, some real, most high-end cosmetic pieces.

Simon and I had upgraded our apartment to a nice two-bedroom on Harrison Street in the South End, walking distance to the shop. It was a community and, though we didn't socialize often with our neighbors, it was nice to know they were there if we wanted to. Life was good, maybe not where I had once hoped it would be, but I thought I had done really well at picking up the pieces.

The phone rang, pulling me from my reverie.

"Teagan."

My heart dropped into my stomach, "Mrs. Marks, hi." Bitterness burned through me because despite the fact that she and the others had tried countless times to reach out, they were still keeping a secret from me.

Silence for a beat or two. "Teagan, I need to talk with you. There's something you need to know, and I've kept quiet about it for far too long."

So she was finally willing to give up the secret. I couldn't deny I was curious, especially since I knew it related to Kane, but so much time had past that it was really of no consequence any more and yet I found myself agreeing. "Okay."

"Will you come home? What I have to say cannot be spoken over the phone. It's very important."

The idea of going home was not pleasant, but then again, neither was the tone of Mrs. Marks's voice. "Is next weekend okay? We have a big sale going on this weekend."

She signed audibly. "Yes, next weekend would be fine."

"Is everything okay?"

"It will be, honey. I think it will be. Maybe you could bring Simon. I would really like to meet him."

"I'll ask him."

"I won't keep you. I'll see you next weekend." She hesitated before she added, "I love you, Teagan."

My heart, the one I didn't think could be reached, squeezed hard in my chest, but the words flowed easily out of my mouth, because they were true. "I love you too."

Colin's name flashing on my phone's screen made me excited—the man knew his way around a woman's form.

"Hey, stranger. You home?" I asked. Colin was a photographer for *National Geographic*, and was usually all over the world for work. We'd met through a mutual friend. When he was in town, we usually got together. It was fun, casual, and comfortable, because he didn't want anything more from me than I wanted from him.

"Three days and then I'm off to Paris." He paused for a moment. "As much as I want to see you, I want you naked and under me more. If I showed up on your door step, would you let me in?"

How I managed to answer without panting was beyond me. "Yeah. I'd welcome you in."

"I'll see you this afternoon. Oh, and Teagan?"

"Yeah?"

"Rest up, sugar, it's going to be a long night," he said before hanging up.

The urge to fan myself almost made me do so. Simon appeared with a pint of ice cream and a spoon. Dropping down next to me, he handed it over. "Colin?"

"Yep." Shoving a huge spoonful of ice cream into my mouth, I handed it back to him.

"You getting lucky tonight?"

"Yep." I *was* going to be getting lucky, quite a lot of lucky since Colin was a stallion. Just thinking about it was getting me hot.

"I guess I should make myself scarce."

"You don't have to. We'll be quiet."

"You shouldn't need to be quiet."

"Are you going to stay at Michael's?"

"No, Michael and I called it quits."

"What? When?"

"Two days ago. He was just too damn needy and jealous. He was even jealous of you."

"I know. He never liked me. I always had the sense he thought I was going to turn you straight and steal you."

"If anyone could, it would be you."

"Well, now, I don't want to kick you from the apartment."

"I'll go hang with Sunshine. Maybe I can get her to bake some brownies."

I smiled every time I thought about our neighbor. She looked like a Sunshine: long blond hair that reached her ass, faded jeans, and tight T-shirts with her Birkenstock sandals. "If you do, I want one. No, two."

"You got it. Have fun. Tell Colin I said hi."

"Will do."

Hours later, I was dressed in a simple black dress minus undergarments, since I didn't have anything sexy clean. A knock at the door signaled Colin's arrival. Pulling it open, I had only a second to enjoy his messy blond hair and green eyes before he stepped into me without a word and sealed his lips over mine. His hands moved to my hips, pulling me close. He was hard and ready, pressing into my stomach, and immediately the place between my legs swelled. His hands moved around my back to cradle my ass; he pulled his mouth from mine.

"You're not wearing anything under this."

"Surprise."

In the next second, the front door had closed and I was pressed up against the wall with my dress around my hips and my legs around his waist. While Colin spread hot kisses down my neck, his hand moved to between my thighs to stroke me in just the right spot. I moaned.

"Front right pocket," he whispered against my lips. My hands moved over him, lingering a moment on the hard bulge, before my fingers brushed against the condom wrapper.

"You come prepared."

"I've been hard since our phone call."

"That couldn't have been very comfortable." My fingers worked his button and zipper before slipping in and finding him—hard and velvety smooth. It was his turn to moan, and when I pulled him free and ran my hand up the length of him, squeezing as I went, he actually whimpered.

He pinned me to the wall as I ripped open the condom wrapper, and, with our eyes locked, I slowly covered him with it.

"This is going to be fast." And I couldn't have agreed more when I moved the head of his dick right where we both wanted it. With a shift of his hips, he buried himself deep inside of me. His body froze, his muscles tensed, and lust took over his expression. "So fucking tight."

My legs pulled him even deeper. "Move, handsome."

"Yes, ma'am."

He was hitting just the right spot with each thrust that, in only a manner of seconds, my body started tightening before my orgasm ripped through me. He pulled me closer, moving harder and faster, until his body jerked with his own release. Resting his head on my shoulder, he gave himself a minute before he said, "That was a good start, but we're far from finished."

By two in the afternoon the next day, I was still in bed. Colin had left earlier after spending nearly twenty-four hours with me as we worshiped each other's bodies. Dear God, the mouth on that man should be bronzed. And yet, as crazy good as Colin was in the sack, he wasn't the best I'd had.

We were kids and really had no idea what we were doing, and yet I had never experienced anything even close to as good as my first. Not that my bedroom had had a revolving door, but I couldn't lie, I wanted to feel what I had felt with Kane, and knew I never would again, because none of them were Kane. It was a vicious circle. I suppose the difference was that I had loved Kane.

I tried not to think about him, but sometimes, like now when my mind was mellow, I couldn't help it. Five years, that's how long it had been since I'd last seen him. Remembering that night always caused a pain that was hard to breathe through. How he became the man he did, when he had been such a beautiful soul when he was younger, I didn't know. I missed him, missed the boy who used to slip into my bed and hold me close, the boy who brought me chocolate milk and whipped cream every morning, the boy who knew when I needed a hug or to have my hand just held. I hated myself for that, that I could be so weak as to still hold a torch for him after everything he'd done. My therapist tried to explain it using technical terms, but I didn't really care. It was what it was: My cross to bear.

Most of the time I was successful at pretending that he never existed, but sometimes, like now, memories of him seeped through. I didn't feel emotion like I'd used to, like most people do, because my mind had shut it down. Remembering him was too much, too painful for me to handle. My therapist reasoned that Kane had become a surrogate family to me, that the pain I felt at his loss wasn't just about him but about what he had come to represent. When our relationship died, it was symbolic of the grief I had felt after losing my parents. And the pain was staggering. Sometimes I feared what would happen to me if I let it in, if I really processed the pain I had so successfully banked. I'd probably go mad.

Life went on, and I came back to Boston and buried myself in the shop. Long hours, late nights, and weekends, focused on nothing but making at least one of my dreams come true. Simon was my anchor; without him I would have been unreachable. Our business was a success, our friendship was top rate, and if there was an emptiness in me that nothing could fill—not success, Simon, or even the men I distracted myself with—what was to be done? Life happened, sometimes it sucked, sometimes you had to start again, and maybe you headed in a direction you never saw coming. The trick was to make it work regardless. I had. But late at night, I cursed Kane for showing me that glimpse into perfect and then taking it away. I hated him as much as I loved him. My therapist was having the time of her life with that conundrum.

I sat in my living room the following night reading through the classifieds while eating one of the brownies Simon had brought home from our neighbor. Sunshine really did like her pot. I wondered if it was the pot that made her baked goods so moist.

Having never smoked pot, I found eating it baked in a brownie was awesome. Feeling mildly giddy since I had eaten two, I giggled as I read. I couldn't believe there was an ad looking for a lady of the night. They used more subtle language, but the "assistant needs to be available in the evenings and open to trying new things" made it pretty damn clear. My eyes nearly popped out of my head at the salary: a grand a week. Sure, I'd probably have to work weekends, but I'd only have to work in the evenings and I could literally lie down on the job. I wondered what Simon would say if I told him I was considering changing careers from coowner of an antique store to prostitute.

"Are you eating all the brownies?" Simon asked, coming from the bathroom with only a towel wrapped around his waist.

"Was I supposed to save you one?"

"It would have been nice."

"Sorry. They're just so good."

He laughed, pressing a kiss on my head. "What are you looking at?"

"I was thinking about becoming a lady of the night."

"What?"

“There’s actually an ad looking for one. Can you believe it? It pays a grand a week.”

“Shit, for a grand a week, *I’ll* become a lady of the night.”

I turned around more fully to look at him. “You’re not a lady.”

My cell rang and I let Simon get it—I so wasn’t in the mood to talk to anyone.

It was a very short conversation, and, when Simon disconnected the call, he walked over and sat down next to me on the sofa. “That was Mr. Clancy. Mrs. Marks has had a heart attack. She’s in critical condition.”

Suddenly I was sober. We were leaving in two days to visit and have the sit-down that she had seemed so adamant about. I jumped up from the sofa and ran to my room.

“I’ll drive and you get us a flight,” Simon called after me.

I poked my head from the room. “What about the shop?”

“I’ll tell the team there’s a change of plans—we’re leaving two days earlier. It’ll be fine.”

He was right, of course. We had wonderful employees.

“Get packed, I’ll call.”

“I love you, Simon.”

“Ditto, now go.”

Nearly twelve hours after the call from Mr. Clancy, Simon and I were driving a rental car through the town I had called home for so long.

“I’m scared, Simon. What if she doesn’t get better?”

“From what you’ve told me about her, she’s a fighter.” He reached for my hand, and my fingers tightened around his.

"I stayed away for so long, and now she could die and she'll never know how much she means to me, how she saved me, how much I love her."

Simon pulled the car onto the side of the road. He barely had it in park before he folded me into his arms. "She knows, Teagan. Family always knows."

The tears fell. "I shouldn't have stayed away."

He pushed me back so his eyes could find mine. "Hindsight, Teagan. It's very easy to fall into the 'should have/would have' game. Don't do that to yourself. What would Mrs. Marks say?"

Wiping at my eyes, I tried to pull it together. "You're right."

"You were hurting, they all know just how much, they understand."

He was right, and I didn't need to say it again since he knew me well enough to know I knew. He asked, "Are you okay?"

"Yeah. And thanks for coming with me."

"There was never a question."

Pressing a kiss to my head, he settled behind the wheel and pulled the car back onto the road. Before long he was making the turn down the long drive for Raven's Peak. I waited for Simon to get his first view of it. As an adult, I appreciated the house in a way my younger self never had. It came into view, the Gothic Revival asymmetric house with its arched doorways and windows, the deeply pitched roof, gables, and decorative bargeboards. The soft yellow light that glowed from the glazed windows looked very much like candlelight and gave the illusion that we had stepped back in time.

"Babe, you did not do this place justice with your description of it. And your description was fabulous. This place is unreal." After parking, Simon climbed out and stared his fill before his gaze sliced back to me.

"You okay?" he asked.

It was hard being back here, but worry over Mrs. Marks trumped every other thought. "Yeah."

The door opened and Mr. Clancy appeared. Nostalgia filled me, and the tears that were still burning my eyes threatened to fall again. I had missed my family. Hurrying up the steps, I threw my arms around him just as a huge German shepherd came barreling out of the house.

"Who's this?" Surprise hit me, since Mrs. Marks had always wanted a dog but feared one would destroy her house. Kane and I had always wanted a dog too. Excitement crept up on me.

"Zeus. He's Kane's."

Ouch. A direct hit.

"It was good of you to come."

Hunching down, I rubbed Zeus's head. My worry for Mrs. Marks extended to Mr. Clancy, because he looked so tired and old. "How is she?" I asked.

"She's moved up to stable condition."

"Thank God. How are you?"

"Rattled, but better now that she is no longer critical. Come in, please. Before I show you to your rooms, I want to bring you to a visitor in the study."

Before I could ask him who, he started down the hall, leaving Simon and me to follow him.

Walking through the house, I really saw it, maybe for the first time. As a child, I didn't appreciate what I was seeing, and the last time I had been there, despite having studied art history at BU, feeling heartsore over Kane continued to keep me blind to the treasures surrounding me. The staircase—five large men could comfortably stand shoulder to shoulder on it. It was constructed entirely of polished mahogany with hand-carved balustrades and newels. As the stairs ascended, it split, curving away from the center to either side of the grand hall. The walls, too, were wood, a paneled wood with a warm patina that seemed to gleam in the light from the cut crystal chandelier that hung three stories above.

"I don't think I ever appreciated just how beautiful this place is," I said to Simon. "And it's so organized. Where are all of Mrs. Marks's knickknacks, Mr. Clancy?" Every room had had assortments of objects encroaching on the floor space, but instead of looking sloppy, it worked.

"She stored them away. She wanted a change," he said and then added, "you're seeing the house with a more practiced eye." He pushed the door to the study open. The study was done completely in a dark burled wood, including the tray ceiling. Built-in bookcases lined the room, the floors were that same dark walnut, and since I'd lived there, several desks had been artistically arranged around the room so that multiple people could work there together. There was one man in a black suit feverishly writing, the sound of his pen scratching over the paper almost comical. He looked up from his work and stood.

Simon stepped into the room, took a turn, and then his focus zeroed in on me. "This is a fabulous room."

"You're not wrong," I said.

"Miss Harper. I'm so happy there is good news for you," said the man.

"I'm sorry, who are you?"

He reached for my hand, squeezing it a little too tightly, and replied, "I'm Dimitri Falco, Mrs. Marks's lawyer."

Suddenly I felt dirty. He screamed ambulance chaser—the kind who ingratiated himself with his clients to get a piece of the pie and then waited eagerly for them to kick so he could claim it. The fact that he was at Raven's Peak now stirred my temper, because he was likely doing just that. Mrs. Marks was fighting for her life, while he sat comfortably in her home waiting with bated breath. Mr. Sleazy was a more fitting name for him. He turned then to Simon, but he didn't offer his hand, just gave him a passing glance as if he was of no importance.

Simon, being Simon, grabbed the man by the hand with both of his and shook vigorously.

"Nice to meet you." And though it would appear Simon was being friendly, I'd bet money he was squeezing Falco's hand just a bit too hard. If riled, Simon could be, in a word, intimidating.

And Mr. Sleazy was not immune. He took a step back, his demeanor clearly shaken. "I'm relieved to hear she is doing so well."

"Why are you here?" I asked bluntly.

"Mrs. Marks recently made some changes to her will."

"What changes?"

"I'm not at liberty to say."

Mr. Clancy cleared his throat from his spot just inside the door. "I'll show you to your rooms now."

"Why did you want us to meet him?" I asked as we started down the hall.

"I wanted your opinion, because something is not right with that guy."

"He certainly seems slimy. How long has he been here?"

"A few days, and what he's doing is a mystery. One wouldn't think it would take days to make adjustments to a will."

"You think he's up to something?" I asked.

He turned. "Not sure, but he's acting suspiciously."

Interesting. "I'll keep my eye on him while I'm here."

Mr. Clancy moved the conversation on. "I was going to put you in your room, unless that's too . . ."

He remembered the last time I'd visited—how I hadn't been strong enough then to handle the memories. I was now. "I'd like to stay in my room." Touching his arm I added, "But thank you."

Contentment settled near my heart when I saw my old room again—the huge canopy bed that was covered in silk and dozens of pillows. After my studies, I now knew the makers of the furniture that filled my room, furniture I had thought belonged in a museum when I was younger—and I hadn't been wrong about that. A Hepplewhite lady's writing desk rested between the massive windows and a Chippendale dressing table was situated on the wall by the fireplace, which was already filled with an impressive blaze. The only change I had made was papering the walls in blue silk, the color of Kane's eyes. I had begged Mrs. Marks to let me change it when I was fifteen. Didn't have to beg too hard. Kane had loved it and, as often as he shared my room, I wanted him to like it. Of course, none of that mattered anymore.

"Breakfast is served starting at eight thirty a.m. in the kitchen, as you remember."

"It's nice that some things stay the same."

The oddest look covered his expression in response. What was he thinking? He turned to Simon.

"Now, for you, Mr. Dale. Your room is this way."

"Oh, I'm coming too," I said and followed. Simon's room was down the hall. It wasn't, thankfully, Kane's childhood room.

Done in a pale-gold damask swirl wallpaper, the room had William and Mary–style furniture—cherry, old, and exquisite. The bedding was navy-blue silk, and the walls were covered in landscapes done in oil colors.

"I could totally get used to this," Simon said as he dropped onto the bed.

"Thank you, Mr. Clancy. We'll be down later after I've given Simon the tour."

"See you soon. Mrs. T is making one of her cakes especially for you."

My heart hitched; Kane had loved her cakes. I hope he choked on them now. "Yum."

As soon as the door closed, Simon rolled off the bed. Reaching for my hand, he pulled me out of the room. "Show me this place."

The sensation that I was seeing the house for the first time lingered as I gave Simon the tour, my education putting a whole new light on the place I had called home for so long. The wall sconces in the large foyer carried the theme of the arch, with beveled glass carved and trimmed ornately in bronze. Their dim ambient light spotlighted the artwork on the wood-paneled walls. The pieces were mostly oil paintings of turbulent seas. Kane and I used to make up stories about the ships in the paintings: One was a foreign princess coming to the New World to marry, but her ship was lost at sea; another was a pirate ship that had just made an impressive haul after raiding ships from the East India Company. Now, looking at the paintings, I recognized the artists—Ivan Aivazovsky, Thomas Moran, Frank Vining Smith, and Thomas Birch—and could appreciate that Mrs. Marks had a very impressive collection. Down the hall from the entrance, the walls were sponged in a muted gold with plaster relief depicting birds on delicate tree branches. The exquisite detail perfectly represented how Mrs. Marks thought of her home. Hopefully she would see it again.

Moving down the hall, we entered the library. As a child, this room had been my favorite, because this was where Kane and I often escaped to. Floor-to-ceiling bookcases lined the perimeter on three sides, the huge stone fireplace taking up most of the fourth wall. The small sofa in the corner was the same one that Kane and I had slept on the first night I'd arrived, and in truth many, many nights after, and still it screamed for occupants to curl up with a book and get lost for a while.

"Amazing. I understand now why you have a love of all things old. This place is incredible. How long has this been in her family?"

"Five generations. Apparently her ancestor had done quite well for himself in the shipping business during the Gilded Age right along with Vanderbilt. He had the house built in the late 1800s."

I answered him almost absently, because his comment about this house and my love of all things old was not one I had ever really thought about. He was right, though. This house, and my life here, had directly affected what I wanted to do and be when I grew up. "I guess I never realized how big an influence the house had on me."

"More than the house, babe, but it definitely played a role."

We toured the entire house, taking far longer than I thought we would, because Simon wanted to see everything—the wallpaper, the woodworking, the paintings, and furniture. We spent almost two hours in the library trying to guess how many books were shelved there. And remembering Kane admitting to doing the same when we were younger sent pain slicing through me. We ended the tour at the cliff. Simon looked down at the crashing surf, and I noticed the shiver that went through him.

"Interesting, see the way the rocks create a sort of wading pool? Would make for a nice place to swim. You ever swim there?"

That had been Kane's and my favorite place. "Yeah, when I was younger."

"With Kane."

"Yes."

His focus moved beyond us to the water that stretched out before us. "What a view."

I wasn't looking at the view, only at the little island where a house stood. It was concealed mostly by trees, but I knew it was there. Did Kane and his wife still live there? Did he have children now, had he then? The thought of seeing little Kanes walking around almost made me step off the edge. God, I needed to make sure Mrs. Marks was okay, and then I had to get back to what was safe and away from Kane Doyle.

"Let's eat, I'm starved." I really wasn't, but I couldn't look another second at Kane's love shack.

We stepped into the large kitchen, the scents making my mouth water, just as two heads turned in our direction.

"Teagan!" I had never seen Mrs. T move so fast to pull me in for a hug. "We are so glad you're home. I wish it was under better circumstances."

My heart moved into my throat. I loved Mrs. T, but I couldn't deny there was a part of me that was bitter that her grandniece was married to Kane, living in my house, living my dream. I suspected she felt that same awkwardness. When she studied me, so many emotions flew across her expression, but they were gone so quickly that I was having a hard time distinguishing them. "We've missed you."

"I've missed you." And, despite my bitterness, I really had.

She stepped back but kept her hands on my arms. "You have grown into a beautiful woman."

My cheeks burned.

Reaching for Simon's hand, I drew him closer. "This is Simon Dale, my close friend and business partner."

"Lovely to meet you," Mrs. T said, and I noticed she stood just a little bit taller.

Simon took her hand, brought it to his lips, and kissed her knuckles. She almost swooned. "The pleasure is mine."

What a ham.

"Are you hungry?" Mrs. T asked while walking back to the stove to check on what she was cooking, which smelled divine.

"You will never eat as well as you will while you're here. This woman, we should steal her and bring her home with us."

"Really? Well, I do love to eat. Seems like a match made in heaven," Simon purred.

Mrs. T was actually blushing—I couldn't believe it.

A half an hour later we were sitting at the large kitchen island eating rosemary encrusted lamb, roasted potatoes, and freshly picked string beans. Mr. Clancy had even selected a lovely Cabernet from the wine cellar.

"We missed seeing your smiling face. It's so nice to have you home. It just hasn't been the same without you," Mrs. T said.

"I'm sorry I didn't come home earlier. I should have. I shouldn't have turned my back on all of you, because you're my family. That was wrong of me." Truth was, with Mrs. Marks in the hospital, it kind of put everything in perspective. Despite my feelings for Kane, these people *were* my family and they deserved better from me.

"Don't. Teagan, what you went through, how Kane behaved, we get it. He hurt you. That's on him regardless of why."

"What do you mean regardless of why?" As if there could be a reasonable explanation for why he'd hurt me.

It was on the tip of her tongue to say more, but she didn't. Instead she turned her attention to Simon. "So tell me, Simon, how did you meet our Teagan?"

"It was a chocolate chip cookie, we both wanted it, and it was the last one."

"Who got it?" Mrs. T asked.

"I did, but I shared it with her." Simon winked at me, his hand finding mine under the table.

Later, Mr. Clancy stopped me from leaving the kitchen with a light touch on my arm. Simon, sensing we needed a moment, continued out of the kitchen to give us some privacy.

"You asked me once why we didn't come with you to settle you in at school but went with Kane. There's more to the story, Teagan. You didn't hear it all. I must encourage you to seek that boy out while you are here and listen to what he has to say, and then you'll understand why we all acted as we did."

"What could he possibly have to say?"

"Please, Teagan. It's his story to tell, but you really need to hear it."

That night, Simon and I sat in my room. "I want to go pound the life out of him. Teagan, give me this. I kept my mouth shut for nine years, but fucking shit, I'm done with this asshole now."

Simon and I were in my room, several bottles of wine later. We were both drunk. I didn't want to feel—feelings sucked. I didn't know what Kane could possibly have to say to me, but realizing I wouldn't be leaving here without seeing him, alcohol was awesome.

"I watched you that first year, a shell of a person, a ghost walking among the living. You pulled yourself out of that, but not by much. He did that to you because he wanted a clean fucking break. I'll give him a clean break when I snap the motherfucker's neck. And now he has something to tell you. Really? I want to be there, so he can astound me with whatever the hell he has to say to you after all this time."

Bending forward, I pressed my forehead into his chest. "God, it hurts. I've done so well at denying this, but being here, even five years later, I can't believe how much it hurts."

"Asshole."

"I'm glad you're here. It will all be a little bit easier with you here." Exhaustion, probably from the nerves that were going crazy in my stomach—fucking feelings, damn them—slammed into me. "I'm tired. Stay here tonight?"

"I wasn't going anywhere." Climbing under the covers, Simon pulled me close. "Sleep. We'll kill Kane tomorrow."

"Painfully."

"Very painfully." He looked down at me. "You can't avoid him. You are going to have to listen to what he has to say."

"I know."

"And after, I'll kill him. Beheading has a nice ring to it."

"Guillotine style or with a large broadsword?"

"Sword, but I don't want to use one of the good ones from our shop. Maybe an old rusty one."

"We could always cut him in several places and drop his body in the water for the fish."

"And let them eat the evidence. Now you're thinking. Love you, Teagan."

The memory of Kane saying those same words to me, especially being back in my old room, stabbed me in my already aching heart, but I forced the words from my throat. "Love you too."

I tried to sleep but I couldn't. Being careful not to wake Simon, I climbed from bed and pulled on my robe. Stepping into my slippers, I headed to the kitchen. Mrs. T had flashlights in a drawer by the back door. Grabbing one, I started outside. With as many times as I'd made this walk, I could probably do it with my eyes closed. Reaching the edge, I noticed a fence had been added, a simple split rail that sat about twenty feet in from the edge. I wondered why it was there, not that it took away from the view, but it seemed unnecessary to me. Taking the path, I noticed another addition, a railing had been installed—wood with square rungs. It was safer, definitely, but again it seemed unnecessary.

Settling on the sand, I switched off the flashlight and looked out at Kane's island. A light was burning, probably his bedroom. Being home, all the memories I had tried so hard to forget were right there, so vivid it was as if they had happened just yesterday and not all those years ago. Was he awake? Was his wife? Were they even now making love? Closing my eyes, I allowed myself to remember how it felt when he touched me, the taste of him, the way our bodies so perfectly fit together, how it felt when he slid into me. I had fooled myself believing I would ever be free of him. He had been there for too many of the moments that forged the person I became. And deep down, despite everything, I loved him—deeply and completely. He was the reason why every man since only ever touched my body; my heart wasn't mine to give and hadn't been for a very long time.

And even loving him, I hated him. Hated that he walked away from something so precious and rare. Not just walked away—never looked back. In the years that came, I wasn't sure how all of this would work. Mrs. Marks was sick and when—because I wouldn't think *if*—she recovered, how many more years did she have? I didn't want to miss any more special moments, but thinking about holidays and birthdays, of seeing Kane living the life I had so much wanted to share with him, made me ill, so how the hell would I ever live through it? Seeing the smiling faces of his children, the look of love he'd give his wife, knowing that once upon a time that look had been solely for me. For Mrs. Marks I would do it, I would suck it up and watch the family dynamic as an outsider again, but I knew I'd die a little bit every time I was forced to. Resting my chin on my knees, my focus stayed fixed on that light, and like a star I wished on it: wished it was me with him, not her, living our dream.

chapter 5

Teagan

Simon and I sat in the hospital waiting room, but we weren't allowed into Mrs. Marks's room. Apparently she was having a bad day, but she was still listed as stable, so that was something. I tried not to think about it, but what if she didn't recover from this? I had missed so many years, and with the thought that she could die with things the way they were between us, I wanted to weep again. Trying to stay positive, I pushed my fears out of my head, but then thoughts of Kane settled in as well as the dread I felt at facing him again. I really didn't want to know whatever it was he had to say, didn't think there was anything he could say to heal the hurt he had caused. And yet I was going to see him and hear him out, because it wasn't possible for me not to.

While sitting there, hoping the doctors would give us at least five minutes with Mrs. Marks, I saw Kane appear at the end of the hall. Everything just seemed to stand still as I got my first look at him in five years. My heart rate sped up at the sight of him. He looked beautiful. His hair was still long, so it brushed his shoulders but, unlike the last time I saw him, it wasn't messy. It looked windswept and sexy as hell. He was taller, maybe even taller than Simon, and his shoulders, always so big, were even wider, his waist narrow, his thigh muscles showing in relief against the faded denim of his jeans. His face was turned away, so I couldn't see his eyes—and I missed those eyes, even though they'd been haunting my dreams. And following that nearly perfect moment of silent appreciation came a stabbing pain that stole my breath. I should have realized that he would have been visiting Mrs. Marks too.

"Shit." I sank lower in my chair.

"What? What's happened?" Simon had been totally engrossed in the magazine he was reading—he could tune out better than anyone I knew.

"That's him." Why the hell did he have to look so freaking good?

Simon's head snapped in the direction I was looking. "Kane? He's hot. Too bad he didn't go bald or get fat."

My head snapped in his direction. "I was just thinking that same very thing," I said. Talk about uncanny.

"Great minds and all. So is that the wife?"

Kane walked along the corridor with one of the nurses, her arm draped through his. Their heads were turned toward each other, and she was laughing at something he'd said. Sweet, almost intimate, and definitely not his wife.

"No, that's not the wife."

"You think he's stepping out? Or maybe they didn't work out. Maybe he's a player—turned into a real Don Juan."

My focus shifted back to Simon. "You're getting a little excited."

"I know, but I do love a good intrigue. So what do you think is going on over there?"

"I never thought he was a player, but he isn't the boy he was, so I don't know. Maybe he is a slut now."

Simon was eyeing Kane, and I knew his thoughts as if he were speaking them out loud.

"He doesn't go your way, and even if he did, would you seriously tap that after what he did to me?"

"No, but a man can dream."

"You're an idiot." They drew closer, so I grabbed a magazine and held it to my face. The last thing I wanted was to have a chitchat with Kane. But he didn't even glance over when they passed by us. Had he seen me and purposely avoided me like we were in grade school? Sure, I was doing that to him but, as the wounded party, I was entitled.

"I guess he doesn't want to talk to you any more than you want to talk to him."

"Fuck that." I stood, dropping the magazine on the table, and started after Kane and his tart. When I was practically on top of him I snarled, "Hey, Kane. How the hell are you?" His whole body jerked like I'd hit him. I wished I had.

Slowly, he turned around, but those eyes were just as lifeless as they had been five years earlier.

"Teagan, you're home." So much for the lessons in giving people eye contact that Mr. Clancy drilled into us. Asshole.

"Not home. Visiting. Home's Boston now. This place has too many bad memories. So who's this? What happened to your wife, Kane? Did you not want that permanency either?"

For just a second I saw what looked like pain cross over his expression, but I just didn't care anymore. "Careful, he won't linger long, this one," I said to the woman. "A rolling stone, always on the move. Best to not get your heart involved. It hurts like a mother when he rips it from your chest and stomps on it. Believe me, I know from personal experience."

"Teagan! You're being rude." Kane had the nerve to call *me* rude? Oh no.

"I'm being rude? Yeah, I probably am. I'm a lot of things I never used to be. Simon, this is Kane, I told you about him. Kane, my boy, Simon."

Simon put out his hand and Kane refused to shake it. "Now who's being rude?" said Simon.

"We should probably get going," the nurse said, speaking up for the first time after having watched the show like a tennis match, her expression horrified.

"By all means, I certainly wouldn't want to hold you against your will. We know how you respond to that, don't we?" I punched Kane in the arm playfully—and not really playfully. I nailed him pretty fucking hard and, damn, that felt good.

A chin lift was all I got from him, a chin lift before he said, "Teagan." And then he turned and left me, again.

"Well, you really handled that well," Simon said, pushing his hands into the front pockets of his jeans.

"I wasn't at my best, but can you blame me?"

"Nope."

"Let's go eat. Being bitter and resentful has made me very hungry."

He laughed, the sound so loud it echoed down the hall. My eyes were still on Kane, and I saw his body tense, even from our distance. Asshole.

Simon was schmoozing Mrs. T, working his wiles so he could get a sample of every dish she was making for dinner. Growing up, I thought Kane could pack food away, but Simon put him to shame. I honestly didn't understand how the man could eat the way he did and still stay so fit. He worked out, but not as much as I would have to. Life wasn't fair.

Standing on the balcony off my room, my thoughts roamed all over the place. We never did get in to see Mrs. Marks. It concerned me how sick she was. I felt guilty for not coming home, even though I knew she understood why I hadn't visited. And seeing that reason the day before—Kane—for the first time in five years, I'd expected to feel anger and bitterness. But under that, there was a longing that had never gone away. I hated that he had that kind of power over me, especially since clearly I didn't have that kind of power over him.

He had moved on, apparently was still moving on, if the scene at the hospital was any indication. I couldn't lie, seeing him with that woman had been more painful than meeting his wife. It sounded crazy, but over the years I had rationalized to myself that he'd left me to be with the one he planned on spending the rest of his life with. She hadn't been, though, and that only threw in my face how right I had been to fear that I had really been no more than a convenience.

He was still so altered from the boy he had been. Why? I still wanted so desperately to know what had happened to him that had changed him so completely. Mr. Clancy had said there was more to the story and, despite myself, I found I really wanted to hear it.

And still my heart ached for him, missed him, missed us. Hated that I would never be free of him, that my love for him had turned into a life sentence. Suddenly the years ahead seemed rather bleak.

Pushing it from my head for now, since thoughts of Kane only led to pain, I left my room. Moving through the house, I marveled over Mrs. Marks's treasures. Having studied art history at school, I couldn't believe I'd grown up in a museum, but had never realized what she had. And yet, it felt like a home: warm and cozy, despite the rare antiquities all around.

Reaching the library, déjà vu washed over me at the sound of voices within, voices I recognized immediately: Kane and Camille. Jealousy, waves of it, crashed over me, even though I had no claim on Kane anymore.

"I'm going to the party too, so I can pick you up, if you'd like." Camille was still sniffing around. Get a life already. He wasn't interested.

"Sure, thanks." My jealousy darkened. He left me, broke my heart over the phone, removed himself completely from my life, and now he was going to parties with Camille, someone I knew he didn't even like. What the fuck? Strolling into the room, I didn't even bother hiding my contempt.

"Camille, how have you been?" She looked terrible. I found comfort in this observation. "You're looking a bit tired. Are you okay?" Mean, petty, beneath me, and oh so satisfying.

Smug was the best word to describe the expression that passed over her face. What the hell did she have to be smug about? Well, besides the obvious that Kane was talking to her and not me.

"Teagan. So you've finally decided to grace everyone with your presence."

"If you want to put it that way, sure. Still got your sights set on this house?"

That got her. Surprise flashed over her face. Take that, bitch.

"Just visiting an old friend. While you were off doing whatever you were doing, Kane and I have become rather close."

"Camille." That one word from Kane held meaning, I was sure, and yet I had no idea what that meaning was.

"Well, it's true. You never looked back, did you, Teagan? As close as the two of you were, you sure as hell severed all ties, and quickly. You should have looked back."

"Enough," Kane barked.

Looked back—what the hell was she talking about? It had come from her mouth first, and in great detail, the developing affection between Kane and Doreen. Camille had relished in telling me *that* news, knew the impact it would have on me—Kane moving on. And it had been him who had moved on, going so far as to get married. Why the fuck would I want to look back on that? "Seems my lack of looking back, as you call it, worked in your favor."

"Indeed, but we're just friends."

"Don't sell yourself short. Kane dumped me, and it seems like the little wife couldn't hold on to him either. His affection is fickle, so you may get your hands on him, after all."

She was like a rabid dog, drooling over the possibility.

"You deserve each other," were my parting words before I swept out of the room.

I fumed as I stomped down the hall, because, of all the people to be sitting in that room with him, it was fucking Camille. As if I hadn't been through enough because of him, and now he was entertaining her? And she just loved throwing that in my face. Stopping dead, I struggled with the need to walk right back into that room and punch him, punch them both, but that wasn't the proper way to handle a conflict, apparently.

Footsteps down the hall turned my attention to Dimitri Falco. Now what the hell was he doing? He moved around the house like he was looking for something as I followed him. His fingers, long, thin, and creepy looking ran along several of Mrs. Marks more valuable pieces.

"Can I help you?"

Snapping around, his startled expression would almost have been comical if not for the underlying hostility that pulsed off him. He'd been so consumed with his thoughts, which I just bet were sinister, that he hadn't noticed he had company.

"Aren't you supposed to be in the study, documenting or whatever?"

His nose went up, honest to God. He tilted his head so he could look down at me. Asshole. "I've recently been asked to perform another service."

"Which is?"

"That's between Mrs. Marks and me."

She'd been in the hospital not taking visitors, so when the hell did he talk to her? Moving past that I asked, "And that requires you to be in this room touching everything like a child in a toy shop?"

His dark eyes turned darker, and a chill worked through me, since he looked evil in that moment. "As a matter of fact, it does."

Crossing my arms, I leaned up against the doorjamb. "So have at it then."

"Excuse me?"

"Well, if you're supposed to be here, then you won't mind if I stand here and watch. I've always been fascinated with the law."

His lips turned up in a snarl. "I don't need to be babysat. I'll return to this at another time."

"I bet you will. See you around, Mr. Falco."

Leaving the room, he glanced at me from over his shoulder and I was scared for a second, because he was not a good man. Why the hell would Mrs. Marks have him as her attorney? When I had a moment with her, I intended to ask that very question.

Sitting on the beach, I noticed a wire that ran from Kane's island to the cliff just a few hundred feet from where I was sitting. I never saw that as a kid and, as many times as Kane and I played there, I would have. I wondered what it was? Could that possibly be the electricity? I always thought they ran that underwater.

I wasn't behaving like myself; every time I saw Kane I turned into a shrew. Rude—I was acting unbelievably rude and I wasn't generally a rude person, despite what I told Kane.

He hurt me; I was bitter. I understood my behavior, but I didn't understand his. He owed me an explanation. After everything we had been through, he owed me that, and yet he didn't seem to have any intention of giving me that despite the fact that Mr. Clancy said I needed to hear it. Was I going to have to pry an explanation from him? The thought was not a bad one. I'd love to inflict pain on him. He had it coming.

The other thought that constantly nagged at me was, what had I done to him to make him turn from me so completely? I had thought he had turned his back on the whole family, but it was just me he avoided like the plague. Yes, I'd been wrapped up in my schoolwork, but that couldn't be what had caused his change, what had made his love turn into hate. I knew there was a fine line between love and hate, but I didn't think it was so literal. And Camille. What the hell had that been all about? She was no different than she had been in school, so why was he now friends with her? Going to parties together certainly suggested they were friendly. It was like Kane was now the anti-Kane. I wish I knew what had happened to my Kane. Maybe he was being held in a cryo capsule in a spaceship orbiting our planet.

Mrs. Marks was doing better, but the docs asked if we could give her a few more days before we came for a visit. I was fine with that. She needed to recover, and that was more important than me getting in to see her, when she would more than likely not even know I was there.

Simon was on the phone in the study, working his magic on a few pieces in an estate sale he was tracking online. Feeling restless, I decided to head into town. The walk was both familiar and comforting.

Before long I was sitting on the pier that Kane and I used to visit all the time. Like when we were kids, my legs dangled over the edge as I looked out to sea. The water was so blue, and the way the sun reflected off it made it appear like diamonds on the surface. Seagulls flew overhead, their distinct cry echoing across the water. Kane wasn't wrong about it being beautiful. I felt that bitterness again, because I really had wanted to call this place home too, but it wasn't big enough for the both of us. Constantly running into him, especially with how dismissive he was to me now, would make living in Blue Hill hell.

A boat was pulling up, docking at the end of the pier. In the next minute, Kane appeared with Mr. Miller, the owner of the boatyard that Kane had worked at as a kid. My heart hitched to see Kane helping the older man from the boat, getting a flash of the boy he had been, the memory of him helping this very same man all those years ago when he was struggling with carrying too much. Why did he get to see the old Kane? Even that nurse—he had been smiling and laughing with her. Why did they get that and I didn't?

I was up and walking down the pier before I could stop myself. Mr. Miller saw me and said something to Kane before he smiled and spoke to me. "Hi, Teagan. Welcome home."

"Mr. Miller, you're looking well." For generations the Millers had run the boatyard, from the days when they built exquisite clipper ships to now where they did mostly refurbishing and maintenance. For a man who spent his days in the sun, his skin didn't have that ruddy fisherman's hue. Though he was balding, he looked at least ten years younger than I knew him to be.

"I'm getting old, but I do appreciate you saying that." He flashed me a smile and placed a hand on Kane's arm. "I'll head up. You okay?"

"Yeah, I'll join you in a minute." Kane's head turned in my general direction. "Teagan."

"You don't call me Tea anymore, why?"

He shrugged. That was the only answer I got.

"Why, Kane? I really need to understand why you've changed so much. What happened to you?"

"Nothing happened."

"You're not the same person you were. You're cold and dismissive. Even though you don't love me anymore, we were the closest of friends. And yet you can chat up other people, including that hag Camille. But with me you've not even attempted to explain why you left the way you did."

His voice sounded hard, but he looked devastated. The contradiction unnerved me. "Let it go, Teagan. Just let it go. We're not who we were. That's over, so just let it be over."

My temper stirred. "How the hell can you dismiss me like this? I'd like to get over you as easily as you did me, but I can't until I understand what I did to turn you from me so completely. Why do you hate me so much?"

"Hate you?" Horror filled his expression. "I don't hate you."

"I disagree. You clearly don't like me. I've been in town for four days, and you have not made one attempt to see me. I wish I could turn it off as easily as you have, I wish the sight of you didn't bring back all the memories I've tried so hard to lock away, and yet somehow they still seep out to torment me. You and me forever, remember? Your idea and mine of forever are very different."

He just stood there like I was invisible. I didn't think my heart could break any more, but it did, the familiar ache burning in my chest.

"Please, just tell me what happened to you. What happened to my Kane? I miss him every day."

"Let it go, Teagan, please just let it go."

His refusal to answer me and the calm, almost callous way in which he addressed me caused my temper to spike and, with it, the words I longed to say just poured out. "You're an asshole." He jerked as if I had slapped him, and I saw pain cross his face, but I just didn't care. "I never would have believed it of the boy I loved, but the man you've become is a big fucking asshole. You broke me, you son of a bitch. You left me shattered and alone and yet you can stand here and tell me to let it go. I've been in therapy for years and I'm still struggling to let it go. I hope whatever it was you needed to do, however you needed to find yourself, was worth the wreckage you left in your wake."

I walked away that time, and yet somehow I was still the one hurt.

That night, I headed to the kitchen to get a glass of water before I went to bed. I had just reached the doorway when I heard Kane's voice. Peering into the room, I watched as he came in through the back door, Zeus at his side. My gaze fell on the harness that Zeus was wearing, one I had yet to see him in, leather with a loop. It wasn't much of a leash, but then I supposed Kane wouldn't want Zeus having too much lead near the cliffs.

"Hey, Mrs. T."

"Evening, Kane."

"Did you bake me a cake?" he asked, which I thought was odd since there was a cake sitting on the one counter.

"I did. Triple chocolate, your favorite."

"You're the best." And though he was trying to act happy, he was failing. Could he possibly be hurt from what I had said to him earlier?

"You want something to drink with it?"

"I'll get it."

Bitterness swelled in me. Despite the sadness that rolled off him, here was my Kane, acting completely normal with Mrs. T, but with me he turned into a cyborg. His hand reached for the cabinet, brushing over the door, before pulling it open. Walking to the fridge, he held his hand suspended for a minute before he pulled out the milk and poured himself a glass, his free hand wrapping around the rim. Moving to the table, his hand bumping along the top of each chair, he took a seat. Mrs. T placed a plate in front of him, the fork to the left of the plate. Zeus settled at his side eating his kibble.

"Delicious as usual."

An alarming feeling of dread moved through me watching him, and then Mrs. T said, "Have you told her?" With those words, my focus shifted.

The smile he had just been sporting died on his lips. "No."

"You going to?"

"No."

"We've all kept quiet because you asked that of us, but she's hurting, Kane. It's not right, you keeping her in the dark like you are."

"Pun intended?" he asked, but there was no humor in his tone, only anger, regret, and bitterness.

"Mrs. Marks intended to tell her. She called her and asked her to come. Mr. Clancy and I encouraged her to do it, but it should come from you."

"Her life isn't here anymore, she's moved on just like I wanted her to do."

"I think you're a fool, and I think you're being very unfair to that girl. She still loves you. It's written all over her face. What if the shoe was on the other foot, Kane?"

He said nothing, only stood and started for the door. "She's better off without me, Mrs. T." And then he was gone, his dog following him out.

It was late. Anger burned, simmering under the surface, and with it, another emotion that was all consuming: disbelief. Everyone was asleep but me. I hadn't noticed it when I came home from school all those years ago, too heartbroken to focus on anything but the pain he was causing me, but since I'd been home, the times I'd seen him, I could tell that something wasn't right. And where my thoughts were taking me as to the cause was what brought on the disbelief.

Heading to the kitchen, I went to the cabinet to the spot Kane had brushed his fingers over earlier. Doing the same, I felt odd bumps on the wood, and looking closer revealed the transparent sticker. I didn't know how long I stood there running my finger over it. Working my way around the space, I saw everything in the kitchen had one.

Pulling the refrigerator open revealed meticulous organization: milk in one section, yogurts in another, veggies and fruits, and each drawer had a sticker. And in that moment I knew my suspicion was correct. My knees buckled and I slid bonelessly down the cabinets to the floor.

The stickers were Braille, if I wasn't wrong. Braille marking the cabinets, which were so organized, every item in precise position. The floor was free of any objects so as to avoid tripping. The wire that led from Kane's island to the beach must be a guide of some kind. They added a fence and the railings on the path. And every time I'd seen Kane since I had been home, he had been with someone, and the harness Zeus had been wearing wasn't for him but Kane. His lack of making eye contact and not shaking Simon's hand. His house, when I'd come home after college, had been tossed. He had done that, done it out of frustration and anger.

Kane was blind.

I was having trouble getting my head around that. What had happened to him? How had he lost his sight? Why would he have kept that from me? Jumping up from the floor and grabbing a flashlight—which caused a wicked case of déjà vu—I ran all the way to the beach. The water swirled from the churning of the little boat's engine as I made my way to the island.

Climbing from the boat, I ran to the house. Zeus heard me before I even knocked, his warning growl alerting Kane. A minute later, the door pulled open.

"Why didn't you tell me you were blind?"

Surprise flashed over his face. "Teagan."

"Why?"

"Come in." He held the door for me. I stepped in, was greeted by Zeus, but I didn't move into the room, staying close to the door.

My pulse was pounding in my throat, the back of my eyes were burning, and I had a thousand questions on the tip of my tongue, but the only one I kept asking was, "Why?" Disbelief had morphed into devastation, but my anger was growing to rival it.

"What gave it away?" A touch of humor laced through his deep voice.

"You were very convincing, but I lived in that house too, I saw the changes. What happened to you?"

He pulled a hand through his hair, his sightless eyes staring right into mine as if he could see me. Somehow he managed to navigate himself to stand on the other side of the room. I didn't understand why he needed to put the room between us, but I moved on from that slight. His face was completely blank, almost as if he didn't hear me. I really thought he wasn't going to say anything and then I saw it, the slip in the armor, the crack that offered a glimpse into the tormented man it hid. His mouth opened, the words tumbling over each other as if he were relieved to finally get it all off his chest. "There was a fire in town, the volunteers were called in. The O'Malleys' old ice cream parlor at the end of Main Street—by the time we got there, the place was completely engulfed. We were going to let it burn, since the risk to the other shops was minimal, and then I saw the kid. My guess, there probably had been a few kids inside smoking, since kids have been doing that since the place closed down. They were most likely the ones who'd set the fire. One of them got trapped when she tried to put the fire out."

Dread rippled over me, like icy fingers down my spine. "A fire?" Kane wouldn't have yanked himself from my life, left me broken and alone, because he had gone blind. No, whatever had happened to him had been significantly worse.

"What happened in the fire? How did you lose your sight?"

"Teagan, there's no point."

"How did you lose your fucking sight?"

"A beam fell, trapped me under it. Retina detachment caused my blindness."

A beam fell, a burning beam. Oh my God. "Lift your shirt."

"What?"

"Lift your fucking shirt."

His face went hard as he pulled his shirt off. I couldn't help but gasp, nor could I stop the tears that spilled down my cheeks. His skin, his beautiful skin, was scarred, twisted and red up and over his shoulder from his left pectoral. My feet forced me around his back, and my tears fell harder, because half of his back and up to his neck were also scarred.

"Oh my God," I said through a strangled cry. And then the reality of what had really happened to him nearly shattered me. Burned, blind, and alone. I had never felt heartache so severely. "Oh my God."

"Tea?"

My teary eyes looked up into his, into those beautiful blue eyes that I had thought were dead. I ran, fled down the beach and back to the boat. Somehow I managed to get to my room before I stumbled, falling to my hands and knees. Curling into myself, I tried forcing air into my lungs, and, when I exhaled, the sound that ripped from my throat was inhuman. All these years I had cursed him, hated him for living the dream without me, but he hadn't been. He had almost died, but then he'd lived: burned, scarred, in excruciating pain, and having to deal with all that horror in the dark. The force of my sobs made my ribs ache. Rocking back and forth, I completely broke down.

chapter 6

Kane

Her scent, that had haunted me all these years, still lingered. I wanted her. My body ached for her.

"Fuck." Clenching my hands, I wanted to smash something, wanted to rage, but I'd been there, done that, and afterward I always had a mess to clean up that I couldn't even see. My Tea had finally come home. Had finally learned my secret, and it revolted her—she couldn't bear to look at me. I didn't blame her, and yet the agony that sliced through me made the pain from my burns seem like nothing.

Needing a distraction so I didn't tear my house apart and despite the fact that it was late, I started toward the backyard. I had spent years learning my house, how many steps to get to any room, to any spot on this island. The high bar I had installed between two large trees had seen me through so many bouts of anger. Pulling myself up was like second nature, curling and lifting, releasing.

How could I have known going into that building all those years ago would have changed my life so completely? Looking back on it, I hadn't been focused. First rule of fire—complete focus. But I'd had Tea on my mind. She had said yes; she had agreed to marry me. I hadn't stopped flying from the moment I'd slipped my ring on her finger. In truth, I'd felt almost invincible; she'd made me feel invincible. And when I saw the terrified face in the window, I didn't even hesitate. How could I not try? It would have haunted me my whole life knowing I hadn't done everything I could have. As it turned out, I was still haunted, but I'd also lost my life, or the one I had so very much wanted, the one that included Tea.

The fire had been so hot that every man who went in had to come back out, none even getting close to the girl. I didn't think; I just ran in and managed to get through the blaze. There was only one kid left, barely a teenager, the O'Malley girl. She hadn't run fast enough, and her friends, not much of ones, hadn't waited for her. We had just reached the door when the beam fell. I feared she had been hit too, but I learned later she had gotten out.

Feeling my skin burning, the smoke suffocating me, I willed the fire to take me, to end it fast, and, even wishing for that, my eyes teared up, because I knew just how devastated Tea would've been from the loss, knew it because the idea of losing her was unbearable.

Lying in that hospital, I'd wanted to die. I was close, knew somehow that everyone was just waiting for me to die. I'd been conscious long enough to demand of Mrs. Marks that she not call Tea. She was horrified, outraged that I would deny Tea her chance at saying good-bye. But I remembered how much she had hated seeing her parents being buried. I wouldn't do that to her, make her last memory of me in a box. I wanted her to see us swimming to our island or laughing over some joke we'd played on each other. I wanted her to remember my body over hers as I moved deeply inside her, connected and bound. I wanted her final memory of me to be on the side of that road when I dropped to my knee and asked her to marry me. I wanted her to remember all that was good and not me burned and broken.

Weeks later, when I was brought out of the medically induced coma, I opened my eyes and saw the same as when they were closed. The doctors explained the burns and the years of treatments I was going to need, explained that the blindness was permanent. I knew I had to set Tea free. At the sound of her voice when I called and told her I had found someone else, I heard her spirit die. I hated myself for that, would always hate myself for that. But she deserved more than the life that stretched out before me.

The pain of the recovery almost rivaled that in my heart. She never came. Even though I had told her I no longer wanted her, she knew how much I loved her—and yet she'd believed the lie. And it was then that I realized she had already been pulling away—not taking my calls, not coming home for Thanksgiving when she had been so upset about leaving me only three months before. Even the way she handled my defection had been almost callously cool. Being away from me, and around so many others with similar interests, she had finally realized that I was just a convenience. I would have dragged my body to the cliff and walked off it, had I been able to see, had I not been as helpless as a child: dependent on everyone around me.

Two years after the fire, Mrs. Marks finished what I had started. I hadn't initially gone off with Tea when she'd moved to Boston, because I'd needed six months for the plans for our house. Mrs. Marks offered me the island, but I wanted to pay for the house myself.

I had hired an architect to draw up the plans for the house that Tea and I had both envisioned. I'd intended to show up in Boston with the blueprints to our home, my engagement gift to her. After the fire, Mrs. Marks found them and had the house built. She gave me part of our dream. Mrs. T came to clean and bring me groceries, my nurse stayed with me for years, helping me to adapt to not only the blindness but the limitations of my body due to the scars. That was one thing I could change; I worked out, rebuilt the muscles, forced my body to adapt.

The town had given me a rather large settlement. I didn't want it. What was the point of it when I couldn't leave my fucking house and the person I wanted with me was far away? So the money sat in my bank account collecting interest.

I was haunted by the memory of my last encounter with Tea when she'd returned home from school. Hearing the heartbreak and pain in her voice at seeing me, I knew I had been wrong, that she had loved me as I did her.

But I had ceased being the boy she'd loved. There was nothing I could give her, and taking her away from the life she was building for herself so she could become a hermit with me was selfish. I felt guilty about lying to Tea, telling her my nurse was Doreen, and worse, my wife, but I'd had to get her to go, and I didn't know how else to make her. In that moment, I was glad for my blindness. Seeing the look on her face, and knowing I'd caused it, would have broken me. She was better off without me, there was no doubt in my mind and heart about that. But hearing her, being near her, only reinforced the simple truth: how much I had missed her, wanted her, only her, always her.

Her words to me earlier, about how I had broken her and callously turned away from her, tormented me. My intention had been to spare her pain, not cause it. I had known my actions from all those years ago would've initially caused her pain, but I'd really believed she would have moved on and found happiness again. She hadn't, though, and I didn't need the words to know the pain she still felt—her voice dripped with it. It took every shred of willpower I possessed to not pull her into my arms at the boatyard, the same reason I'd had to put the distance of the room between us just now. I wanted her, but I wasn't just burned and blind, wasn't just battling all the insecurities that came along with my life now. I had other lingering problems from the trauma that made me unfit to be around people. Limited exposure was okay, but building a life with Tea when I was so fucked up was not fair to her, despite how much I still really wanted that.

I dropped from the bar, my muscles sore and tired, and yet still my body ached for her. Moving to the bathroom, I turned on the water and stripped. I liked the water as hot as I could stand it, because it forced me to feel. A dispenser for soap and shampoo hung from the wall, something Mrs. T filled for me during her weekly visits. Feeling the cold liquid in my palm, I massaged it into a lather before wrapping my hand around my erection, my other hand pressing against the tile, my head lowered as I thought of my Tea.

Teagan

I lay on the floor, staring at the ceiling. I'd cried so hard and for so long, I was numb. Shock had settled in, part of the reason the pain I had felt seeing Kane's scars had ebbed.

Maybe it was wrong of me to feel anger, but I did. I should have been at his side, and instead he had pushed me from his life—not just pushed but ripped me out of it. I understood, as much as

I hated it, what had motivated him. Had it been me, I would have done the same, spared him from the agony and horror, and yet I was still pissed.

Blind. I still couldn't quite believe it. He walked around very well for a man who couldn't see. For someone like him to have to live in perpetual darkness—someone who loved looking out at the sea, loved watching the sun rise and set, loved seeing the world—was cruel.

He'd gone into a burning building to save someone. That was my Kane. Always the first to lend a hand, always offering so much of himself. And despite how it all turned out, love burned in me to know that the boy I adored was still there, in the man he had become.

How had he survived the nightmare? Even trying to put myself in his shoes, I knew I couldn't possibly appreciate the terror he must have felt and lived through for so long. And was still living through, being forced to learn how to live with limitations he never thought he'd have.

Wanting to understand, wanting to find that connection, I stood and closed my eyes. Trying to walk to my door, I hit my shin on the corner of the bed and nearly face-planted when my toe got caught on the edge of the rug. It was too easy, though. I knew this room. Making my way to a wing of the house I didn't know as well, I kept the lights off, closed my eyes, and tried to find my way back to the stairs. At first, I thought I could do it, but I got disoriented, my hands reaching out for something, anything, to give me some indication where I was in relation to the door. Panic gripped me, the darkness so complete, so scary and lonely. The urge to open my eyes was strong, but Kane would never be free of the dark. My heart was pounding in my chest, and an icy chill covered my skin. True fear filled me, overwhelmed me, nearly crippled me. Even being in a room full of people, you could feel all alone: Who was near? How did you get out if you needed to? How did you find your loved ones? I couldn't even find my way out of a room in a house I had grown up in. I fumbled around in that room for God knows how long, but I never made it to the door. Anguish accompanied my fear even knowing that Kane was adapting and learning how to compensate for his blindness. And he had learned all of this while healing for years from those burns. How much pain had he been in? And he had no ability to draw comfort from the faces of those he loved.

Defeated, I opened my eyes and made my way to the kitchen and lit a burner on the stove. I watched the blue flame come to life, grow strong. I placed my arm over it, but I couldn't hold it there longer than a few seconds. The pain was excruciating, and the smell . . . Tears I didn't think I had left to cry started filling my eyes again. This burn was small and it still hurt like a mother. Half of Kane's back and chest were scarred. The fact he'd survived the pain alone was a testament to his strength. Tending my wound, I waited for morning before returning to Kane.

As his house came into view, my heart stopped beating in my chest. The house was painted green with window boxes gracing the front windows. He had built our house. Climbing from the boat, I walked to the front door and knocked. Zeus came from around the back.

"Hey. Your daddy here?" I asked, scratching behind his ear.

Following him around back, I found Kane doing pull ups on a pole anchored between two trees. The memory of him doing this when we were younger nearly brought me to my knees. We were older, different, and yet the continuity of seeing him doing something so familiar comforted me. Like in our youth, his muscles bunched and corded as he curled up and down, though they were significantly larger now.

"Kane."

His body tensed a second before he dropped to the ground. "What are you doing here?"

"We need to talk."

"Not sure what there is to say," he said and reached for his towel, a clear dismissal.

"Really, nothing to talk about? The boy I loved is injured and blind and I, too, was left in the dark for nine years, but there's nothing to say?"

"For what purpose, Teagan? Your life isn't here anymore."

The fact that I didn't shoot fire from my eyes with my fury was amazing. "It isn't here because you pushed me away. I don't have the burns or the blindness, but I suffered all these years too."

"They didn't expect me to live. I didn't want you to watch me die. I couldn't let that be the final memory you had of me."

"But you lived and still you made no attempt to reach out to me. Why?"

"I didn't want this life for you."

"It wasn't your call to make. If you really had died . . ." My sob came out in a gasp, tearing at my throat, making it so hard to get the words out. "I would have wanted to be there right at your side, would have wanted you to feel me there, would have wanted to be able to tell you how much I loved you. I would have wanted to watch as you left this world and maybe a little part of you would have stayed with me, in me."

"I didn't want your last memory of me to be ugly."

"There is nothing about you that is ugly. Watching as you moved on to whatever is out there wouldn't have been ugly, it would have been beautiful, life changing, heartbreaking, soul stealing, but not ugly. When I came back four years later, why didn't you tell me then?"

A single tear rolled down his cheek. "I can't be what you deserve. Eventually you would have figured that out." Before I could say anything, he continued. "It took years for me to heal, years of pain and agony, completely at the mercy of everyone around me. I didn't want that life for you, didn't want to strap you to an invalid. And maybe it was vanity, but I didn't want you to see me like that, to see what I had become. I wouldn't have needed to see to feel your pity. I didn't want that. Not from you. I begged Mrs. Marks to tell you I'd died, but she wouldn't. That was her line in the sand. So I had to improvise."

"Who was the woman?"

"My nurse. You have no idea how many times I've played that conversation over and over again in my head. Telling the one person I wanted most that I didn't want her. It took everything in me not to grab you and never let go. But then reality returned, and I knew that tying you to me, to this life . . . you deserved better than that."

"And Doreen?"

"I knew you were jealous of her. I could hear it in your voice. My guess is it was as potent as my jealousy over Simon. I knew you'd believe me. Your emotions would make you believe the lie."

"So you wanted a better life for me and, to do that, you broke my heart."

"Watching me die would have broken your heart anyway, but it would have also left you with memories that would have haunted you for the rest of your life. What I did seemed the lesser of the two evils."

"And what about what I wanted?"

"You wouldn't have wanted me, Tea. You don't want me now. You saw my scarred body and you ran. Who wants to be strapped to a blind, burned freak?"

"I didn't run because of your scars. I ran because I had just learned that the boy—no, the man—I love, suffered horrendously. I saw the evidence of that suffering and broke down, completely lost my shit. You shouldn't have pushed me away, should have trusted in what we felt for each other to know I would have never walked away."

His voice cracked, his eyes drifting down. "Your rejection would have killed me."

"Why do you think I would have rejected you?"

"Look at me!" he roared. "Who the fuck wants this?"

"Me, Kane, I do."

"You should go."

"I don't want to go."

"Leave! Just fucking go back to your life and forget me. Please just fucking forget me."

"I can't forget you. I've tried, believe me I have tried, but I can't."

"You deserve more than I can give you."

"Bullshit."

"I've got nothing, Tea."

"You could have me. Once upon a time that meant everything to you."

"Once upon a time, I was a whole man. I'm not that man anymore."

"And that's it? All those dreams we had as kids, you're just willing to let them die? I don't understand—you're here, I'm here, I still love you. Why can't we try?"

His next words were softly spoken, but there was no denying the finality of them. "I don't want to. What we had is gone."

My gasp came out, even though I tried to stop it. I had thought there was nothing more he could say to hurt me. Clearly I was wrong. I started to walk away from him but stopped myself because damn it, *he* was wrong. Turning back to him, he looked defeated: his head bowed and his hands resting on his hips.

"You're wrong."

His head jerked up.

"Maybe what was between us is over, maybe we really can't go back, but telling me to walk away, to forget you, is wrong. We're family, Kane, whether you want to accept that or not. Family pulls together during a tragedy, we don't push each other away. Mrs. Marks is in the hospital and here we all are, together, praying for her recovery. That's how it should have been with you too, and you damn well know it."

I started away from him again, but I just wasn't finished, so I turned back. "And it needs to be said, what you suffered through, what you endured all these years, I can't even begin to imagine, but you act as if you're the only one who suffered. I suffered too, Mrs. Marks, Mrs. T, and Mr. Clancy did as well. Not to the mention the strain you unintentionally put on my relationship with Mrs. T, forcing me to believe her grandniece was living my life. It isn't all about you, Kane, it isn't all about what you want—not when you belong to others, not when you mean something to people. You're acting selfish and a bit cowardly and I have to say those are two characteristics I never thought would ever describe you."

And then I walked away on unsteady legs.

"Jesus Christ." Simon pulled a hand through his hair, pacing back and forth while we stood on the cliff overlooking the island. I had just told him about Kane

"How bad are the burns?"

Every time I saw Kane's body in my head, my eyes stung. "Almost his entire back, from midway up, and his left pec to his shoulder are scarred. I burned myself. I wanted to see what it felt like." I lifted my arm to show him the wound.

"Teagan, that's looks awful." His attention moved back to my face. "How bad did it hurt?"

"Like hell. I can't even imagine what he went through, Simon. I can't . . . I wasn't there for him. At the worst moment in his life, I wasn't there." And that destroyed me. I hadn't said as much to Kane, but I felt it. In his darkest hour, he'd pushed me away instead of pulling me close.

Simon's arms came around me. "He wanted you there, he just didn't want you there. But you're here now. Don't rush him. In his shoes, I would have pushed everyone away, but you were his friend before you were anything else, so be his friend and let him come around at his own pace."

"You're right." And he was. Being Kane's friend had never been hard, but I knew Kane wasn't on the same page. He had closed himself off to the world, living on the island in isolation. Had told me to go back home and leave him. But hope burned in me, because I knew he journeyed off his island sometimes. Maybe his words really were all bravado; maybe he wanted to reach out but was afraid. Fear was not an emotion I would have pegged for Kane, but then he wasn't the same person he had been. Was it possible that I might be able to reach him?

Not realizing where my thoughts were going, Simon grinned. "I usually am."

"He built our home. We talked about living on that island, separate from the world when we wanted to be. Just him and me. I'm happy he has that at least." My focus shifted to Simon. "I would like you to meet him. In a real way, this time."

"I would like that too."

"Maybe we can try to get him to engage," I said.

"How?"

"I don't know. Nine years is a long time to let pass without telling me about the secret hell he was living, so telling me to go back to my life could be how he truly feels. But I think he might still be in there, that he might be pushing me away to avoid having to witness me walk away at a later point. I don't want to walk away. He isn't living. The Kane I knew wanted so much more from life. Maybe he and I will never get back what we had, but if I could help him find his way, offer him a hand like he did with me when I was younger, I'd be giving him back a small measure of what he's done for me."

What I didn't say was that, though his body was scarred and he was blind, the damage was even greater, damage not seen on the outside. He was different, harder, more closed off. I understood the change. I had changed too, and I hadn't lived through the ordeal that he had, but I couldn't help but mourn for the boy he had been. And yet deep down I hoped there was still a chance for us, once he realized I was here and I wanted to be here. But my fear was that we would never get back what we'd lost, because the fire had destroyed us too.

"We can at least try," Simon said, though he didn't sound hopeful, and he was probably right not to be. Kane was pretty set in his ways now, and I was, after all, just a girl from his past.

"I'm going to see Mrs. Marks today. Would you like to come?" I asked.

"Yes. And then we'll brainstorm and see about getting Kane off that island," he said, knocking his hip lightly into mine, trying to ease the tension.

"Okay."

He reached for my hand. "Teagan, you're hurting, I get that. Knowing now why Kane wanted a clean break, that it was for you, not him, I know that seeing his scarred body and learning he lost his sight must fill you with all kinds of emotions. It's okay to cry, to feel conflicted, to be angry at him and yourself. But don't overthink this. You fell in love once before, so just because you're both different now doesn't mean you won't fall in love again."

"Are you reading my mind?"

"Maybe." He wrapped his arm around my shoulders and squeezed. "It's been nine years, Teagan, give yourselves time to find each other again."

"You always know exactly what I need to hear."

"I'm brilliant, it's true. Now let's get some food. Mrs. T is making pastrami sandwiches."

Mrs. Marks was sleeping when we arrived at the hospital.

"She's been in and out, so please don't be surprised if she doesn't wake during your visit," the nurse said after showing us to her room.

"How is she doing?"

"Remarkably well. She's a tough cookie, that one." Admiration rang in the nurse's voice. I couldn't help but agree with her, because Mrs. Marks was an extraordinary person.

Simon stood at my side as I took the chair next to the bed. Her hair was not in her signature bun but down around her shoulders. I never realized how long it was. Sitting there, holding her pale hand in mine, I thought about Kane in a bed much like this, the skin of his body wrapped in protective cloth, his eyes no longer seeing.

Tears pricked my eyes and I wiped them away.

"Even lying there, she's got an air about her," Simon said in awe. "She looks like a Hollywood starlet."

"Wait until she wakes and you meet her. You are going to love each other."

"I've no doubt."

Mrs. Marks stirred, and her eyes opened. Her hand moved, squeezing mine lightly.

"Teagan."

"Mrs. Marks. Yes, I'm here."

"You came home."

"I'm sorry I stayed away so long. I shouldn't have, I should have visited, shouldn't have turned my back on you. Forgive me."

"Nonsense, you were hurting. I am so glad you're home."

Her focus shifted to Simon, so I made the introduction. "This is Simon."

A slight smile touched her lips, and then her hand squeezed harder. "Kane . . ."

"I know, Mrs. Marks. I know about Kane."

"He made me promise."

"It's okay, please don't worry about that now."

"I didn't agree with him, you know . . ."

"It's okay, Mrs. Marks."

"So bad, understand why he didn't tell you. Loves you. Needs you to heal him."

Her words were turning disjointed from exhaustion, even though they touched me and gave me hope. But she needed to focus on getting stronger. Her eyes were already having trouble staying open.

"Are you staying?" she asked.

"Until you are better, yes."

"That's good, the family's together. Kane . . ." she said.

"Would you like me to ask him to come see you?"

"Secret . . . can't keep it."

"I already figured it out, so you didn't tell his secret."

"No, not his secret. My lawyer . . . Lawson."

I thought her lawyer was Falco. Glancing at the heart monitor, I saw her pulse soaring. Trying to reassure her, I vowed, "Lawson and secret. I've got it."

The nurse appeared, eyeing me like I was somehow upsetting Mrs. Marks.

"She's trying to tell me something, and it's getting her upset."

Gentleness replaced the woman's censure. "That happens. Her mind is working, but her body isn't on the same page. She's getting stronger every day. She'll be able to tell you whatever it is she needs to soon enough."

"Did you hear that, Mrs. Marks? Just rest now. I'm not going anywhere."

She seemed to hear me. Her hand loosened around mine and her eyes closed.

"She's sleeping now and will probably sleep through the night," the nurse said.

"See you tomorrow. Mrs. Marks." Pressing a kiss on her forehead, my lips lingered there.

Stepping out of her room, my head was spinning. *Who was Lawson? What secret?*

"Are you going to see this Lawson guy?" Simon asked.

"Yeah, though I'm not really sure how to start that conversation, since it's unlikely her lawyer is going to share a secret with me. Isn't that against what they do?"

"It would seem."

Let's go talk to Mr. Clancy. He knows Mrs. Marks the best, so maybe he knows something about this secret. If nothing else, he can probably lend some insight into who Lawson is."

"I like this plan. Wonder what Mrs. T is making for dinner."

Even with all the conflicting emotions I was feeling, I laughed. "I'm really glad you're here."

Wrapping his arm around my shoulders, we started down the hall. "Me too."

"Mr. Clancy, we need your help." I'd found him in the kitchen, sipping a cup of tea. Mrs. T was baking something that smelled divine.

"Mrs. T, we need to talk about whatever that is you're making," Simon practically purred and off he went, right to her side, hoping for a sample. He was ridiculous.

Pulling the chair out next to Mr. Clancy, I dropped my elbows on the table and sighed. "First, I know the secret."

"It's about time."

Mr. Clancy actually sounded disgruntled, which earned him a smile. I wanted to talk to him about Kane, but first I needed help. "When I visited Mrs. Marks, she mentioned that she had a secret she needed to tell Kane, and mentioned Lawson. Who's that?"

"Her lawyer."

"I thought Mr. Sleazy was her lawyer."

He nearly choked on his tea. When his face was no longer pink from lack of oxygen, he actually grinned. "You don't like him either."

"No, like you, I don't trust him. He seems slippery. How did Mrs. Marks find him?"

"He was recommended by Mr. Lawson's law firm. Lawson has been her lawyer for thirty years, but he's semiretired, keeping only a handful of clients, and Mrs. Marks is one of them. Mr. Sleazy, I'm guessing, assists Mr. Lawson so the firm is up to date on her affairs. When Lawson retires fully, the transition to the new lawyer will be a smooth one for Mrs. Marks."

"Wonder what Lawson thinks of Mr. Sleazy. Where does Lawson live?"

"He has a small cottage at the other end of town."

"What do you think it is Mrs. Marks needs to tell Kane?"

Curiosity crossed his face. "Not sure."

"So the question is, do I talk to Lawson or should I tell Kane, since whatever this is about, it's about him?"

"Tough one—he's been through so much already. I'd hate for him to have something more dumped on him."

"My feelings exactly. So should I visit Mr. Lawson?"

"Neither situation is ideal, but yes, I think it should be you. I believe Kane would want you to tell him whatever it is Mrs. Marks needs to share."

Sitting back in my chair, I studied Mr. Clancy from across the table. "I'm not so sure Kane wants me anywhere near him. I understand now why you all stayed silent. Mrs. Marks said he made you promise."

"Yes. He didn't want that life for you."

"Can you tell me what it's been like for him? He's not feeling particularly chatty, at least not with me."

Simon settled next to me, as if he knew I was going to need his support.

Mr. Clancy placed his cup back on its saucer, his smile fading as his expression turned a bit solemn. "In the beginning, we all just waited for him to die." He reached for my hand. "We weren't here at the house, because we stayed close to Kane, spent most of the early weeks at the hospital, leaving only to shower at a nearby hotel. There had been so much damage to his body, the doctors were sure infection would set in before his body ever had time to heal. He was isolated to prevent germs from doing what we all feared. He was put into a coma for the first few weeks, and, after, when he was conscious again, the nurses told us he called out to you, often."

My heart squeezed, the pain caused by Mr. Clancy's words stealing my breath.

"To everyone's surprise, he survived and grew stronger, and that's when they started skin grafts. He had so many surgeries and recoveries, and yet he got through all of them. He was released from the hospital almost a year after the fire and brought here. He stayed in your room, found it like he was sighted and wouldn't leave it for months. He mourned the loss of you. I think he still does.

"Mrs. Marks grew concerned because, though his body was healing, his soul wasn't. That was when she had the house built on the island; she even tried to get him involved with it, but not being able to see, he only grew frustrated." Mr. Clancy's inhale sounded like it pained him. "He had the plans for your house drawn up, Teagan, while you started school. It was why he needed the time before moving with you to Boston. He was working with an architect on your house. And, even knowing he had months before he could join you, he'd packed up his room so he could leave as soon as the plans were done."

Those words started to crack the walls surrounding my heart. I'd thought he was unsure about our future, when really he'd been working on building our future. I was a fool. "I didn't know that."

"When you came back after school and had the falling out with him, we thought we had lost him. He plunged so far into himself that he was unreachable. For almost a year, we had to sit and watch as he died a little each day. I honestly don't know what the trigger was, but one day he got out of bed. Started memorizing the floor plan of his home. Kane had been seeing a therapist quite regularly after he returned home, but she wasn't having an impact on him, because he didn't want to hear it. When his attitude changed, so did their sessions, and he just soaked up what she had to say to him. She helped him to understand his blindness and how he needed to learn to live in the world again."

"Can he see anything?"

"No, only darkness. When he was ready to face the reality that he would never see again, we poured over the websites the therapist recommended to us. Activities we take for granted can be unimaginably hard when you're blind. And it isn't just the lack of sight that's an adjustment, but the reality that you've lost your independence. In order for Kane to accept his blindness, we needed to help him get to a place where he didn't feel so dependent. We ordered the Braille labels so that Kane could feel his way around the house. We also added washable labels to his clothes so he wouldn't need help dressing, and purchased talking clocks so he would know the time. Even little changes like installing the soap dispensers in his bathroom, which are easier for him to use, and, as an added benefit, he wasn't fumbling around with bottles, a tripping hazard if he should drop one, made him feel more in control. And then we organized both his house and this one. We put everything in specific locations, so he knew where to locate what he needed; we cleared the floor, adding measures for his safety, and eventually got Zeus. He was so motivated to not be a burden that he even worked with Silas Miller from the boatyard, figuring out how to navigate the boat from the island to the beach on his own. The markers and wire from the island to the beach are there for him. Silas rigged something so Kane's boat travels along that wire. When he feels tension, he knows he's deviated from the course. The first time he appeared in the kitchen, having come from the island on his own in that boat, I swear we all cried.

"People in town know. They think of him as a hero for saving Kathy O'Malley and almost dying in the process. Because of that, people have respected his wish to be left alone. No one pushes. We all take what he's willing to give. He wears your ring around his neck."

Wiping my eyes, I held Mr. Clancy's stare, but I was confused. I hadn't seen my ring. I wasn't even sure it had made it back. I'd mailed it home after learning from Mrs. Marks that Kane had really moved on. "I had to take it to the jeweler—the prongs needed to be tightened." He reached for my hand. "He understood, Teagan. He understood why you gave it back. He's come a long way, but he was such a confident young man, so independent, and he isn't anymore. That's an adjustment for anyone, but he's also very proud, so it's doubly hard for him."

"When I came home after college and saw him so angry and bitter, I couldn't believe the change in him. I even called Mrs. Marks and demanded to know what had happened to turn the beautiful boy he had been into such a hard man. Now that I know he's blind, I keep trying to imagine what these years have been like for him, and I can't get my head around it. And as terrible as it is to say, I don't even want to know what it was like. The thought of him in so much pain. . . it hurts so much to know all this time he wasn't living the dream, that he hadn't moved on, that he was isolated and in the dark. I hate knowing that he's hiding from life, hiding from me."

"Don't let him." Mr. Clancy's words made it sound so simple.

"Kane was as stubborn as a mule, and I suspect he's even more so now."

"True, but that never stopped you before."

"He doesn't want me anymore, Mr. Clancy, and I just know that if I spend any time with him, I'm going to fall just as hard as I did when we were kids. I can't have my heart broken again. I almost didn't survive it the last time."

He reached across the table and took my hand. "He loves you, he never stopped. His body has healed, but his soul is still hurting, and there is only one person who can heal that. I hate what brought you home, but I'm glad you're here. He needs you. Once upon a time, he walked into your room and comforted the little girl you were. He needs you to do that for him now."

chapter 7

Teagan

"Are you sure this is going to work?" Simon was dubious, which I totally didn't get, since my idea would have worked on him.

"Yes."

"He doesn't really seem the type."

"Trust me." Stepping off the boat, we were greeted by Zeus, who came running down to the beach.

"Hey there, handsome. Your daddy around?"

Zeus started back up the beach, but my eyes were already looking toward the house where Kane stood on the front porch, leaning against the post.

Simon said, "You're right; the house is the color of your eyes."

"Teagan."

How did he know it was me? I wanted to ask, but now wasn't the time. "Kane, I wanted you to meet Simon officially. Simon, this is Kane."

Simon moved to Kane, who stepped off the porch and offered his hand. "Nice to meet you, Simon."

"Likewise. I've heard a lot about you."

"Nothing good, I'm sure."

"Quiet the contrary, Teagan's your biggest fan."

An emotion flitted across Kane's expression, but it was gone too fast for me to discern. "Do you need something?" he asked.

Nerves turned my stomach inside out. He sounded so remote. Now I wasn't so sure my plan was going to work. It would have worked on my Kane, but I no longer knew this Kane. Yet we were here, so . . . "There's a new bakery in town. They're giving out free samples all day today. We are planning to go stuff our faces with cake. Want to come?"

Hope sparked when I saw the flash in his eyes. My Kane was in there. "Ah, I don't think—"

"You shouldn't think, nothing good ever comes from that."

Simon's head snapped to me, but my focus was completely on Kane. *Take the bait, Kane.* He wanted to, I could see it, and my heart felt a lightness I hadn't experienced in far too long.

"Fine, we'll eat it all without you. Mrs. T asked that I invite you to dinner. She's making your fave—potpie. I helped her make yours."

A slight grin, just the barest of lifts, but it was there.

"Come on, Simon, whoever eats the least cake has to help Kane with dishes tonight. Bye, Kane. See you later." I called, walking backward, watching him. He didn't go back inside. He stood there like he was conflicted.

"So?" Simon asked from my side.

"Progress. He grinned."

"Saw that. Are we still going to the bakery?" he asked.

"Oh my God, you are . . . there are no words. Yes, we're going to the bakery. I want cake and lots of it."

"Race you to the boat," he said.

Simon was getting a cooking lesson from Mrs. T. I wanted to go to Kane, but knew I needed to tread lightly, so instead I decided to visit the Lawsons out of restlessness. I didn't tell Kane about Mrs. Marks's request, because I agreed with Mr. Clancy that it might be best to see what the news was first. The town looked just like it had when I was younger. I loved Boston, loved the life I had created there. I'd been born just outside of Boston, but it wasn't home. Maine was now my home.

Passing the diner, I saw a face I would be happy never to see again. Camille. She wasn't alone. She was engaged in a conversation with a pretty blond who looked rather upset. It was so tense, I was half tempted to walk over to defuse the situation, but in the next minute, Camille turned and walked away.

The blond shifted, so I could see that she was crying. I didn't recognize her, but that didn't stop me from crossing the street toward her. When I was within speaking distance, I asked, "Are you okay?"

Her blue eyes turned to me, startled. "Teagan?"

Then I was the startled one. "Yes. Do I know you?"

"Oh, no, sorry. I'm Kathy O'Malley."

My legs went numb, and a coldness swept through me. Bitterness, which was completely unfair for me to feel, moved through me. Bitterness that she was whole and healthy while Kane wasn't. Not her fault, I knew, but I felt it anyway. "Hi." It was all I had.

"I always wondered how this would go."

Tilting my head, I studied her for a minute. "What do you mean by that?"

"If we ever met, I mean. I cost you so much." Simply stated and so profoundly true. And yet it wasn't really her who had cost us so much. Kane had assumed the risk when he'd signed up to be a volunteer firefighter.

"He knew what he was getting into, Kathy. I didn't like it when he joined, but he knew the risks."

"Doesn't change the fact that he got hurt because he was saving me. I never should have been in that building."

"You could probably find all kinds of ways to beat yourself up over it, but it won't change the outcome. I think Kane, despite his injuries, takes satisfaction from the fact that he got you out. And knowing how he used to be, that's what's important."

"That's very generous of you to say."

I wanted so badly to know what had happened, the minutes up to and including when it all went to hell. She apparently was a mind reader.

"I was in the kitchen. There had been a few of us, but they ran as soon as the fire started. I tried to put it out but I couldn't. It spread so quickly. I really thought I was going to die. He appeared like some kind of superhero. He was smiling. I thought I was going to die until I saw that smile. He was trying to distract me, and so he told me we were going to be fine because he had a surprise for you and nothing, not even the fire, was going to keep him from giving it to you. He said something about a dream. He sounded so happy. I heard the crack before I saw the beam. He glanced up and pushed me so hard out of the way. I'll never forget his face right before . . . it was like he knew."

Tears welled and spilled down my cheeks. "Knew what?" My words got stuck in my tight throat.

Her eyes shone as bright as my own. "That with the falling of that beam, he had lost the dream."

Closing my eyes, I just let the pain roll over me. It was the past, it was over, and yet in that moment I felt as if I was right there next to him, experiencing it with him. Wiping at my eyes, I tried to regain control, since dwelling on the past was painful and pointless. "He didn't lose it, he just took a detour."

She sounded hopeful. "Really?"

"I love him. I always have. He's not there yet, but I'm nothing if not tenacious."

"Oh, wait until I tell Dad."

It was possible that Kane didn't want anything to do with me, but if it helped her with her guilt, I had no problem with sharing my intentions. And they were my intentions. I lost him once, and I wasn't about to lose him again. I'd give him time, but not a lot of it since he'd had nine years.

Changing the subject, I asked, "Are you okay?" She still had tears clinging to her lashes.

"I lost my job. I was managing a small clothing store, but the owners decided to retire. I've been with them since I graduated college."

"Kind of like a family away from the family."

"Yeah. They're moving to Florida. I'm happy for them, but now I'm back to pounding the pavement."

"I'm sure you'll find something." I didn't want to ask, but I was dying to know: "Was that Camille I saw you talking with?"

"Yeah," she said, disgust clearly lacing through her words. "I've known her my whole life. Our parents are close . . . She's not had an easy time of it, failing out of school, the estrangement from her dad, but even still, she's just so . . ."

So what? There was clearly more she wanted to say, but she didn't. Instead she said, "I need to get home. I have to start looking for a new job. It was really nice to meet you. Could you tell Kane I said hi when you see him?"

Estranged from her dad, now that was interesting. I'd have to think on that later, but for now I said, "I will. It was nice to meet you too and don't worry about the job, you'll find something."

Mr. Lawson's house was a small saltbox cottage just off the beach. Painted a cheery yellow, with a white picket fence, it was charming. Two rocking chairs sat on the front porch; he and his wife probably rocked there in the evening. A stone path led to the front door. I knocked. A woman who looked to be in her late sixties answered. Mrs. Lawson, no doubt. Curious brown eyes stared out of a face with surprisingly few wrinkles, but I didn't suspect surgery aided in that. Her white hair had been cut into a bob. She was petite, dressed in wool slacks and a pink cashmere sweater.

"Can I help you?"

"Is Mr. Lawson available?"

"Can I give him your name?"

"I'm Teagan Harper. I'm here about Mrs. Marks."

Her face immediately softened. "Oh, please come in. How is she?"

"Better, getting stronger every day."

"So relieved to hear that." She led me out back to a flagstone patio surrounded by gorgeous garden beds filled with a riot of color.

"Are you the gardener?" I asked.

"No, that's all Larry. There he is."

He was coming from a shed, dressed in old jeans and a flannel shirt. It was hard to imagine this man being a lawyer, and then his eyes landed on me and I saw the intelligence. Interest rang from his words when he said, "Hello. Can I help you?"

"This is Teagan Harper, dear, she grew up at Raven's Peak."

"Oh yes, of course." He gestured to the iron patio table with peridot cushions. "Please, let's sit. My legs aren't as steady as they used to be. Would you like something to drink?"

"No, thank you."

"So how can I help you?"

"When I visited Mrs. Marks, she got very agitated about a secret that possibly had to do with Kane Doyle."

His expression changed from friendly to pained. Leaning back in his chair, he ran a hand over his head. "I wondered."

"Wondered what?"

"She hated keeping the secret about Kane from you. It ate her up, but she's been keeping another secret for far longer. I wondered if she'd let that one go too."

"Do you know what she's talking about?"

"I do. The secret is about Kane's mother."

A coldness moved through me—anxiety, fear, and maybe a little anger. "Mrs. Marks has information on Kane's mom?"

"Yeah."

I stood, needing to pace. Kane did not need this. "Is it bad? He's been through a lot already."

"I'd rather I spoke to Kane about this. Does he know you're here?"

"No, we weren't sure what the news was, and he's been through enough."

"We?"

"Mr. Clancy and I."

"Right. I understand, I do, but I think this is something he's going to want to hear. Can you tell him when he's ready to come see me?"

"Yes, but can you answer something for me?"

"If I can."

"Does his mom have other children?"

"No."

That was something. "Okay, I'll tell him, but I can't guarantee that he'll come. He made peace with his mom's desertion a long time ago."

"I understand."

"Since I'm here, I was wondering what you know about Mr. Falco?"

"What has he done?"

I didn't expect that question. "You think him capable of doing something?"

"I'm not sure."

Irritation moved through me. "So why is he working with you for Mrs. Marks?"

"He really isn't. I've kept him on the periphery on purpose. My practice was merged with another, one where Mr. Falco was an associate. When I semiretired, the firm recommended him. They wanted someone shadowing me, so when I did fully retire they could take over with little effort."

"And why don't you trust him?"

"For one, he enjoys living outside of his means, and in so doing he's made some not so very wise choices."

"Meaning?"

"His business associates are not all respectable."

"And his firm knows this?"

"I'm not sure how they wouldn't. It's not like he keeps it a secret."

"Why would a practice hire a man like that?"

"I would guess that Mr. Falco has information that one or more of the partners in that firm isn't interested in having shared. Leverage to a man like Mr. Falco deludes him into believing he holds all the power."

A disturbing and cryptic comment. "When you do fully retire, do you think you'll be able to get Mrs. Marks another lawyer?"

"I'm working on it. I have a few things I'm looking into."

"What firm is Mr. Falco with?"

"Connelly, Drake, and Bowen"

"Bowen as in Camille Bowen?"

"Her father."

"Well hell."

On my way back from the Lawsons, my mind whirled. Mr. Lawson knew something about Kane's mom. I really hoped it was good news, though I couldn't imagine how the news could be good, considering she'd left years ago and had never tried to contact her son. The old Kane felt his mother's abandonment deeply, but I wasn't sure how Kane felt now. Did he even care?

Sleazy worked for Camille's father. I didn't know much about Mr. Bowen, but the man had a reputation for being a good lawyer, so why would he hire someone so shady?

I tracked Kane down the following morning while he was walking Zeus on the beach. I hated that I had to have this discussion, especially when I was trying to draw him out of the hole he'd put himself in, but I couldn't hold on to this knowledge. It wouldn't be right or fair.

"Teagan, morning."

"How did you . . . never mind. I need to talk to you. Do you have a minute?"

"Sure."

I fell into step next to him, déjà vu washing over me with how many times we had done this same thing in our youth. "When I went to visit Mrs. Marks the other day, she was conscious for a part of the visit. She became very agitated . . . needed you to know something."

I felt his body tense, but he didn't say a word.

"I went to see her lawyer—Lawson, not Falco. He knows the secret." Stopping, I touched his arm. "It has to do with your mom. Mr. Lawson said when you're ready he'll tell you what he knows. I asked, because it would matter to me: it turns out she doesn't have other children."

Silence.

"I also ran into Kathy yesterday. She's nice, but she has lots of guilt about you and the fire. I can't say I blame her for feeling the way she does. Anyone in her shoes would. I tried to ease her pain a bit by telling her you knew what you were getting into, knew the risks, and in the end you saved her.

"She told me about the fire, about you coming for her, all of it. How happy you were, happy that you were going to be joining me, and when the beam fell, she saw your expression and could tell that you believed the dream was lost." His arm turned rigid under my hands, every muscle tensed.

"You didn't lose the dream. I'm here, Kane, and I love you. I never stopped. You said you didn't want that, that what we had was over. If you really truly feel nothing for me, then fine, once Mrs. Marks is better, I'll go back to Boston. But if you still feel for me what you once did, give us a chance. If all you can offer is your friendship, I want it. I miss you. I've missed my best friend all these years."

"You have Simon." Bitterness and hurt radiated off him.

"Simon is a close friend, yes. He was there to force me to pick up the pieces. I wouldn't have survived without him; I was that lost, that broken. But he isn't my best friend. I've only ever had one of those. You're not the only one who suffered. Seems stupid to continue suffering if we both want the same thing. I want you back in my life any way you'll have me. If you want that too, take the step. You need to make the first move, but know that if you do, I'm all in."

Lifting up on tiptoe, I pressed a kiss on his cheek. "Love you, Kane."

And then I left. I knew he needed time to think.

Kane

I heard the boat moving away, but I stood frozen in my spot. I never thought I'd hear those words from her again. She loved me. Maybe I didn't deserve it, but damn if I wasn't greedy to hear her say it again. Having her near stoked the flames that never died in me. I loved her, always had.

I wasn't good for her, though. I couldn't give her all the things she deserved and I couldn't be the man she deserved. At some point it was going to cause resentment, probably on both sides. And beyond that, I was a mess, an emotionally fucked-up mess. My therapist called them panic attacks, but they felt more like I was dying—fear so intense that I couldn't breathe. My heart raced, my body shook, and for however long it lasted, I was completely crippled with fear. There were signs to alert me I was about to have one, heart palpitations, sweating, and shaking just before the full out attack. Apparently it was common after what I'd been through, but I knew from Mrs. Marks and the others that witnessing one was terrifying. When I'd told Tea what we'd had was over, I'd meant it. That died in the fire when the boy I was died. I wasn't sure she'd be really thrilled with the man I'd become.

And even knowing that, I felt hope, because she wanted me—damaged and scarred, she still wanted me, and I wanted her. I'd take her any way I could have her. She was right that I was hiding from her, from life. She'd called me a coward and selfish, and at the time her words had felt like a kick in the gut. A kick that I'd apparently needed, because she wasn't wrong about that either. I hadn't realized my insecurities had morphed into cowardice until I saw myself through her eyes. A nasty reality check, but one I'd definitely needed.

Yet I honestly didn't know if I'd ever conquer all of my insecurities. Even after nine years, I still found myself struggling to relearn everyday activities. The first time I went grocery shopping was a day-long event, locating what I needed in the store, buying the items, and getting them all home. The grocer had said I could call in my order and he'd get it ready for me, and sometimes I took him up on it. And sometimes I wanted the challenge, wanted to be able to buy my groceries like a sighted man. So I had learned to fold my money in different ways to distinguish the various denominations. I knew now I needed both Zeus and a person with me to help me locate the items that weren't easily distinguishable by touch. I was adapting. It got a bit easier every day, but having lost my sight so abruptly, there really weren't words to describe the fear and panic, the realization that my life was forever different, and the struggle to adapt to that life in the darkness. To make Tea struggle with me as I found my way again seemed wrong. Not to mention that if she ever witnessed me in a full-on panic attack, it would probably traumatize her and send her running back to Boston. And maybe that wasn't being fair to Tea, but then again, she had no idea what life for me was like now. And even listing all the negatives, I wanted to try. I wanted her back, wanted to hear about her life, wanted to hear her laugh again. I wanted to sink myself deep inside of her and appease the hunger that never went away. I wanted to touch her, to feel her face, to see the woman she had become. To taste her on my tongue while hearing the sounds of loving she always made that drove me wild. I wanted my Tea, all of her, every inch of her, body and soul.

But to really have Tea, I needed to stop hiding and find my niche: somewhere I could still add value. I was limited in what I could do, but I knew myself well enough to know that, if I didn't make something of myself, Tea and I were never going to work—my disability would always be there between us, at least for me.

Tea's unexpected news about Mrs. Marks and her apparent secret about my mom was startling. My mom had left, for whatever reason, and stayed gone. Perhaps there was a perfectly logical explanation, but I wasn't able to find one. No matter what the cause, she'd removed herself from my life. How does someone forgive that? I wasn't sure I wanted to take Mr. Lawson up on his offer. I suspected that leaving that part of my past in the past might be the wiser choice.

The same couldn't be said about Tea, though. She had visited the other day, offering the olive branch about the bakery. She'd even insulted my intelligence, and I knew she was trying to get me to engage. She said I needed to make the next move.

What should my next move be? I wanted to get to know who she was now . . . and there was the double-edged sword. If I learned all that she had accomplished in the time we'd been apart, I would understand exactly what she would be giving up to be with me. That seemed not only unfair but really fucking selfish on my part. I knew Tea loved me enough to give it all up, and that fact settled like lead in my gut. Tea was a college graduate, a business owner with a social life in Boston. How the hell could a blind guy with no job compete with that? And still, none of that was going to keep me from trying to win her back.

Teagan

Simon and I had just returned from another visit with Mrs. Marks. The doctors had planned on releasing her but decided to hold her for a few more days. Some of her numbers weren't where they'd like them to be. I thought this wise—her speech was still disjointed, and she couldn't focus for long. I wondered if maybe she'd had a stroke along with the heart attack, since her mind wasn't quite there. I asked her doctors, but they didn't readily answer.

Simon was in his room dealing with a problem from the shop. There was a chance he was going to need to leave for Boston. I hadn't expected that he was going to stay with me the entire time, but I was going to miss his company. We'd never been that far from each other since becoming friends almost a decade earlier. It was going to be strange not seeing him every day.

It had been two days since I'd spoken to Kane regarding Mr. Lawson. He hadn't made any attempt to talk to me. His absence was my answer, and, boy, did that hurt like hell. It seemed like the Kane I knew really was gone.

Walking down the lane around Raven's Peak, I unsuccessfully tried to put Kane out of my head. I remembered Kane's wish to turn the place into an inn. He was right, it would make a wonderful retreat for people, away from the beaten path but close enough to enjoy the offerings in town. And the town was different now—it had more trendy shops and sights worthy of seeing. We had always been a shore resort town, but in the years since I'd been gone, we'd turned into a resort, period. Any season held interest for visitors, whether it was the whale migration in the fall, the theater troupe that put on productions that were recognized as far down as Boston, or the holiday open houses where many of the older homes celebrated the season with a walking tour. An inn would do very well here, especially one with the view that Raven's Peak had.

A warmth burned down my spine, drawing me from my thoughts, as I saw Kane walking down the lane. Zeus was with him, guiding him as Kane held on to the loop of the leather harness. My eyes burned at the sight—Kane was blind. I still hadn't fully gotten my head around that, but there was a healthy dose of pride burning in me too, because, despite what had befallen him, here he was walking down the lane. Had it been me, I don't know if I would have bounced back as well. Why *was* Kane walking down the lane? Was he looking for me? The thought was intoxicating.

Zeus barked as they approached, right before Kane said, "Tea?"

He was calling me Tea again; my heart swelled. "Yeah. How did you know where to find me?"

"Zeus found you."

Smart dog. "Handsome *and* clever."

The slightest of grins curved Kane's lips. "Zeus or me?"

"Both."

"Do you have a minute?"

"Yeah. I was just walking. I went to see Mrs. Marks earlier. They're going to hold her for a few more days. She's not quite herself; I think she may have had more than a heart attack."

Concern clouded his expression. "Why do you say that?"

"She's just out of it—not forming words, struggling with trying to communicate and not being able to. I don't know, she's just off."

"Last time I was there, she was sleeping," Kane said.

I wanted to know if he'd like to go with me to see her, but I didn't let myself ask. He needed to make the next move, even knowing how much it would mean to Mrs. Marks to see the two of us together.

"You said I needed to make the first move. I want to make that move, Tea. I just don't know if I'll ever be the guy you deserve."

"You already are."

"I'm not, though. You loved the boy I was. He's gone. The man in his place is bitter and angry. He can't support himself the way he would like to and is constantly depending on others. He's not much of a man."

"Seems harsh. You can't see; it's a challenge, yes, that you need to rely on people more than you would like, but I don't see how that makes you less of a man."

"I lost the keys for the boat once. It took me two hours to find them."

"You have people around you who, had you asked, would have helped you."

"I shouldn't need help finding fucking keys."

"Again, you're blind. Asking for help doesn't make you helpless."

"The fuck it doesn't."

"And that is where we disagree. You need to get past that, Kane, for your own sake, because you are always going to need help with something. Most people do. Why you see that as a weakness, I don't know. You lost those keys, and yet you can drive that boat by yourself from the island to here. You sought me out and found me despite being blind."

"Zeus found you."

"But you walked from the beach here, yes? Nothing remarkable for a sighted person, but you are not a sighted person anymore. I didn't even realize you were blind, even though I had seen you several times. You get around incredibly well for someone who can't see."

"How did you put it together?"

"I overheard your conversation with Mrs. T and watched as you got yourself a glass of milk."

Another grin. "You and the eavesdropping."

He was referring to our youth when I'd listened in on his conversation with Camille. "I only seem to do it when it relates to you."

"I lied when I said I didn't want to try."

Hope stirred.

"I just don't know where to go from here," he added.

"Well, that makes two of us."

"And I'm . . ." His head dropped, his shoulders slumped, and I knew what he was thinking. He was afraid, afraid to let me in, afraid to share the darkness with someone, because in doing so he would grow to need me. Which meant that losing me would destroy him.

"I'm not going to leave you."

"I'm not the boy I was." His words were barely audible.

"I'm not the girl I was." I didn't want to ask. I almost couldn't get the words out, but I had to know: "Do you still love me?"

He looked up, his eyes aflame. "Never stopped, Tea. Mine forever, remember?"

Relief washed over me, so profound my legs nearly buckled under me. "Then give us a chance."

We had just reached the house.

"Will you come upstairs with me?" I asked.

He hesitated, but I saw the answer before he nodded. Taking his hand, we started up the stairs. Zeus, realizing he wasn't needed, went in search of food. I heard Mrs. T greeting him. We reached my room; he stepped into it a few paces farther than me.

"We can sit on the balcony," I suggested, and he moved to it like he knew exactly where he was going.

"How did you do that?"

"I stayed here after the fire and memorized the room."

Settling next to him on the little sofa, I asked. "How long did it take for you to heal?"

"Four years, closer to five."

"Do you still feel pain?"

"No, the nerves are dead. It looks awful, but I feel nothing."

"I don't think it looks awful."

He obviously didn't agree, but he said nothing. I wanted to ask him about the fire and his recovery, but I just didn't think he would tell me. Avoiding it completely seemed rude, so I said, "If you ever want to talk about that time in your life, I would really like to hear it."

Nodding his head, so I knew he'd heard me, he still remained silent.

"Mr. Clancy mentioned you had been working with an architect back in the day, and that was the reason you didn't join me right away when I left for Boston."

"Yeah, I wanted to surprise you."

"I love the house. It's exactly as I saw it every time we discussed it."

"I never saw it built, but the plans were perfect."

"I love the window boxes."

"Are they like the ones your dad hung for your mom?"

They were far nicer, because Kane had hung them for me. "Better."

"I don't think there's anything in them, so if you want to add flowers, that would be nice," he said.

"I'd like that."

He turned toward the view, his shoulders sagging a little. "I missed you, Tea. No, that's not a fair statement. That day when I called and told you I had found someone else, my spirit died right along with yours. There's never been anyone else for me but you."

I wiped at my damp cheeks. "It's only ever been you for me. I tried to move on, tried to put you in the past like I thought you had done with me, but I never could. No one ever measured up. I didn't want second best."

"We lost a lot of time. Do you think we still have a chance?"

"I love you. You love me. Yeah, I think we have a better chance than most. You just can't be afraid to reach for it, though I understand your hesitation," I said softly. "You've been through a lot and, even though we've lost so much time, you're still finding your way back. Maybe now I can be at your side while you figure it out."

"I'd like that. We always were better together than apart," he said.

"True."

He stood and put some distance between us, his hands coming to rest on the balcony railing. I moved to join him, and, sensing me, he turned in my direction as I approached. I needed to see his scars, needed him to know they didn't disturb me. Because he knew me so well, he knew what I wanted when I simply asked, "Kane. Could you remove your shirt?"

After a slight hesitation, he lifted his shirt over his head. When I saw his beautiful scarred skin, tears stung the back of my eyes, but I didn't see anything ugly. Just the opposite.

"You're beautiful, Kane. I hate what you went through, hate that I wasn't there, but you are still as beautiful as you were when we were kids. You are not a burned freak, you're mine. My Kane, remember?" My fingers ran over his scars, causing his body to tense. His eyes closed, and I realized that he hadn't known the touch of a woman since me. And in that moment, all the men I had been with, the men I had used to bury my pain, every one of them felt like a betrayal to him. The tears just kept coming, but it didn't stop me from pressing my lips to him, over the skin that was lasting proof of all he had given up to help another. His hands fisted at his sides.

"Touch me, Kane."

Always so sure when they were on me, his hands were now reluctant, hesitant. Taking them into mine, I lifted them to my face. "It's still me."

His fingers gently traced me, learning me again: a delicate brush over my cheeks, lips, jaw. Feeling his touch again, my eyes closed. The emptiness that nothing ever seemed to fill no longer felt so vast.

"So fucking beautiful," he whispered.

Lifting up on my toes, my mouth found his—a brushing of lips until his arms wrapped around me, pulling me close as he took the kiss deeper. His tongue ran over mine, tasting me, remembering, reclaiming. He pulled away from me to lift my shirt over my head, and my bra followed. His hands moved over me, touching me in that way that always made my body ache. His thumbs brushed over my nipples, his mouth moving to my neck and shoulder before meeting his fingers. His tongue flicked me, then he closed his mouth over one of those aching peaks and pulled it deep into his mouth.

Mindless with need, my fingers worked the snap of his jeans. I couldn't believe I was feeling him under my fingers, couldn't believe I was tasting him again. When he lifted me into his arms, neither of us saw my shirt; his toes must have gotten caught on it, and he fell on top of me so hard all the air was forced from my lungs. I couldn't draw a breath. When his hands reached for me, they were shaking.

"Tea, are you okay?"

I couldn't answer because I couldn't breathe. I reached for his hands, but he knew something was wrong.

"What's wrong? Jesus fucking Christ, Tea. Talk to me."

I had never heard him so scared; he was shaking and yet he was furious. Air was slowly pushing into my lungs, and after a few minutes, I was finally able to speak, but he was practically mindless with worry and anger.

"I'm okay. Just had the wind knocked out of me."

"Fuck! What are you doing? I can't even carry you to the bed without causing you harm."

He stood then and moved away from me.

"It's going to take some time for both of us to adjust, but we can do this."

"What happens if we're swimming and you start to drown? How the fuck do I save you if I can't even see you? What would happen if we ever had a child who got hurt, and I couldn't find them? You're not getting a man, you're getting an invalid."

"Stop hiding."

"I'm not hiding, I'm being practical. My life has limits now. Yours doesn't have to."

"Don't pretend you don't want me with you. You built our home. I'm not giving up, Kane. I'm not ever going to give up on us." Reaching for my bra and shirt, I dressed, my body aching but my heart aching more.

He turned from me, his beautiful scarred back and neck the vicious reminder of how everything was different now, how he was different, and how I was too. Different enough that I might not ever get my Kane back, but I didn't care. I wanted him in any way I could have him. Grabbing his shirt from the floor, I pressed it into his hands. "I'll send Zeus up."

I started for the door but glanced at him from over my shoulder. "Love you, Kane." His shoulders tensed, the only reason I knew he had heard me before I walked away.

Kane

I listened to Tea's soft footsteps fade. Jesus, I could have really fucking hurt her. I hated being blind, hated the impotence more than the damn scars. Jerking my tee back over my head, I heard Zeus's nails clipping on the wood.

I should be in her bed right now, buried in her, feeling her around me, hearing her come. Instead I'd knocked the fucking air from her lungs. She was right, we both needed to adapt, but the thought of unintentionally hurting her—fuck. I hadn't, not this time. And if she were willing to take the chance, knowing she was the one likely to get hurt, I'd be the fucking coward she'd called me if I pulled away, knowing I wanted her more than anything.

And as much as I would like to claim that my knee-jerk reaction of pulling away from her was all in the name of wanting the best for her, it would have been a lie. I *was* a bit selfish and vain, because I wanted her to see me as a man, not as a blind man. And as unfair as it was for me to feel it, I hated that Tea was more careful around me now. It was subtle but undeniable. Like coming to me to ask me to dinner instead of just calling. I knew she was trying to be helpful, that she was offering to assist me because I was blind. But I was trying to prove to her that I was still capable, which was negated every time she put my blindness between us.

I couldn't help but smile, though. She really had accepted without question the man I was now, and she still wanted to be with me. Suddenly my conviction of not wanting to force my life on her fell flat. She was right, the choice had been hers, and denying her that choice had been the height of selfishness on my part. And yet, even knowing I had put both of us through hell, separating us when we could have weathered the tragedy so much better together, a part of me still believed I had done the right thing. Knowing how strongly it had affected Mrs. Marks and the others being forced to watch my recovery, I think it would have been even harder on Tea. In fact, I think it would have been so hard on her it would have scarred her permanently, which would have forever altered our relationship. How would she be able to look at me and not see where I had been and just how far I had sunk? In the end, I think reconnecting with her as the man I was now, damaged and altered but not broken, gave us a better chance at rekindling what we'd had.

And I wanted us back; it was time to move forward, no more hiding. She'd said asking for help and being helpless weren't the same. I wanted to believe that, and once upon a time I had, but I sort of lost that lesson in the years since the fire.

I knew the direction I wanted to go, had known for a long time where I saw my niche. Mrs. Marks was getting too old, as were the others. Running Raven's Peak was becoming more than they could handle. She and I had discussed the idea of turning the place into Raven's Peak Inn. She liked the idea, more if I was in charge of it, since I knew the place and would respect it. I wanted it too, and I knew she suggested it because she knew I needed to get back up on the horse. I had kept myself busy with things, but nothing that tested what I could and couldn't do. I needed to understand my limitations. I feared they were far more than I wanted to admit, but I would never know until I tried.

Having a plan was one thing, but I didn't know where to start. There was someone who could help me, however. "We're going to the O'Malleys', Zeus."

I had walked the same way to town ever since I was a kid. I was sure I could do it without Zeus, not that I would ever attempt it. The O'Malleys lived just off Main Street. It was early, well, early for the O'Malleys who liked to sleep in whenever possible, but I needed to talk to Mr. O'Malley. He could help me hash out the ideas for the inn, since he had run his own business for years before the economy had crashed. Stepping up to the front door, it took me a minute to find the bell.

A few moments later, I heard the sound of feet, the unlocking of the door, then felt the swish of air as the door opened and heard the startled intake of breath.

"Kane? You okay?" Kathy asked. "Come inside. Hi, Zeus."

Walking into the foyer, I stopped and waited for Kathy to close the door. She was always tense around me. I could feel the stress coming off her. I'd always had the sense that I made her uncomfortable, which made sense given how all this had happened. But there always seemed to be more to her discomfort than that.

"Is your dad home?"

"Yeah, I'll go get him. Would you like to wait in the kitchen? I just made some coffee."

"That'd be great."

Following after her, I leaned up against the counter and listened to her moving through the kitchen as she prepared my coffee. "Black, right?"

"Yes."

I felt her hand on mine, then the warmth of the mug as she pressed it into my palm. "Thanks."

"I'll go get my dad."

Sipping the coffee, I listened to the stillness. The house wasn't up yet. I felt bad about that. Cinnamon wafted toward me; Mrs. O'Malley had probably made one of her cinnamon Bundt cakes for dessert the night before. It was a damn fine cake, almost as good as Mrs. T's creations.

Heavy footsteps down the stairs signaled the arrival of Mr. O'Malley. As was his way, he walked right up to me, taking my hand in a firm shake. "Kane. Everything okay?"

Lowering my head, I found my words caught in my throat for a moment. "Not entirely. I want a life with Tea and to do that I need to move forward—I never had a dad, but I kind of think of you as one. I've been stagnating." My head lifted. "I need to stop hiding. I need to enter the world again as a blind man, need to find how I fit, but I'm not sure where to begin."

He was crying. I could hear the tears in his voice. "You are a strong man, son. I can't tell you how long I've, hell, how long we've all waited to hear you speak those words. Make no mistake, Kane, you've been through hell and you've come out on the other side. Maybe you disengaged, but I wouldn't say you were stagnating. I realize much of the work you've occupied your time with since the accident were more hobbies than jobs, but you never stopped trying. And in the trying, you learned that your blindness isn't as debilitating as you feared. Now that you're ready, a good way to find where you fit is to figure out what you want to do with your life. Do you have any ideas?"

"I want to turn Raven's Peak into an inn. I want to learn the ins and outs of a venture like that."

"Sounds like a plan to me. So now you just need to learn the business."

"How?"

"I can help. There are also online classes, but a lot of it is intuitive. Knowing you, you'll pick it up really easily."

"Will you help me?"

"Yes, I'll help you." I felt his hands on my shoulders. "I think of you as a son, Kane. I'm here for you. We all are."

"Thank you."

Teagan

I had no idea how much dirt a window box required. Simon and I had purchased four large bags, and each box took two. He was off buying us more so I could fill the four boxes that graced the front of the house. I hadn't seen Kane since he'd suggested this—that was a few days ago. Hopefully he wasn't having second thoughts; with how things were left, I wasn't really sure.

The bright flowers looked so pretty against the creamy white of the box. I finished the two boxes and, while I waited for Simon, dug a little garden near the front stoop. Unlike the dirt, I had purchased too many flowers and thought a colorful garden by the door would be welcoming. Digging through the dirt, I uncovered so many worms. I grinned at the memory of Kane and his worm potpie when we were kids. I had never seen him look so grossed out. I lifted one of the little guys in my hand and felt its wet little body squirming. A heaviness settled in my chest remembering Kane when we were kids—he'd had so many dreams, like his wish to build a boat, and the fire had cost him all of them. Zeus appeared at my side. I was so startled I nearly tossed the worm.

"Tea?"

Hearing Kane's voice pulled me from my forlorn thoughts. "By your front door. I was adding a garden just off the steps."

"Sounds nice."

A few seconds later, he was on the ground next to me. Reaching for his hand, I dropped the worm into his palm.

"Don't eat him," I teased.

The smile came in a flash. "I never did get you back for that."

"You teased me enough growing up."

"Maybe, but that trick was really disgusting."

"Yeah, lucky for you that you didn't just dig in to your dinner."

"And that's what made it so disgusting. The what-if."

"The look on your face was classic. I should have gotten a picture."

"You would have had it turned into wallpaper and papered your room with that instead of the blue silk."

"Nope, the blue silk matches your eyes perfectly."

"Could have had my whole grossed-out face."

"Nope, your eyes were the very first thing I noticed about you when we met. Did you know that? Just those eyes, so blue."

His smile faded. Touching his chin, I turned his head to me. "Just because they don't see doesn't mean they aren't still the windows to your soul. I still see you, Kane. I can still see inside you."

A light brushing of his fingers over my face told me he was reading my expression and could see that I wasn't kidding. I meant every word. Cupping my chin, he brushed his thumb over my cheek. "Sorry about the other day. I could have really hurt you."

"You are bigger than me Kane, but I'm not a doll. I've taken your weight before."

"Not like that."

"I'm still here. I still want to be here. I'm still going to eat all the cake Mrs. T has made for dinner."

"Not if I get there first."

"Is that a challenge, Kane Doyle?"

"Maybe not if it's just cake, but for a kiss, absolutely."

"Let me get this right. If you beat me back to the house, you get to kiss me?"

"Yep."

"If I conceded you the victory, would you kiss me now?"

His voice grew hoarse. "Yeah."

"You win. Kiss me, Kane."

Cradling my face again, he kissed me like it was his job. His tongue pushed past my lips, stroking and warring with my own. I had never forgotten his taste; I loved it, was addicted to it. His fingers tightened on my scalp as he kissed me deeper. Pressing myself against him, I gave back as good as I was getting. We were both out of breath by the time we ended the kiss.

"Missed that," he whispered.

"You and me both."

Zeus growled. "Simon's back. He went to get more soil for the boxes. Help me finish, and then we'll get dinner and cake, and, later, maybe you'll kiss me again," I said.

"I like this plan."

"I like you."

The previous day had been a really good day. After we'd finished the window boxes, the three of us had gone to dinner at the house and after, while cuddling in the library, Kane had kissed me again. Simon had gone to bed early, but I suspected he hadn't even been tired; he just wanted Kane and me to have time alone. For almost an hour, we'd made out like school kids on the sofa. On the surface, we were healing and finding each other again, but we weren't scratching below the surface. I had a life in Boston, a life I wanted to share with Kane, but one I suspected he didn't want any part of, since he barely engaged in his hometown. The idea that he'd travel all the way to Boston was laughable. And more than I perceived his need to separate himself from life, I knew he was holding a part of himself back from me—a part of him I no longer could touch. I'd had all of Kane. I wasn't going to settle for just part of him. I knew that at some point, we would have to address where we saw ourselves going.

That morning I was helping Mrs. T make breakfast. She was preparing a coffee cake, one of Kane's favorites, and teaching me as she went. The door opened and Kane appeared, Zeus at his side. He was carry something; it looked heavy and, from the flush on his face, I suspected he'd brought it all the way from his house.

"Let me get that for you," I said as I approached him. He had done the hard part and could probably use the breather.

"I've got it, Tea."

"I know, but you looked wiped. Let me help you."

"Tea, I've come this far. I can finish." I relented at the bite in his words.

"Okay."

"Smells good, Mrs. T. Is that my coffee cake?"

"It is. I'm teaching Teagan, so she can make it for you herself."

He grinned. "Nice."

"Would you like some coffee?" I asked.

"I'll get it."

"Kane, I'm standing right here next to the coffee maker."

"Tea, I've been making my own coffee since I was eleven, I can do it."

Why was he being so stubborn?

"Fine." I sounded like a child, but he was being difficult. He stiffened at my tone, but I couldn't tell what he was thinking.

"I'm going to the boatyard later. Do you need anything from the market, Mrs. T?"

"Apples. There aren't as many as I thought, and I plan on whipping up an apple galette for dessert."

A walk into town sounded nice, especially since the doctors were still running tests on Mrs. Marks. "I'll come into town with you, and I'll get the apples while you're at the boatyard."

"I'm going to be in town already. I can just as easily get the apples," Kane replied, and there was definitely hostility coming off him now.

Throwing up my hands, a pointless gesture, since he wouldn't see it, I said, "I'm just trying to help."

"When I need your help, I'll ask for it," he snapped.

"But you don't ask for help, because you think asking for help makes you look weak."

There was no question what emotion fueled the thunderous expression on his face. "I'll be in town if anyone needs me. Come on, Zeus."

I wanted to stomp my foot, because I honestly didn't know what I'd done wrong. Simon walked in at that moment. "Is Kane all right? He looked pretty angry just now."

"He's stubborn. I'll be in my room."

I heard Mrs. T as I left the kitchen say, "I guess there's more coffee cake for you."

"That is not a bad thing." But I heard the worry in Simon's voice.

chapter 8

Teagan

The next morning, I woke and, out of habit, looked to my nightstand, but there was no chocolate milk waiting for me. Climbing from bed, I wrapped my blanket around my shoulders and stepped out onto the balcony. The sun was shining. The waves crashing against the cliff could be heard even from my distance. Inhaling the salt air, I took a minute to savor being home.

I hadn't seen Kane since he left to go into town the day before. He was avoiding me, at least I thought so. He always was so stubborn, but unlike when we were kids, I couldn't read him anymore.

The sound of voices drew my attention to the backyard, where Mr. Clancy and Mrs. T were having breakfast under the shade of a tree. But the sight of Kane took my focus. Dressed in shorts and a tee, his hair back in a ponytail, he wasn't alone. A man, similar in build and size, was circling him. Just as I realized they were fighting, the man lunged. But it was Kane's reaction that nearly sent me over the railing of the balcony; I was stretched that far to see what was happening. He deflected the hit. How the hell did he do that if he couldn't see? As I watched, I realized that Kane was using his other senses to get a fix on his opponent. Watching him, I realized he had grown his hair to cover his scarred neck. Even though he couldn't see it, I guessed he didn't want others to.

The man stopped the lesson and offered Kane direction, to which he listened with rapt attention, soaking up what he was being taught. For almost an hour I watched from my place above him, watched the life Kane had made for himself despite the tragedy that had befallen him. I had always thought he was incredible, but that word just wasn't good enough.

They looked to be finishing their session and wanting nothing more than to be near him, I hurried and got dressed. Running down the stairs, I flew out the back doors and around the house. The man was just leaving, shaking Kane's hand. By the time I reached Kane, the man was pulling down the drive.

"Morning," I said, a little out of breath.

"Tea. Morning."

"I saw you from my window. That was pretty amazing."

He grinned. "Thanks, it helps me with my balance, among other things."

"What are you up to now?" I asked.

"I need to get a shower."

"I'll walk you. Maybe I could make you breakfast. Remember my world-famous waffles?" They weren't, really—never could get them to hold their shape, but the flavor had always been perfect.

There was a slight hesitation before he said, "Thanks, but I'm not really hungry. I'll come up to the house later."

"Well, at least let me walk with you to the beach." We hadn't made that walk together in far too long.

"I don't need your help."

I recoiled from the harshness of his statement. He didn't need my help, but I wasn't offering to help him. And even if I were offering, what was up with him not wanting my help, but taking it from the man who was just helping him not ten minutes ago?

"I wasn't suggesting you needed help. I just wanted to take a walk with you."

"Another time."

"What the hell is going on, with you blowing hot and cold, Kane? Make up your goddamn mind. We've wasted nine fucking years. Are you seriously going to waste more time by doing this?"

Anger rolled off him. "If it's such a waste of your time, then what the hell are you doing still sniffing around me?"

"Whoa. Sniffing around you? That's Camille, don't get us confused. You know what? Go to hell."

"Been there already."

A direct hit, but I was so pissed I didn't react. Turning on my heel, I walked back up to the house. Not surprisingly, my heart ached as if on command. I wondered if I could just rip the thing from my chest and be done with it.

Simon chose that moment to appear, all smiles. "Hey. You just talking to Kane?"

"Not talking, yelling." Simon kept pace with me easily as I strode to the house, though I didn't have a clue where I intended to go once I got there.

"What happened?"

"He's kissing me senseless one minute, and the next he's getting all bitchy because he thinks I'm trying to suffocate him with my need to help him. I wasn't even offering help—just wanted to take a walk with him. God, I'm so frustrated."

"You have that look. What are you up to?"

I stopped walking, turned, and pondered his question. Here I was, exactly where I wanted to be, in arm's length of the man I wanted to be with, and still he was keeping me at a distance. This knowledge, coupled with the persistent pain in my chest, my stomach being one big knot, and a headache constantly just behind my eyes, was the final straw. I needed a goddamn break from life. "I'm going to get drunk, like roaring, head-in-the-toilet drunk. Want to come?"

"Yes, someone's got to hold your hair back."

"You're the best."

"Where are we going?"

"No clue, but we'll figure it out. The town isn't that big."

We discovered Dahlia's, a dive bar right on the water. It was mostly a hangout for locals, but since I'd been MIA for nine years, no one seemed to know who I was. And I was okay with that because at the moment I was dancing. Yep, to music only I could hear. Simon, bless Simon, had been laughing, but now he was growing concerned, because, with each shot, my legs had grown a little less steady. I had never spent the day drinking, likely wouldn't again, but that day it was exactly what I needed.

"Maybe you should sit down."

I stopped mid-Riverdance and studied Simon as if taking his suggestion under advisement. "Buy me another shot and I'll sit."

"Then sit." Calling to the bartender, he said, "Another tequila shot."

Dropping onto the stool, I watched as Tammy, the bartender,

poured the drink, but since there were three of them, I wasn't sure which one to reach for.

"Need help with that?" There was no mistaking the humor in his tone. "You are going to hate the world tomorrow."

"I hate the world now."

"What happened with Kane?"

"Sneaky. Asking me to reveal my secrets while under the influence. Naughty, Simon."

"So, what happened?"

"Nothing. Like nothing happened. I offered him breakfast, he turned me down, I offered to walk to the beach with him, he turned me down, and then he snapped that he didn't need my help, which I find extremely hypocritical—whoa, that's hard to say. Is my tongue too big? Hypa-critical, hypa-cricketal . . ." I giggled. That wasn't even a word.

"Teagan, focus. What did you find hypocritical?"

"That he didn't want my help, but he doesn't seem to have a problem accepting help from others." I twirled my glass around in a circle; it escaped my fingers and slid right off the bar. I pointed to Simon when Tammy's eyes sliced over to us as it crashed to the floor. "He did that."

Simon rolled his eyes heavenward. "Don't do that, they'll get stuck up there," I said. Spinning in my stool, I lifted my leg every time I came around to Simon and nailed him in the shin.

He grabbed the stool so abruptly I almost went sailing right off it. "Home," he said. Tammy slid him the largest bottle of water I had ever seen. "If I drink all of that I'll float home. That might be fun. Let me have that. Thanks, Tammy. Simon will pay you back for the glass he broke."

She grinned at me. Halfway to the door, I remembered who she was. Grabbing the doorjamb as Simon was trying to pull me out of it, I called back to her. "Health class, eighth grade."

"Yup. You were clearly out for the lesson on overdrinking."

"Yeah, I was probably out drinking." I roared with laughter. Simon, having had enough, tossed me over his shoulder.

"You Tarzan, me Jane. Or do you want to be Jane? I think I could be a pretty macho Tarzan."

"I love you, Teagan, but if I live through this night, it will be a miracle."

"Sometimes I wish I had been in the car with my parents. Especially these last nine years—never coming here, never meeting Kane, how much easier that would have been."

I felt Simon roughly pull me from his shoulder, his hold on me like a death grip. "I never want to hear you say that again. You fucking hear me, Teagan?"

"I'm not saying I want to die, only that I don't think it would have been so terrible if I had."

"We aren't talking about this now, with you drunk, but when you're sober, we're going to have a nice long chat."

"Okay, with cookies, or maybe Sunshine will bake us one of her chocolate cakes."

"You're assuming we'll back in Boston."

"Probably. Once Mrs. Marks is better."

"And Kane?"

"He's not my Kane anymore. I think that ship has sailed—was attacked by pirates and then sunk to the bottom of the cold, dark sea."

"Is this the alcohol talking?"

"Maybe, or maybe I'm just tired of having my heart broken by the one person I actually offered it to. He loved me once. If he still did, wouldn't he be pulling me close now? Wouldn't he have come for me, found his way to our door, and begged me to come home? If he loved me like I love him, how could he bear knowing I was out there and all he had to do was reach for me. No, I was right, feelings suck. I'm getting five cats when we get home. I hope you aren't allergic."

No response from Simon. He helped me into the car before he climbed in and started up the engine. He didn't pull from the curb, though. "Again—when you're sober, we're going to talk."

"And when I'm sober, I promise to listen."

Unlocking the door, I put my fingers to my lips and said in a really loud whisper, "We need to be quiet."

Starting up the stairs, I had the most excellent idea. Before Simon could stop me, I ran to the landing of the stairs, before it split off to either side of the foyer, and straddled the railing. I remembered wanting to do just this that first night I'd arrived at Raven's Peak.

"Teagan, what the hell are you doing?"

"I always wanted to do this." And so I sailed on down the railing and landed at the bottom hard on my butt. The sharp pain that radiated up my back felt oddly good.

"Are you hurt?" Simon was at my side faster than I'd ever seen him move before.

"I'm fine."

"Tea?" I loved the tingles that worked down my spine whenever Kane said my name. Looking past Simon, I saw Kane standing in the hall by the kitchen.

"Hey, Kane. What are you doing on the mainland?" And for some reason I found this question hilarious. I rolled onto my back, which hurt like a mother, and roared with laughter.

"Is she okay?" Kane asked Simon.

"Drunk, really fucking drunk."

"She do that often?"

"Only when she's hurting."

Zeus joined us and started licking my face. "Simon, we should get a dog too, a dog and five cats. Maybe I could train them to retrieve baked goods from Sunshine."

Simon lifted me to my feet. "Time for bed."

"Yeah, you look tired," I said, then giggled again because *I* thought I was funny.

"Night, Kane," Simon said as he started to lead me up the stairs, but I stopped walking and turned to Kane.

"Why are you here?"

"I was playing chess with Mr. Clancy."

"You play chess? How?"

"I tell him where I want the piece and he places it. He tells me the moves he's making. I see the board in my head."

"He helps you with playing chess and you're okay with that? No barking at Mr. Clancy on how you don't need his help? No, of course not, you save that for me. You went through hell and kept me at a distance, but did it ever even occur to you that I was in hell too? You had everyone here—the whole damn town—to help you through it. You left me broken and alone. You claim you don't want this life for me, and yet you have no idea how bad the life you forced on me was. If not for Simon, I don't think I'd be standing here right now."

Pain washed over Kane's face. Wiping at my eyes, bitterness fueled my next words. "I'd offer to help you home, but I don't want to be mistaken again for a dog. You were my lap dog once, remember? It shouldn't still hurt after all this time, and yet it does." I started back up the stairs. "We got any of those bottles from the other night, Simon?"

I didn't look back at Kane, but I knew he was still in the same spot looking in the direction he had last heard me. And in that moment I really just didn't care what he was thinking.

"If I ever do this again, kill me. Just take a spoon and scoop out my brain."

My head was in the toilet. I'd made it to my room before the entire contents of my stomach decided to rise up my throat.

"I'm not going to scoop out your aching brain, but I am going to so enjoy rubbing this in your face. I got video of you dancing. YouTube, baby."

"Maybe it will help sales at the store."

"Well, with the grace you exhibited sliding down the banister and landing quite soundly on your ass, I'm thinking no." Simon stopped gently stroking my back. "Are you okay? That was pretty intense down there."

"I honestly don't know. I know he's pushing me away because he's afraid, but I really don't want to hurt anymore. I'm so tired of hurting." And then my stomach roiled. I was going to either vomit or turn myself completely inside out. And just taking a moment to visualize that—gross.

Long fingers threaded through my hair, holding it gently from my face, but they weren't Simon's fingers. Kane caressed my back as I dry heaved. He didn't want my help, but he was willing to offer his own. What was that all about? I opened my mouth to ask that very question, but before I could speak, Kane asked, "Water?"

"Where's Simon?"

"Went down to get you some aspirin."

"Maybe the timing is wrong, but you need to tell me. If you really don't want me here, I need to know. I thought you were going to try, but you aren't trying, so are we really over?"

"It's not that simple."

"Explain it."

"I want you here, Tea, want that so bad at times it nearly chokes me. I'm trying. You were right when you said I've been hiding. I have. It was easier to isolate myself, partly because I couldn't find my way anywhere else, but also because being seen as Kane the Blind Man, rather than as just Kane, is hard.

"I want a life with you, and I know that to do that I need to step out of the shadows. Yet sometimes it's just too easy to fall back on what's familiar, to push away rather than pull close. And with all that being said, you have a home in Boston, a business, friends. How can I ask you to give all that up for me?"

"Who says I have to give them up?"

"I can barely make my way around here, finding my way in Boston . . . I'm not there yet and may never be."

That hurt, but I moved past it. "There are options. It is possible to have your cake and eat it too. I'm willing to investigate those options. Simon is as well. If we're on board to find a compromise than you need to be too. Maybe we are different, Kane, but I know it doesn't matter, because you are the one for me. Your hesitation is really only yours."

His head lowered so I couldn't see his face. I knew he did it on purpose, but I couldn't say why.

"Why won't you let me help you?" I asked. "You will have to answer that question eventually." His face lifted to mine. I didn't have a clue what he was thinking.

And then my stomach pitched and the conversation was over.

Later, after copious amounts of water, I slid into bed. Simon had offered to stay with me, but it was late and he had done enough. My thoughts turned to Kane. I really had no idea what was going on in his head, but whatever it was, he really seemed to be struggling with what he seemed to want and what he thought he could have. I knew what I wanted. I wanted Kane. I was willing to fight for him, for us, and, at the same time, if he wasn't willing to fight for me, I was prepared to let him go. And just the thought of that was devastating.

I was just slipping into sleep, when I felt my bed dip. At first I thought it was Simon, ignoring my suggestion that he sleep in his own room for the much deserved rest he had earned from babysitting me, but as soon as I felt the body pressed up against mine I knew it was Kane. His arm wrapped around my stomach and pulled me closer, the familiarity of the movement making my throat tighten. It had been far too long. "Love you, Tea," he whispered in my ear.

For that night, it was all that mattered.

Waking in the morning, only I was in my bed. Perhaps Kane had never been there. Maybe I just imagined him in my drunken stupor. My head pounded, my stomach ached, and . . . so did my ass?

Climbing from bed, I didn't bother dressing. I spotted Simon first as I entered the kitchen—sitting at the table stuffing his face with waffles. He greeted me with a big, stupid grin.

"Hey, sunshine. How you feeling?"

I wanted those waffles. I flicked him off.

"Rough night?" Mrs. T asked, but since she and Simon had become BFFs, I was certain she had had a play-by-play of my adventures.

"Not my best morning."

"Can I get you something to eat?"

"Please. Bacon and sausage and fried eggs and a bucket, since I'll probably not hold that down long."

"Delightful," she muttered as she started for the fridge.

It was my turn to smile. "That's me, a real charmer."

"How's your ass?"

Narrowing my eyes at Simon, I asked, "Why did you ask me that?"

"You don't remember your graceful slide down the banister last night?"

"I really did that?"

"Yep."

"Well, that explains the pain in my ass. It's not just you this time."

"Cute." Simon stuffed half a waffle in his mouth and chewed it with his mouth open, for my benefit.

"I'll hurl on you," I warned.

"I'm like a cat, you'll never hit me."

"Was Kane there last night?"

Mellowing, Simon said, "Yeah."

"I thought he was a hallucination brought on by too many tequila shots." And yet feeling as shitty as I did, a lightness filled me as I remembered our conversation. Kane was trying, was willing to try for us, and that was a step in the right direction.

At that moment, Mr. Sleazy walked into the kitchen. The sight of him at the house so early annoyed me, so much that I didn't check myself and asked, "What the hell are you doing here?"

To say he was surprised at the hostility rolling off me was fair. "I'm working."

"What exactly are you doing that requires you to be in the house as often as you are? Correct me if I'm wrong, but you are only updating an existing document, yes? You aren't writing Mrs. Marks's life story, or the sequel to *War and Peace*, so why are you here? Specifically, why are you here now at"—glancing at the clock, I saw it was only seven thirty in the morning—"this hour?"

His feathers were definitely ruffled. Guess he wasn't used to being questioned. "I was given full access to the house."

"For what purpose?"

"As I mentioned, I'm working on something else for Mrs. Marks, and I shouldn't be saying this since it's privileged, but she wants everything cataloged."

"Why?"

"To sell."

The clatter of the spoon against the floor was a good indication that the news came as much of a surprise to Mrs. T as it did me.

"She wants to sell her things?"

"Everything, including the house."

"Really? And when did you discuss this?"

"Before her heart attack."

"And was anyone else around when you discussed this?"

"Teagan, stop," Simon interrupted. "She's not feeling very well this morning. Please excuse her."

Mr. Sleazy lifted his nose in the air, like a bad smell had just offended him. I knew I was the bad smell, but I didn't care. He turned on his heel and left. My focus shifted to Simon.

"Why did you do that?"

"Confronting him isn't the best way to handle the situation."

"Meaning?"

"If he's working something shady, give him enough rope to hang himself."

Resting my head on my hand, I just stared at my friend. "You're like Kojak."

He flashed me his pearly whites. “Seriously, I’ll look into him, into his credentials. We’ll watch him. Mr. Clancy already is. If he’s up to something, he won’t get away with it.”

At that moment, Mrs. T placed my breakfast in front of me. “Sorry I didn’t help you with making it,” I said.

“You can help when you aren’t hungover.”

“Deal.”

And then I dug into my breakfast. As I suspected, I threw it all up a half an hour later.

Simon and I climbed from the boat on Kane’s island two days after my bender. He was looking back from where we came.

“You used to swim from there to here?”

Remembering the countless hours Kane had taken to teach me to swim brought a smile. “Yeah.”

“Impressive.”

Studying the house, I wondered who kept the place for Kane. Right as I thought that, the front door opened and out walked Mrs. T, which prompted me to ask, “Hi, Mrs. T. You tend to his house?”

“I buy his groceries when I’m in town if he hasn’t yet and work the gardens. The boxes and that garden near the door are lovely.”

“Thanks.”

“Kane does quite a bit on his own, but there are just some jobs that I can do so much faster and this way he’s free to pursue other things more exciting than cleaning toilets.”

It felt as if her last comment was a verbal hand slap, but I still asked, “Other things?”

“Yeah. He’s there now, the boatyard. Go see.”

A half an hour later, my heart swelled with joy to see Kane working on a beautiful boat, his fingers sure as he moved slowly up and down, sanding the long strip of teak. He was building his boat; even blind, he was building his boat. He hadn't lost that dream.

"I've never seen anything like that. To look at him, you'd think he could see," Simon said.

"He always wanted to build a boat."

"When there's a will, there's a way."

Mr. Miller saw us walking toward Kane and said something to him. His head lifted, like a sighted man's would. His hand stilled on the wood he worked.

"Hi, Kane."

"Tea."

"You're building your boat," I said.

"Yeah." His hands moved lovingly over the wood. "It's taking far longer than it should, but I love it."

"It's beautiful."

"Is it?"

"Very. The grain of the wood has lots of striations and the color is a warm brown. The curve of the hull, softly sloping comes to a gentle point. You've stained it darker, a rich mahogany, which is the exact color of the boat you showed me once."

I was so focused on the boat, I didn't notice Kane until I saw the look on his face as I described his boat to him, knew he was seeing it exactly as I did. "It really is beautiful, Kane."

And then I saw the name, penciled on the backboard. He had

told me that the name needed to mean something. Seeing the name he chose, my heart ached with love. *My Tea.*

I wanted to throw myself into his arms, wanted to proclaim my love for him, wanted him to pull me close, to love me, to take up where we'd left off, but instead I banked all those feelings, put them aside for later, and focused on the part of me he needed now.

"Simon and I were going to the diner for lunch. Will you come?"

No was on his tongue, I could see his lips practically forming the word, but he stopped himself. Instead, he placed the paper he was using down and stood.

"I may need a hand finding the place." My heart sighed.

Slipping my hand into his, I smiled up at him and knew somehow he knew I was. He squeezed my hand and smiled back.

Simon moved to join us. "Lead the way, Teagan."

The diner looked exactly the same, and I was happy to see our booth was unoccupied. Once we'd settled, I found our names that Kane had carved into the table when we were younger and traced them with my finger.

Reaching for his hand, I pressed his finger on the carving.

"Our booth," he said softly.

"Yep. Place looks exactly the same."

"Same lights, those horrible orange globes?"

"Exactly the same."

"God, someone needs to tell Henry it's time to update."

When our waitress approached, I couldn't quite believe what I was seeing. Camille. The girl who'd wanted to live in Raven's Peak, the house on the cliff, ruling over the town, was instead serving the town fast food. If that wasn't karma in action, I didn't know what was. Kathy had mentioned the estrangement between Camille and her dad. She hadn't been exaggerating. As I'd noticed the other times I'd seen her since I'd returned, she didn't look good. Her dye job wasn't being kept up regularly, as evidenced by the dark roots. She was a bit heavy in the middle, and, though she was wearing a uniform, her street shoes were not of a high quality. Clearly part of the estrangement included not keeping her in the lifestyle to which she'd become accustomed.

"Well, as I live and breathe. Kane and Teagan. How nice." Venom dripped from her words, or maybe it was jealousy. I couldn't help but think of Kane entertaining her in the library when I'd first arrived. Why had he? She had known the truth about Kane all those years ago and took great delight in lying to me. She was a bitch. Why did he allow her in the house?

"So you've reconciled. Guess it will be the three of us going out now"—her eyes drifted to Simon—"or four. I must admit I've enjoyed having Kane all to myself. I think he liked my company too. Didn't you, Kane?"

I hated that she knew exactly where to stick the knife. Kane said nothing, his silence speaking volumes, and in that moment I wanted him to explain how he could spend time with this person. She was vile. But I wouldn't put him on the spot, wasn't going to give Camille the satisfaction.

"So how long have you worked as a waitress, Camille? Didn't you want to rule over this town at one time? What happened with that?" I asked sweetly.

Direct hit. If her eyes were laser beams, I'd be toast. "This is just temporary. I've had a tough time of it lately, but I'll be just fine. You'll all see." Her focus drifted to Kane. "Oh, or maybe not."

I was nearly out of my chair, but Kane's hold on me tightened like a vise.

Simon, being Simon, leaned back and, though he looked calm, I saw the anger. "Really? This is temporary. I'm guessing you're older than Teagan, here, by quite a few years, to look at you. So you're over a decade out of high school and this is a temporary gig? If you say so."

She looked about ready to launch. I waited for the steam to come from her ears, but laughter came from my side—Kane was laughing—a deep, throaty laugh. A laugh I had not heard in far too long. "I approve of your friend, Tea."

Simon's smiling eyes met mine. "What's good here?"

Kane and I said "the chowder" at the same time.

He closed his menu. "Three bowls of chowder it is." Simon stared pointedly at Camille's name tag before adding, "Camille." It was a clear dismissal.

Kane laughed again. "Yep. Really like your friend."

Kane and I sat on the beach of Raven's Peak. Simon was packing; he needed to get back to the shop. I wanted him to stay, but I knew he had to go. I had offered to help him pack but he claimed he didn't want me hovering, though I suspected he didn't want me to witness his attempt at sweet-talking Mrs. T into some food for the road.

My thoughts shifted to Kane and I asked, "Why were you entertaining Camille at the house?"

"She comes occasionally to chat. I feel bad for her. She doesn't have any friends—not even her dad talks to her."

"I understand her lack of friends—she brings that on herself, but why doesn't her dad talk to her?"

"No idea. I tolerate her visits. Enjoying her visits, as she claimed, is a stretch, but I didn't say anything to refute that—it's pointless. Silence is more effective with her."

"I'm happy to hear that—thinking you two have been chummy all these years really pisses me off."

"I feel the same about her as I did when we were kids."

"Good." And it was wrong of me to feel that way, but I did. Camille was a bitch, always would be.

His head turned in my direction. "What's your life been like, Tea?"

"That's a loaded question." Leaning back on my hands, I looked out at the sea. "College sucked because for the whole of it I felt like a zombie, going through the motions of life, but not actually living it."

"Tea."

"No, I need to say this. I need you to understand. When you left me, I wanted to die. Simon wouldn't let me give up. He forced me, berated me, strong-armed me into living without you. When my feet were back under me and I had come to terms with your wish to move on, I came home to find you had returned and were married. And worse, you cut me completely out of your life—every part of it, including our friendship.

"That was even harder than you leaving me, but somehow I moved past it, started a business, tried to find joy in life again. Simon helped a lot with that, but no matter how much I tried to fill the hole left by the loss of you, I always felt empty. Being here with you, I don't feel empty anymore. For me, it's always been you, Kane. And I know we have a long way to go, but I want—no, I need—you in my life. Maybe you don't want me the way you used to, but I meant what I said. I'll take you any way I can have you."

"I've never stopped wanting you. You need to know that." His head was lowered so I couldn't read his expression. "It's not my place to ask, but you must have dated in all that time."

"I did. Nothing meaningful, nothing close to what we had. I never wanted that again, not the beauty of it or the pain when it was snatched away."

His hands clenched, and I knew what he was thinking, that he hated that it hadn't been him with me all those years. "I wanted it to be you. Sometimes I closed my eyes and pretended it was, but never did anyone ever come close to giving me what we shared."

"I hate that others have known you that way. I know it's unfair, since I was the one to push you away, but I hate it. You're mine."

"I am. Still am, Kane."

He closed his eyes as he settled back on his hands, his face looking up to the skies. "I really like hearing that."

chapter 9

Kane

Working out with the bar, I tried to move past the jealousy I felt knowing that Tea had slept with other men. It was wrong of me; I'd driven her to it, but the ugly emotion still twisted in my gut. She was mine, no other man should know her taste, the feel of her skin, the sounds she made when she came. I hated knowing that there had been others, I hated that I had asked. It was the one thing that only I had given her, but I had fucked that up too.

I sensed her friend Simon before I heard him calling my name. I liked him, liked that she had him to help her through all the shit I had done to her. I couldn't deny I liked it more that he'd never had her.

Dropping from the bar, I turned.

"I'm about to leave, so I wanted to say good-bye."

My hand reached out. He grasped it, hard and fast. "It was nice to meet you. I'm glad Tea's got someone like you watching her back."

"Happy to do it." Silence fell, which always made me uncomfortable. You don't appreciate how much you read from someone by just watching that person. Losing that ability put me at a disadvantage.

"Teagan loves you, has always loved you. Even when she hated you, she loved you. I never want to see her suffer the way she did again. I knew her when she was with you, and I knew her when she was without you. Seeing the two of you together, I understand now why she reacted so severely. I don't know what it's been like for you—can't imagine going through what you've gone through."

"But?"

"If you can't move past whatever is holding you back—whatever is keeping you from taking her into your arms and loving her, making up for all that time you lost—let her go. Her life has been on hold for nine years; she needs to start living it and that includes love and family. She wants that, I know she does. If you can't give her that, you need to let her find it somewhere else."

"How do you know that I don't want that too?"

"I think you do, but I think you're afraid to reach for it. I get it, you're blind, you're scarred, and you think that makes you less of a man to her."

Even though he nailed it on the first try, it pissed me off just the same. He steamrollered right past my angry expression.

"Look, if it was me in your shoes, *I* would have thrown in the towel a long time ago. But she deserves all, not part, of you. She's waited long enough for it."

She hadn't waited with everything. It was completely unfair, and yet it was still how I felt.

He chuckled and fuck if he hadn't read my mind.

"You would deny her sex? You fucking told her you were married to another person, living in the house that should have been hers. Yeah, she's had sex, Kane. Far less than I would have had in her shoes. And now she feels guilty, like she's betrayed you with those men. You took it all away from her, you gave her no choice, and now *you're* jealous? If that's the best you can do for her, leave her alone. Cut the cord now and set her free for good. She'll find her way. She's stronger than she gives herself credit for, and I'll be there to get her through it, *again*. She can and will find happiness without you."

"Are you purposely trying to piss me off?" If I could see, I would have fucking knocked his head off.

"Yeah, I am. Fight for your woman, Kane, before you lose her again."

I knew he was gone even before I heard the sound of the engine firing up. Fucking asshole. He wasn't wrong, I had been holding myself back. That he would go to bat for her, to confront me and hold the mirror to my face, so to speak, yeah, I liked him. His pep talk came a few days too late, though. I had already pulled my head from my ass. I wanted Tea, and I planned on fighting like hell to have her.

Walking back inside, I headed for the shower. I had a meeting with Mr. Lawson in the morning. I wasn't sure what he could share with me about my mom that I'd find interesting. The woman had left and never looked back. A knot formed in my stomach, apprehension that I wasn't going to like whatever it was he had to say.

Teagan

Kane went to see Mr. Lawson—I heard Mr. Clancy mention it to Mrs. T in the kitchen. Kane hadn't asked me to come with him, and

that kind of hurt. Standing on the back patio, I watched as Kane came around the house, Zeus at his side. I started to step off the patio to call to him, but the sag of his shoulders and the downward tilt of his head kept me from doing so.

His mother had been absent for most of his life, so what could he have learned from Mr. Lawson that would open up the wound again? I could feel his pain even from my distance.

He needed time, and I'd give him that, but then I'd offer him my shoulder. Give him the comfort he had given me after my parents had died. Turning, I went back inside. Mr. Clancy usually had tea now; maybe I could join him.

I tracked Kane down a few hours later at the boatyard. He got around really well, but then I suppose he'd had nine years and was determined to not be a burden to anyone, as if he could ever be. Fool.

He was working on painting, Mr. Miller right at his side to help guide him. I was happy to see that the sadness I had spied earlier no longer seemed to haunt him. I waited until he pulled his brush from the boat, so I didn't startle him and screw up his work.

"Kane."

"I wondered how long you would wait." Placing his brush down, his head turned in Mr. Miller's general direction. "I'll come back later, if that's okay."

"Sure thing. I'll seal everything up, so if you don't make it back, we can work again tomorrow."

"Thank you."

Kane stood. Mr. Miller helped him around the boat. "Hi, Teagan."

"Hi, the boat looks beautiful."

Mr. Miller smiled, admiration and pride in his expression. "It sure does."

Kane held his hand out to me, and I immediately linked our fingers.

"Where's Zeus?"

"Home. I had Sam drive me."

Sam—the same man who had driven Kane and me to school as kids. The few times I had seen him since I'd been back, he hadn't seemed to have aged at all. Kane and I started to walk, not really sure where we were heading, just around, I guessed. He was upset. I didn't need to hear his voice to know this.

"You went to see Mr. Lawson," I said.

"Yeah."

"Tell me," I urged gently.

"My mom lives two towns over. She's married and apparently has been for over ten years."

Clenching my jaw to keep from hurling the curses that I was choking on, I pressed myself against his side, offering comfort. There could be any number of reasons why his mom had moved away and remarried, but none of them were acceptable, given that she'd abandoned her child. He was better off without her. He had found a very loving family at Raven's Peak; and, while logically that all made sense, the heart of the nine-year-old left behind still beat in his chest. Logic didn't mean shit to him.

"All this time, and she was right there, so close and so far away. Not a phone call or a birthday or Christmas card. How can a woman bring life into the world and then turn from it?"

The scenario sounded awfully familiar—like mother like son. Kane had done that to me, his intent to protect, his goal my well being. What if his mother had done the same? I wanted to say this to him, but he wasn't ready to hear it. He was angry, and I understood that feeling all too well. When he was calmer, when he'd had more time to think about it, I'd broach the subject.

And even with that course of action in mind, I opened my big mouth and blurted, "Maybe you should contact her."

"No."

Stupid. "Sorry."

"For years I wondered—hell, I still find myself wondering—what did I do wrong? How could she not love me enough? How could she just forget about me? Why did she hate me?" He stopped walking, and his entire body went so taut that I thought he was going to break. Pulling his hand from mine, his expression turned to one of profound disgust.

"I fucking did that to you. Jesus, I made you feel exactly what I have spent my entire life feeling."

Well, yes, he had. He could have been describing me for the past nine years, but I wasn't about to confirm that.

"Your intentions were in the right place," I whispered, leaving it to him to make the inference.

"And you're here with me now. Why?"

"I can't stay away from you, never could."

His arms lifted. I walked right into them, and they closed me in for a tight hug. "Love you, Tea."

It wasn't necessary for me to respond. For a few glorious minutes we stayed like that, exactly my favorite place to be. His voice was soft when he asked, "You think I should see her?"

"I think you might find there was a reason she left."

"Lawson has her address and number. We'll have to call him."

"Okay."

Silence fell for a moment; Kane clearly had something on his mind. He said, "I'm sorry. I'm sorry I made you feel all the things I did. I wanted to protect you, but I didn't realize I was hurting you anyway."

"We're here. It took us a long time to get here, but we're here. Let's leave the past in the past, okay?"

"Okay." A slight smile touched his lips. "Wise words."

I rolled my eyes. "Don't roll your eyes," he said.

"How do you—"

He laughed, the sound easing the tension I hadn't realized was stiffening my shoulders. "You always rolled your eyes at me when you thought I was being a clown."

This was true. My smile faded when I thought about him never seeing me roll my eyes at him again, never seeing the boat he was building, or the sea he'd so loved to look at.

His hands moved up my back, his fingertips finding my lips. "Why the frown?"

"What's it like?"

"Dark." Trying to lighten the mood, a grin pulled at his mouth, but looking into those beautiful eyes and knowing he couldn't look back caused an ache in my chest.

"At first it was maddening, frustrating. I broke so many things, both unintentionally and intentionally. Lonely is a good word to describe it, and terrifying. Disorienting—places I thought I knew with my eyes closed"—another grin—"I learned I didn't know, because my sense of direction was completely screwed up. I couldn't make it from my bed to my bathroom without walking into something and stubbing my toes."

"But now you walk through your house like a sighted man."

"Because I forced myself to learn it again. Counting the steps to get to the bathroom, listening to the sound of the water and knowing it needs to be on my left side if I'm heading to the bathroom. Even smells help to guide me.

"I've adapted, but I miss it. I miss seeing the horizon. I miss the sunrise and seeing the full moon in the sky. But most of all, I miss your face. I wish I could be looking at you right now, but"—his fingers ran along the curves and lines of my face—"I do see you."

Emotion tightened my throat at his beautiful sentiment. My hands covered his, expressing silently just what his words meant to me. "I've developed a lazy eye. It's probably best you can't see me."

A second passed as my words sank in, and then that fabulous face tilted back and he laughed, a deep belly laugh. I loved his laugh. His hand moved down my arm for my hand. "Let's get something to eat, my lazy-eyed love. And then we'll contact Lawson and get my mom's information."

"Sounds like a plan."

Kane

My hands were actually shaking as I reached for my phone to call my mom. Ever since my meeting with Mr. Lawson, I had played countless versions of the conversation I was about to have in my head. I was angry and bitter, and yet I could no longer ignore the fact that I had acted similarly toward Tea. My intentions had been in the right place, so had my mom's been too?

Resolving to actually have the conversation didn't make it any easier. Realizing there was no point in dragging out the moment, I dialed her number. Along with memorizing the floor plan of my house, I had also mastered the keypad on my phone.

My heart felt like it was going to pound right out of my chest when the call connected. The line was answered on the second ring. "Hello."

Mom. Her voice sounded exactly as I remembered, and the memories that voice stirred were countless.

"Hello?" she said again.

Emotion tightened my throat but I did manage to say, "Mom."

A gasp sounded over the line, followed by a few seconds of silence before a whispered, "Kane?"

I heard disbelief in her tone, but I also heard hope and what sounded an awful lot like longing. "Yeah, it's me."

"Oh my God, Kane." Her voice broke and the sound of her crying filled the silence. Her pain came over the line, so intense and heartbreaking that I felt my own eyes stinging with tears. Her reaction was so unexpected, so raw, and, on top of that, confusing as hell. If she hurt so badly at the sound of my voice, then why did she stay away for so long?

"Please don't cry, Mom."

"I'm sorry, I just never thought I'd hear your voice again."

I was confused and, honestly, pissed too. She never thought she'd hear my voice again, but she'd been the one to walk out. "Why not?" I asked curtly.

"I don't deserve to be near you."

A shock went straight to my core. There it was . . . she had left me for my sake, just as I had done to Tea. My eyes were no longer stinging but actually filling.

She asked, "How are you?"

I couldn't answer that, not over the phone, and drop the shitload of suck that was my life on her, so I lied: "Good." But I immediately followed that up with, "Actually, not good. I've spent my life wondering why you walked out. I'm all grown-up now, not the boy I was; I think you owe me an explanation."

"I do, you're right." There was silence for a beat before she added, "My intentions were in the right place, but you're right, I owe you an explanation. Maybe you would like to come here for dinner?"

I hadn't expected her to be so willing to see me, regardless of her intentions, after she had stayed away for so long. I answered almost out of shock. "Okay."

"Oh, Kane, sweetheart." Hearing her endearment for me sent tears rolling down my cheeks. She asked, "Are you doing okay?"

"Honestly, Mom, there's just so much we have to say, and I'd really rather we say it face-to-face."

"That's fair. You have my address?"

"Yes."

"I love you, Kane. I never stopped."

The sincerity I heard in her voice touched a place in me that had been empty for far too long. I needed to end the call, because I was about to lose my shit. I hastily offered a few days that I was free for dinner, and she picked one. Then I said, "I'll see you soon."

"I look forward to it, Kane, more than you can possibly know."

"Bye." I hung up before she could reply. Dropping the phone, I sat back in my chair and let the tears fall, because the impossible had happened twice. Not only had I gotten my Tea back, but I had just spoken to my mom for the first time since I was nine years old. And what was even more shocking, it sounded as if she had missed me as much as I had missed her.

Teagan

Hearing noise coming from the back of his house, I walked around it and saw Kane. When he'd called the house earlier, he'd mentioned that he'd called his mom the night before, and a visit was scheduled. It wasn't enough information for me, which was why I had sought him out. I suspected he was working out his issues through exercise.

His high bar seemed to be his fallback. The way he so effortlessly pulled himself up, I suspected he used it often. The second he realized I was there, he dropped from the bar and turned to me.

"Tea."

"How was the call with your mom?"

"She sounded genuinely happy to hear from me. She asked me to visit even before I could suggest it."

"That's good."

"I was thinking more along the lines of odd."

"Not odd, not if she really was doing as you did, staying away because she really believed it was better for you."

"Maybe." He sounded conflicted, and I understood what he was feeling. I understood what it felt like to be denied seeing someone, someone you wanted in your life, all in the name of what was best for you. It sucked even if her heart was in the right place.

"Her voice sounded the same; I felt a flood of memories just hearing it across the line."

"You've missed her."

"Yeah, and I think she really missed me too."

"Not surprising," I said and saw the smile that flashed over his face.

He said, "I've missed you more."

Tears were imminent—I needed to change the subject. "Mrs. T is making you a triple chocolate cake. Will you come up for dinner?"

"Tempting." The fact that he was able to switch gears so easily meant the phone call hadn't upset him as much as I feared it had.

"Need me to sweeten the pot, Kane?"

"Yeah."

"How so?"

"A night on the sofa in the library with you."

My heart twisted at the memory. "Done."

His smile faded. "I want a life with you, Tea. I don't want to know another day when you're not near me."

"I want that too." I'd make it work somehow, having both Kane and the life I started in Boston. When there was a will . . .

There was time before dinner, so Kane and I visited Mrs. Marks. She had been so agitated the last time I saw her that I thought it might bring her comfort to see us together, working on fixing what had been broken.

She was sleeping when we arrived, her head turned slightly, her hair down around her shoulders. She looked so frail lying there; it scared me to think that she might not recover. Kane's hand tightened on mine, and I knew he was thinking the same thing.

A nurse entered to check on her IVs. Seeing us, she smiled absently. "Evening."

"Hi. Has she been awake at all today?" I asked.

"A little this morning. Her lawyer was here. He seemed awfully itchy to talk to her. But she doesn't stay awake for very long."

"He been here before?" Kane asked.

"I don't think so, at least not during my shift."

At that moment, Mrs. Marks's eyes fluttered opened and, though she was looking right at us, she didn't see us immediately. It was clear the minute she did, since a smile touched her lips.

"That's a sight," she whispered.

Moving closer to her bed, I reached for her hand. "How are you feeling?"

"Better." Her focus shifted to Kane. "Kane, you told her?"

"Yes."

"Thank God."

"I'm sorry we put you through that. I didn't agree, but I believed it was his dying wish. It broke my heart to keep you out of the loop—but I understood his intentions. Watching him struggle, the agony, it would have been very hard on you to watch that."

I was happy to hear that her speech was more clear and her words less disjointed. Zeroing in on her last comment, I replied, "Not as hard as it was for him to live through. I would have been there every second if he had let me."

"I know, but it would have broken this old lady's heart having the ones she thinks of as hers hurting so. Kane in pain and you watching that pain."

What could one say to that?

Her gaze moved to Kane. "Kane, did you speak to Lawson?"

"Yes."

"I'm sorry, your mother made me promise."

"I did the same to you with Tea."

Surprise crossed her face. "I guess you did. You okay? Your mom?"

"I called her. We're meeting next week."

"Good. She loves you. This I know."

Sensing that Kane didn't want to discuss the topic any further, she changed it. "Mr. Clancy told me Simon went home. I'm sorry I didn't get a chance to chat with him."

"He'll be back. We have another person completely in love with Mrs. T's cooking."

She chuckled.

Kane asked, "Is it true you want to sell Raven's Peak?"

"I'm getting older, so are the others. We're having trouble maintaining such a huge house, as you know, Kane."

"So you asked Mr. Sl—I mean, Falco, to inventory your house?"

An odd look moved over her face, suspicion maybe, reminding me that this woman didn't let anything pass her notice. "Yes."

"And?"

"And what, dear?"

"There's more to what you asked of him, isn't there?"

Surprise greeted that answer before she smiled. "I didn't realize I was so easy to read."

"You're not, but you're also not a fool. Falco is a fool."

"There may be another reason behind my request of him, but we don't need to get into that now."

"He's inventorying in the event you need to sell. What are you hoping to do with the place?" I asked.

"I would like to give it to Kane and you. His inn idea is brilliant."

Turning my attention to Kane, I could tell he was startled by the news. "You still want to turn the place into an inn?" I asked.

"Yeah. Most of the foundation is already in place, and, with the elegance of the place and its location, I think it would be a very successful inn."

"I absolutely agree. I'm just surprised."

Kane's voice turned noticeably cooler. "Surprised at the idea of a blind man running a business?"

Whoa. What the hell? That pricked my temper. "Surprised because the first and last time I heard you mention the idea was when we were kids, and the fact that you knew yourself that well at twelve surprises me. I didn't figure myself out until I graduated college." I stood. "Suddenly, this room is just a bit too small. I'll see you tomorrow, Mrs. Marks."

"Teagan, don't leave upset," she whispered, and I felt terrible that she had to witness that when the whole point of the visit was for her to see that Kane and I were mending our fences, but Kane had been out of line.

"I'm sorry," was all I offered as I started from the room.

"Tea?" Contrition laced through Kane's words, but I was angry, so I just kept on walking.

I didn't go right home. I walked around town to clear my head and ended at the boatyard. I knew what fueled Kane's outburst; he was having doubts himself and feared I was too. Running my hand over his boat, I knew I didn't have doubts. I believed he could do whatever he set his mind to. He always could. The fact that he was blind now added another layer of complexity to his goals, but that wouldn't be enough to stop him from succeeding. Pushing his doubts on me, though, that wasn't going to work.

"Tea?"

My head whipped around and I saw Kane standing a few feet away. "How did you know I was here?"

"You always came here when you were upset."

"Where's the car?"

"Sent it home." He moved his hands into the front pockets of his jeans. "I'm sorry. What I said was wrong."

I appreciated the apology, but his quick reaction made me suspect this wouldn't be the last time he did so. "You're blind, a challenge, but I don't doubt you for a minute. Undermining me, us, putting your doubts on me, is not cool."

"I know."

"I'd like to help you, and not because I think you need it, but because I want to. I want to witness you make your vision a reality."

"I'd like that."

"Can I ask you something?" I asked.

"Anything."

"Outside of Mrs. Marks and the others, did you have visitors when you were in the hospital?"

"Yeah, most of the town. Why?"

"Including Camille?"

"She may have visited, but I never saw her. You're not answering my question, why?"

"Walking in on you two when I first arrived was like a wicked case of déjà vu. Hearing you talk, laugh, plan outings together. That hurt a lot."

"I'm sorry, Tea. It isn't what you—"

I didn't let him finish. "I came home, in college, right before you called me to end it, because I hadn't been able to get in touch with anyone. Camille was at the house, collecting the mail. I couldn't understand where everyone was, why there was not one person in the house. In the nine years I had lived there, the place was never left empty. She was the one to tell me you'd moved away, moved in with your girlfriend and everyone had gone to help get you settled. She spared no detail regarding your developing relationship with Doreen, even paralleling it to ours. When you called, you only confirmed what she had said. She enjoyed it, hurting me. Knowing now she lied, made it all up, pisses me off, but worse, the fact that she knew what really happened to you and I didn't . . . that burns."

"Son of a bitch," he hissed. "I always wondered why you believed the lie so easily, why you didn't hunt me down. Stupid, because I had broken your heart, but knowing how I felt about you, it seemed like you gave up on us rather easily. I didn't know what she did, how she played you, but I'm not fucking surprised. The whole town knew of the accident, and Camille, being the cunning bitch that she is, somehow arranged to be the one to look after Raven's Peak while the family was with me. Her learning about the Doreen ruse isn't a surprise either, nor is it a surprise that she enjoyed hurting you. I'm so sorry, Tea. I can't even begin to imagine how that must have felt, coming from her, of all people."

I couldn't lie, I was relieved to hear that Kane hadn't included Camille in his plan, but that she had gained the knowledge through her typical nefarious ways. His belief, though, that I had believed the lie so easily needed to be addressed. "I *didn't* believe the lie, even after your call. It was only after I spoke to Mrs. Marks and she confirmed it that I believed."

He said nothing; I assumed he was thinking the same thing I was. For two people so in synch with each other, we had allowed ourselves to be persuaded rather easily.

"And the party you two were discussing, whose was it?"

"Just a mutual friend. She was going to give me a ride."

"Mutual friend?"

"The girl from the fire, Kathy O'Malley."

Oh . . . Oh . . .

"Every birthday, Christmas, holiday, school plays—I've become an unofficial member of their family."

"Makes sense. You saved her life." And it cost him his own. I didn't say it, but I knew he was thinking that too. "And Camille?"

"She knew Kathy when they were kids. Kathy is a few years younger than her, but their families were close, they still are."

"I guess it was nice of Camille to offer you a ride."

He chuckled. "That's generous of you."

"I told you I met Kathy a couple weeks ago. She's very nice. In fact, it's nice of all the O'Malleys to include you."

"They've done more than that. They insisted on helping to pay for the building of my house. They set up a bank account for me and deposit money every month. I told them it wasn't necessary, but they felt compelled to do it. It isn't their fault I got caught in the fire; I don't think I did anything that countless others wouldn't have done."

"I disagree. You were always the first to jump up and offer a hand. It's just part of who you are. I think what you did wasn't ordinary but extraordinary, just like you."

Tenderness washed over his face. "Come here," he whispered, and I didn't hesitate, reaching for him so he knew I was close. His hands cradled my face, "Can you forgive me?"

"Yes. Can you forgive me?"

"Yes." To seal that, he brushed his lips over mine, allowing them to linger.

chapter 10

Teagan

“That cake was ridiculous.” Kane could say that, since he’d eaten almost half of it. Our walk home had been so reminiscent of old times; a few times, along the way, he’d squeezed my hand, and not just in affection but for assistance. The small gesture meant the world to me.

“I should hope you liked it, you did have three slices.”

Kane patted his flat stomach. “So damn good.”

We were snuggled up on our sofa. We didn’t fit as well as we had as kids, but I loved having his body so close to mine. Dinner had been like old times, except for Mrs. Marks’s absence. Zeus was curled up on the floor.

“I’m going to see Mrs. Marks again tomorrow. I don’t like how I left. She’s recovering and I’m adding stress. It was thoughtless and stupid.”

"It was human, Tea."

"Will you come with me?" I asked.

"Yeah. What time were you hoping to go?"

"Around noon. I can come get you."

An edge rang in his voice when next he spoke. "I'll come to the house."

Sitting up, I turned to him. "Okay. So you tell time by a clock that speaks?"

"Yeah, and I have a watch that opens so I can feel the hands."

I touched his face, his cheek, his lips, and he closed his eyes. "I asked Mr. Clancy about the fire and what happened after. I wanted to know, but I didn't want you to live through it again."

His eyes opened and in them I saw torment, the memory haunting him still. "It was as close to hell as a person can come."

Sympathy and bitterness caused an ache in my chest. "I would have never left your side."

"I knew that's how you'd feel, and that's why I didn't tell you."

"Not to beat a dead horse, but I'm going to anyway. Had it been me, in that hospital bed, alone, scared, hurt, blind, would you have wanted me to keep you in the dark about it?" I asked.

Every muscle in his body reacted to that. "Fuck no."

"Now you understand how I feel. It should have been me at your side."

"If it had been you in the hospital bed, would you have wanted me to sit and watch as you suffered, struggled to live, only to witness you die? To have my final memory of you be in the burn unit of the hospital?"

Just the idea of it made my eyes burn. "No."

"Now you understand how I feel. We're here now. Let's move forward. Looking back won't change anything."

"I can do that."

"So, why antiques?"

"This house. My life here. You. For the longest time all I wanted to do was look to the past, and eventually I learned that sometimes it is healthy to look to the past. Maybe you'll come to Boston and see the life I've made there."

He didn't answer, because we'd had this discussion already. I knew his answer to traveling to Boston was a no, and he knew I knew. I understood, I really did, but it hurt that he would never know that significant part of my life. I brought it up again with hope that maybe he'd feel differently after he'd had time to think it over.

I was pushing it, but I added, "I'll be with you. Think about it?" And though he said what he knew I wanted to hear, I knew his mind was already made up.

"I'll think about it."

Watching Kane work was an experience. He listened to recorded books and translated them into Braille. He had started the practice as a way of learning Braille, and now he found comfort in the work. He offered the books he translated to the public library, which distributed them among the other branches who had a need for them. He had a trusted group of people around him—Mrs. Marks and his family at Raven's Peak; the O'Malleys; his lawyer and accountant, who took care of all his bills and legal matters; and Mr. Miller, who helped him with his boat.

As I watched him work, I couldn't help but think as wonderful as this was for him, he was limiting himself. There was a big world out there, and yet he stayed here, where it was familiar and safe. I suppose I understood that, but the Kane of our youth had wanted to see the world. He'd dreamed of driving his boat up and down the coast. Sure, he wouldn't see it in the same way, but it seemed he was giving up so much.

I wanted him to come to Boston. The topic was over. I knew he had no intention of coming to see the life I had made for myself. Maybe it was selfish of me to ask it of him, but it seemed to me that if you wanted to share your life with someone, you would want to know everything about that person. I'd been doing that with Kane, asking everyone about him, trying to really get the picture of his life when I wasn't in it. His refusal to make the trip hurt. I got that he didn't want me to treat him differently because he was blind, and yet he was treating himself differently, using his blindness as an excuse to disengage. He couldn't have it both ways.

"You're thinking too loud."

Glancing over, I saw that Kane was no longer working but staring in my direction. My heart tripped in my chest like it did every time I looked at him. I couldn't believe I was here with him, had thought the day would never come.

"Are you okay, Tea?"

"More than okay."

"I'm almost done, and then we can go for a swim, if you want," he suggested.

"I'd like that."

His smile stopped my breath. "So would I."

He kept pace at my side, never more than a foot away, his long strokes easily cutting through the water. He knew the area so well there was no anxiety, and as long as he could hear me next to him, he didn't worry about me either. I loved that he still swam and that he had taught me how to so I could share moments like this with him. I knew how much he enjoyed swimming.

He wore a swim shirt, something he had never done before. He was covering his burns, I knew, but I wished he wouldn't. Scarred or not, he was beautiful to me. And then I realized that he had never seen them. He didn't know what they looked like, and I guessed that what was described to him by the doctors was technical and not for the layman.

After our swim, we sat on the beach, the sun drying us, and, though there were long periods of silence, it wasn't uncomfortable.

"Kane, has anyone told you about your burns?"

His muscles flexed; the subject was clearly not a favorite of his. "The doctors, but I tuned them out because I wasn't ready to hear it. As I healed, I didn't really see the point in having my head filled with the image of what I had become."

That broke my heart—his scars weren't as bad as he clearly believed them to be. I wouldn't coddle him; he'd hate that, so instead I asked, "Aren't you even a little curious?"

Every time those eyes found mine, I marveled at how well he was able to do that. "Maybe a little."

"Would you like me to describe them for you? And before you say no, I think you are beautiful, scars and all. I wish you wouldn't hide them from me."

He said nothing, and I knew he was considering my words.

"Take off your shirt and let me tell you what I see."

He hesitated, but he did as I asked and removed his shirt. He wouldn't look at me, even though he couldn't see. I got it. He was embarrassed.

My fingers were gentle when I ran them over the scar tissue. "It's darker than the rest of your skin. Twisted and red, stretched in areas. Just above your nipple, across to your underarm, and up the center to your collarbone. Your neck down to midback, concentrating mostly on the left side; the edges are less pronounced and almost blend into the rest of your skin. To have survived this, to be the man you are, having lived through something so horrifying . . . yes, your skin is scarred, Kane, but it's your skin, so it could never be ugly."

He moved so fast, turning and drawing me to him, his arms coming around me like steal bands. His mouth found mine, his tongue pushing past the barrier of my lips to taste. My arms moved around his neck, holding him closer. His hands roamed down my body, over my breasts, and across my stomach, and everywhere he touched burned, aching for more. I felt his fingers on the strings of my top, felt when they stilled.

"Please don't stop. I want you . . ." The memory slammed into me, the words came out before I could stop them, not that I would have. "I want you to poke me, Kane. Please."

His entire body stilled, even the air in his lungs seemed to still before he started shaking. Concerned, I tried to pull away, until I realized he was laughing. The sound was so glorious, I closed my eyes and just soaked it in.

When he was able to speak, he said, "Are you begging me to poke you, Tea?"

"I really am."

And then he was kissing me again, turning me, and lowering me to the sand. He worked my top off, his fingers tracing my collarbone, down my shoulder. He was learning my body, seeing it through his fingers. His other hand moved over my stomach, down my thighs. Straddling my legs, he cupped my breasts in his hands, his thumbs brushing over the nipples just like he had done before. His head lowered, and his mouth closed over my breast. It was heaven feeling him touch me again. His fingers danced down my stomach and slipped under my suit bottoms. When he touched me, just the tips of his fingers on the nub that ached, my back arched. His mouth was on my other breast while his thumb took up the stroking, his fingers sliding over my aching flesh until he found me and pushed a finger in, slowly, as if he was savoring the sensations as much as I was.

His mouth moved lower, down my belly. Untying the strings of my suit bottom, he removed the fabric that separated me from him. Moving down my body, he lifted my ass and pressed a kiss right where his fingers had been.

"Kane." My body was so oversensitive that, feeling his mouth on me again, I already felt the start of an orgasm. I fell completely over the edge when he pushed his tongue in deep, just as he squeezed that nub.

His mouth drifted back up my body, his lips lingering over mine. Reaching for him, my hand slipped under his waistband, finding him and wrapping around him. He moaned. His eyes closed. Shifting us, so I was straddling him, I moved lower down his body. His eyes opened, his focus on where my hand held him.

Pulling his shorts off, following the fabric down his legs, I slid back up his body and took him into my mouth. The sexiest sound rumbled up his throat as I worked him, twirling my tongue around the tip before sliding it under his shaft, while fondling the sac between his legs. He was close but he moved, pulling me up his body, and turned to pin me under him. Pushing my legs apart, he gripped my hips and slid into me. Feeling him inside me, being connected to him again, rocked me, and the emotions that burned through me were staggering. I realized he wasn't moving and one glance confirmed that he was experiencing the same profound moment I was. And then he started to move, a slow, easy glide, in and out, until it wasn't easy but hard, fast and frantic, to reach that moment together.

"Come for me, Tea."

And I did at the exact moment he did.

Leaving the beach, we returned to his house for a shower. In the bathroom, he turned on the water before he held his hand out for me. Grasping it, he drew me into the shower with him. His mouth was on me before I even felt the spray. His hands moved over my body, which was sleek from the water. Cradling my face, he kissed me deeply, like he needed to kiss me or he'd die. My hands found his stomach, the chiseled muscles of his abs. His body wasn't the body of the boy I'd known, he was a man, a beautifully defined man. He broke the kiss and reached for the dispenser, filling his palm with shampoo, and his fingers on my scalp nearly made me moan in pleasure. No one had every washed my hair before, and no one could ever make it feel as wonderful as he did. My bones turned to goo.

Rinsing my hair, he moved on to my body, washing me so tenderly. When he was done, I washed him as thoroughly and sweetly as he had done for me. He tensed when I moved over his scars, and I felt his discomfort in every muscle. But he needed to get past that, because he was mine, all of him. He lifted me into his arms, pressed me against the shower wall, and when he entered me this time it was as tender as his washing had been. Kissing me as if I were the most precious thing in his life, he slowly and deliberating brought me to orgasm. My name passed his lips in a whisper when he followed shortly after.

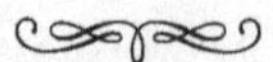

I woke up in Kane's bed and reached for him, but he wasn't there. Stretching, my thoughts turned to the night before. After our shower, he'd brought me to his room and made love to me again. In the middle of the night, he'd reached for me twice. And just before dawn, we'd made love again. And it was love, not sex, it was a sharing of not just our bodies but our souls. That was what every sexual relationship I'd had since Kane had been lacking. No one but Kane had ever touched my heart or my soul.

Sitting up, I reached for the robe he'd left for me, but I got distracted when I saw his nightstand, or rather, what was on it: a glass of chocolate milk with whipped cream. My heart sighed at the sight, and then I saw what else shared the nightstand, his pictures. Ones he could no longer see, but still they were there, pictures of me, of us, through the years.

"Tea?"

Kane was leaning against the doorframe, his voice questioning, wondering if I was up yet. "I'm awake," I said.

He walked into the room, his steps sure, before he sat down next to me. I took a sip of the milk, then reached for his hand to pass him the glass. "Do you still drink a glass of chocolate milk with whipped cream every morning?"

He didn't seem to want to answer, but reluctantly he did. "Yeah."

"So do I."

This earned me a smile. "You looking at my pictures?" he asked.

"Yes. Where did you get all of them?"

"Mrs. Marks. I asked her if she had any. I wanted you close."

"At home, I have a picture of you too."

"Did you throw darts at it?"

"That was the intention, but no. When it got to the point that I missed you so much I ached, I'd pull it out and wish that it was me here with you instead of the woman who was."

"There has never been anyone but you."

"For me either. I know you don't believe that, I can see that clearly on your face. Yes, I dated, I had sex, but that is all it ever was. I never had what we shared last night, never, only with you."

"I'm jealous of those other men. Really fucking jealous."

"Nothing to be jealous about. They got my body but never my heart or my soul. Those have always been yours."

"I still don't like knowing other men have touched you, tasted you, seen and heard you as you came."

"You'll drive yourself crazy thinking about it, so please don't. There will never be another, I can promise you that."

"Damn straight." But he said that with a little smile. He wasn't over it, but he was trying, and that was all that mattered.

The following morning found me at the boatyard. Kane had gone to the public library in town, but for what, he didn't say. I'd asked if he wanted company, and he said he thought I'd get bored. This gave me the perfect opportunity for my mission. Silas Miller stood in a boat hangar where a sailboat was being refinished.

Hearing me approach, he turned and smiled.

"Teagan, hi." He looked past me. "Is Kane with you?"

"No. I came alone. I wanted to ask you for a favor."

Placing down the mechanical part he had been working on, he wiped his hands with a towel he had stuffed in the front pocket of his work pants.

"What can I do for you?"

"I was hoping you could teach me how to drive a boat."

Interest moved to understanding and settled on approval. "For Kane."

"He always wanted to build a boat and drive it up and down the coast. He's building the boat, but I imagine, as self-sufficient as he is, he won't be able to drive it." Looking down for a minute, my throat tight thinking of Kane losing so much more than his sight, I added, "I want to be able to give him that."

"He would love that." Mr. Miller's words were so soft, my gaze met his. "He often mentioned it, you and him, his boat."

Knowing he had still been thinking of me, still wished for the dream, even with all that had happened, settled very comfortably in my chest.

"Let's go check my calendar and we'll schedule some days. You'll need to get your boater's license, but I can help you with that."

"Thank you."

"Damn sad turn of events, tragic, but seeing the two of you together is just proof that some things are meant to be."

Kane and I were finding our way, and I was happier than I'd been in a long time. I wasn't sure what he was doing when he went to the library, had asked him a few times, since he went daily, but he said it was a surprise. Whatever it was, he was happier after doing it, more confident and aware, so whatever he was doing, I hoped he kept at it.

Mrs. Marks was feeling almost back to normal. She had been in the hospital for nearly four weeks, but the last few times that I'd visited her, she wasn't disoriented and was able to speak with no apparent struggle. The doctors were talking about discharging her. Hopefully in the next few days she would be coming home. It had been far too long since the five of us were all together in the house. The visit with Kane's mom was coming up, and I knew he was nervous, but I sensed a vein of excitement in him too. I hoped that their first meeting, after all these years, wouldn't be a disappointment for him.

The only blemish in my nearly perfect world was Mr. Sleazy. I couldn't stop thinking about him—he was up to something. Simon had hired a PI a few years ago after someone had come into our shop and sold us a fake. When Simon left for Boston, he'd planned on contacting the PI to have him look into Mr. Sleazy. I had the sense Mr. Lawson was doing so already, but I was still uneasy and, with Mrs. Marks in the hospital, I wanted to make sure the man who was in her home wasn't planning something nefarious. Wondering if Simon had heard from the PI, I reached for my cell phone and called him. He answered on the first ring.

"Hey, how's it going? How's Kane?"

"Better, good, really good. He's more open with me, and his instinct to push me away seems to be occurring less and less. He's working on something new—he won't tell me what, but I love seeing him look less haunted."

"That's good, that's what he needs."

"Simon, we made love."

"And?"

"It was perfect."

His voice sounded deeper, softer. "You love him, that makes all the difference."

"So how are you? How's the shop?"

"We've been busy as hell. I uncovered a couple of treasures that the previous owners were clueless about. I think I should be able to tie everything up in a few days. I'm thinking about shutting it down for a month. What do you think?"

"A month?"

"Double, Teagan, we've made double what we normally do in a month. I'd like to close up and join you in Maine."

"I'd like that."

"Now's not the time, but we need to talk about the shop, especially if you're thinking about staying in Maine."

Thinking about the future caused my stomach to twist into a knot. I wanted Kane, so if that meant staying in Maine, I was fine with that. But for Kane to not even consider living in Boston, to just want to settle at Raven's Peak—I didn't think that was the healthiest option for him.

"We'll talk, just not now."

"You know, we can always open a branch in Maine. There are options."

I had thought of that, but I didn't want to make any decisions now. When it came time to think about what was best for our business, I wanted the only factors to be the ones that were directly related to the business. My personal life shouldn't have an impact on my professional decisions. It wasn't fair to Simon or our business. "You're right, and when I'm more comfortable with where Kane and I are heading, then we can sit down and figure it all out. Whatever happens, Simon, I don't want to lose you."

"Not going to happen, so don't worry about it."

"I needed to hear that. So I called . . ."

"Not just to hear my sexy voice?"

"That, and have you gotten anything back about Sleazy yet?"

"Not yet, but I'll be with you soon, so when our PI calls, we can hear it together. Tell that lovely Mrs. T I'll be returning in a few short days so she can prepare a feast in my honor."

"You're an idiot, but I'll tell her."

"Teagan, Kane." A worried Mr. Clancy pulled me from sleep. Kane stirred at my side, his head turning in the direction of the voice.

"What's wrong?"

"It's Mrs. Marks. The hospital just called. She's had a stroke. I don't know the details, or how severe."

Kane and I jumped from the bed. I was wearing my nightie, and Kane wasn't wearing a thing. Mr. Clancy started for the door. "Car will be in the drive in five."

As soon as the door closed, Kane's head turned in my direction. He sounded serious, but I saw his slight grin. "He got an eyeful."

He looked embarrassed, so I said, "A fucking nice eyeful."

We dressed quickly and hurried down the stairs, my hand in Kane's for support as well as to guide him, since being in a hurry could make him miss a step. I didn't want to be visiting him in the hospital too.

The car was in the drive, Mr. Clancy and Mrs. T already inside it. Once Kane and I climbed in, Sam, the driver, didn't hesitate to peel out.

"I don't understand how she could have had a stroke when she's being so closely monitored," I said.

"My thoughts too," Mr. Clancy said, his focus on the window. He was nervous or maybe scared. He and Mrs. Marks weren't just employee and employer, they were friends, best friends, as near as I could tell. Covering his hand, I gave it a reassuring squeeze. "She's going to pull through this."

"I believe that too, I really do."

Mrs. T chimed in. "I owe her a hundred bucks. She ain't going let me slide with that."

And just like that, the tension in the car dropped drastically.

Kane's fingers linked through mine and I could feel his discomfort in the rigidness of his fingers.

"You okay?"

"It's times like these that I really hate my blindness. Someone I love is in trouble and I feel completely useless."

"There isn't much for any of us to do."

His voice took on an edge. "At least you can find the fucking building without needing help."

How did I respond to that? I didn't, just held his hand tighter in mine.

As soon as the car pulled up to the curb, we filed out and headed to the front desk. It took a good fifteen minutes for the doctor on call to come see us. What he had to say was better than I was expecting, however.

"She's had a mild stroke, her left side is affected, and her ability to speak has been impaired. This could just be temporary—it most likely is—but we'll know more by morning."

"How did this happen? You ran all those tests. Weren't you thinking she'd already had a mild stroke?" I demanded.

"She exhibited signs of a stroke, yes, but the tests all came back negative. What's happened now isn't uncommon, a piece of the clot that caused her heart attack traveled through her bloodstream to her brain. It happens, but the good news is the stroke was mild and so the effects will be minimal if not completely temporary."

"Can we see her?"

"Only one visitor. Too many will be overwhelming to her."

"You should go, Mr. Clancy," Kane said, and Mr. Clancy didn't hesitate to follow the doctor down the hall. "I'm going home."

"What's wrong, Kane?" I asked, but he ignored me.

"Sam?" Kane asked.

"I'm here."

"I'll come with you." I said.

"You should stay."

He barely got those words out before he turned and allowed Sam to lead him from the building.

I stood for a while in the same spot, my mind on Kane. One step forward, two steps back. I wanted him in my life and I knew he wanted the same, but maybe his blindness was just too big a hurdle for us to overcome. Maybe our love just wasn't enough anymore. With a heavy heart, I sought out the others.

Kane

As soon as we were out of hearing distance, I told Sam, "I'm about to have an attack."

"I'll get you in the car." Sam practically hauled me to the car, opening the door and helping me in, since he knew it was mere moments before I'd be fully consumed. I barely heard the door close before it was on me: pounding heart, sweating, pins and needles breaking out over my body, and the fear, the fucking fear that stole my breath. Lying back on the seat, I tried for calm, but I knew I'd have to ride it out.

"Are you okay, Kane?" Sam's voice penetrated, the last of the sensations fading.

"How long?" Was that my voice?

"Almost fifteen minutes."

Damn, that was definitely one of the longer ones. "Yeah, I'm okay. Thanks for getting me to the car. I didn't want to freak everyone out, especially with Mrs. Marks in the condition she's in."

"Understood. You want to go back inside, or should I take you home?"

"I think home."

"You got it."

My legs were still unsteady by the time we reached home, so instead of going to my house, I decided to crash in Tea's room. "Thanks, Sam."

"Do you need anything?"

"No, I'm going to sleep, but thanks."

I heard the lock on the front door click and felt the air stir when Sam pushed the door open. "I'll head back to the hospital. You've got your phone right?"

"Yeah."

Zeus greeted me at the door and assisted me up the stairs. Kicking off my shoes, I climbed into Tea's bed and felt as Zeus settled in next to me before I was out.

When I woke, I knew Tea was in the room by her scent. "Tea?"

"Yeah, I'm here. You okay?"

She couldn't have been wearing shoes, because I didn't hear as she approached until I felt the bed dip as she settled next to me.

"How's Mrs. Marks?"

"She's good, the doctors were really happy with all her numbers this morning. Kane, what happened last night?"

I should have told her this already. I hadn't because it was another sign of weakness. "Ever since the fire, I'm overcome with anxiety at times—panic attacks are what my therapist calls them."

"Oh my God."

"I didn't mean to snap at you yesterday, but I really didn't want to freak you out. I knew I didn't have much time before I was completely overtaken by it."

"What happens?" Her voice was soft, concern lacing through her words.

"It feels like a heart attack. You're completely out of control for about ten minutes—your heart races, you feel numb or get pins and needles, you break out into a sweat or get the chills, and, even being unable to stop it, you are cognizant of what is happening."

"That sounds horrible. How often do you get them?"

"I used to have one almost every week, but now they're few and far between. In fact, it's been a while since my last one. I've found that exercise really helps to reduce the occurrences, which is why I use my bar as often as I do."

"Oh."

"What?"

"I thought you were working out your anger issues."

She knew me so well. "In the beginning I absolutely did, but now it's more therapeutic. Except recently—" I stopped midthought. No need to go there.

"What were you going to say?"

"Nothing."

"Kane, talk to me. Recently it's more than therapeutic, so what's causing the anger you need to work through?"

The words just tumbled out. "You and the men you've slept with. I'm having a hard time dealing with that."

"I have slept with five men including you." The sharpness of her voice was proof enough that she was pissed.

"Tea, you don't . . ." And yet hearing that there had been four other men, I wanted to hunt them down and kill them.

"You'll listen because you need to get over it. The first man was Erik. We dated for six months, four and half years after you broke up with me, six months after I learned that you were married. The second man's name was Drake, we dated for a year, Donovan lasted five months, and then there was Colin, on and off again for two years. Every single one of them was sex. I didn't love them, I didn't want a life with them, but I enjoyed them. I'm not sorry for that, Kane. I was, I felt guilty that it was them and not you, but you know what? You're the one who made your bed. Every action that's happened after you broke my heart falls completely on your shoulders. You can't change the past and you can't change me. Just as you are not the same person, neither am I. I've slept with four other men, that's who I am now. Deal with it."

She was gone, her scent fading. "Tea."

"No. Seriously, Kane, it's enough. I was angry at the hospital, because I thought you were pushing me away again. But I can't say that this is any better. You're dealing with a panic disorder but you didn't think to mention that? What would have happened if you'd had an attack when we were alone? Don't you think that would have scared the shit out of me?

"You say you want a life with me, but you need to let me in, all the way. It worked for us before, because we held nothing back, but all you seem to want to do is hold back. And as far as the beauty of what we share, I never had that with anyone but you. Having sex and making love are two entirely different things. We make love, those men gave me sex—scratched an itch—nothing more. You want to move forward and leave the past in the past, then fucking starting living those words. I'm sorry your life turned out so far from how you saw it, I'm sorry you've endured all that you have, but you can only use your tragedy as an excuse for so long."

I don't know how the hell I found her as easily as I did, but I was out of the bed and across the room, pressing her between the wall and my body, in a heartbeat. Her muscles quickened against mine, but it wasn't out of anger or fear, it was desire.

"Am I being unfair? Absolutely. I fucking love you, hell, I'm damn near obsessed with you. I have been ever since I heard you crying on the night you arrived."

"And yet you cut me free." Her voice was barely over a whisper.

"I never should have."

"A point we can agree on."

"I don't want to linger in the past, but I can't help my jealousy. Had it been me who'd slept with others, you can't tell me that wouldn't feel like acid burning in your gut."

"It would, but I can't change the past."

"I know, and that's why I work out the anger on my bar. Eventually, I'll come to terms with it. I'll never like it, but I'll learn to accept it."

"And in the meantime?"

"I want to love you so completely that those other guys are forgotten."

"They already are, Kane. It's only your taste I crave, your touch I seek, your body I want, and your heart that I need. You, only you, always you."

My mouth slammed down on hers, my hands yanking her shirt over her head. Cupping her breasts, I licked the swells, teasing her nipples through the silk of her bra with my thumb. As I flipped the clasp, her breasts spilled out into my hands. There were so many fantasies that had sustained me over the years, so many visions of us that had haunted and teased me, and one of them was that I wanted to fuck her breasts, wanted my shaft cradled between them and the head in her mouth as she sucked me off.

My expression must have given me away. "What do you want, Kane?" I felt her soft hands on my face. "I told you I was all in and I am. I'm not holding back, not with anything. Tell me what you want?"

My hands tightened on her breasts. Without my saying anything, she seemed to understand and directed me to a chair.

"Sit," she ordered.

And I did, happily. I felt when she dropped to her knees between my legs. Her fingers worked my zipper before she pulled the denim down my legs. We'd dressed so quickly earlier I hadn't bothered with briefs. My eyes closed when her hand wrapped around me. I moaned when she moved closer, pushing me into her cleavage as she sucked the head of my dick into her mouth. My hands moved back to her breasts, pressing then together as my hips rocked and, coupled with her sweet, hot mouth working the tip, it wasn't going to take me long. I heard her, the soft mewling in the back of her throat, and I knew she was getting off on pleasuring me. I didn't deserve her, but she was mine. Her hands moved to my thighs, her fingers digging into the flesh, her head moving faster, her beautiful breasts cradling me and I came, loud and long. She swallowed and I growled.

"Stand up and take off your jeans and panties." That came out as more of an order than I intended.

I heard the rustling of her clothes a few seconds before she said, "Okay."

I stood and offered the chair. "Ass on the edge, Tea." As soon as she took it, I dropped to my knees, spread her, and ate her until her scream nearly shattered the windows.

chapter 11

Teagan

Sitting on the floor in the library, resting between Kane's legs as he reclined back against the sofa, contentment settled over me. The scene earlier in my room had been intense, but it had also been cathartic, tearing down the last of the unseen barriers that held Kane and me back. The road wasn't going to be smooth all of a sudden, but at least we were both all in.

Zeus was on the sofa, stretched to take up most of it, his head resting against Kane's thigh.

"So about the inn, what are you going to do with all of the collectibles? Seems risky leaving them out with so many passing through."

"Agreed. Part of the house will be the residence for Mrs. Marks and the others. All the antiques will go with them."

"I like that idea, that they'll still be here but as permanent guests themselves." Turning around so my arms could rest on his thighs, I said. "I really only was surprised before because you hadn't mentioned this idea since we were kids. But I'm guessing you and Mrs. Marks have spoken about it far more often."

"Yeah, after the fire, when I was finally on my feet again, I needed to get involved, keep busy. Even blind, I could sense them all slowing down. They're in their eighties, and this house is a lot to keep up. Mrs. Marks and I discussed it. I knew I was going to need help setting it up, but it seemed like the perfect solution. They don't have to move, and the money we'd make could keep the place going."

"It's brilliant, and you have your house, so you can escape all the people when it gets to be too much."

His head dropped a degree, his eyes on where my hands rested on his legs. Though he couldn't see them, he did feel them. "Our house, Tea. I want the dream, but that doesn't mean I'm not scared of what comes next—of limiting you because I am limited with what I can do. I don't want you to come to resent me. I don't know if I'll have the courage to leave what is familiar to me. I don't know if I'll ever have the strength of will to chase the dream with you. I've been lost a few times, right here in town, and I can't tell you how debilitating it is."

My throat tightened on hearing the insecurity and doubt he felt, another scar left from the fire. "After I saw your burns, learned you were blind, I tried to walk from my bed to the door with my eyes closed and nearly face-planted. Then I went into the west wing and tried to find my way to the door. I was so scared, wanted to open my eyes, but I knew you would never be free of the darkness. I never even found the door. I burned myself too."

"What? Where?" I reached for his hand and brushed his fingers over the healing wound. "Why would you do that?"

"I was trying to see what it had been like for you. I couldn't stand the pain, and it's just a small burn. The thought of you . . . the pain, the darkness." Tears welled in my eyes. "You say you don't know if you'll have the strength of will, but you already do. To have come as far as you have, overcoming all that you have, you leave me in awe."

He pulled me into his lap, cradled my cheek with his hand, and kissed me. He molded his lips to mine, tasting and savoring. His other hand lifted to frame my face, and he kissed me deeper, his tongue sliding into my mouth to stroke my own. Straddling him, I reached for his shirt. His mouth pulled from mine to object.

"Don't," was all I said before discarding his shirt. My fingertips moved along his scarred skin. "Can you feel that?"

"Not in the sense you mean, but because it's you, yes."

My lips replaced my fingers. He inhaled, his fingers on my thighs tightening. Moving up his neck, my tongue ran along his jaw, my hands roaming over him, feeling him with my fingers like he now did with me. Trailing down his stomach, lower to the bulge pressing against his jeans, I rubbed him through the denim, heard the groan that rumbled up his throat. Like in our youth, my breasts felt fuller and the ache started. I needed him. I couldn't wait another second to feel him inside me. I didn't care that we were in the library, didn't care that the door wasn't locked.

Unzipping him, I pulled him free.

"Tea."

"Please," was all I said. His fingers curled around my waist, sliding my pants down my legs, only the one leg sliding off completely. Pushing my panties aside, he pushed up as I sank down. My moan couldn't be stopped as he filled me so completely. For a moment we didn't move, savoring being connected. Lifting up, he was almost completely out before I sank back down again. We found our rhythm as we slowly brought each other to climax. With all the times we had made love, this was the most profound. Wrapping me in his arms, still inside me, we stayed like that for a long time.

⁂

As I sat in the kitchen with Mrs. T, Simon came strutting in with Mr. Clancy right behind him.

"Look who I found loitering outside," said Mr. Clancy.

Jumping from my spot at the table, I threw myself into Simon's arms. "Hey."

"Hey, sugar. How's Mrs. Marks?"

"She's good, better."

"I'm happy to hear that." He hugged me hard, his lips brushing over my ear to whisper, "I brought back a chocolate cake from Sunshine."

Jerking away, I beamed. "We have to share with Kane."

"Oh yes."

He looked past me to the others. "Hello, Mrs. T. So, let's discuss the feast you're preparing in my honor."

⁂

We were at Kane's—Simon on the chair, Kane and me on the sofa. Sunshine's cake was on the table, though mostly gone. Kane had me pressed so closely to him while he laughed at whatever it was Simon was talking about. I had never seen him so relaxed, smiling without reservation.

"My parents want to throw us a party at the shop."

This comment from Simon pulled my wandering mind back to the conversation. "Why?"

"To say 'Congratulations, you're a success,' appeasing their ever-present guilt. Who knows?" Simon's parents took an active role in their son's life and, by extension, mine.

"Not necessary, but it'd be good for business," I said.

"That was my thought too."

"Will you come?" I asked Kane and knew his answer as his body tensed next to mine.

"Never mind," I whispered, not wishing to bring up a subject I knew we didn't see eye to eye on.

"I'm going to crash on the sofa, you okay with that, Kane?"

"Yeah."

Standing so Kane could follow, I moved around the table and kissed Simon good night. "See you in the morning."

"Sleep well." His eyes were twinkling more than usual. Idiot.

Back in Kane's room, I stared at the pictures on his table. Maybe it was wrong of me to want him to leave what was familiar to him, but I did.

"Tea?"

"Yes."

"I can sleep in the other room."

"Why?"

"You're mad."

"I'm not mad. I just . . . I hate that I can't share so much with you about my life. I can't tell you how many times in the past nine years I've thought 'Kane would love this'—a restaurant, a walk along the water, the sight of the sailboats anchored there."

His words were so softly spoken. "I can't see those sailboats."

"Not with your eyes, but like you told me, you can see with more than your eyes, you can see with your heart and I'm your heart, Kane. I could give that to you."

The door closed, the lock flipped, and then he was across the room. His hands framed my face, and his fingers threaded through my hair a second before his mouth sealed over mine. As soon as our lips touched, an electric jolt burned through me, starting where our lips were locked and traveling over every nerve from the very tip of my head to my toes. Shock and the most intense feeling of want kept me from reacting. His mouth was soft yet demanding, his taste was intoxicating, and his tongue insistent, running along my lips, tasting me with each pass. This was a different Kane, a more primal, wild Kane, and I loved that he was allowing himself to let go, that he was comfortable enough with me to let go. So consumed by him, I hadn't realized I wasn't kissing him back.

His voice sounded raw when he demanded against my lips, "Kiss me back."

At those words, I snapped out of my sensory overload. Reaching around him to hold him close, my mouth opened, my tongue touching his. It wasn't frantic, our kiss, even though that was how I was feeling, the overwhelming need to touch and taste every inch of him; it was more a leisurely exploration.

His fingers tightened on my scalp, then one of his hands moved to the back of my neck, applying pressure at the nape, which sent chills shooting down my spine. Forgetting everything except the man in my arms, I molded myself against his hard body as my hands moved under his shirt to touch him, the warm skin hard with muscle. In response, he trailed his hand down my back, along my spine, then over my ass to pull me hard against him.

His kiss was drugging, pulling me under into sweet oblivion. The moan that escaped my lips was a plea begging for more. He responded, taking the kiss deeper, sweeping my mouth with his tongue. Pressing me to him, he ground his hips against me while his mouth feasted on mine.

So consumed by what he was doing with his hands and mouth, I didn't realize he had backed me up to the bed until I felt it hit the back of my legs. His fingers were working my nightgown strap, and with a good tug, my dress pooled at my feet. Without missing a beat, he cupped my breasts, his thumbs running over the nipples that were so hard they hurt. Pulling his mouth from mine, he looked hungry. Running his tongue over my nipple, his pulled it between his teeth, applying enough pressure to make the ache between my legs throb, before sucking me deep into his mouth. My knees went weak. Grabbing his arms to keep myself up, he moved to the neglected breast, turning me boneless with just his mouth.

"Touch me," he commanded softly. Lifting his shirt over his head, I licked each one of the muscles of his six-pack, moving my mouth up and over him, kissing every inch of him. I felt his muscles quicken when I reached his scars, but he didn't pull away. Working the snap of his jeans, I moved them down his legs, my hands sliding down his thigh muscles.

"Touch me." Again the command, but since I wanted to touch him, I did. Palming him through his boxer briefs, I rubbed his hard length. Wanting to feel him, I pulled his briefs down and loved seeing him so hard with his need for me. Wrapping my hand around him, hard as steel and soft as velvet, I watched his face as I worked him.

Long fingers danced down my stomach and between my legs, I widened my stance so he had better access to the aching nub. His thumb moved over that pleasure point as his fingers slid lower and pushed into me. My hips moved, pushing him deeper, as my hand moved up that hard shaft, squeezing the tip before sliding back down. My stomach muscles tightened as his fingers brought me to the edge of orgasm. Swelling in my hand, his hips rocked along with mine and I wanted to feel him come, wanted to see his face, but he moved.

Tossing me onto the bed, he pounced so all that magnificent, muscled maleness surrounded me. Lifting my hips, he rubbed himself over my wet heat, focusing the tip on my aching nub. He pushed into me, only the tip, before pulling out. My body was clenching, desperate for him, and yet he continued to play, driving me crazy with his teasing.

His expression turned darker, his need overpowering his teasing. Lifting my hips, he slammed into me hard. So hard it hurt a bit, but the pain coupled with the pleasure had me spiraling into the most intense oxygen-depriving orgasm of my life. His thrusts were relentless, hard, fast, and deep, prolonging the pleasure just as he came, his body tensing and his muscles flexing. The low growl from deep in his throat was the sexiest sound I'd ever heard.

I awoke in the middle of the night to the feel of Kane tasting me on the inside, his head between my legs, and his tongue buried deep inside of me, his hands on my ass, lifting me up so he could more fully feast. Shamelessly, I grabbed his head and moved my hips against his mouth. He stroked me to yet another orgasm and then lapped at me like a cat at a bowl of milk. When he climbed from the bed, I rested up on my elbows.

"Where are you going?"

Standing just to the right of me, he was a picture—every inch of him naked and so fucking beautiful, including his scars. My eyes drifted lower; he was aroused, big, hard, and thick. As I stared, his hand wrapped around his erection, his legs spread a bit, and he started stroking himself.

"Kane?"

"For years, all I had was this, my hand and my memories. Can't go back to that, can't spend the rest of my life away from you, your body, your heart, or your soul."

My heart was aching right along with my body. Moving to sit on the edge of the bed, I reached for him and pulled him closer.

Pushing aside his hand, I touched him, a gentle touch, tracing the veins, running over the tip, then down to the base. The muscles of his abs flexed when my tongue touched the tip of him, then ran under the shaft and back up again. Gripping his hips, I moved to the edge of the bed and took him into my mouth.

His hips jerked, his eyes closed, and his hands moved to my hair, his fingertips applying pressure while I pleasured him. Stroking the length of him with my tongue, his hips started to move as he thrust into my mouth.

"Tea," he growled and moved so fast, pulling from me, then lifting me as he fell onto his back, gripping my hips and yanking me down onto his mouth. Surprised at the intensity of his loving, the wildness of his need, I lost myself to the sensation burning through me. Arching my back, I rode his face for a minute as his tongue drove into me. Bending forward, I took him into my mouth again as my hands squeezed the sac between his legs. My hips were pumping, his were rocking, and just when his saltiness filled my mouth, I came again.

We laid cuddled into the other, my head resting on his shoulder. My body had never been so sated, my heart never so full.

"I'll come with you to Boston."

Shifting myself so I was partially sitting up, I studied Kane's face. "Are you serious?" I was almost afraid to ask.

"Yeah, its time I broke with the familiar."

No words would come, so instead I kissed him with everything I was unable to say.

In the morning, I took a shower while Kane was still asleep. I was guessing he was really tired after our night of lovin', and then the door of the shower opened.

"You didn't wake me." He pressed me against the tile wall, my breasts flat against that cold hard surface, his mouth on my neck, and his erection between my legs. Tilting my ass back, he teased me by slipping just the tip in. He played like this for a while before his hand reached for the dispenser of soap. Lathering, he proceeded to wash my body, taking a good long time between my legs: the sting of the soap coupled with his fingers pushing into me felt so good. Before I wanted him to, he stopped and turned me to him. His hands palming my breasts, squeezing and teasing.

Returning the favor, I reached for the soap and lathered him up, sliding my hands down his body, over his chest and abs, to the hard length of him. Up and down I worked him, squeezing and pumping, until I felt his shaft getting harder and thicker. Watching his face as he came, feeling his hot seed spilling out over my hand, was brilliant. His hand joined mine, our fingers linking, as his orgasm moved through him. And then he was moving my hand with his down my body to between my legs.

"Touch yourself here," he ordered just as he dropped to his knees, spread me, and pushed his tongue deep. Brilliant, fucking brilliant.

Kane

Tea went back to sleep after our shower. I had worn her out, and I felt damn smug about that. Our lovemaking had been more raw. I liked that too. Finding my jeans, I pulled them on. Zeus at my side, I headed for the kitchen. Simon was there. I heard him moving around.

"Just put on the coffee. I'll make some scrambled eggs, if that's okay," he said by way of greeting.

"Yeah."

"Can Zeus have some?"

Zeus barked. He never barked unless it was about him and food. I chuckled, "Yeah."

"Is Teagan still sleeping?"

I could tell by Simon's tone that he knew how we'd spent most of the night and morning. We hadn't been particularly quiet.

"Yeah." Resting up against the wall, I listened as Simon worked in the kitchen like a man who knew his way around one. I had been hoping to get Simon alone. I had wanted to talk with him ever since he had come to see me that day. As much as I didn't want to hear the details, I needed to. I needed to know just what I had put Tea through. "What was it like for Tea, after . . ."

I heard the skillet pulling from the heat and knew that Simon had turned to face me. "Honestly? Terrifying. She was lost. She'd given up. She wouldn't get out of bed for weeks, wouldn't engage, almost flunked out. Looking into her eyes—forgive the expression—you'd see nothing, no sparkle, no humor, no Teagan. Emptiness and, just beneath that, pain. I really believed that she wasn't going to pull through it."

"She did, though," I said.

"Yes, after I pushed her to get professional help. She learned to move on, learned to cope, but she never got over it. There was always a part of her held back from people. She never stopped mourning you, the life you two were supposed to have. She never missed a sunrise. I'd catch her staring at it like it was the first time she was seeing one. I asked her once what was so fascinating about seeing the sun coming up that she never missed one. She said it wasn't the sun, but the memories that drew her to the window every morning. I never understood what was so damn special about the two of you that it deserved such loyalty, especially after learning that you had moved on and married another. But being here, and seeing the two of you, I get it now. And Teagan . . . that spark's back."

My chest ached. It was worse than I'd imagined, and I'd imagined it was really bad. "I thought I was doing the right thing."

"I know. I hated you, wanted to pound the shit out of you for hurting her so callously, but knowing now why you did it, I think you were right."

My head snapped up at that. "Really?"

"I think if she had been there, if she had seen you right after the fire and the months and years after, where you struggled just to live, it would have changed her. She would have been there, no question, but seeing the one she loved going through something so horrific would have altered her. And with everything that came after, it wouldn't just be you dealing with the feelings of helplessness, but her too. Can you imagine how she'd be now? She'd smother you and you'd grow resentful. It sucks not having the one you need most with you, but in the end, I think you made the right call. Despite all the pain it caused on both sides."

Hearing my own rationale being validated eased some of my guilt. "Have you said this to Tea?"

"She isn't ready to hear it, but she's a smart cookie. Of course, I'm a single gay man who has had only one meaningful relationship, so I may not have a clue what the fuck I'm talking about."

"You agree with me, so I think you're a very wise man," I managed to get out without laughing.

"Let me get these eggs on. I'm not liking the way Zeus is eyeing my leg."

"Thanks, Simon."

His voice sounded a little funny—"Yeah, no problem."

chapter 12

Teagan

Kane had left earlier to work at the library. My feet hadn't quite touched the ground since he'd told me he'd come to Boston. He was making that step for me. What was even better, he seemed excited about the trip.

Simon and I had just returned from the hospital, and, though Mrs. Marks hadn't regained her ability to speak, she was staying awake for longer stretches, even though she was still a bit out of it.

"Have you heard anything from the PI on Mr. Sleazy?" I had googled Sleazy and, though there was all kinds of press shit out there on him—the man really seemed impressed with himself—nothing I'd learned helped me understand how he'd heard of Raven's Peak.

"I did, he called last night. We have a phone meeting with him . . ." He looked at his watch. "About now, actually."

Sitting in the study, I listened to Simon's PI on speakerphone. "Dimitri Falco, born 1986 to Francesca and Joseph Falco in Greenwich, Connecticut. Got decent grades, parents are pretty affluent, went to Yale for undergraduate and graduate. Estranged from his parents after a few priceless pieces from their home went missing, parents convinced he took them. Logical, since the man likes the finer things but doesn't usually have the money for them. Bought himself a top-of-the-line Jag a year ago, when he was floating on a wad of cash; the cash dwindled, and he couldn't afford the payments, so it got repossessed. Passed the bar on the first go, worked as an associate for a year before getting hired by Connelly, Drake, and Bowen. I've been looking for the connection between Falco and Bowen and found something, Bowen's daughter, Camille, also attended Yale at the same time as Falco. She flunked out early into the second year. They may not have known each other, but the connection deserves a closer look."

"Thanks for getting on this so quickly," Simon said.

"You bet. I'll call when I know more."

Simon hung up the phone. "So what do you think about the lovely Camille going to school with Sleazy?"

"Not a coincidence. I couldn't figure out how he'd learned of Raven's Peak, but now we know. I'm guessing his interest is getting his hands on some of Mrs. Marks's priceless pieces, like he allegedly did with his parents. It seems to fit what we know about him. Learning there was a treasure trove like Raven's Peak ripe for the picking was no doubt too tempting for him. That I get."

"And Camille?"

"She loved this place—she wanted to live here with Kane. When we were younger, she threatened him that she'd get him back for not sharing her ridiculous plans for the future. She's still nosing around, stopping by to chat with him." The lightbulb in my head flashed on. "Maybe she isn't really here to chat with Kane. Maybe she's eyeing some of the pieces she's drooled over since our youth. Maybe she plans on getting Sleazy to steal them. I wouldn't put it past her."

"Well, she did claim that her waitressing gig was temporary. Maybe her little scam with Sleazy was what she was alluding to."

"Possibly, but what I don't get is her father. Why would a well-respected man hire someone with a past like his? There had to be something that forced Bowen's hand."

"You're right. You think it could be related to Camille flunking out? Embarrassment for her old man? Maybe he brushed that failure under the rug and Sleazy found it?"

"I don't know, I don't get how the minds of the super rich work. Maybe. Seems kind of stupid to stake the reputation of your firm and yourself on the fact that your daughter isn't the sharpest knife in the drawer. All anyone has to do is talk to her to figure that out."

"Ha! True but funny." He laughed, leaning across the table. "Maybe we should hang a shingle and go into business."

"Investigation? Nah, leave that for the Scooby gang."

"Tell me you're ecstatic that Kane's agreed to come to Boston."

"Yes. He's going to love it. I can't wait to take him to the marina, and I know he can't see the boats, but I'll describe them to him, and he can run his hand over them."

"You're really good about that with him."

"What do you mean?"

"Without being asked, you describe a scene for him so he's a part of it. And having never been around a blind person before, it's instinct. I think that's what I find so fascinating about the two of you. You move as if you're attached, effortlessly from one to the other. It's like one mind and two bodies. I had never believed in soul mates, but now I've seen it with my own eyes."

A warmth moved through me hearing Simon describe how he saw Kane and me, because he was exactly right. "It's been like that with us since our very first meeting. I never felt uncomfortable with him, actually quite the opposite. I only ever felt truly comfortable with him."

"It's the same for him. He isn't one to show emotion, but whenever you're near, he's more relaxed—the hardness of his jaw eases, his shoulders aren't so square."

"That's love, Simon. It isn't just a feeling, it's a state of being."

"I need to find me that."

"Usually happens when you're not even looking for it."

"Good to know. All right, I'm smelling something sinful, so let's go pester Mrs. T to let us sample it."

He rose and started for the door, and I followed. "Kane's probably back. I'll go see if he wants to join us."

He stopped in the door and turned to me. "Call him."

"What?"

"Call him. He has a phone. You don't need to go get him. I know your instinct is to keep him close, to hold his hand, to be his eyes. But, Tea, you're also the woman he loves and, as a man, he needs to feel in control of himself. He needs you to see that just because he's blind, it doesn't mean he can't be all the things you need him to be. You undermine that every time you act in any way you wouldn't normally, placing his blindness right there between you."

"I didn't . . . I . . ." Pulling a hand through my hair, I felt ill, because Simon was absolutely right. "I didn't realize I was doing that." Clarity came. "That's why he doesn't want my help."

"Yep."

"God, I'm an idiot."

He wrapped his arm around me. "Not an idiot, just overprotective. But he's the man in the relationship, and he needs you to know that he can protect you sometimes."

My arms wrapped around his waist, happiness making me feel almost giddy. "You are a very wise man, Simon."

"You are not the first to say that, and it's true—wise, handsome, charming, witty—I've got it all, except for food in my stomach, so let's call Kane and get some before I wither away."

Later that night, Kane and I were spooning in my bed. Zeus was at the foot, stretched out and snoring. My stomach was full, my body sated, Kane's naked body pressed up against mine. Life was good. Remembering the phone call from the PI, I turned to Kane, my head resting next to his on the pillow.

"Want to hear something interesting?"

His fingers drifted up and down my spine, the sensation so soothing. "What?"

"Camille and Mr. Sleazy both went to Yale at the same time. And now Mr. Sleazy works for her dad. And he's here in the house that Camille coveted as a kid."

His jaw clenched. "You don't think it's a coincidence."

"Nope. He has a habit of spending beyond his means. He's estranged from his parents because of stealing some valuables from them. Seems to me he's not here to update documents but to case the joint."

"Well, shit. You couldn't have picked a better mark, three old people and a blind man watching over the place." Bitterness dripped from his voice.

"Stop."

"Seriously, I could be sitting right there in the library and he could be stealing us blind, fucking pun intended."

"You said it yourself—your life has limitations now. The fact that you can't see some criminal invade your home under the guise of a friend . . . most sighted people wouldn't be able to see that either."

"You did."

"Only because Simon and I often have encountered people like Sleazy in our business, grifters who come with 'rare' treasures that they're willing to sell to us at a discount. The first few we fell for, but after getting burned a few times, we got wise to it. Had I not experienced that, I wouldn't have picked up on Sleazy's intentions either."

Leaning over him, I rested my arms on his chest. "You're blind."

"Thanks for pointing that out."

I slapped him, but playfully. "Let me finish. You're blind, and yet you know every inch of this house without needing to feel your way around. You can get into a boat and cross a body of water, climb the steps up to Raven's Peak, and find your way inside like a sighted man. You're building a boat and doing whatever kind of fighting you are with that man, often kicking his ass. You're beating Mr. Clancy in chess, and you make love like a god. Don't be so hard on yourself."

He was silent for such a long time that I had no idea what he was thinking. "There's somewhere I'd like to take you. Will you come with me?"

"Yes.

"You don't even want to know where?"

"I'll be with you. Where doesn't really matter."

He rolled so I was pinned under him, a grin tugging at the corner of his mouth. "Tell me more about me making love like a god."

"Why tell when you can show me?"

"I like the way your mind works."

"Shut up and kiss me."

Walking down the brightly lit corridor, my stomach roiled and my hands were damp from nerves. The place Kane wanted to take me was the burn unit of the hospital, the place where he had spent almost a full year of his life. As soon as we entered the sealed doors, the nurses at the station moved from around the desk to greet him warmly.

"Kane, you're early this month," one nurse, whose name tag declared her to be Lydia, said affectionately. "And who is this?"

"This is Tea."

At the announcement, three sets of eyes flew to mine like I was a celebrity or something. In the next second, I was being hugged hard by Lydia. "So nice to meet you."

Clearly. "You too." I sounded lame, but I had a suspicion there was more to the pointed stares I was receiving. Mr. Clancy had mentioned that Kane had called out for me; was that why they were looking at me the way they were?

"You'll have to suit up. Kane knows the way," Lydia said before adding, "it means so much to the patients. Thank you for coming."

Since I didn't know what I was doing yet, I only smiled at her. Kane reached for my hand and started pulling me down the hallway. We entered a locker room with gowns wrapped in plastic and boxes of latex gloves.

"Kane?"

"I come every month, sometimes a few times. Remembering what it was like, I come and sit with some of the more severe cases. Just the sense of another human presence can make all the difference."

My eyes stung and a lump formed in my throat. "Who came to see you?"

"More than I needed and not the one I wanted."

"I would have been camped in your room, would have handcuffed myself to your bed."

"I know."

I needed to be calm for these people, but I suspected I was going to have a major crying jag, which, considering the amount of crying I'd been doing lately, wasn't that much of a surprise.

"Okay. What do I have to do?"

⁂

The patient's name was Jerry Beck. He had been on vacation with his girlfriend when the gas grill they were using malfunctioned and burned part of his upper body. The girlfriend didn't stick around after that, and Jerry had been in the burn unit for over two months. His skin was so tender, the pain in his eyes so pronounced, I actually felt his pain in my own body. And yet, he was smiling and laughing, finding something to be happy about despite his circumstances. People based strength on physical ability, but real strength comes from within, like with Jerry and Kane. People who find the will to continue on, even when they're at their very lowest.

"You're here with Kane?"

"Yeah. He's with another patient."

"Don't know what I would have done without him."

"He visits you often?"

"Yeah, he arranged for my mom to visit too."

"He did?"

"My mom's alone and she doesn't have money, so when she heard what happened, she couldn't get to me. I know it just tore her up. And then one day she's here. Kane paid for her trip and even set her up in some place for the duration of her visit."

I was going to start crying right there in Jerry's room.

"I guess having been where we all are, he gets it. Not a lot of people would do that, take such an active interest. He's a good guy."

"You have no idea."

I managed to make it out of Jerry's room, discarding my gown and gloves in the red can marked for them, and down the hall to the locker room before I lost it. Sliding down the wall, pulling my knees toward me, I cried. I cried for Jerry and his mom, I cried for all those other beds filled with burn victims, but mostly I cried for Kane, because I could see him in Jerry's place.

The door opened; I jerked my head up, expecting to see Kane, but it was Lydia. She settled next to me on the floor.

"He used to call out for you. Every day, all day long. I couldn't imagine what kind of person wouldn't come to the one she loved when he'd needed her the most. Years later, he explained who you were and why you never came. And then I hurt for you too, being so ruthlessly pushed from his life.

"I've been doing this job for a really long time. I know people handle grief differently, but that first day Kane came walking into the unit, holding on to the wall because he couldn't see where he was going, he stood just in the doors, asking if it would be all right for him to sit with one of the patients. At first I thought he was acting out of contrition, that he had some horrible things in his past he was trying to do penitence for, but that isn't it. With all he's suffered, including the loss of you, he comes in here looking to offer comfort to strangers."

Now I wasn't just crying, I was weeping.

She reached for my hand, her hold strong but affectionate. "Got to tell ya, I'm really happy to see you walking through those doors with him. If anyone deserves to be reunited with his loved one, it's that man."

And before I could say anything, she stood and slipped from the room. I washed up—though one look at me, and it would be clear I'd been crying—and then I went in search of Kane. He was sitting in a little kid's room: the child's face was wrapped, his hair mostly gone. His parents were in the room too, sleeping, as Kane held a book in his lap, his fingers moving over the pages. He was afraid he wasn't the boy he had been, but he was so wrong. He was my Kane, older, wiser, maybe a little more hardened, but he was still the boy who came to me and offered comfort, the boy who used to help our elderly neighbors carry their groceries home, the boy who ran into a burning building to save the life of another. We were better together than apart. We were apart when he'd walked into that burning building, apart for the past nine years that were filled with so much pain. No more. No more sadness, no more tears. We were together again, finally, and that was something to celebrate.

A half an hour later, he too was dumping his gown in the can. I stepped up next to him and took his hand. Pulling him down the hallway, I led us to the stairwell, and, as soon as the door closed at his back, I curled into him, wrapped my arms around his waist, and kissed him. It took him a few beats to respond before his mouth was moving, his tongue searching for mine, his fingers threading through my hair, his palms settling behind my ears in both possession and tenderness. We were both breathing heavy when we finally ended the kiss many, many minutes later. "What was that for?"

"Just because."

Even though he couldn't see, his gaze searched mine. "Can you tell me what I did, so I can do it again, and often?" he asked.

"Just being you."

"So I have more of those in my future."

"Oh yes, you do."

"Excellent." His fingers traced the features of my face. "You're blushing."

"How can you possibly know that?"

"There's heat right here." His thumb trailed over my cheek. "I loved making you blush, watching your cheeks turn all rosy."

"Now you feel it."

"Yes, almost as good. Thank you for coming with me."

"I'd like to come again."

"I was hoping you would."

Wrapping his arm around my shoulders, we started down the stairs. "I've been thinking . . ." I said.

"A dangerous pastime."

I punched him in the gut playfully. He used to say that to me all the time growing up.

"You hit harder." At least that's what I think he said, since he was laughing.

"Anyway, I think it's time to properly welcome Simon to the family. What do you say?"

He looked downright wicked in response. "Oh, I think that is a brilliant idea."

"We can get started as soon as we get home."

His arm on me tightened. "Yeah, home."

"Are you serious?" Mrs. T looked conflicted, not knowing if she should laugh or discipline Kane and me. "You do realize that you are all grown adults."

The way Kane's head turned to mine like he was confused, the same very way he did when we were kids, made me roar with laughter. His face was so serious, as if we were discussing the cure for cancer.

"Come on, please?" Again Kane was talking just like he used to when we were younger; that particular voice had always worked and, as it happened, it still did.

"Fine."

Kane grabbed my hand as we ran out the back door.

At dinner, Kane and I sat at the chairs closest to the doorway. Mrs. T placed Simon's potpie in front of him. "It's tradition in our house to break off the top crust. My homemade churn butter is just delicious with that warm crust."

"That does sound good. You guys aren't eating?" Simon asked, but he wasn't really that interested, because he loved food. The fact that we weren't eating was of no matter.

"No, we ate on the way home from the hospital," I lied.

"God, this smells really great, Mrs. T."

Kane's hand was wrapped around mine; I was supposed to squeeze it when Simon pulled off the crust. And as Kane had done when he was a kid, Simon lifted the crust, and then his eyes went wide and he looked across the table, but Kane and I were already halfway out the door.

"What the fuc—Teagan!"

He was in pursuit, pie in hand, but there was no way I was wearing worms. Kane and I had grown up in that house; we knew every room. We tucked into a small room off another room. "How long do you think he'll look?" Kane asked.

"Not long, maybe five minutes, before he's back in the kitchen sweet talking Mrs. T into something to eat."

"So we've got some time," Kane said cryptically.

"For what?"

And then he was kissing me. It started off as fun but quickly turned hot. His hands on my bare thighs curled my toes as he moved my skirt up my legs. As he lifted me, my legs wrapped around his waist, and my arms sought his neck, pulling him closer. Sucking his tongue into my mouth, I stroked it with my own. Pressing me back against the wall, one of his hands left my body to work his zipper. He slid into me, and I yanked my mouth from his, bit my lip, closed my eyes, and rode the waves of pleasure. Tightening my thighs, my calves pressing against his ass, I urged him to go deeper, move faster, and when I came, he swallowed my cry just as his own orgasm burned through him.

We found Simon after our interlude and, as I suspected, he was eating with the others, completely undisturbed by the worm potpie. We apologized for the trick. He forgave us after some posturing. Much later, we all went off to bed. But as soon as Simon disappeared into his room, we snuck out to stand just outside his door. Five minutes after he closed his door, Simon screamed, "I am going to kill you, Teagan."

We ran back to my room and slammed and locked the door.

"What number was that?" Kane asked.

"Kane 226."

A toad in the bed—classic.

Kane

I didn't know if I wanted to follow through with this. Tea and I were parked down the street from my mom's new home. Whatever had caused my mom to run from me, she was thrilled at the idea of seeing me again. I wasn't on the same page. She had left me and now she had a new life. No children—I think if there had been children, I wouldn't have reached out to her. To leave your kid only to have more, no, I wouldn't have understood that. The fact that

Tea had asked about children when she had spoken to Mr. Lawson just showed how well she knew me.

Without having to ask her, Tea was describing my mom's house to me. "It's a small Cape, painted white with black shutters. There's a small postage-stamp lawn with gardens and a seminew-looking blue car in the driveway. It's cozy."

I loved that she did that, brought me into the scene without having to be asked. She knew exactly what I needed.

"Are you ready, or do you want a few more minutes?" she asked.

"No, I think I'm ready."

"Okay." I heard her car door open, so I opened mine too, holding the door for Zeus. We waited for her to come around the car. She handed me Zeus's leash, taking my other hand and linking our fingers. We started down the street.

"There are about ten houses on each side of the street. It's a small little neighborhood off one of the major roads that runs through the town. It's lined with maple trees, the leaves all red now. There are a few kids playing: some at a basketball net that's set up on the curb in front of one of the houses, and others are riding their bikes or playing ball. Several yards are fenced in, many with dogs who look like they want to jump the fences so they can play. We're going to cross the street now."

Her hold on my hand tightened, and, as much as I loved the gesture, I also felt bitter that she needed to guide me, that I wasn't able to do it myself. It was stupid, but, of all the people in my life, I wanted to be strong for her, wanted *her* to be able to rely on *me*.

Her next words shouldn't have surprised me, but they did. "I love you blind or sighted, so stop overthinking it."

It was my turn to ask, "How did you know what I was thinking?"

"I've known you since you were eleven. Plus, your hand stiffened a bit in mine. I knew you were having a negative thought, probably about me needing to help you across the street like a little old lady."

"Little old lady?"

"Well, I imagine whatever you're thinking isn't very flattering to you. But you should know, Kane, a person looking at us would see two people in love walking their dog."

I just knew the face I was getting, had seen it countless times growing up. In that moment, it really hit me: She was back, she was with me, she was my Tea again. Emotions tightened my voice, turning it rough. "Glad it's you walking me across the street."

Clearly she liked what I'd said, "Me too. We're just at their driveway. There are three steps to reach their front door. I'll let Zeus take over." Her voice had turned warm, with a husky edge that lit a fire in me.

Zeus was amazing. I had been dead set against the idea when Mrs. Marks had suggested it. I'd been in denial, believing I could get along just as well as I had when I was sighted. Now I didn't know what I'd do without him. Smart and loyal, he had kept me company and made the darkness seem not quite as dark. Reaching the door, I felt Tea at my side.

"You ready?" she asked.

"Yeah."

I heard Tea knock, then heard the sound of feet coming from down the hall, the rate and clip of them suggesting the person was excited. Then the sound of the lock disengaging, the swoosh of air as the door opened, and the subtle scent of her perfume—a scent that took me back to when I was a kid. Memories bombarded me; luckily Tea had a hold of my hand, or I'd have likely been swept away by the rush of them.

"Kane?" I never forgot the sound of her voice. And though I had recently heard it over the phone, it wasn't the same as hearing it in person.

"Mom."

Her voice pitched deeper; I could hear the tears in it. "Sweetheart, are you blind?"

Again, she used an endearment for me; rarely did she call me Kane. "It's a long story. Mom, this is Tea."

"Hello, Mrs. Nesbit. It's very nice to meet you. And this is Zeus."

"Please, come inside."

Tea led me inside, her soft voice guiding me through the house, describing what she was seeing. We settled in a room painted a pale blue with Queen Anne–style furniture. I had no idea what Queen Anne–style furniture was, but I didn't mention that. Apparently, a tray was already set on the table with iced tea and cookies.

"The sofa is right behind you—feel it on the back of your legs?"

"Yep, thanks Tea."

Once settled, Tea sitting pressed right up against me on one side and Zeus on the other, I heard my mom offering me a glass of iced tea.

"Please." Something cool and wet to help ease the dryness in my throat sounded good.

When she touched me, guiding the glass into my hand, a sharp pain erupted in my chest and my eyes stung. I didn't realize until that moment how much I had missed my mother's touch, even for something so simple as handing me a glass. I took a sip and found the table with my free hand to place the glass down.

"Please, you must tell me what happened." Her voice sounded a bit hysterical, and I understood. It had to be a shock to see your child so many years later and so altered. So I summed up the nearly two decades that had passed, everything from Tea's arrival to the fire to her return. And in sharing my story, I realized that every major moment had been with Tea. I wanted Tea to share all my major moments, and I was glad she was there with me then. She must have realized the same thing, because her warm hand found mine, and she held it tightly. I wished I could see her face in that moment, so I touched her with my free hand, along her lips that were tilted slightly up, along her cheeks that curved a bit from her smile, along the small indents near her eyes that were smiling right along with her lips, along the silky brows that were arched every so slightly.

"I like to see you smile."

She pressed her face on my shoulder, sending a dampness through my shirt. Unlinking our fingers, I moved my arm around her shoulders and pulled her against me.

"You're beautiful together." I had completely forgotten my mom was watching us.

"I worried, after I left, but Mrs. Marks assured me she would take care of you. It looks as if she did."

Bitterness pierced the moment, reminding me of why I was there. "Why did Mrs. Marks agree to take me?"

"I suppose I need to explain why I left. I didn't want to go. I loved you so much, but I was ill. My bipolar disorder was not under control. I'd take my meds, but they made me feel so out of it. I really thought I could control the swings, that I didn't need the meds. I'd go off, and everything would be great, and then I'd drop, sink far lower than I ever had before. I worked at Raven's Peak, and one day, when I knew the others were gone for the day, I was on the cliff. I planned to walk right off it. Mrs. Marks hadn't gone off with the others; she had stayed behind to watch me. She was the one to stop me; she brought me back into the house and called my doctor. I thought she was going to have me arrested, I couldn't blame her if she had, but instead we talked about her son."

That came as news. "Mrs. Marks has a son?"

"She probably doesn't talk about it because it's too painful, but I know she wouldn't mind me sharing with you what she shared with me. She had a son. She had him later in life after a brief affair. The man didn't last, but the way her face lit up when she talked about her son, she had clearly been thrilled to learn she was having a baby. When he reached his early teens, he started showing the early signs of schizophrenia. It was years later that he went off his meds, because they made him feel like mine made me feel. The hallucinations got so bad that he ended up killing himself. He hanged himself in his room."

So that was why she had those odd sad days growing up, every year on the same day. That day must have been the anniversary of his birthday or of his death. Tea must have realized the same thing, since I heard her soft gasp.

"She didn't want to see the same thing happen, couldn't bear the thought of someone else losing their battle with their own demons. She paid closer attention to me, making sure I was seeing my doctor, urging my doctors to make sure they found the drug combination that didn't make me feel so out of it. Everyone at Raven's Peak took a more active role with you—Mrs. Marks never told them why. She didn't need to, because they just loved spending time with you, so I had some space to find my balance.

The day you fell down the stairs, I had gone off my meds again. It was my day off, and we were home. We were playing, and I pushed you. I hadn't meant to, and you probably don't remember. All you remember was the fun we were having. I called her, before I even called nine-one-one. I hadn't hurt myself—I'd hurt my beautiful son. I will never forget the look on your face, staring at me in such pain, wanting me to make it go away. And I was the reason you were in that pain. I waited until I knew you were going to be okay. I visited you when you were sleeping, signed over my parental rights, and then two days later I committed myself. Never again would I put you at risk. Mrs. Marks and the others had raised you with me, so it was never a question that she would adopt you."

"Why did you stay away? Why didn't you ever try to see me?"

"I thought you were better off, safer, without me. And you were so young. I really believed you would forget me, that I would become just a distant memory. I didn't trust myself around you—even having the support of Mrs. Marks and the others, I'd still brought harm to you. What if the next time I did more than break your leg? I couldn't bear it."

"I spent my life wondering why my own mother didn't want me."

"Telling you would have made you seek me out. I know you well enough to know that, and I wouldn't have been able to stay away if I'd seen you. Me being near you was not in your best interest."

It was on my tongue to tell her off, to rage at her thoughtlessness. In trying to keep me safe, she had ended up doing more damage. But, feeling Tea against me, I couldn't. I had done to her exactly what my mom had done to me. My intentions had been in the right place too, and yet I'd ended up hurting the one person I loved most in the world.

"As much as I would like to argue the stupidity of your decision, since I also exhibited the same idiotic thinking with Tea, I can't. Are you happy with your life now?"

"Warren and I met in group. He's wonderful, kind, and patient. He was one of the rotating therapists, and we started dating when he rotated out. He keeps me grounded, and I like to believe I help him with letting his hair down. He disagreed with my wish to stay out of your life. Argued until he was blue in the face that I needed to reach out to you. He was thrilled when he learned of your call, and he was very eager to meet you, but we thought for this first meeting, it should just be me.

"There's been a hole in my heart that could never be filled, Kane. I want you to know that. Mrs. Marks sent me your school pictures every year; I have them hanging in my room. Seeing you grow through the years, knowing you were happy, made me happy.

She told me about Teagan, how quickly you bonded, how you were always there for each other. It gave me solace, knowing something good came from all the bad."

I couldn't argue with her on that. Tea wasn't just something good—she was everything.

"Can you stay for dinner?"

I felt Tea's agreement in the way she moved into my side, settling to be there for a while. I held her closer. "We'd like that."

chapter 13

Teagan

As we traveled home from visiting with Kane's mom, his head remained turned away from me, a sign he was processing and wasn't ready to talk. I used the time to reflect on the visit. There was no denying his mom's joy at seeing her son, nor could she hide her pain when she'd learned what Kane had been through. Watching her, I could see so much of Kane: the same eyes and black hair, even some of their mannerisms. And it was also clear that she loved her son and truly believed she had acted in his best interest. I wondered why Mrs. Marks had never told her of the accident. Was she trying to spare her the pain?

Thinking about Mrs. Marks's son, I think I understood now why she went by Mrs. Marks. She had been a single, unwed mother in the sixties; my guess is that she used "Mrs." for her son's benefit. After she'd lost him, being called Mrs. Marks kept him with her.

Before we'd left, his mom had asked Kane if she could see his scars. The sight was etched into my brain, and Kane's blindness had been a blessing, sparing him from seeing her completely collapse. She didn't crumble so much in words or tears, being mindful of Kane, I was sure, but the devastation and despair clouding her expression was very hard to watch. She was probably even now playing the what-if game: What if she hadn't left, what if she had stayed or come to visit. Would Kane still have found himself in that burning building?

And Mrs. Marks losing her son . . . I had noticed two other angels on the tree in the years that followed the ones Kane had suggested I hang for my parents. I now knew one was for her son and one was for Kane's mom. It seemed kind of fitting that we had all lost our families and had found a new one in each other.

"Thank you for coming with me."

Glancing over, my gaze collided with his blue one. "You okay?"

"Yeah, I am." His hand moved from his lap, searching for mine. Slipping my hand into his, he linked our fingers and lifted our hands to kiss my knuckles, his lips lingering for a few seconds.

"I suppose an argument for nature over nurture could be made from this," he said.

"How so?"

"She left to protect me, and I did the same to you, even though I hadn't been in her company for over a decade when I left you."

"I think the need to protect the ones you love is universal. Instinctual, like breathing. There was love in her face when she saw you."

"I could sense it in the way she moved, how she breathed."

"What will happen now?"

"We'll probably take this slowly, but I'd like to have her in my life again. I hadn't realized just how much I really missed her until she came back into my life."

"I think she'd like that very much. Maybe you could even bring her to Raven's Peak when Mrs. Marks is up for visitors."

"Good idea."

"Why do you think Mrs. Marks didn't tell her about the fire?"

"I guess since my mom never tried to see me again, why mention it? The news would only bring her pain."

"That's my thinking too. Did Mrs. Marks ever mention her son to you?" I asked.

"No, never. And I never saw any pictures of him either, unless they're in her rooms. I've never been in her rooms."

"No, me neither. It's sad but happy because we all found each other."

He squeezed my hand. "Really glad you were with me today."

"Me too."

Sitting in the library, Kane filled Simon in on our visit with his mom.

"That had to be a sobering moment for her, seeing you at the bottom of the stairs and knowing she was the one who put you there. At least it sounds like the reunion went well, so maybe you'll have a chance to be a part of each other's lives."

"What did you do while we were away?" I asked, since I could tell Kane was done sharing.

"Mrs. T made me a killer lunch—filet mignon sandwich. I'll never eat anyone else's steak sandwich again."

"With horseradish sauce?" Kane asked.

"Yep."

"Yeah, there's no going back after one of those."

"I've never had one of those. Why haven't I had one of those?"

"It's a recent addition to her repertoire," Kane said.

"Oh, Teagan, you are missing out." Simon wiggled his brows at me. "If you're nice to me, maybe I can sweet-talk her into making them tomorrow for lunch. Oh, I almost forgot. I can't believe I almost forgot—I've been waiting for you to get back to tell you. The sandwich is just that good."

He had a one-track mind. "Simon, focus," I said.

"Right. Mr. Sleazy was here to finish up the inventory. It's shopping day. No one was supposed to be home, and I suspect he knew that. Shocked the hell out of him when I answered the door. I followed him—didn't even bother being subtle about it. He really does not like me, but I think you're right in that he's looking to finance his next big purchase from pieces he lifts from here. He had a nice big satchel with him, and yet there wasn't a thing in it when he opened it, no laptop, not files, no inventory sheet."

"I knew it. So he must have a buyer," I deduced.

"That would be my guess."

"What are the chances his buyer is Camille?" Kane said from his spot near the fireplace. "Think about it—she stops in for visits all the time. How much do you want to bet she's really been scoping out the pieces she wants Sleazy to steal?"

"I thought the same thing," I said, "but how can she afford to pay him on a waitress's salary, since Daddy seems to have taken a step back?"

"Good question. And why did Daddy take a step back? It'd be interesting to talk to the man," Simon said.

"I wonder if he *would* talk to us." I was speaking mostly to myself.

"Maybe not to us, but he'll talk to Kevin O'Malley. It wasn't just Kathy and Camille who were friends—their families are as well," Kane said.

I couldn't deny I liked the idea, but . . . "What would you say to Mr. O'Malley?"

"The truth. Camille's been coming around, Mr. Sleazy is always around, I know about his checkered past, and do I need to be concerned."

"And you're okay with asking him that?"

"Why not? If something shady is going on, the three seniors who live here and I are vulnerable."

There was an edge to that last comment, and I knew it stemmed from frustration—that he couldn't defend his home as well as he'd like. There wasn't a thing I could say to ease those feelings. I knew he'd only get mad if I tried.

"I'll call him," he said before he started from the room. "I'll see you both at dinner."

He was gone before we could respond.

"He okay?" Simon asked.

"I'm guessing he's just frustrated, and I get it, but it's hard watching him be his own worst critic."

"Considering the circumstances, I think he's coping rather well."

"Agreed. So if it is Camille who Sleazy wants to sell to, where do you think the money is coming from?" I asked.

"Don't know. The woman we saw at the diner didn't look like she had two pennies to rub together, so I don't have a clue where tens of thousands of dollars is going to come from. Not to mention: What does she plan on doing with the stolen items? She couldn't possibly think to display them in her home, because items like Mrs. Marks's would stand out," Simon speculated.

"Like I've said, she isn't the sharpest knife in the drawer, so she may not have thought all of this out."

Simon was rubbing his chin. He did that when he was thinking something through. "The whole situation just seems off. Sleazy, I think, is pretty transparent, but as for Camille, I don't know. I have the sense there's more to her involvement. Maybe her affection for Kane is sincere, and she really is coming here to see him, and because she's cold and callous, her attentions seem forced."

I didn't like thinking about it, but I remembered her coming right out and saying she wanted Kane when we were younger; she hadn't hedged at all. And the tires. "She slashed his tires when we were kids."

"*What?*"

"Right after he told her it was never going happen with them."

"What the fuck?"

"Maybe you're right, maybe she's got a warped attraction thing going on for Kane. That's unnerving. I'd rather it be that she was only looking to steal from us."

"Agreed, a thief is far easier to deal with than a loon. Anyway, after I saw Sleazy off and the others came home, I walked into town. I think this could be a great place to open a second store."

"I think so too."

"The Boston shop is firmly established—speaking of which, don't forget the party is approaching. I think we need to branch out, and here seems just as good as anywhere."

The party. I wondered if Kane remembered and was still willing to travel to Boston with me. I'd have to remind him. Moving past that, I focused on Simon's suggestion. It was true, Blue Hill had seen significant growth during the years I'd been away, many high-end boutiques now had storefronts along Main Street. Antiques would do very well. "I like the idea of opening a shop here. We should call a realtor and see what's available."

Kane never did join us for dinner, so I found my way to the island. Zeus greeted me as soon as I stepped off the little boat. Walking around back with him, I found Kane, but he wasn't working out with his bar. Instead he was sitting on one of the Adirondack chairs, a beer in his hand, seemingly lost in thought. Not wishing to disturb him, I stopped walking, debating if I should stay or go.

"You don't have to leave."

Uncanny how he did that. He answered my unasked question. "Your scent, not just your perfume but your natural scent, is unique and it drives me crazy. I can always tell when you're near."

Moving around to face him, I saw that his eyes were closed, his head resting back. He looked really comfortable. I had feared he was brooding again.

"You missed dinner," I said.

"More for Simon. That guy eats."

"I know. You okay?"

"Yeah, just thinking."

"About?"

He placed his bottle on the table next to him and reached for me. Climbing into his lap, he wrapped me in his arms. I sighed. I couldn't help it, since this was my very favorite way to sit.

"I was thinking about you," he said.

Tingles moved down my body, like fans in the stands doing the wave. "Me?"

"Seeing my mom, knowing it was because of her illness that I found a permanent home at Raven's Peak and met you . . . how one small change can have such drastic effects. I don't know if things would have been different if my mom hadn't left. Would I have volunteered for the fire department and ended up in that burning building? Would I have stayed here after graduating high school? I honestly don't know, but what I do know, even with everything that's happened to me, is that I'd go through it all again if it meant I could be with you."

An involuntary sob ripped from my throat; as horrible a thought as that was—him going through it all again—the sentiment was the most beautiful thing I'd ever heard.

"I mean it, Tea. Being with you these past few weeks has made me realize how wrong I was to push you away. How life, my life, is so sweet with you, and so empty without you." He reached into his pocket, my ring appearing. "Marry me, Tea."

Tears were falling now; there was just no stopping them. "Yes."

Reaching for my hand, he slipped his ring on and, like he had done before, he kissed it. "I won't fuck it up this time."

Crying, I buried my face in his neck, but the tears were happy ones.

I woke up in the middle of the night, Kane over me, his mouth trailing kisses down my neck and collarbone, down the valley between my breasts to my stomach. My hands moved over him, up his arms, over his shoulders, and down his back. He tensed when I reached his scars but only for a second; he was getting used to my touch. I still felt the sting of tears when my fingertips moved over his scarred skin, thinking of the pain he had endured, and hearing that he'd endure it again to be with me, there just weren't words.

His tongue dipped into my navel, licking down my stomach to the apex of my thighs. His fingers curled at my waist a second before he pulled the silk of my panties down my legs. His hands found my legs, moved up to my calves, and draped my legs over his shoulders. Spread for him, I watched as his head lowered and he kissed me right where I was aching. His fingers tightened on my ass as he lifted me higher, his tongue running down along my wet heat, tracing me and dipping in only slightly. Returning to the nub, he sucked on it, and I felt the start of the orgasm tightening in my belly, and then he was pushing into me, hard with his tongue, as he rubbed and squeezed the pleasure point with his fingers. Stealing my breath, the orgasm seemed to just keep coming as he continued to feast, working me until another orgasm followed the first. As I came down from the second one, he moved up my body and slid into me. He moved slowly, in and out, almost leisurely. His mouth found mine, and I tasted him and myself. He rolled so I was astride him, my hips taking up the motion, riding him as I slowly brought him to climax. Sitting up, he held me close, his body flexing with his orgasm, his seed pumping into me. Neither of us were willing to break the beauty of the moment, so we stayed like that for a good long time.

Kane

Tea had fallen back asleep after we'd made love, but I couldn't sleep. My thoughts were on our lovemaking. It had been different, more profound. We hadn't used protection since she returned, and I hoped that I had planted my baby in her. I wanted that, wanted to have a family with her. Even though we had taken the long way to get where we were, she was in my bed and wearing my ring. She had told me once that all of her happiest memories were with me, and I understood the sentiment completely, since I felt the same way. We had a lifetime to make more memories. I wasn't going to let her go, wasn't going to lose the best thing in my life again.

I wished I could see her, really see her. In my head, she was still that eighteen-year-old, her thick copper hair falling past her shoulders, her eyes the color of summer grass, with a smile that took my breath away. Her body was different, her breasts larger, her hips rounder, and her waist thinner. There was muscle under her soft skin, defined from working out. She had been gorgeous at eighteen, at twenty-seven, she was stunning.

The party in Boston was next month. I was nervous. It was a big city. I didn't know it at all, but it meant everything to Tea that I come. I could hear that so clearly when I'd agreed to join her. I'd go and do my damnedest to not embarrass her.

She had accomplished so much in the years we were apart. Even knowing how much I had hurt her, she hadn't let it get the better of her. She'd pushed on and made something of herself. I had yet to do that. I needed to set up and run the inn—needed to know I could. The librarian, the same woman who'd worked at the library when Tea and I were younger, gave me my own room so I could listen to my classes and take notes on my recorder and not disturb anyone. I was churning through the online classes and even had a few interviews with owners of inns in neighboring towns that Mr. O'Malley offered to drive me to. There was much to learn, but I found I was thirsty to learn more. For the first time since the accident, I felt anticipation, a real belief that not all of my dreams were lost.

We would visit Mrs. Marks in the morning. She was awake and speaking more clearly. Luckily the stroke had been mild, so mild that the effects were all but gone. It was scary how close she had come. Mrs. T was already working up a new menu that was lower in fat, but she wasn't going to forgo taste. Simon, as her taster, was very honest. So there was no doubt the end result was going to be a winner.

Mrs. Marks was scheduled to come home at the end of the week. I wanted to tell her about the visit with my mom. Needed to thank her for taking me in, for giving me a family, for giving me Tea.

Sometimes I wondered if she hadn't planned it, if she had figured out just what we would come to mean to each other, and that was why she had allowed us so much freedom growing up. It would explain why she had taken our breakup almost as hard as we had. I'd never be able to pay her back for that gift, but I could start by taking the pressure of running Raven's Peak off her shoulders.

Mr. O'Malley hadn't been home when I'd called, but his wife had promised she'd have him call me in the morning. I believed Camille was working with Sleazy. She always had been a schemer, even with something as simple as going to the movies. She would try to get in without paying. Never did she just do something the right way; there was always an angle. I wasn't surprised she hadn't changed, but I'd be damned if I let her steal things from Mrs. Marks.

Tea stirred, and I pulled her closer. Zeus, rolling in his sleep, settled against my other side. For the first time in a really long time, I was happy.

"Mrs. Marks, you look wonderful." Tea sounded relieved; I knew she'd feared that Mrs. Marks was worse than the doctors were saying.

"I feel wonderful. Simon, I'm sorry I wasn't up for a visit the last time you were here."

"Nonsense. It's wonderful seeing you looking so well."

I sensed when Simon moved. I heard Mrs. Marks's breathing speed up.

"Lovely to officially meet you," Simon said. I wasn't surprised to hear a giggle from Mrs. Marks.

Tea chuckled. "We need to bottle that, Simon, and sell it. We'd make a fortune."

"Bottle what?"

"Your charm."

I grinned. I couldn't help it. Tea was right. Simon could charm the panties off a nun, I'd bet. Not that he'd want to.

Tea's hand squeezed mine. "Would you like a few minutes with Mrs. Marks?"

My chest felt tight, but not in a bad way. I hadn't mentioned my wish to talk with Mrs. Marks alone, and yet my Tea knew me, knew without me having to say anything. Bringing her hand to my lips, I brushed my lips over her fingertips. She moved into me, just slightly, seeking a closer connection. I could feel her pulse pounding in her wrist, felt her breath coming out faster: excitement, lust, desire. Her eyes would be a darker green and her full lips slightly open. Beautiful, even in my head, she was fucking beautiful.

"Just a few minutes."

It took her a minute to respond. She was still lost in the moment and, I couldn't lie, I liked that her desire for me left her off-balance, aroused. "Ah, okay. Simon and I will get some coffee."

Her breasts pressed into my chest when her soft lips brushed lightly over mine. My dick stirred to life. I could tell when she'd left, and not just because her scent wasn't as strong—my body just knew. Another connection.

"I'm so happy you two have found your way back to each other." Mrs. Marks pulled me from my thoughts of Tea.

"There's a chair here, about three feet in front of you," Mrs. Marks directed.

Zeus moved and I followed, until my toe touched the leg. Reaching out, I felt the back of the chair, then felt the seat on the back of my legs before I sat down.

"What did you want to talk with me about?" she asked.

"I saw my mom."

"I hate that I kept that from you. A pattern seems to be forming in my behavior."

Mrs. Marks meant it as a joke, but I could hear disgust for herself in her tone.

"She asked you to keep the secret and so did I. We shouldn't have. That's on us, not you."

She didn't reply, but I suspected there was a part of her that agreed with me. I continued. "Thank you for taking me in as a kid, for giving me a home and family, for indirectly giving me Tea."

Tension stilled the air, and I could feel her stiffening. After a moment of silence, her words were soft, tormented. "I lost my son—having your child die before you is the hardest thing there is for a parent. It isn't right. I was there when that beautiful soul was brought into the world, and yet when he died, he did so alone. I had thought we were managing his illness, thought he was finally happy and getting some control. For years, I blamed myself. Had I done something differently, taken him to different doctors, watched him more closely, would he still have taken his own life? Later, I realized he wouldn't have wanted that. Playing his nurse and not his mom would have put his illness between us.

"Seeing the parallel of my own life and your mom's, seeing the similar patterns of my son in her, knowing she had you to care for, I couldn't not get involved. I wished it could have turned out differently, wished you didn't lose all that time with your mom, but I was glad that I could be there to help both her and you."

My throat hurt, and unshed tears burned the back of my eyes. I could hear the pain in her voice, the regret. "You saved both of us."

She was crying softly. I could hear the tears in her voice. "Thank you for saying that."

"I'd offer you a tissue, but I don't see any," I said in an attempt to lighten the mood. Hearing her chuckle eased the knot in my stomach.

"Making light of your blindness is a good sign."

"I'm coming to terms with it, but I wish I could see Tea now that she's older."

"She looks the same, her hair is the same, her face, her smile. And she still looks at you like you hung the moon. From the very beginning, you and she . . . 'two peas in a pod' is how Mrs. T and I described you. You're stronger together."

I grinned at Mrs. Marks's description.

"She's wearing your ring."

"It never should have been off her finger. Fuc—Messed that up. Won't again."

"Good catch." Mrs. Marks didn't like swearing. "Makes an old woman's heart light to see the righting of a wrong. Kane," she said almost urgently. "You hurt her. I know why. I understand, but for a long time I wasn't sure we would get her back. You can't do that to her again. You can't yank yourself from her life. Teagan's a strong woman, but I don't think she'd survive that again."

Pain stabbed through me. I didn't like thinking about what I had put Tea through. I knew she had lived in her own hell during the years we were apart. I really believed she was over it now, had dealt with it and put it all in the past. I liked to think we both had. But doubt nagged at me.

Tea entered then, and my body jerked, and then I smelled her, sweet and spicy. Her voice was deeper, a little hoarse, so I knew she had heard the tail end of our conversation.

"We brought coffee." Her hip brushed my shoulder, her soft hand reached for mine to wrap my fingers around the cup. Her lips pressed against my ear, and her breath fanned out over my skin. "Miss me?"

"Hell yeah." I wanted to pull her into my lap, wanted my mouth on her and my hands all over her, but now wasn't the time. She moved.

I felt her behind me, her hand on my shoulder almost absently, like she needed the connection. Since I, too, sought that connection to her, I understood her reciprocal need.

"Simon, tell me about this skill of yours in finding treasures," Mrs. Marks asked.

"I can sense them or almost smell them out. It's like they call to me," said Simon.

"Oh God, here we go," Tea said. Clearly she'd been through this conversation before.

"She's jealous, since she doesn't have my gift."

"Tell me about this rolltop desk. I might have a need for one."

I knew Simon had settled on the edge of the bed. I heard the springs give. "So glad you asked."

Tea leaned over me. "This could be a while."

I wanted to pull her from the room, to find a closet so we could use the time in a far more enjoyable pursuit. If I could see, we'd already be halfway down the hall.

"Maybe we should find a closet," she whispered in my ear. My dick pressed into my jeans.

"I was just thinking that."

"I know you were."

"Later, Tea."

Goose bumps rose on her skin as her arms wrapped around my shoulders. "Can't wait."

Tea straightened, because Simon and Mrs. Marks were done with their powwow. "Let's talk about your lawyer," Tea said. She never was one to pull a punch.

"You want to know why I asked him to inventory the house."

"You were hoping to catch him trying to steal from you."

I heard surprise in Mrs. Marks voice. "Yes, how did you know that?"

"Just made sense based on what we've learned about him. But if you suspected he was up to no good, why didn't you just fire him?"

"I was going to, but I was asked not to."

It was Tea who sounded surprised now. "By who?"

"Richard Bowen."

Now I was surprised. "Camille's dad asked you not to fire him?"

"He was the one who suggested I tell him I wanted to sell, that I needed him to catalog the contents of the house."

"He's looking for his own leverage." It was Simon's voice this time, full of admiration.

"What do you mean by that?" Mrs. Marks asked.

Tea leaned into me, probably cocking her hip. She did that when she ranted. "We believe that Mr. Sleazy, your lawyer—"

Mrs. Marks interrupted Tea. "You call him Sleazy?"

"*Mr.* Sleazy. I'm respectful," Tea said. There was silence for a beat, which was followed by a genuine belly laugh from Mrs. Marks.

"Well thank goodness you're being respectful."

A touch of humor laced Tea's voice when she continued. "We think Mr. Sleazy has something on Bowen, which is why he hired the man despite his shady past. Mr. Sleazy and Camille went to Yale together. We think she told him about Raven's Peak. He has a penchant for stealing. He used whatever he has on Bowen to get into his firm, so he could represent you and get into Raven's Peak. He's never allowed in the house unaccompanied, and he doesn't like that."

"Interesting. So my lawyer *is* trying to steal from me."

"You don't sound all that surprised," I said.

"I'm not. Lawson's been looking into Falco, because he thought the situation odd, and Richard's a friend. We decided to dangle the carrot, so to speak, and see how Dimitri reacted."

"What do you mean by that?" I asked.

"He's supposed to be inventorying, but Lawson hasn't gotten

one thing from the man, and he's been at it since I've been in here. He isn't even trying to be surreptitious. So if he's not inventorying, what's he doing in my house?"

"Isn't it a risk to have him there at all? I mean, we've been watching him, but he could come when we're not around." Tea was still angry.

"The house is covered. Lawson's made sure of that."

"You're loving every second of this detective stuff," Tea said with admiration.

"Oh, I absolutely am." Mrs. Marks's voice softened. "You all got involved because of worry for me, didn't you?"

"Yeah, we aren't going to let them steal from you." Tea sounded a bit incredulous.

"Them?"

"Oh, we think Camille may be selecting the items she wants whenever she visits Kane," Tea said, but there was a note of skepticism in her tone.

"You don't sound so convinced of that, Tea. What's up?" I asked.

"Remembering Camille from when we were younger, I don't know, she really may be coming to see you."

"I always had the sense she liked the house more than me."

"Or maybe she just wants you to think that so you don't object to her friendly visits."

"To what end?" Mrs. Marks asked.

"Kane and I weren't together; maybe she was hoping to wear him down, get him used to her company, so he'd actually want her company." Silence reigned for a beat before Tea continued. "We've kept you too long, Mrs. Marks. Sorry. We'll let you get some sleep."

"I enjoyed the visit, but I am tired. It was nice to meet you, Simon."

"Likewise."

Standing, I felt Zeus follow. Tea's hand found mine. She moved us forward to the bed, placing my hand just above Mrs. Marks's head. Leaning over, I pressed my lips on her forehead. "Sleep well."

I didn't need to see to know she smiled.

"Tea, I forgot there's a thing tonight at the O'Malleys'. I'm going to talk to Kevin there. Will you come with me?" I asked.

"Yep." We were in the library, and Tea was looking for a book. We had just made love on our sofa, my body still sated, and yet her scent was turning me hard again. Amazing how one could improvise, making love without shedding clothes. When there was a will . . .

I heard the footfalls first, Mr. Clancy's even, determined stride, and another, shorter pace, heels on the wood. A woman.

"Kane, Teagan, you have a visitor." I rose from the sofa, glad Mr. Clancy hadn't arrive five minutes sooner; he would have gotten an eyeful, namely Tea riding my dick. Tea joined me, pressing herself to my side.

"Sorry to just drop by, but I just visited with Mrs. Marks and wanted to see how you were doing."

Mrs. T's grandniece, the woman I'd claimed I had left Tea for. Doreen. Shit.

"Hi, I'm Doreen. You must be Teagan. I've heard so much about you."

Tea went still, every muscle in her body rigid, and her voice was cold. "Nice to meet you."

I felt the air stir around me, the tip of Doreen's shoe touching my foot, her body leaning into me, her lips brushing over my cheek. "You look good, Kane."

Tea was gone, the warmth of her body no longer close. She was still in the room, but she wasn't at my side anymore.

"How are you, Doreen?"

"Good, I'm really good. How about you? I heard you were doing it, turning this place into an inn. That's wonderful."

"I'll leave you two," Tea, but not my Tea, said. Her voice was dead. What the hell was she thinking? Fear clawed at me. I didn't like hearing her sound that way.

"Sorry, you've caught us at a bad time, Doreen," I said hastily.

"I understand, I should have called first. I'll be around for a few days. If you have the time, I'd love to catch up. I'm so glad to see you doing well." I could hear disappointment in Doreen's voice, but she needed to leave. I needed to talk to Tea.

She was gone, her footsteps hurried. I had hurt her feelings. I felt bad about that, but Tea was my priority.

"Tea?"

I knew she was in the room, I felt her, and yet she stayed quiet. "Talk to me."

"I hate her."

I wasn't expecting that, or maybe I was. "Doreen?"

"I hate her." Her voice was barely a whisper, but it was full of conviction—it had an edge. "I fucking hate her." She was louder now, and there was anger laced through her words. But under the anger there was pain, so much fucking pain.

"I never dated her, that was a lie. There's no need to hate her."

I never heard Tea sound the way she did when she spoke again. Broken. "It doesn't matter. She took my life, you made me believe that. I hate her. I'll always hate her. That's on you—you set the stage and placed the players. My whole world's happiness was taken away by Doreen. Hearing her name brings it all back. The hours, months, that I contemplated ending it because I couldn't bear the thought of life without you, that I hadn't been good enough for you, that you had moved on, that you had left me. She will always be all of those horrible, nightmarish feelings rolled into one. I moved on, I picked up the pieces, but I never got over it. I hate her, Kane. And there's a part of me that hates you too for making me have to live through the lie."

I knew she was gone. I felt her leave and my heart bled. Sinking back onto the sofa, my head in my hands, tears fell from my sightless eyes. In trying to protect my Tea, I'd broken her.

Teagan

Sitting on the beach, I tried to work through all the emotions tearing me up. My reaction surprised even me, but seeing her, the woman I believed was the source of all my pain, I couldn't help it. I felt all of it again, the helplessness, the despair. I knew she hadn't done anything, but it didn't matter.

The look on his face when I'd told him I hated him hurt worse. I didn't want to hurt him, but in that moment I did. I wanted him to feel some of the pain I had lived through, wanted him to know what it felt like. I didn't have his scars and I could see, but I had lived in hell too.

"You okay?" Simon asked as he settled next to me on the sand.

"I met Doreen."

"Shit, that couldn't have been fun."

"I flipped out on Kane. Told him I hated her, hated him too."

"I'm sure he understands. He knows at least in some measure what he put you through."

"I should be over it. We've moved past that."

Resting back on his hands, he focused on the sea. "Why? You're human. Seeing the woman you believed was the cause of your world crashing and burning would have pissed off anyone." His head turned in my direction. "There's more. What's wrong?"

"You told me I couldn't keep putting his blindness between us, but that's what he does. He disengages. I get it, he's learning to live an entirely different way, but he's still pushing me away. Not as drastically as he did before, but there's still a part of him I can't reach."

"And that's a problem."

"Yeah, I've had all of Kane. I'm not going to settle for most of him."

"That's fair. What are you going to do?"

"I'm hoping he figures it out on his own. He can't hold me to a standard and not follow it himself."

"Where is he now?"

"I left him in the library."

"I think he left. I heard the car before I came down here."

My heart squeezed in my chest. I'd told him I'd come with him to the O'Malleys', and then I left him alone.

Simon reached for my hand, my gaze turning to him. "What you've both been through—there's no rule book, Teagan. There's no right way to handle it. What's important is that you're here together, that you work through the lingering issues together. There's nine years of baggage, sweetie; it's going to take more than a few weeks to heal those wounds."

"You're right, I do know that."

"So don't be so hard on yourself or him. And give him some space. You could both use it. Once emotions cool, you can talk. Until then, just be glad you found each other again and are willing to make it work this time. The rest will come."

Resting my head on his shoulder, I grinned. "I've said it before, but I'm saying it again. You are very wise."

"Yes, I am."

❧

It was late when I felt the bed dip, felt Kane—his arm coming around my waist, pulling me back into the cradle of his body.

"I'm sorry," I whispered.

"You've nothing to be sorry for. I'm the one who's sorry, sorry I put you through that."

Turning to face him, I tried to speak, but he stopped me. "My intention was to protect you, but if I'm being completely honest, it was more than that. I was being selfish. I wanted to preserve the beauty of what we'd had. I didn't want it blemished with the nightmare. I was so consumed by my own hell, battling my own demons, that I didn't really think about what I was doing to you. I should have pulled you close, but bringing you into all of that would have altered all the memories of you that helped pull me through to the other side. Sounds stupid, but it's the truth. I needed to find my way without you. I always knew the way with you, but I needed to know I could do it alone. Does that make sense?"

"Yes."

"I'm sorry I broke you."

Tears filled his eyes, and one rolled down his cheek. I wiped it away and pressed a kiss there. "I don't hate you."

"I'd hate me."

"You always were very hard on yourself."

His arms tightened around me. "Are we okay?"

"Yeah, we have some shit to work through, but I love you, so we'll figure it out."

He exhaled. "You have every right to be angry. You're right. It's on me. I'm sorry."

Lifting his hand, I pressed a kiss in his palm. "Did you go to the O'Malleys' house?"

"Yeah."

"Sorry I didn't come with you."

"Under the circumstances, I wasn't expecting you to."

"Did you talk to him?"

"I did, but he didn't have much to say—only relaying to me that Mr. Bowen wants to talk."

I perked up at that. "Really?"

"Yep, have a meeting scheduled with him on Monday. He wanted to meet sooner, but Mrs. Marks is coming home tomorrow. I wasn't going to miss that."

"I bet Mrs. T is baking a cake," I teased.

"I know she is."

Leaning up on my elbow, I saw the grin curve his lips. "How do you know?"

"I may have asked her to, even given her some suggestions."

"You and that sweet tooth."

He moved so fast, pinning me under him, and then his mouth was on my neck and he started moving slowly down my body. He looked wicked when his head lifted. "Sweet."

I laughed. He moved lower. I moaned and spread my legs wider.

"It's so good to be home." Mrs. Marks was settled in the kitchen. She wanted to be in the heart of the house and not alone in her room.

Mrs. T feverishly cooked her homecoming meal, Simon helping, though he was doing more eating than helping. Mr. Clancy was at the table with Kane and me.

"It has been too long since we've all been together like this," Mrs. T commented as she whipped egg whites for the soufflés she was making.

"You're not wrong, Mrs. T, and I'm glad for it, because I have an announcement," Mrs. Marks said, gaining the attention of everyone in the room. "I've worked with Mr. Lawson and have had papers drawn up. I'm deeding the house to Kane and Teagan."

"What?" Kane and I said at the exact same time.

"I was doing it anyway, and, after this scare, I decided not to wait. Now, before everyone goes crazy, this is as much for me as it is for you. I want to see Raven's Peak as an inn, but mostly I want to witness its transformation. I love this old, drafty place; it's been in my family for a long time and it will continue to be as long as Kane and Teagan, and hopefully their children, have a part in it."

"Absolutely, it'll never fall out of the family. But are you sure?" I asked. I couldn't believe she was handing over Raven's Peak. I knew how much she loved her home.

"I had intended for my Danny to have it, but he died, and for so long I worried what would become of it, and then I was blessed with you. I remember when you both came here. Kane, when your mom brought you with her to work that first time, you were just a baby, so beautiful—from the very beginning you were a source of joy, bringing laughter back into this house. I know you think you are the lucky one, but I am the one who was blessed. You're a beautiful soul, Kane, and I have so enjoyed seeing you grow from that small little bundle to the man before me, honored that I was there to help you along the way when your mother felt she no longer could be."

The expression on Kane's face gave me a glimpse of the wide-eyed boy he had been.

"And you, Teagan, arriving with such sadness in your eyes. Watching you find each other, comforting and healing your hurts, turned us from a group of old folks into a family. I would be honored for my ancestral home to go to you, because you are all the family of my heart."

I was full-on crying, blubbering without words. Kane pulled me up against him. "You took two lost children and you gave us a home. We'd been honored to carry on your legacy," he said, voicing exactly what I was feeling.

Mrs. Marks was crying too, and Simon was alternately handing her and me tissues. "Excellent," she said through her tears. "Now, I'm starving, what's for dinner?"

That night, Kane and I lay silently in bed, both of us thinking about Mrs. Marks's words from earlier.

"I want children with you, Tea."

Sitting up, I turned to him. His hands behind his head, his sightless gaze shifting in my direction. "Where did that come from?"

"I've been thinking it for a while. I want to feel my baby growing in you—our child, the blending of us, the enduring symbol of what we feel for each other."

"I want that too. I'd like a bunch of kids."

"Now that she's made it official, we need to start working on the inn," he said.

"Yeah, any idea where we start?" I asked.

"I've a few." He grabbed me and pulled me down on top of him.

"But first, let's work on that baby." And then he was kissing me. Work had never been so much fun.

"Places," I called from my spot near the fireplace. "Simon, let me explain it to you. When the lights go out, you run. Only the murderer knows who his or her victim is. If you are the chosen one, scream loudly so we can discover your body. And that's when the guessing on who did it begins."

"Okay, I got it," Simon said. He sounded cheerful. Maybe he was the murderer.

"Mrs. Marks, are you ready?" I asked. She was dressed as Miss Scarlet and sitting in her favorite chair. She wasn't going to be moving around—the game would come back to her. She looked good, though, stronger than she had when she'd returned home a couple days ago.

"Yes, dear. I'm ready for some good old-fashioned bloodshed."

I laughed. "That's the spirit."

"All right, ready and action."

I ran, déjà vu swamping me, because damn if I didn't feel Kane right behind me. His arms wrapped around me and pulled me close. "How the hell did you find me so fast?"

"You're in my world now, babe. I rule the dark."

"Oh my God, you're so weird."

"Maybe, but you're about to die."

"Again?"

"Yep."

"And how exactly will you mete out this death? Tickling?"

"No, nothing so easy."

Someone approached, which threw me off, since murder in our game was always a solo gig. I heard Simon's cackle as he appeared just in front of me. In his hand was what looked like a potpie. My gaze flew to his.

"No, I'm not eating worm potpie."

"No, doll, but you're going to wear it," Simon said with sinister intent.

"Death by fright, good idea, Simon," said Kane.

"I'm filled with them," Simon countered.

"You're teaming up, that's not fair."

"Whining won't get you out of your fate, Tea. Suck it up and take it like a man," Kane said and glanced at Simon, like he could see him and was confirming they were ready to proceed. "You ready, Simon?"

"All good here, Kane."

In the next second, I had worms in my hair. The sensation was so disgusting that I wish I *had* died of fright.

Kane

Tea came with me to visit Mr. Bowen. The smell of pine cleaner and coffee greeted us when we stepped from the cold foyer into the heated space of his law firm. The sounds of an office echoed around us: fingers tapping on a keyboard, phones ringing, a copy machine, the soft hum of voices.

"The receptionist is walking toward us," Tea said softly.

"Kane Doyle?"

"Yes."

"Please—this way. Mr. Bowen will be right with you."

The noises became muffled with the soft click of the door closing, separating us from the office activity.

"It's a nice conference room: big walnut desk, leather chairs.

Oh, here he comes. He's tall, about your height, balding, trim, sharp brown eyes. He's wearing a gray suit, white shirt, and burgundy tie. Looks like silver-and-onyx cuff links, nice."

"What about his shoes? Why did you leave out his shoes? Doesn't he have feet?"

She picked up on my sarcasm and bumped me with her shoulder. "Clown."

I grinned, couldn't help it. She was adorable.

"Mr. Doyle. Thank you for coming."

"Sure."

"And you're Teagan Harper, yes?"

"Yes, sir. Nice to meet you."

"Please, call me Richard."

"You're here about Dimitri Falco, aren't you?" I heard as he settled into his chair, the jovial tone of his voice turning flat, laced with guilt.

"Yes. We've talked to Mrs. Marks, so we know you and Mr. Lawson are looking to flush him out, but she's an old woman and doesn't need this brought into her home."

"Agreed. I wasn't thrilled with Larry's plan, but we had to do something."

"Maybe you should start from the beginning," I said.

"I didn't know any of this, not until Falco showed up. I want you to know that."

"Okay." Apprehension twisted in my gut.

"When the ice cream parlor went belly-up, Kevin O'Malley tried to sell the building and couldn't. So not only was he not making money, but after he sold everything to cover his losses, he was still paying the mortgage and taxes on the property. He'd say now and again how he wished the place would burn down—it was something we'd all chuckle at a bit. Then there was the fire, and Kathy was caught in the inferno along with some other kids.

"Kids had been hanging there, smoking and drinking, since it closed down, the not-so-best-kept secret in town. The fact that Kathy was there was surprising, but she always had a tendency to want to fit in, to be with the cool kids.

"It wasn't until later that I learned the truth. The fire hadn't been an accident. It had been set on purpose. Kathy had overheard her parents talking and decided to take matters into her own hands. She had no idea the chain of events she was setting off."

"How did you learn of it?" Tea sounded horrified and angry.

"Camille. She brought Dimitri here about a year ago. I didn't like him from the moment I saw him. He laid it all out precisely. He's smart—arrogant, lazy, and shiftless—but smart. Explained to me how the fire had been set on purpose. He knew this because there had been an eyewitness."

"Camille," I said.

"Exactly. He listed the charges Kathy would be brought up on, since there is no statute of limitations on arson. Knowing how devastated her family already was, and then dumping it on them that their daughter had done it on purpose . . . They'd have been forced to watch as she was carted off to jail, when all she was trying to do was help . . . She was just a kid. I couldn't do it."

"So he blackmailed you?" I had suspected the fire had been started due to carelessness. Either way, the end result was the same.

"He wanted inside Raven's Peak. I was his means."

"Why Raven's Peak?" Tea asked.

"I honestly don't think he cared as long as he had access to valuables, but Camille wanted in and created a shared goal with Falco. The fact that he blackmailed me for a job pisses me off, but what's even more infuriating is his arrogance in believing that I would just sit back and allow him to steal from a client and a friend. His arrogance will be his downfall."

"How do you mean?" Tea asked what I too was thinking.

"I've been playing him too. I stalled when he first 'started'—didn't want to expose Mrs. Marks to him for any longer than necessary—by claiming he needed to go through our new employee training. Falco was smart enough to go along since I do have partners and they would have become suspicious if he didn't follow our normal hiring procedures. I gained an additional few months by insisting that he become familiar with Mrs. Marks's file, one that was streamlined for her safety. Again my partners would expect him to study up on the cases he was taking over, and Falco was willing to play the game since he knew the outcome would be favorable."

"You said Camille had created a shared goal with Falco. To what end?" Tea asked.

"I'm guessing to steal."

"You didn't want to expose Mrs. Marks to a criminal and yet you did." Tea was seething.

"In a way, yes, but she knew what we were doing. We didn't keep her in the dark. Larry continued to represent her, and we gave Dimitri enough rope. She was actually enjoying the intrigue."

She would. "Enough rope?" I asked.

"Like I said, I've been playing him too. It was why I agreed to his demands. While he thought he had me over a barrel, Larry was having him investigated."

"Do you have something on him?" It seemed to me that the jig was up with Mrs. Marks' home and Raven's Peak passing down to me and Tea.

"Yeah, in his arrogance he didn't think we'd do some digging, but we did and found the fence he used to sell the stuff he stole from his parents. They are fully prepared to press charges."

"Does he know?"

"Not yet, but that's about to change."

"Is that why you and Camille are estranged?" Tea asked.

"I spoiled her—I was trying to make up for the fact that her mother had left, but I created a monster. If she has been trying to steal from Mrs. Marks, then she was looking to profit from your tragedy, and that sickens me. My own child sickens me."

I suspected she was a bad egg whether he'd spoiled her or not. "If Camille was using Dimitri to get the pieces she wanted, and he's expecting to get paid, how is she funding this? A waitress salary isn't going to cut it. Are you giving her money?"

"No, and that's the part that doesn't make sense. She loves Raven's Peak. I can't imagine she'd want to see pieces of it being sold off to strangers, so if she has no intention of buying what Falco is stealing, then what's her motive?"

"To see Kane," Tea said.

"I thought she was over that crush, but then, I don't know my daughter like I thought I did."

On the street a little while later, I stopped and just breathed deeply. What a fucking web.

"You okay?" Tea asked, her voice rounding out some of the edges.

"Yeah, a little in shock."

"Understandable." Her hand tightened on mine. "Are you upset about the fire being set on purpose?"

"No, why? The outcome doesn't change whether it was intentional or not. She thought she was doing the right thing, and, having spent time with that family, I know they're very close. I'm trying to understand Camille's intentions."

"So you aren't convinced she's trying to steal from Mrs. Marks either."

"I don't know. Unless she's conning the con artist, how could she?"

"Conning the con artist, interesting. She doesn't have the money, but she told him she did, and, based on who her father is, why wouldn't Mr. Sleazy believe her? Who would have thought we'd have such an underbelly of crime in our small town?"

I laughed in spite of myself. "You're adorable."

"Why are you laughing?" She sounded almost whiny. The look that used to accompany that voice came clearly into focus in my mind's eye.

"I don't think one case of blackmail rates as an underbelly."

"It should." She sounded disgruntled but quickly turned serious. "If Camille is really after you, that scares me. Last time you thwarted her efforts, she slashed your tires."

"You think she might try something?" I didn't know if I agreed with Tea, but there was no mistaking her tone: She was worried.

"I don't know, but it makes me nervous. *She* makes me nervous. Anyway, you're taking this all very well." Her voice now had an edge of hope.

I was going to need to think about Tea's concern. She was usually pretty spot-on with people, so something wasn't sitting right with her. She clearly wanted to change the subject, so I did. "What's done is done. I've got you, and our lives are where we always wanted them to be. Let's not dwell on what can't be changed."

"That's very mature thinking, Kane, and, coming from you, eater of worm potpies, I'm impressed."

"At least I don't wear them in my hair." Pulling her close, I kissed the top of her head.

"Never intentionally." Humor flickered in her tone.

Yep, no point on dwelling, I had everything I ever wanted right here.

Teagan

We were at the O'Malleys' celebrating Kevin and Sally's anniversary. Kane had asked me to go with him, and I couldn't deny that part of my excitement for the day was getting the chance to see Kane interacting with the O'Malleys, because they really were like a second family to him. Their house wasn't a big one, but it was so nicely decorated: drawings that the kids had done as children hung on the walls, and the rooms were cozy, made for a family to settle into and be comfortable. I think I was even more moved by what I saw because I was late, and my period was never late. I hadn't taken a pregnancy test yet. I was procrastinating just a little, because I wanted to enjoy the high of possibly being pregnant for just a little while , in case I actually wasn't. The scents coming from the kitchen made my stomach growl—my appetite had definitely increased—a fact that was not lost on Kane.

"Hungry, Tea?"

"No, my stomach is just making noises like a small wild animal."

"You always had a very colorful way of describing something. I'll introduce you, and then we'll get something to appease the small furry animal."

"I didn't say my stomach was furry, I said it was wild. It's wild as in sexy, not furry."

Then it made that noise again, and he responded by laughing. "Yep, that's sexy."

I slugged him, not hard but hard.

"Kane, so happy you could make it," said Sally O'Malley. The petite woman greeted Kane with affection and love in her dark eyes. Yep, definitely a second family for Kane.

"And you must be Teagan. It is so nice to finally meet you."

Finally. Did Kane talk about me to the O'Malleys? And then, as if she'd read my mind, she added, "Kane speaks of you so often I feel as if I know you."

My attention shifted to Kane, whose head was lowered. Taking a play from his book, I ran my finger over his cheek and felt the heat blooming there.

"If you meet my friend Simon, he'll tell you that I speak incessantly about Kane, but then again, since he's my favorite person in the world, I guess it's not really a surprise."

His head jerked up at that, his eyes turning in my general direction. "Really?"

"Yes, but you already knew that."

"Still nice to hear," he whispered.

"Oh, please, you must let me introduce you to Kevin," she said as she reached for each of our hands and started pulling us along.

Kevin was a large man, almost as tall as Kane and big in the shoulders. His wife only reached his chest; they were so opposite, and yet, watching them, there was no denying the affection.

"Kevin, look who I found. Kane and Teagan. She was just saying how Kane is her favorite person in the world. Doesn't that sound familiar?"

Kevin grinned. You could tell he thought his wife was the cat's meow. "Sure does." His focus turned to me. "It's nice to officially meet you, Teagan." His hand engulfed mine, but he was gentle when he shook it.

"Nice to meet you."

"Would you like a drink, Teagan?" Sally asked.

"Sure, a Coke would be nice."

"Okay, Kane and I will get drinks. Be back in a jiff."

Watching her go, her husband said from my side, "She wants to pry information from Kane about how things are going with you two."

"I guessed. It's nice he has you."

"I wish the circumstances that brought us together weren't what they were, but he's been like a son to us."

"He looks to you both as something akin to parents. Regardless of what brought you together, you are together, and you don't treat him differently. I suspect that's why he really enjoys your company. You see him and not his scars or his blindness."

"So do you."

"Yes, but I've known him since I was nine and been in love with him for nearly that long."

Approval shone in his eyes. "So is it true you had Mrs. T make him a worm potpie? Do tell."

Later, while Kane was chatting with Kevin about something, I walked through Sally's gardens. Someone came up next to me. Glancing over, I saw it was Kathy.

"So glad you could make it," she said.

"Happy to be here. Last time I saw you, you were in need of a job. Any luck?"

"Not yet, but I've gotten a few leads." She nodded toward Kane. "How is he?"

"He's great. Happy."

"I can see that. I'm so glad you two are together again. I remember you in school, how you were like Frick and Frack."

Leaning closer to her, I said, "Kane knows about the fire. Mr. Bowen told him. He isn't upset. Just thought you should know."

Her jaw dropped; I had never seen that in real life, but it dropped, hanging open wide enough to catch flies. "So he knows it was Camille who set the fire?"

Now my jaw dropped. "Wait. What?"

Suspicion lit in her eyes. "What exactly did he tell you?"

"That you started the fire, because you heard your parents talking and wanted to help them. Camille witnessed it. She brought Falco to her dad last year, and they threatened to tell the police you started the fire if he didn't hire Falco."

"Son of a bitch. I just knew it, knew she was up to something. I didn't start the fire. She called me and asked me to come with her, to hang with her friends. It was the weekend after Thanksgiving. She was already home, already kicked out of Yale because of her grades, but some of her high school friends were home for the holiday. Since all I'd ever wanted was to hang with her, I went. She was so off that night, just ranting on about Yale, her father, you going off to school, Kane following you to Boston. It was her idea to start the fire. She wanted Kane to come. I thought it was some twisted idea she had that if he saved her in the fire, he'd grow feelings for her, especially since you were out of the picture temporarily. Once the fire got started, it burned too fast to stop it. She came to me after and begged me not to say anything. She told me to think about what would happen to her dad's practice if his daughter was found guilty of arson, so I said nothing. Everyone thought it was my carelessness anyway."

"And all the while she's been lying to her father to get access to Raven's Peak. Unbelievable."

"What do you mean?"

"Falco's terms for the blackmail were to get hired into the firm so he could represent Mrs. Marks and get access to her home."

"For what purpose?"

"To steal from her, we're guessing. It seems awfully vindictive, but having never gotten her hands on Raven's Peak, I'm guessing she wanted to take it in pieces. But then again, the few run-ins I've had with Camille, she's always been vindictive."

"What do you mean?"

"When Kane rejected Camille's affections when we were younger, she slashed his tires."

"What?"

"Creepy, right?"

"I wonder if her intent for that fire wasn't more malicious," Kathy said, but she seemed to be thinking out loud.

"Meaning?" Chills went through me.

"Nothing specific, but knowing her better, everything she does has a purpose. Kane loved you back then, and she knew it; she'd be more inclined to make him pay for that than seeking to win his affections, especially since her happy, pampered world was crumbling around her while you two were living the dream."

Dread and fury warred inside me. Kathy was right. If Camille had set that fire, she'd had an agenda, and I remember her threatening Kane that he'd be sorry for his lack of interest. If she'd purposely harmed him, it was likely I was going to kill her.

"She shouldn't be allowed to get away with that," Kathy said.

"I agree. Where is Mr. Bowen?" We both scanned the yard for him. "There he is," I said, but I was already making my way over to him. That bitch Camille may have intentionally set out to harm Kane. The idea of it was vile, disgusting, and so completely something she would do.

"She lied to you. Camille started that fire," I said by way of greeting to Mr. Bowen.

"What?"

"I was just talking with Kathy, and I shared with her that Kane knew she had set the fire. She remembers the event entirely differently."

His focus sliced to Kathy. "Camille set the fire?"

"Yes."

"Are you kidding me?" Mr. Bowen roared.

At the sound, Kevin and Kane ended their conversation, both walking to where the furious Bowen paced. Camille had cost us so much, and if she had set that fire with malicious intent, I wanted her in prison. "She isn't going to get away with this," I demanded.

Mr. Bowen stopped his pacing and leveled me with a haunted expression. "No, she won't."

In the next minute, Camille and Mr. Sleazy arrived, oblivious to the undercurrent. I would have thought her father would have told her that the secret was out about the blackmail. But maybe her lack of knowing fed into whatever her father and Mr. Lawson were working on the side for Dimitri. Sparks started flying, and though few words were said, the tension was insane. Kane's expression set me in motion because he had clearly caught on to the meaning behind the tension: that there had been more to Camille's involvement with the fire than just having been there. He looked like he wanted to commit murder. I went to him and wrapped my arm around his waist.

"She's not worth it," I whispered. And yet, even as I said that, my mind was working. She'd pay if she set that fire on purpose. Whenever I had encountered her, it always ended in a pissing contest. Her need to one up, to get the last word, could be used against her.

"How did you know what I was thinking?"

"It's all over your face. And I was thinking it too, but she is seriously not worth it." Turning his face to me, I pressed a kiss to his lips. "Remember, you said it didn't matter how the fire was started. It was done, in the past. And it is. Don't let this set you back. She's taken nine years from us, don't give her any more."

"Easier said than done."

"Agreed, but killing her won't change the outcome, and, as much fun as it would be before, during, and after her death, we'll still be right where we are now. That said, I've a thought."

"I know that tone. You have a plan?" I felt some of the tension drain from him.

"I do."

"I'm hungry. Feed me woman," he said, his hand finding mine. "And then we'll discuss this plan."

"Delighted to. I think I saw a few nice juicy worms in the garden."

He pulled me closer and kissed my head. "Thank you."

"For what?"

"Being here."

"My pleasure, Kane Doyle, it truly is. Now, let's eat. The small wild animal that is my stomach is growling again."

Kane and I were sitting in the kitchen with the family. We'd briefed them on what had happened at the O'Malleys' the night before. Mrs. Marks looked about ready to launch. "If she set that fire, so help me, I will use every cent of my money to see her put behind bars."

"I think we can do that without you needing to spend a cent." It might not work, my idea, but I wanted to try. If Camille had deliberately set the fire, she needed to be held accountable.

"I'm listening."

"It'll be like Clue but better. And we're going to need a few more players."

Mrs. Marks's eyes sparkled. "I'm all ears, dear."

The best china was set, the silver on the table, and Mrs. Marks was dressed to the nines. Mrs. T had spent the day cooking as Kane, Simon, and I cleaned the house. Everything was in place; we were just waiting for our guest to arrive.

The sound of the bell sent Mr. Clancy to the door with determined strides. He pulled it open for Camille. She didn't wait to be asked in—she walked in as if it were her home. Pulling her coat off, she handed it to Mr. Clancy without even making eye contact.

"Camille, how lovely that you could make it," Mrs. Marks said. "Please, let's go to the drawing room. We'll have tea there. It's one of my favorite rooms."

Standing out of sight, I watched the two head down the hall. Mrs. Marks addressed Camille as they went: "Had I known you had such a love of my home, I would have asked you here more often. There is nothing I like more than talking about Raven's Peak."

I followed after them and stood near the entrance once used by the servants. Camille walked around the room, her fingers running over several priceless pieces. What was her endgame? Conning a con artist for works of art she really had nowhere to place seemed so odd, which was why I really believed her goal was Kane—to get close to him and win him over. Had I not returned, would she have succeeded? She took the place across from Mrs. Marks, who was serving the tea. On cue, Kane and Zeus walked into the room from the door exactly opposite to where I was standing.

"Kane." Surprise and, if I wasn't mistaken, longing rang in that single word.

"Camille, I didn't know you were going to be here today."

"Mrs. Marks invited me for tea."

"May I join you?"

Mrs. Marks hesitated, then said, "Of course, dear." Her solicitous reply had me biting down on my lip to keep from laughing; she was really getting into her character. "Will Teagan be joining us as well?"

I saw his eye roll from my place at the door. A little overdone in my opinion, but Camille ate it up. "No," he said.

Camille perked up.

Mrs. Marks pressed. "You look upset. Everything okay?"

"Yeah, it's . . . yeah." Kane would not be winning any awards for his acting.

"Did you and she have a fight?" Mrs. Marks put her hand to her mouth, feigning contrition. "Sorry, I shouldn't be asking such personal questions in front of company."

"It's okay. Camille's not just company." He actually got those words out without laughing. Camille, now rather smug, leaned back in her chair and smiled deviously. I wanted to throw up.

"It's true. Kane and I have grown rather close. Do you want to talk about it, Kane?"

He pulled a hand through his hair before resting his elbows on his knees. "I don't know, as misguided as Kathy's actions were, she set that fire out of love for her parents. Tea would have done that for me once upon a time, but I don't think she would now. She's different. Her life is different, but I miss that passion. To love someone enough to act so recklessly is remarkable."

Right on cue, Simon walked into the room. Now, unlike Kane, Simon should win an award. He stopped suddenly, his eyes growing wide before narrowing. His voice was the perfect blend of surprise and scorn.

"Well, isn't this a picture. What the hell is she doing here?" He was improvising, so Simon.

"I invited her for tea." Mrs. Marks was holding her own, her disdain coming across loud and clear. "It is my house, after all."

"Thought you had better taste than that, Mrs. Marks. Where's Teagan?"

"She's not here." This came from Camille, who was clearly not happy with Simon's interruption.

Simon stared at Camille as if her head were sprouting a plant. "You figured that out all on your own, that's surprising."

I bit down on my lip so hard I drew blood; Kane was turning an unhealthy shade of red and Mrs. Marks was grinning behind her teacup. Stay on script, Simon. Moving from my spot, I waited a beat or two before I entered.

"Hey, Simon . . ." Taking a cue from Simon, I widened my eyes. "Camille, here again?"

She snarled, her lips curling up to bare her teeth. "Teagan."

"Looking to the steal the silver?" I asked sweetly.

"Hardly."

"Kane, don't you look comfortable. Am I interrupting?"

"Nope, just friends having tea," he said.

"Friends now, really? That's a surprise. I thought you found her tedious, at least that's what you said the other night."

Kane's head lowered, and Camille looked like she wanted to kill me. I moved on. "Did you enjoy the O'Malleys' party? I did. I learned something interesting. Is it true you flunked out of Yale? It's a real shame that Daddy greased some palms for nothing."

"How dare you?"

"We know you didn't get in based on your brains, I mean, seriously. A person only needs to talk to you to know you aren't Ivy League material."

"You think you're so great, but you're nothing."

"I disagree. Unlike you, I managed to stay in college, even graduated with honors. I own my own business, I'm engaged to *him*, and

I live in this fabulous house. All the things you wanted. In fact, I'm living your dream. That must sting a bit."

Steam was coming from her ears, and she looked about ready to scratch my eyes out. "He should have been mine. He liked me until you showed up."

"He defected awfully quickly, so he couldn't have liked you very much."

"You bitch."

"Maybe, but I'm only speaking what I see. Speaking of which, where's Sleazy? I mean, Dimitri. Now, he's more your speed. So what was the plan? He steals things from here, but how were you planning on paying for them? You've got no money." Looking her from head to toe I added, "And if you're bartering for the items with your assets, Sleazy's getting the short end of the stick."

She launched to her feet, and I honestly believed she would have attacked me if Simon hadn't placed himself between us.

Her next words were hissed. "So smug, but I sure as hell had a big influence in your world, no matter what you think."

I turned cold at the venom in her words, but this was what I wanted, so I acted blasé and confused. "What do you mean by that?"

"I didn't get the dream, but neither did you."

My skin crawled at how callously she offered that tidbit. "Like you had anything to do with that."

Her eyes turned to Kane. "I only ever wanted you, Kane. The house would have been nice, but I wanted you. You had nothing, came from nothing, but I wanted to offer you the world. And then she came into your life and she was all you could see. You never gave us a chance."

"I'm hearing an awful lot of whining and jealousy, but that's a far cry from having any control over Kane's and my lives. Delusional much, Camille?"

"I set that fire. Set it to get Kane there." She turned imploringly to Kane. "I had that passion, not Kathy."

Fury burned through me. Simon held me back from attacking. My gaze moved to Kane, who stood, his body rigid with rage, then to Mrs. Marks, who was fisting her hands in her lap. "You set the fire intentionally?" I asked.

"I wanted him . . . I couldn't have him . . ."

"So you set a fire?"

Her gaze looked a bit wild, and she turned it on Kane. "You didn't want me. I had to make you understand."

"Understand what?" Ominous was the only word to describe Kane's voice.

"I always get what I want."

In that minute, Mr. Bowen, Mr. Lawson, and the sheriff came walking into the room. Shock kept Camille from speaking. She stared at her father as if confused as to why he was there. Pain shone in her expression, so I guessed there was still someone who she actually cared about.

"Daddy, what are you doing here?"

"I always knew you were selfish and spoiled, but this? I don't have words."

"You're under arrest, Camille Bowen, for arson," the sheriff said. It grated that we could only get Camille on arson due to the time that had lapsed since the fire, but Mr. Lawson explained that arson was without a statute of limitations and, in Maine, was punishable by up to thirty years in jail. He was certain that if we got her to admit to starting the fire with the intent to cause harm to another, the prosecutor would push for, and win, the maximum sentence.

"What?" Her confusion turned to panic. "What are you talking about?"

I answered her. "You intentionally set a fire to harm Kane, a fire that almost killed him. You should be tried for attempted murder, in my opinion. You cost him his sight and caused the burns that he spent years recovering from. Did you honestly believe you were going to get away with that?"

"But . . ."

Mr. Clancy arrived at that moment to show the sheriff and Camille to the door, Mrs. Marks following, after talking to Mr. Bowen and Mr. Lawson. Simon stepped up to me as I reached for Kane's hand.

"Well, I don't even have words. I can't believe she did it, can't believe she confessed," Simon said. His attention turned to Kane and me. "She really didn't get that what she did was wrong. That is seriously fucked up."

Simon wasn't wrong. "You can say that again, but what I don't understand is if she was after Kane all along then what was the point of the whole blackmailing ruse with Mr. Sleazy? It's not like she needed access to Raven's Peak, she's been making herself at home here for years."

"No idea." Simon replied, but Kane remained silent.

Squeezing his hand, I asked, "You okay?"

"She's a fucking bitch. I want a few minutes with her."

"The sheriff agreed to it, right?" I understood where he was coming from.

"Yeah."

"What are you going to say to her?"

"I don't know, but something will come."

Kane

Camille was being transported to Portland. Before she left, I had a few words to say to her, and then I intended to put her out of my mind forever. She had been brought into the visitor room of the local jail, just her and me. Zeus was with me. He helped me to find the chair.

I wished I could see her in that moment, wished I could see the expression on her face. Though I suspected it wouldn't be as contrite as it should be, just belligerent.

"Come to gloat?" She sounded just like the spoiled child she was.

"Gloat? Have you noticed I'm blind?"

"I didn't mean for that to happen. I thought you'd get wounded, but I never imagined you'd get trapped."

"You fucking set a building on fire when there were people in it. It wasn't just me you put at risk, not even just Kathy and the others—you put yourself in danger."

"Well, I clearly didn't think it all the way through." She sounded dismissive, like that was of no matter.

Rage burned through me. If I'd had my sight, I would have likely reached across the table and strangled her with my bare hands. "Didn't think it through?"

Standing up, I lifted my shirt and heard her gasp. "You did this! You intentionally did this. Have you any idea the pain associated with burns like this, the months of agony, the years of recovery, the surgeries where they take skin from other parts of your body to graft? I lived in hell for years because you didn't fucking *think it all the way through*."

Still no tears, but something sounding like remorse came through now. "I had no idea."

"You stole nine years of my life, and not only did you make me live through hell, you put Tea through hell as well, when I attempted to protect her from the nightmare you caused. I love Tea, you know just how much I do, and yet you can sit there with barely any remorse in your voice. As if it's all a big misunderstanding. Understand this, Camille, I've already been called as a witness. I fully intend to show them what you've just seen. Dimitri is testifying. Kathy is as well. You're going away for a long fucking time. And once I walk out this door, I'll forget all about you, because I have a life, a family, and Tea waiting for me. And you, you'll be here miserable and alone. You brought that on yourself.

"Oh, and as a parting gift . . ." I pulled the Polaroids from my pocket and tossed them on the table. "So you don't feel as if you've walked away empty-handed. Here are some pictures of Raven's Peak. Hang them on the wall in your jail cell—that is as close as you'll ever get again."

I knew Tea was waiting for me as soon as I stepped out onto the sidewalk; I smelled her, felt her. She sounded unsure when she asked, "How did it go? You okay?"

"Absolutely. Let's go for a walk on the beach."

"Sounds perfect."

We started down the street, Tea pressed up against my side, letting me feel her words before she said them.

"I never liked Camille, not from the first day I saw her talking to you outside of school. I hated her."

"What day?"

"My first day of school—you took me for ice cream, but before, you were talking to her. It's why I started to leave. I didn't want you to feel like you had to hang with me."

"That's why? I wondered. I was only talking to her while I waited for you. I saw you come out of the school, watched you walk away, and realized my plan backfired."

"We were so young," she said.

"Yep."

"I love you as much now as I did then—more."

"You better." But I tucked her closer and held on to those words for the entire walk home.

Teagan

Simon peppered the man next to him on the flight to Boston with questions about where he got his shoes. It was amazing to me how he could befriend anyone. He just had the kind of personality people were drawn to. Zeus was lying on the floor at our feet, his head resting on a pillow I'd brought just for him.

Mr. Lawson had called before we left with the answer to the mystery regarding the role Mr. Sleazy had played in Camille's game. It was out of spite—she never intended to buy the pieces Mr. Sleazy planned to steal, she just didn't want Kane to have them. And I suspected she forced her father to believe the lie about Kathy setting the fire so that the focus, or guilt, never shifted to her. Like I had said countless times before, Camille was a vile bitch but not a very clever one. Her own stupidity had ensnarled her and it helped that Mr. Sleazy had cut a deal for a lesser sentence by coming clean about the entire sordid mess. Of course he still had to deal with his parents and their charges against him.

Kane had been quiet since we'd left Raven's Peak a few hours before. I knew he was nervous. I couldn't blame him, remembering the terror I felt the day I'd pretended to be blind. It meant so much to me that Kane made the trip despite his fears. I had so many places I wanted to show him. The tour was for me too, since I had decided not to return to Boston.

Simon and I had talked, and he knew my home was with Kane. When Kane returned to Raven's Peak, I intended to be with him. I'd start the legwork for space for our second store, since Simon and I were definitely going to move into phase two. He'd take care of adjusting our Boston store, bringing our employees, Christy and Matt, up to speed on their new roles as managers. When he was comfortable that everything in Boston was good, he'd join me in Maine. I liked that he wanted to be there too. It wasn't just for the store either. He liked it there, the people and the town.

"What are you thinking about?" Kane's voice pulled me from my thoughts.

"How much I can't wait to start my life with you."

His grin was adorable. "I thought we already had."

"I mean officially. I want to move into our house. I want us to work on setting up the inn, but before that, I want to share Boston with you. I can't wait to show you the Harborwalk and the Commons. We can go to the harbor and check out the *Constitution*, which is docked there." Leaning into him, I touched my mouth to his. "Thank you for coming."

"I like hearing you happy."

"I like you."

Getting out of the crowded Logan International Airport had been a bit overwhelming. Zeus was incredible, guiding Kane easily through the bodies. Once Simon and I had grabbed our bags, we headed out for a cab. As I settled in the cab, I took a deep breath. In truth, getting through the airport was the part that had scared me the most. Kane was quiet again, his face turned toward the window. I wondered what he was thinking. This was his first trip outside Blue Hill since he'd lost his sight. Later, when we were in bed, I'd try to get it out of him.

"Sunshine left us some baked goods as a welcome home." Simon supplied that lovely little tidbit.

She had been bringing in our mail and checking on our plants. We loved Sunshine's baked goods.

"She's the one who made that cake?" Kane asked. He sounded hopeful.

"Yeah. Wait until you try her brownies."

I saw a smile, the first one since we'd left Maine. So another fan of Sunshine's baked goods. Reaching the apartment, Simon offered to take the bags so Kane and I could walk Zeus. Poor baby had been cooped up in some type of transportation all day.

The air was cool. Fall was coming. We walked along Harrison Street down to Massachusetts Avenue. The silence felt comfortable, but I was still curious, so I asked Kane, "What are you thinking?"

"It's strange, being completely unfamiliar with where I am. Even the scents are different. But it's not as bad as I was expecting."

Relief washed over me. "Really?"

"Yeah, I've adapted far better than I'd thought—using my other senses more than I knew I was."

"I'm so happy to hear that. I was nervous that you were hating every minute of this."

"Not possible—I'm with you. But I'm going to enjoy myself more than I thought."

"Yay."

"You can't let go, though, Tea."

My hand tightened around his. "Never."

Kane

Stepping into the space that had been Tea's home for so long—the place where she'd found sanctuary after I'd broken her heart—took a will I didn't know I had. I hated knowing this place existed because of what I had done.

Her scent was in the space, faint but undeniable. Simon's too. Wasn't sure how I felt about knowing her friend by his scent. I was turning into a fucking woman.

"So in front of you is the living room." She walked me to the sofa, and I ran my hand along the back of it. "There's a big chair, an ottoman just to the right of it, and a coffee table separating them," she said as she walked me to each piece, showing me the lay of the land. It wasn't really necessary, Zeus knew what he was doing, but she sounded so adorable, so I didn't stop her.

"There's a television against the wall. The kitchen . . ."

"What's it look like?" I needed to know the space she surrounded herself with.

"Oh." She sounded flustered. Reaching for her, my thumb brushed over her cheek and felt the heat there.

"You're blushing."

"Maybe a little."

"Describe your space for me, Tea."

"The walls are a deep plum, with white crown moldings. The sofa is a gray chenille with throw pillows in ivory and plum. The coffee table and TV armoire are medium cherry wood and the floors are a lighter cherry. There are prints of Boston, some watercolors, and a picture of Raven's Peak and . . . our island."

My head turned in her direction. "You have a picture of our island on your wall?"

I could feel her hesitation by the stillness of the air. Her voice was soft, a touch sad. "I asked Mr. Clancy to send it to me about a year after we broke up. Some dreams you can't let go."

I didn't deserve her, after what I'd put her through, but I wasn't going to let her go. "I never let it go either."

She was crying. I could hear it in her voice. "My room is this way."

Taking my hand, she walked me down the hall. Her scent grew stronger—this was her domain. "The bed is an old white iron bed, the comforter is white eyelet."

My pulse pounded in my throat. "What color are the walls?"

Her reply was so soft, barely a whisper. "Blue, a clear crystal blue."

Curling my fingers around her arms, I yanked her to me, my mouth sealing over hers, my tongue driving into her sweet mouth, my arms pulling her close, locking her there. She kissed me back, her hands moving around my waist. Her tongue warred with my own. We were both out of breath when we ended the kiss. My fingers traced her face, seeing her, the swollen lips, the slight smile.

"I like your room, Tea."

"I like that you're in my room, Kane."

It was still early, so after the tour, we sat on a bench in Christopher Columbus Park, splitting a sandwich. A light breeze was blowing, the scent of the sea surrounding us.

"There's a red one, probably around thirty feet, double mast, white sail. Lights along the masts and main sheath—looks like they're having a party." Tea finished describing the scene, and I could see it exactly as she described it.

"And we weren't invited," I said.

She leaned closer to me. "You look happy."

"I've got my woman, my dog, and food—what more do I need?"

"When you go back, I'm coming with you." My head snapped toward her, my heart beating hard in my chest. "I thought you were going to stay in Boston for a few weeks."

Her next words swelled my chest again, making my heart beat in an uneven rhythm. "Can't. I've been away from you for too long. I don't want to be away from you any longer."

"But the shop?" Why the fuck was I arguing with her?

"Simon's got it. I'll start looking into our new place in Maine. Is that okay?" Nervousness rang from her words, and no wonder, because her idiot man was arguing with her over something we both wanted.

"Okay? You're coming home with me to stay . . . yeah, that's fucking okay."

I heard her sigh.

"I want you with me, Tea. I just don't want you to have to give up anything to do that."

"I'm not. Simon has everything well in hand, and I need to start looking for a new storefront."

"You don't have to convince me. I'm all for you coming home with me."

In her room later, I rested in bed while she finished her nighttime ritual. She had always been like that, had to wash her face, brush her teeth and hair, lotion her skin. I wasn't complaining, I enjoyed every part of her ritual, but I wanted her in the bed now.

"Tomorrow, I'll take you to the shop." She was sitting at her dressing table across the room as she spoke.

"Okay."

"The party is on Friday. Seven at the shop."

"Looking forward to it." What I was looking forward to was experiencing her in the world she had created for herself. The bed dipped slightly, her scent surrounding me, and her soft body brushed up against mine.

Reaching for her, I ran my fingers over her shoulder, along her clavicle, my fingertips brushing over the soft silk of her nightgown.

"What are you wearing?"

"It's a black nightie, lace and silk."

"Lace?"

"Yeah." She took my hand and placed it over her breast. My dick hardened instantly. "Lace here"—she slid my hand lower to her belly—"and silk here." Moving my hand even lower, I felt the curls between her legs, the wet heat. "Nothing here," she said.

Growling, I pushed her onto her back, spread her legs, and buried my face between her thighs. Sweet Tea, my favorite flavor. I loved the sounds she made in the back of her throat as I teased the nub, flicking my tongue over it before sucking. Her hips lifted, and her fingers laced through my hair. Moving through her fold, I pushed my tongue deep into her, wishing it were my dick. I felt her clench around me, felt the tremors, the start of her orgasm. Rubbing that nub, I pushed my tongue in farther and pressed down, and she came on a cry.

Kissing my way up her body, I lifted her nightgown up and pulled it over her head. Running my hands down her body, I cupped her breasts, pushed them together, and licked her, teasing the nipples until I closed my mouth over one and pulled it into my mouth.

"On your hands and knees." My request came out in more of an order, but I was hard and wanted to be inside her now.

"Okay." Lust turned her voice deeper.

"Wrap your fingers around your headboard. You holding on?"

"Yeah." I wished I could see her. My Tea, on her knees, her tits brushing the pillow, holding on to the rails of her bed, her legs spread, her ass tilted, waiting for me.

Moving behind her, I ran my hand down her spine and over her ass before I gripped her hips. "Wish I could see you like this."

"Please, Kane."

"Anything for you." I wanted to pound into her, but instead I eased in, slow and deliberate.

"Oh God."

My hand moved to her back again, running over her spine and up along her arms, before I wrapped my hand around hers, her grip so tight I was sure her fingers were turning white. My other hand found her breast, rolling the nipple, twisting and turning it as my hips moved harder and deeper. And then there was no thinking, just feeling. Grabbing her hips, I pounded into her, hard and fast, until I felt her spasming around me, and then I stilled as I emptied myself into her. Like always, my release was fierce and lasting, my body pulsing in pleasure. Still buried inside her, I bent forward, curling around her to hold her close.

She was satisfied, maybe a little smug, when she said, "That was incredible."

So incredible I took her again ten minutes later.

I heard excitement and pride in Tea's voice as we walked to her shop the next morning. She was different, more confident and animated. Clearly she loved what she did, and it was comforting to know that; even though it wasn't where she had intended to be, she had made the most of it. Hearing Tea, experiencing the world she had created for herself, wasn't just humbling—it was eye opening. She had once said I was hiding and she'd been right. I had been. I hadn't accomplished a damn thing since my accident: nothing substantial, nothing that someone could build a life on. Tea had made a life in Boston, had friends there. And because of me, she was going to give all that up. In theory, I loved the idea, until I realized just what she was going to be giving up. Especially since she only had this life because of me.

"Here we are. So the front is all glass, and the displays are switched out every month. Right now we're featuring a bedroom set, circa 1880. Cherry wood, Chippendale style. An old patchwork quilt with faded deep colors—red, blue, green—covers the mattress. Our sign, hunter green and muted gold, hangs over the door. 'New to You Antiques.' I kind of stole that from Mrs. Marks."

The door opened and I could smell the history, the scent of wood and parchment, linens that had spent time in mothballs, lemon wax. "Everything is set up like rooms, every piece for sale."

"Hey, Teagan. Welcome back," a male voice called. I tensed; it was stupid but instinctual.

"Matt, this is Kane, my fiancé."

I heard the footsteps approaching, so I stuck out my hand. "Hi, Matt."

Hesitation and a slightly damp palm greeted me when he shook my hand. He was uncomfortable. Blind people tended to draw that reaction from people. "Hey, Kane. Nice to meet you."

"Christy's in the back. I'll go get her. We made a sale—the Shaker bookcase and desk."

"Really? How much did you get?"

"Eight thousand dollars for the set."

"Nice."

"Yeah, we were pretty stoked."

A breeze, the jangle of the bell, and then I heard Simon's voice bellowing as he entered, "Greetings! Coffee and donuts have arrived."

"Why do you always have to make a grand entrance?" Tea asked. My lips twitched.

"Is there any other kind?"

I felt the shrug from Tea before she said, "I guess not. You're really a ham."

"Kane, coffee." Lifting my hand, he pressed the cup into it.

"Thanks."

"Matt and Christy sold the Shaker. Eight thousand dollars."

"Sweet." Simon's footsteps moved away, the strong smell of coffee going with him. When Simon spoke next, he was across the room. "I bought a doggie bagel for Zeus. Is that okay?"

"Yeah, thanks." He'd thought of my dog. Another hit. Not only had she made something of herself, she'd managed to surround herself with good people. Even broken and adrift, she'd *lived*, and the same couldn't be said of me. I felt very undeserving of her.

"My mom's like a dog with a bone anyway, but when it's one of the parties she's organized, she becomes a bit much. No worries.

When the party is over, we have Sunshine's brownies to look forward to. I have a feeling we're going to need them."

"It's very nice she's doing this."

"Yes, blah, blah, but it'll be mostly her clients and friends, so it's going to be a bit dry. You know I'm not wrong. Good for business, yes, but entertaining, I don't think I'd go that far."

Tea's silence was a clear indication that she agreed with Simon, if reluctantly.

Simon was right, the party was definitely good for business, at least in the several transactions I overheard, but entertaining it was not. Zeus and I stood off to the side; Tea had just left me to show a couple a bedroom set they had their eyes on. I liked how spirited she sounded, how knowledgeable she was, and I realized I had never asked her about school, about what she'd studied. It had sort of slipped my mind as we'd been finding our way, but later, after I peeled her dress from her and made us both happy, I'd ask.

Earlier she had run my hands down her body so I could feel the clingy black material that hugged her figure. I'd been hard since. She had done it on purpose, giving me something to think about during the party, in case she wasn't at my side. Not a bad way to spend my time, visualizing her in that dress and her out of it—but damn uncomfortable.

I smelled her before I felt her small hand on my chest. "Hey. Would you like something to drink? Wine, scotch?"

"No, thanks. It sounds like the party is a success."

She moved right up against my side. I loved when she did that.

"It is. Everyone's dressed in gowns and tuxes. You look incredible, by the way."

I had purchased a tux, endured the fittings, and, hearing her compliment, it had been worth the aggravation. "This old thing."

"Sexy, you look incredibly sexy."

Her fingers were working down my chest to my stomach, my hard-on turning even harder. I might need to wear the tux more often.

"You need to stop that or I'm taking you to the back and easing the ache you're causing."

"Promise?"

Despite the fact I was blind, my eyes still widened. "Don't tease me."

"Who's teasing? I have an office—"

"Where?"

She moved us through the store, as eager as I was, if her near run was any clue. Reaching her office, she pulled me into it.

"Zeus, stay," I said. I may have growled it, I wasn't sure.

The door closed at my back, her mouth on mine, her fingers working my zipper. Grabbing her, I moved the fabric up, pulled her close, my fingers slipping under her panties to stroke her ass.

"Where's your desk?" I asked in a way that sounded more like an order.

Taking my hand, she led me to it.

"Hands flat on the desk."

"Okay."

My hands moved to her shoulders, pulling the straps of her gown down her arms, pinning them to her sides. Cupping her full breasts, I worked her nipples while rubbing myself against her ass. If only I could see the sight of a naked Tea on her knees, watching as her breasts shook, while I fucked her mouth, her own fingers stroking herself to climax. I'd had that dream countless times over the years. Later tonight, even without sight, I'd make that fantasy a reality. And after, she could have me any way she wanted me.

"I want you inside me now, Kane."

"Impatient."

"Very."

Laughing, my fingers moved between her legs and I stroked her. She was already so wet. Finishing what she'd started, I pulled myself free, positioned myself, and pushed into her. We both moaned in pleasure. Tight and wet, I pushed in deep before pulling out, rubbing her own arousal over her.

"Please, Kane."

"Chest flat on the desk, arch your back for me, Tea."

She didn't hesitate, and I felt as her ass tilted upward. I didn't hesitate either as I slammed into her, over and over again, until she spasmed around me, a sexy sound rumbling low in her throat. I was right there with her, my body jerking as I came.

Breathing heavy, our scents filling the room, she purred, "That was awesome." She sounded so fucking hot.

"I need to clean you."

"No. I want your scent on me, want to feel you between my legs. Anticipation for later."

I grew hard again. Easing out of her, regret filled me. I wanted to be buried inside her still. Stepping back, I heard her move, heard the fabric slipping down her body. She leaned into me, and her natural scent mingled with our lovemaking was not helping my erection. Pressing a kiss on my mouth, she said against my lips, "See you out there."

The door opened and I heard Zeus enter. It took a few minutes for me to get myself back in my trousers, and then I lingered a few minutes more until I could actually walk. Voices came from down the hall, soft like a whisper. I hadn't intended to listen until I heard what they were discussing.

"Such a shame. Poor Teagan. She's worked so hard getting this shop open. I heard she was moving back to Maine, giving up her life here to be with him. I think it's a very romantic concept, but it seems to me that he should be the one to move since he doesn't have a job, instead of forcing her to give up everything for him."

"Teagan and Simon are opening a shop in Maine?" The voice sounded surprised and concerned.

"Only so she can be close to him. It could sink them, this move—the expense of opening a second store, when they've only just gotten this one off the ground. But she's determined to do it and Simon backs her."

"Such a tragedy."

They continued to talk, but I moved away from the door, stumbling until I found a chair and dropped down into it. Zeus nudged my leg with his head, his fur touching my numb hand. I hadn't realized the impact moving to Maine would have on her business—she'd been happy talking about that second store. I hadn't really thought a great deal about what I was asking her to give up to be with me. And I couldn't argue with those gossips, since they were right. I'd pushed her into this life, and now I was asking her to give it all up, and for what?

Teagan

Simon saw the last partygoers to the door, but my thoughts remained on Kane. Our moment in my office had been incredible. I wondered what he had been thinking, what fantasy he was having, because there had been a deliberateness to his actions, a longing that I'd sensed hadn't quite been quenched with that fast but fantastic ride. I was up for anything, would do anything, have anything done to me, as long as it was Kane doing it. Just thinking about the possibilities made my body respond in a very pleasant way. Since that moment in my office, though, he had been acting odd. Distant. I couldn't wait to get him home so I could ask him what was troubling him. Besides, I had a surprise for him, one I knew he was really going to like.

"Have to hand it to my mom. She outdid herself. We made some really good contacts tonight."

"We did, and we sold quite a bit too."

"Added bonus. Where's Kane?" Simon asked exactly what I was wondering.

"Not sure. I saw him earlier, but that was over an hour ago. I'll see if he's in the back."

Nervousness, or maybe it was worry, had my heart pounding in my throat. Checking my office, I discovered that he wasn't there, nor was he in the small room we used to consult with clients. After a quick sweep of the store, my worry turned to panic.

"Simon, he's not here."

"What? He's got Zeus. Maybe he just went for a walk."

"He's doesn't know the way and neither does Zeus."

"Does he have his phone?"

"Oh, right." Hurrying to the counter, I grabbed my phone out of my purse. Dialing Kane, my hands shook as I put the phone to my ear. It went right to voice mail. Fear clawed at me. He could be anywhere and, not being able to see, he wouldn't know which direction was up. Even with Zeus, how would he know where he was?

"What do we do?" I was bordering on hysterical.

"Calm down first. He's a grown man. If he gets into trouble, he'll figure it out. Seriously, Tea, he isn't a helpless child."

I knew that, and still I couldn't stand the thought of him out there alone and blind in a strange city, especially since he was only in Boston because I had asked him to come.

"My guess, Zeus knows the way home, if nothing else, so let's check the apartment first."

"Okay." A rational move. I needed that, since I wasn't thinking clearly at all.

Throwing the door open, I called out. "Kane, are you here?"

He came out of my room, dressed in jeans and a tee. He was wearing sneakers and a jacket.

"Are you going somewhere?"

"Home."

"Now?"

"Yeah."

Simon moved past me into the apartment. "I'll be in my room," he said before disappearing down the hall.

"What's going on?"

"I never asked you about college, about your studies. Hearing you tonight, I realized how much you love what you do."

"I do."

"I'm proud of you, proud of what you've accomplished despite what I put you through."

"Kane, what's going on?"

"I need to do the same. You're right, I was hiding, afraid of living, so I buried myself on that island in a solitary life. Asking you to give this all up for that isn't fair."

"You're not—"

"Let me finish, please. I'm blind. I've finally come to terms with that. I won't be the man I thought I'd be when I was that eleven-year-old. There are so many things I'll never be able to do. I mourned for that for a long time—up until a few hours ago, if I'm being perfectly honest. But though I'm not who I thought I'd be, I can still do so much. Witnessing the life you created here only reinforces that. I don't want you to have to give anything up, and I don't want to be a burden. I want to be able to make it on my own, to find my own niche, to be self-sufficient, so we're stronger together, and it's not just me pulling you down. I've been working toward that, taking classes online, learning about business and finance."

I hadn't known he was doing that. I was happy to hear he was. "For the inn?"

"Raven's Peak to start, but I want to open multiple inns, if I can."

"I think that's a wonderful goal."

"I'm going home, Tea, going to work my ass off to be the man you deserve."

And just like that, the happy glow faded, the familiar knot in my stomach returning. "You're pushing me away again."

"No, just trying to stand on my own two feet."

My head got it, but my heart wasn't on the same page. "Call it what you want, but you're holding yourself back. I can't do this again, Kane. Can't be left again."

"Can you not see that I need to do this for myself, and, in doing it for me, it will be for you too?"

"What I see is you pulling back into yourself. You don't want my help. You don't want me to treat you differently because you're blind, and yet at every turn you place your blindness right there between us."

"I'm not pulling away, Tea."

"You are, you're here, dressed to leave without me. You're leaving me again." The ache I had lived with for years was back, and even more devastating.

His face turned fierce, and he stepped closer to me. "I'm not leaving you."

"You are." I wanted to curl up in a ball, wanted to disappear again.

"Tea."

"Go, just go. Find what I can't give you. Put your demons to rest, but know this: You leave here now, I won't be following. You want me, you know where to find me."

He looked incredulous as well as hurt. "Of course I want you."

At that moment, I honestly couldn't agree with his heartfelt declaration.

"I don't want to leave things like this," he whispered.

I couldn't stop the tears even if I'd wanted to. It was all too familiar, too much like the last time. "Please just go."

He turned and walked into my bedroom, and my heart cracked open. I couldn't believe this was happening again. When he returned, he had his bag over his shoulder and his dog at his side. Watching as he headed to the door, I was screaming inside for him to stay, to stay with me. He reached for the doorknob, his voice so soft I almost missed it, "Love you, Tea."

And then he was gone, walking out of my life again.

Teagan

Lying in bed the morning after Kane left me, I stared up at the ceiling. Simon lay next to me, his arms folded under his head.

"He didn't leave you."

"You keep saying that, but it sure as hell feels like it."

"He'll be back. He needs to do this, needs to know he can do it, can manage without you, so being with you won't feel like helplessness."

"I get it in theory, but it still hurts like hell."

"Yes, well, that's why I suggested eating Sunshine's brownies."

"I'm pregnant."

Simon nearly fell out of the bed. "What?" His eyes moved down to my stomach. "You are?"

"Yep. I took the test before we left Maine. I had planned on telling Kane last night after the party."

"Kane doesn't know?"

"Nope, and during his speech about needing to stand on his own didn't really seem like the best time to drop it on him."

"You need to tell him."

"I realize that, but how's that going to go? He'll come back because he's responsible, and then he'll grow to resent me and our child, since he never did find whatever the hell it is he's looking for."

"You're upset, I get that, but deep down you know what he's doing is what's best for him. You're just upset that you can't be at his side while he does it."

"What if he can't? What if he never finds what he's looking for?" It was my biggest fear.

"I don't think—"

Sitting up, I looked back at Simon. "Seriously, what if he can't? What if his blindness is too much for him to overcome?"

"I don't know."

"I agree with what he's doing. Ever since I returned, I've been thinking he needed to do something like this, but I'm afraid that he won't find his way to the other side. He's had so much time already."

"He never had the enticement he has now."

"What do you mean by that?"

"You. He didn't have you. He does now, and he has that one," Simon said, touching my belly. "Amazing what a good incentive can accomplish. When are you going to tell him?"

"Don't know."

"Don't wait too long."

Dropping back on the bed, I really wished I could have two or three of Sunshine's brownies.

Kane

Two months ago, I'd left a heartbroken Tea. I'd called her every day and, though she sounded hopeful, there was a sadness about her. I wanted her with me, but I understood why she wouldn't come. She was right. I needed to go to her. And when I did, I'd be a man more deserving of her.

Breathing deeply, my hands actually shook a little, but it wasn't just nerves, it was also excitement. I was having the first staff meeting for the inn. I won't lie, when I first returned home the whole idea seemed incredibly daunting—turning Raven's Peak into an inn given my lack of sight. How did I work with the contractors? How did I create and follow a project plan or check status updates when I couldn't see? Mr. Clancy and I did a bit of research on the sites left to me by my nurse, into the technology available to aid those without sight—software that allowed for voice commands, apps that actually spoke what was on the computer screen through synthesized voices, other apps that converted documents into Braille. We even had the floor plans drawn up in Braille, tactile graphics they were called. Once we got a system set up and trained the various contractors on the uniqueness of my project management style, it was surprisingly easy to mange the transformation of Raven's Peak into an inn. I also learned that sighted or not, I was going to need help and more, I had learned it was okay to ask for it.

Kevin O'Malley had helped me hire the contractors, and Mr. Lawson and Mr. Bowen had helped with the legal parts. Mrs. T and Mr. Clancy had helped me interview the staff members who would be assuming their roles now that they were officially retiring.

I hired Kathy to manage the inn. It made me feel good, despite all that had happened, that she was there because I had walked into that fire: The ends absolutely justified the means.

We were meeting in the kitchen. Zeus walked with me down the hall from the library where I'd set up a temporary office. I'd thought about using the study, but I felt Tea in the library, felt her around me, and I drew strength from that.

I could hear their voices and knew that I wasn't the only one who was excited about this venture. Mrs. Marks had been very outspoken the past couple of months, thrilled at the activity going on in her home and the direction I was taking the place.

The voices immediately softened as I stepped into the kitchen.

"Is everyone here?" I asked.

"Yes," Mr. Clancy said. He had become my right-hand man. It wasn't helplessness to ask for help—Tea had been right.

"There are only a few rules that will be strictly enforced: We all help out, because Raven's Peak is big and can be a handful. If you need something, ask; don't go without because you're afraid to ask. The customer is always right, even if they aren't. We want the experience to be so outstanding that they return year after year and tell their friends about us. And lastly, we eat cake for every staff meeting."

I could feel Mrs. Marks's eyes on me, even though I couldn't see her. Mrs. Rainer was the new chef. Mrs. T raved about her pudding and sauces. From what I had sampled of her work, she was worth the rave reviews. "So, Mrs. Rainier, what cake did you bake for us?"

"Mrs. T gave me her recipe for your favorite: triple chocolate."

I flashed her a smile, "Excellent."

Two slices of cake later, I hunted down Kevin. Well, Zeus did. He was staying close to help oversee the contractors.

"What can I do for you, Kane?"

"I need the name of the uniform cleaners you used for the ice cream parlor—will they handle linens?"

"We'll call and see. How's it going?"

"Good, all the permits are in place, plus the insurance and legal agreements with the town. The contractor is making some renovations in the west wing for Mrs. Marks and the others. The new fence is up, and we've placed a locked gate on the stairs—legal demanded that. A sign is being made, a few vans purchased to transport guests to town." I'd finally found a use for the money the town had given me after the fire, and it seemed fitting to use it on the inn, since it was going to bring tourist business to the town too.

"Sounds like it's all coming together. How's Tea feeling about it?"

"We talk, but there's a distance. I hope I did the right thing, that I didn't hurt her one more time than she can forgive."

"She loves you, son, I imagine she'd forgive you anything."

"I hope so."

Teagan

"If I throw up one more time, I swear to God, Simon, my stomach is going to come out."

"That is really disgusting. Thank you for putting that visual in my head." Simon was rubbing my back, which caused a case of déjà vu to wash over me as I remembered the night I'd gotten stupid drunk at Dahlia's. "You haven't told him yet. You're almost three months along, Tea, you got to tell him."

"I know."

"So?"

"I think it should be done in person, but I'm waiting for him to come to me. Stupid, I know, since asking him to travel to me is kind of rude, but he left. Every time he leaves, I somehow come back to him. He needs to come to me."

"I understand, but you're carrying his child. He has a right to know that."

"I agree, and every day I reach for the phone and every day I stop myself."

"We haven't talked about the shop in Maine. You still want to do that?"

"I think business-wise, it's a good investment, but if Kane and I don't . . . Maybe it won't be Maine, but I think opening a second shop is smart."

"Me too."

"I almost told Mrs. Marks about the baby yesterday, but Kane should hear it first. There's a lot of activity going on at Raven's Peak. She sounded excited."

"That's good news."

"I hope so."

Kane

"The florist is here and needs the order," Mrs. T called, hurrying down the hallway. Opening day was in one week. In five months, we'd turned Raven's Peak from a private home to an inn. I hadn't felt this kind of pride in something I had done in a really long time.

"Kane, the inspector needs you to sign off," Mr. Clancy said as he, too, hurried past me. Moving through the house, Zeus at my side, I felt more like the kid I had been, the optimistic wide-eyed kid. I had driven it, planned it, organized it, coordinated it, seen it through, and countless people had helped. My blindness hadn't stopped me, hadn't been the obstacle I deep down feared it would be. And having accomplished this, I was eager to try for some of the other dreams Tea and I had.

I wouldn't do another thing without her, though. I was done with life without my Tea. There was the very real possibility that she was going to take a play from my book and push me away when I saw her again. Well, she could try to push me away, but I wasn't going anywhere. I might have a fight on my hands, but I was prepared to fight dirty if necessary. I loved her, wanted her, and I knew she felt the same despite the anger she may have been feeling toward me at the moment.

"Four more reservations on the wait list," Kathy called from the library.

"The contractor needs you," Mrs. Marks said, startling me, since I hadn't heard her approaching.

"Why aren't you wearing your heels?" I asked.

"Oh, so last year. I am all about Crocs now. I can garden in them, walk in the water and across the sand, and with no squished toes."

"I don't have a clue what a Croc is, and I think I will live a very happy life if I never do."

"They make them for men too."

"Never going to happen."

"Your loss. The contractor is in the kitchen. He needs you to sign off on the work done to your house. I like the changes a lot, Kane, and I just know Teagan will too."

"You're sure you're okay with me redistributing some of your things?"

"They're yours now, yours and Teagan's, but yes, I am very okay with it."

I had a surprise for Tea. I'd had the idea since we were kids and, with Raven's Peak turning into an inn, now seemed like the best time to turn the idea into reality.

"Car's here," Sam called from the doorway.

"Thanks, Sam. I'll be right there." Time to finish this up. There was somewhere I needed to be.

Teagan

It had been five months. I had a baby bump and I still hadn't told Kane. I didn't want to do it over the phone, so I was going home. I planned on purchasing a ticket on Monday. I hadn't wanted to be the one to go to him. He left, shouldn't he have been the one to come back? In the long run, I guess it didn't matter, and yet, to me, it did.

Simon had been off the grid for the last month—he told me it was a guy. Seemed odd that every time I walked in on him talking to this guy on the phone, he got all cryptic. He had never done that. He always shared with me. Was he moving on? Had he found his Kane? I wished him better luck with it. My Kane was slipping through my fingers. Simon was moving on and I was once again alone. Not really alone, though. My hand touched my baby bump. I had this little rascal.

I was happy for Kane, happy that he was happy. I could hear it in his voice when we spoke on the phone—hopefulness that I hadn't heard since we were kids. I couldn't deny that, as much as I'd hated being alone the past five months, I loved hearing that again. Maybe he was finally finding his way. And maybe that way wasn't with me. Seemed stupid, but then, with how our lives had been for the past ten years, at this point I didn't know shit about our futures.

Simon wasn't home and I didn't want to be alone, so I went to Sunshine's. I hung out with her until dawn, before dragging my butt home and going facedown for a while. When I woke up, I called out to Simon, but he was still MIA. It was Sunday, so the shop was closed. Being in the apartment alone was depressing, so I headed off to Christopher Columbus Park. The bench Kane and I had sat on was unoccupied, so I took a seat and looked out at the water. No sailboats. The water was a little rough, the sun bright. There was a boat, docked at one of the slips, with beautiful lines and colors. Kane would have loved that boat; in fact, it looked a lot like the one . . .

And then I stood to get a better look. It didn't just look like Kane's boat—it was. I could see the name *My Tea*, registered in Blue Hill, Maine. My heart pounded in my chest. His boat was here, so where was he? How did his boat get here?

Looking around the harbor, I didn't see him immediately. And then I saw Zeus, running toward me, and just behind him was Kane. He was here. He'd come for me. He'd come for me in his boat. Tears burst from my eyes. I watched as he moved effortlessly toward me. Impatient, I hurried up the grass toward him. I stopped myself from launching at him, my breath coming out in pants.

"Tea?"

"Yeah."

"Where the hell have you been?"

Not the reunion I was hoping for. Before I could speak he went off.

"No word? You just up and left. What if something had happened to you? How would we know where you were? How would we find you?"

"You did find me. How did you know I was here?"

"You brought *me* here—like the pier at home, it's your place."

Good guess. "I did call you repeatedly with no answer."

Some of the ire left him. "Must have been out of range."

"Really great to see you too."

"Sorry, I've just been a bit worried."

"I was in my apartment for the past several hours."

"You must have come back right after we left it."

"We?"

"Simon."

Oh, Simon. That was just rich. "Let me guess. You found yourself and now you prefer Simon."

He chuckled, his blue eyes sparkling with mischief. "I'm not gay." His hands reached for me, his fingers running over my face. "It is nice to see you." Pulling me to him, his arms started around me, until he stepped back like I'd hit him. His hand moved to my stomach. "Tea, are you eating too many sweets again?"

"Are you calling me fat, Kane Doyle?"

"Darling, you *are* fat."

I punched him, hard, and he laughed.

"I'm not fat, I'm pregnant."

His laughter died. "What?"

"I'm carrying your baby, I'm over five months along. I think it was that night after we met your mom, that perfect night. I'm hungry all the time, want to cry all the time, pee all the time, and, for the first few months, I was puking. It has been so exciting."

"You're pregnant?"

"*We're* pregnant."

A hardness came into his voice, darkened his eyes. "Why did you wait to tell me?"

"You needed to find yourself. It didn't seem fair to dump that on you then. Honestly, I didn't think it would take you this long to find yourself, since I didn't think you were lost to begin with."

And then I was in his arms, pressed so tightly against him, and I just sank into him because it felt so good to be there again. I'm not sure how long we stayed like that, not long enough, as far as I was concerned, before he stepped back, his hands reaching for my stomach again.

"A baby." His head lifted, his eyes finding mine despite not being able to see. "I love you, Tea."

My hands covered his. I didn't say it back because I didn't need to. "Your boat's here."

"I came to bring my woman home"—his voice choked up as he added—"and my baby."

"You drove the boat alone!" Now I was pissed. "Of all the irresponsible things to do—"

"Simon drove it."

"Simon?"

"Yeah, he came up to Maine to drive it down here with me. I heard a rumor that you got your boater's license, so I was hoping we could drive it back up the coast together."

"You want me to drive with you up the coast in your boat?"

"Just like we talked about as kids. Better 'cause it's the three of us," he added with a grin.

"I love that idea. My bag is at the apartment. I'm already packed. I was catching a plane in the morning."

"You were?"

"Yeah, I missed you and I needed to tell you about the new guy," I said.

The most serene expression covered his face, a peacefulness I had never seen in him. "You okay?" I asked.

"Never better. Really, never better." Reaching for my hand, he kissed his ring. "We'll call Simon to get your bag. He's catching a flight to Maine." Whistling for Zeus, we started toward his boat. "Shall we? O captain, my captain!"

So this is what it felt like when a dream came true. "Absolutely."

Kane

It felt unbelievably good—the wind in our faces, the scent of the sea and of Tea, her laugh as the boat skipped over the small swells of the ocean. I could feel her happiness from my spot next to her. It almost rivaled my own. We were having a baby. Tea was carrying my child. The day I'd hoped for had finally come. We were going to be a family.

I couldn't wait for her to see what I had done to our home—she was going to be thrilled with the changes.

"This is amazing," she called to me. "Do you want the wheel?"

I did, but I wasn't going to risk her, my child, or Zeus. "No, I'm okay. It's almost as good being the passenger."

"She's beautiful, Kane, you did an amazing job on her."

I didn't answer, knew I didn't need to.

"We're almost there. Do you want me to dock at the island or on the beach?"

"Beach."

Thirty minutes later, she was tying us off. "Do you want to take the path or the stairs?" she asked.

"Path—you're pregnant."

"Okay."

As soon as Raven's Peak came into view, I heard her exhale. "Oh my God, Kane, it's beautiful."

I knew what she was seeing, had walked around the gardens with Mrs. Marks, repeatedly, familiarizing myself with what had been done. The gardens now wrapped around the house, bursting with color. A fountain sat in the middle of the circular drive, the water cascading down the sides. Tables and umbrellas dotted the green grass, little clusters elegantly arranged and perfect for staring at the view beyond. Vans, with Raven's Peak Inn painted on them, sat parked near the front door ready to take guests into town.

A section of the yard, farther from the cliffs, had lawn games and additional sitting areas right off the terrace, so people could dine outside and play games. Everything had been planned to accommodate additional people, without looking crowded.

"You've been very busy," she said, and I heard admiration and love.

"Let's walk down the lane. You need to see the sign."

It was familiar, walking the lane like we used to as kids. I missed this, missed having her at my side. I could tell when we'd reached the sign, because she not only stopped walking but her body pressed into mine in contentment.

"You couldn't have picked a more perfect sign as the introduction."

"Describe it to me."

"It's deep green, with gold letters, a bare tree branch rises up along the right side of the sign and over the name 'Raven's Peak Inn.' Perched on the highest branch are two ravens. Mrs. Marks must love this."

"She does. She cried when we unveiled it. Ready to see our house?"

"You made changes to the house?"

"Yeah."

"I thought it was perfect just the way it was." She sounded a bit miffed now.

"Trust me."

"I do, but I still don't think you needed to change the house."

A half an hour later, we were walking up the beach toward home. "Looks the same from here," she muttered. But then I heard her intake of breath, and I knew it was for the gardens, namely the window boxes I'd had the gardener fill with plants. I knew how much Tea loved what had been done with them last summer, and the gardener assured me it was stunning.

"It's beautiful. The colors are exquisite—hot pink, purple, yellow, white against the green of the house—it's a picture."

"Come inside," I said, eager now for her to see the rest. Pushing the door open for her, she jolted to a stop. I'd had the living space changed. We'd fashioned the library in Raven's Peak on a smaller scale and the sofa, our sofa, was right smack in the middle of it.

Her exhale sounded harsh in surprise. "Our sofa." Her voice was soft, tenderness edging her words.

"Seemed only right that it be in our house."

"But you've changed the floor plan. You're going to have to memorize it all over." Concern—how like her to be more concerned for me.

"Babe, I rule the dark. Remember?"

Her next words dripped with humor. "You're a clown."

I grinned and said, "Let's go to the bedroom." Her hand tightened on mine as she led me to our room, where most of the work had been done. The back of the house had been moved out, and the bedroom had been expanded so her bedroom furniture from Raven's Peak would fit. The walls were done in blue, just like her old room.

She was so quiet I almost said her name to make sure she was still with me, and then I heard soft crying, deep as if from her soul. "Tea?"

"You brought our room to our house."

It was our room. I'd always thought of it that way too. I felt my own eyes stinging. "Did you see the terrace door?" I asked softly.

A small deck had been added to the back with a little sofa, so we could continue to watch the sunrise together.

She threw herself into my arms, buried her face in my neck. "It's perfect, Kane, it's absolutely perfect."

"I want to marry you."

"I know, me too."

Pushing her back, I cradled her face in my hands. "No, I mean now, in two days."

"What? I don't have a dress, and there's no pastor."

"I can get the pastor, and does the rest matter?"

I felt her answer in the way her body relaxed into mine. "No, it doesn't. You look happy. I'm guessing you found what you needed to."

"Who I really am didn't go very far. It was just lost for a while. The satisfaction of making Raven's Peak come together, to know I managed it, helped me to understand that needing help doesn't mean being helpless. You were right. I had to learn that lesson."

"And you've learned it?"

"Yes. And now I want my life with you, the life we talked about as kids. You, me, the family on the beach—here, in two days, we say our I dos." I couldn't stop touching her stomach, loved that what we felt for each other had created life. Humbling and oddly a major turn-on. "I need to make an honest woman out of you."

"Finally."

"Seems a crime our bed is just sitting there empty. It's been too long. I've a need, woman."

"Oh, I just bet," she said, but she was pulling me toward the bed.

"What are you wearing?"

"Does it matter? It's going to be off in a minute."

And then she was pulling me down on top of her, my body cradled in hers. Exactly my favorite place to be.

Teagan

I don't know how we pulled it off in two days, but we did. Kane was even now standing on the beach with Mrs. Marks and the family, waiting for me. The O'Malleys were there too, as was Kane's mom and her husband and Mr. Miller. Simon was with me, helping me dress, since I was so nervous my fingers weren't working.

I was wearing a simple white sundress and my hair was down, a ring of daisies around my crown. I was holding a cluster of hot pink peonies, and my feet were bare.

"You have his ring?" Simon asked.

"Yes, no. Oh shit, what did I do with it?" Frantic, since I was already running late, I starting digging into my jewelry box.

"Oh, wait, I have it," Simon said, which earned him a growl. "Relax, Teagan, you're just getting married."

"Just?"

"To the boy you've been in love with since you were . . . what? Ten? Seriously, this was a foregone conclusion, so take a deep breath and chill."

He was right, of course, but I couldn't believe we were actually here, finally. It was eleven years after he'd first proposed, but we were here.

Remembering the first time I'd seen him, when he'd come into my room to comfort me, I think I knew then that he was going to be a very important person in my life—the most important. A knock at the door brought me back to the present. Mrs. Marks entered, dressed in one of her vintage gowns in a pale pink. She looked beautiful, except for her feet and the hot-pink Crocs. It really didn't work, but I didn't have the heart to tell her that.

"You look beautiful, Teagan. You wanted to see me?"

"Yes. I was hoping that you would walk me down the aisle, so to speak."

Tears smarted in her eyes, her hand coming to her mouth. "I thought Simon was going to walk you down the aisle."

"I've two left feet. I'd probably take her out long before we ever reached the beach. Nothing says 'here comes the bride' like a face full of sand."

"He babbles when he's feeling emotional," I said helpfully.

"It's true." Leaning over, he pressed a kiss on my forehead. "See you out there."

I grabbed his hand before he could leave. "Thank you, for everything. I wouldn't be here if not for you."

"My pleasure, Teagan, truly."

Passing Mrs. Marks, he squeezed her arm before he pulled the door closed behind him.

"There was never any question that I wanted you to walk with me, Mrs. Marks. My life could have gone so differently, but you took me in, gave me a home and a family. The night I arrived, I was so sure I wouldn't know happiness or joy again. How wrong I was. Not only did I find love and family, I found Kane. And he is to me, well, everything. I owe that, all of it, to you, for reaching out to a young girl you didn't even know and offering her a hand when she so needed one."

"Oh dear, you've made me cry."

"You still look beautiful. Will you?"

"Like you need to ask."

She stepped up next to me, her hand reaching for mine. "I love you, dear." Her shoulders squared and her chin lifted. "Here comes the bride, finally."

Kane looked beautiful in his linen suit, his white shirt open at the collar, his pants rolled up, and his feet bare. Zeus was on his one side and Mr. O'Malley, his best man, was on the other. As I neared, his head turned in my direction and a smile curved his lips up on the one side. Reaching him, Mrs. Marks kissed my cheeks and then Kane's before placing my hand in his. We turned together to face the pastor.

"You look beautiful."

"You can't see me."

"I'm seeing you with my heart, Tea, so yeah, I can."

"You're going to make me cry."

"You're crying a lot these days."

"Hormones."

His face tilted to mine. "You sure it's just hormones?"

"I'm finally marrying the boy I've wanted to marry since I was ten, so that may play a small role in my feeling emotional."

"I still want my life with you, want to wake up next to you every morning and go to sleep next to you every night. We're gonna finally make that real."

"So it's real for you?" I asked.

"Very fucking real, and I want it, all of it."

"Good."

The pastor cleared his throat. I had completely forgotten he was there. "Are you both ready now?"

Kane leaned over and whispered in my ear, "He sounds annoyed."

"He looks it too. We're ready," I said.

"More than ready," Kane said, "so get on with it."

epilogue

Kane
4 months later

My hand was going to fall off. I had lost blood flow about a half an hour ago. Tea had a grip. She was in the seventh hour of hard labor. The past hour she had been pushing. I had to say, knowing all the pain I had lived through, I was thinking childbirth might just top that.

She had gone all crazy too, crying one minute and then screaming at me. She actually threatened to cut my dick off. I mean, what? I liked my dick, she liked my dick, and yet I think if she had a scalpel, I'd be singing a few octaves higher.

"The head's crowning." The doctor's announcement had Tea's hand tightening on mine.

"Black hair," she panted through her pushing.

"Tea, just focus." I couldn't believe she was trying to describe our child while she was still pushing him from her body.

"No." And another deep breath, her body going tight, another push.

"Shoulders are out, the next push will do it," the doctor encouraged.

And she did, one last push. I heard the sigh rip from her throat.

"It's a boy," the doctor said.

"He's beautiful, Kane," she said through tears.

In the next minute, someone was standing in front of me. "Open your arms, Kane. Hold your son."

I didn't even think, just went with instinct. Opening my arms, I felt the tiny life placed there. Wrapping him close and tight to my chest, I felt my heart swelling with love. So small, so delicate. Using the tip of my finger, I traced his face, his little lips, his chin and cheeks, his eyes. "You're right, Tea, he is beautiful."

"He has your eyes," she whispered. "We still need to name him."

"Christian Simon Doyle. After your dad and your idiot friend."

Her voice sounded raw when she spoke again. "That's perfect."

"*You're* perfect. Thank you, Tea, thank you for my son, for our life, thank you for not giving up on me."

"You made me make a promise once, remember? You made me promise I would never leave you. I meant it then and I mean it now. I'll never leave you. Now you need to make that promise to me."

"Never, Tea, you're my home."

Teagan
One year later

Kane was sitting on the patio off the bedroom, Christian in his arms, watching the sunrise. I started into the bedroom with our chocolate milk but stopped just inside the room to watch them. We had come a long way; for so long, I never thought we'd get here, but we had and life was idyllic.

Simon and I opened our second shop just off Main Street in a beautiful little place. Christy and Matt were now officially running the Boston shop and both stores were in the black. I thought I'd feel more melancholy about leaving Boston, but I loved being home. Simon and I sold our apartment, and Simon moved into one of the rooms in the west wing of Raven's Peak. Mrs. Marks had insisted. She said there were so many extra rooms, and it was stupid for him to pay rent for a place in town when he spent most of his time at Raven's Peak anyway. Having access to Mrs. T, who insisted on cooking occasionally . . . Simon was all over that.

Raven's Peak Inn was booked nonstop, a raging success. Kane had found his niche too: project management. He was hired to set up inns: to manage the steps from conception to the grand opening. Since Raven's Peak Inn, he had managed two others in the area and now he had an assignment on the West Coast scheduled to start in a few weeks. Mr. O'Malley was his partner and they made a hell of a team. The fact that Kane was not only willing to leave Blue Hill but travel across the country, showed how much he had healed in the year since Christian had been born. He was so much like the boy he had been, that sometimes I forgot all the trauma he had lived through. His beautiful body was scarred, his eyes sightless, but his soul had healed, and having him back, all of him, was bliss.

There were still times when he brooded, when he got frustrated that he couldn't do something, but he was learning that it was okay to ask for help.

Mrs. Marks and Mr. Clancy got married. None of us could believe it. They came home hitched one day after an afternoon outing. They were off in Italy now, touring through Europe.

Doreen visited a few times since we'd married, and I had learned to let go of my grudge against her, since it was completely unfair. But being truthful, I avoided her, because seeing her made me remember and, though I had forgiven her, there was a part of me that would never forget.

I'd never been so happy. I had Kane and Christian, my family at Raven's Peak, Simon, and a life that was even better than I had ever imagined.

"Tea?"

"Sorry, got distracted, you two together are a sight."

Stepping out onto the patio, I placed a glass of chocolate milk with whipped cream on the table and lifted Christian into my arms before settling into Kane's lap, his arms coming around both of us.

"This is as close to heaven as I'm ever going to get," he whispered into my ear.

Remembering there was a time he had been as close to hell as a person could get, my chest squeezed. Reaching for the glass, I gave Christian the first sip before taking one, and then held the straw to Kane's lips.

"Never grows old," he said.

"You're not wrong." Placing the glass down, I snuggled deeper into Kane's embrace, holding Christian tighter. "I'm pregnant."

Kane's arms tightened around us. "You are?"

"Yeah, about a month along."

His finger touched my jaw, turning my mouth to his so he could kiss me. "Hope it's a girl."

Then he stood, lifting me and Christian—his strength surprised me sometimes—before gently placing me on my feet. "Let's go for a walk."

Christian had started walking at ten months. Walking along the sand with Mommy and Daddy was his favorite. Each of us taking a little hand, we started down the beach, Zeus trotting along beside us. Little Christian guided his daddy as much as his daddy was guiding him.

Kane looked thoughtful when I glanced over at him. "You okay?"

"Yeah. We did it, Tea. We're living the dream." His head turned to me, his eyes so beautiful and filled with love.

He was right, we had caught a glimpse of the dream as kids, but, finally, we were living it.

about the author

L.A. Fiore is the author of several books, including *Beautifully Damaged, Waiting for the One*, and *Just Me.* Her favorite condiment is salt, due to its versatility as both a food enhancer and a form of protection against supernatural visitors, especially since her ill-mannered cats are dropping the ball in their roles as guardians of the underworld. She loves hearing from readers and can be reached through Facebook at: www.facebook.com/l.a.fiore.publishing